Jim Reaper

Paul Kelly

Dedication

For Mum & Dad
My moral compass. X

Chapter 1

Lorraine Fuller sat and watched her washing come to the end of its cycle in the near deserted laundrette. The only other person there was an old lady wrapped in layers of cardigans and a tartan blanket across her lap. She too sat in silence, head bowed, watching her spinning clothes. Lorraine shuddered as she looked at the pensioner. It had gone 10pm on a Saturday night and the old lady was here staring blankly at a spinning vortex of vests and support tights. The younger woman felt quite disturbed by this possible vision of the future. She told herself she would never end up this way. Yet the fact of the matter was, they were both here on a Saturday night. The pensioner was probably widowed and was ending her days here after a lifetime with a good man by her side. Lorraine was 28 and had never married. And here she sat in the same laundrette passing judgement while the rest of London were out dancing, abusing narcotics or having hot sweaty jungle sex. She sighed wearily and pulled the damp washing from the machine and transferred it to the huge dryer as the front door opened and a man in a long grey winter coat walked in.

She loaded towels and stopped suddenly as she held up a pair of her red silk panties. In the bright neon lit laundrette this flimsy garment mocked her. Apart from the pensioner and the man who just walked in, who was actually going to see these? This thought made her surreptitiously glance out the corner of her eye at the man, only to find he wasn't just looking at her, but staring right at her. She checked again to be sure. This time she noticed he looked nervous, his hands fidgeted, but most important of all, he had no washing. He just sat there staring at her. Lorraine quickly scanned the rest of the washers in the laundrette, apart from the pensioners; every machine's door was open. Same with the dryers. So, he had no washing; he wasn't picking any up, so what the fuck was he doing here? He was still staring at her. She checked the old lady was still there, sat mesmerised at her own drawers rotating in soapy water. Her presence somehow made Lorraine feel safe. This potential attacker wouldn't molest her with a witness, surely? Realising this, any anxiety she had about being attacked, turned to contempt. It was her turn to stare now. A thin smile played on her lips as she looked this pitiful pervert in the eye. I mean, is this how he spends his Saturday nights, voyeuristically getting his rocks off looking at women's knickers? Feeling more empowered by the second, she twirled her red panties round her index finger as she sneered at him. "Want a picture?" The dark-haired man suddenly looked down at his feet and withered under her stare. Ha! Girl power one, pervert nil. Her euphoria was cut short by the chilling male voice behind her.

"Fucking do it now!"

She spun around expecting to see a second pervert flanking her, only to be faced with the old lady, inches from her face. Lorraine blinked rapidly trying to comprehend what she was looking at. The old lady's face was contorted in a hateful sneer, and for the first time, Lorraine could actually see her full profile; the long angular nose, the thick eyebrows, the square jaw and to her surprise, the Adam's apple? Her eyes went wide, and the scream was stuck in her throat, but the man was too quick for her. In a swift move, he grabbed the collar of her jacket and yanked her sideways and forced her head into the open dryer. Lorraine's heart was pounding as she grabbed at the side of the dryer as her face was pushed down into the pile of damp washing, stifling her screams. Then, panic gripped her as she felt a rough hand reach between her legs and grab her groin. Her terror was consuming her as she kicked out and fought against her rapists. Only as she felt herself being lifted off her feet by the hand holding her groin did she realise it was going to be much worse than rape. The attacker bundled Lorraine into the dryer and slammed the door shut.

Thrashing about in wild panic, she flailed her arms to untangle herself in the damp washing. Through the circular glass door her attacker stood there with one hand leaning out of view at the side of the dryer, near the start button. She wanted to kick out, to smash through that glass door and into this transvestite's face, but her legs were shaking uncontrollably with fear. The metallic click of the latch startled her as the door opened up. A desperate hope gripped her; he'd had a change of heart, then the long black object was tossed into the dryer and landed in her lap. It buzzed and shook as she touched it. Bewildered she looked up at the man who

3

just gave her an evil grin as he slammed the door shut for the final time and turned on the machine. She screamed as the huge drum slowly started to turn and heard the repeated sounds of coin after coin being loaded into the dryer. The wet washing was tangled round her neck on the second rotation of the drum as the metal cylinder started to get hot; she saw her killer sat smiling opposite her tomb, clearly enjoying the show...

Chapter 2

Nobody likes an appraisal. Being summoned to sit in front of a desk whilst being talked down to, like a child. Every fibre of your being wants to tell your appraiser to go fuck himself, that you are an adult and this subtle form of corporate bullying is counter-productive and actually makes you want to fuck over not only your employer, but the face of the smug bastard with a baseball bat who is currently appraising you. Unfortunately for Jim, he could never make that fantasy a reality; because his appraiser was his employer, and also, a professional killer. Jim's colleagues, although not professionals, were also killers. Alas, as shit at his job as he was, so too was he a killer. For Jim, was a Reaper.

This was the third time this month Jim had been summoned to his boss's office to discuss the reasons why he had failed to meet his targets. Or more importantly, why he has failed to kill them. Jim hates his job, but there is no way out. Knowing what he knows, working for a department that officially does not exist. If he openly voiced his desire to leave, or yet again failed to increase his work ratio, he would find his name on "The List". Yet again, the same chastising monologue assaulted Jim's ears, and as a coping mechanism, Jim played "Bullshit Bingo" and mentally ticked each one off in his head. His boss droned on about how Jim's co-worker Singen Lime (who Jim nick named "Slimey", quite apt as the man was more reptile than human) has had to repeatedly help clear Jim's workload, this really rubbed his nose in it. There were the clean-up squads who had to mop up and cover up after him and his half-hearted botched kills. Jim nearly had a full card ticked off on his Bullshit Bingo, one more and he could jump out of his seat and shout "House!" The sharp crisp tones of his bosses raised voice brought him out of his daydream. "Jim! Are you listening to me?" He jumped at the sound and focused on the stern-faced man in front of him. He had to appease this seriously pissed off killer who regarded Jim as deadly as a pacifist snail on Horlicks.

"Look, er... th... there are plenty of nasty people in the world who really do deserve to die. I'd have no problem making the world a better place..." He was cut short.

"No! It is not our place to play God. All the names are supplied by random computer selection. That is the fairest way this difficult task can be done."

No, not God, but Ceaser. That was the name of the computer program that was stored on his boss's laptop. So, nicknamed because when a victim's name appears on screen, a little cartoon hand with a "thumbs up" icon appears next to it. As soon as the kill is confirmed, a cartoon "thumbs down" logo heralds their demise. And who said merciless cold-hearted killers had no sense of humour?

His boss continued, "The computer is not biased, it is not corrupt, and it is not emotional... and it would have no problem with adding a woman's name to the list." And there we have it, 20 minutes of waffle before we reach the real reason why Jim was here: his inability to kill a woman.

"Singen informed me that you froze in the laundrette and that if he hadn't acted quickly, Miss Fuller would still be alive." Jim stared at his feet, and the plastic sheeting that covered the whole office floor.

"Your colleagues will only carry you for so long Jim, before they get sick of it and carry you shoulder high out the door in a box. So, we are going to put you back on the straight and narrow and assign you a mentor."

Chapter 3

Jim stood outside his boss's office on the aging metal gantry overlooking "The Kill Zone". A corporate rebranding misnomer for the shop floor where he and his co-workers planned and prepared to murder innocent strangers in cold blood. He sighed wearily as he looked at the 40 desks below. All had state of the art computers, all had the usual stationary, all had in and out trays. "In" meant you had made The List and were targeted for death, "out" meant...

His shoes made a clanging sound as he descended the dark grey metal staircase. The noise brought back chilling memories, as he reached the bottom, he crossed the room to slump at his desk. Around him, his colleagues milled about, coming and going, tapping away at keyboards, chatting away to each other, sometimes raising their voices to be heard over the sound of gunfire. Sometimes Jim would delude himself that he was back working in his old dull office job at the department of statistics, for this was an office workspace like any other. Then a member of staff would walk by loading a Glock handgun, or you'd be given a blueprint, a set of keys to a flat and a photo of a stranger.

Or every now and again, as a very stark reminder of how this "office" differed from others he'd endured, there was the horrific spectacle of one of his fellow office workers being dragged unceremoniously down the metal staircase from his boss's office… wrapped in plastic sheeting. The sound of their skulls bouncing off every step on the way down announced to all that they were leaving the company and new applicants were to be recruited shortly. Recruited, kidnapped at gunpoint, same result. No, this office space was a tad different to most. The one piece of security this office could offer any newcomer is that it could withstand a 5 mega tonne blast from a nuclear bomb.

Through office gossip and overheard conversations, Jim had learned that his office was in fact a facility… a nuclear bunker left over from the cold war, acquired by his nefarious employers. This ghostly relic buried deep below ground was accessed by one way in and one way out. All guarded by armed men. From his desk, Jim gazed around The Kill Zone, 40 desks in arcs of 10 in a semicircle facing a huge 15-foot-high by 30-foot-wide high-resolution digital screen. This screen was linked to every computer terminal in the facility and was dominated by a huge interchangeable map of London. This map was peppered with neon dots. Green for targets being hunted… red for confirmed kills. Off to the sides of the screen were mini pie charts denoting monthly quotas.

A moving stream of typeface from Reuters news agency flowed from right to left across the bottom of the screen; this was filtered showing only world birth rates, advances in medicine, new technologies to prolong life, health programs, do gooding rock stars feeding the third world. A second strip from Reuters ran parallel to the first, directly below it. This was the one that everybody in the bunker paid particular attention to; it contained stories and statistics of world deaths. A train went off a bridge in Mumbai killing 768 passengers, 81 refugees drowned fleeing a war zone, terrorist bomb in Belgium claims 26, serial killer in Sweden decapitates and eats a 6th victim. Not quite double figures, but every little helps. A cheer goes up around Jim as his colleagues scan the latest deaths coming in on the screen like they were watching the football results come in as the latest death toll read: High school shooting in Texas claims 47. Ah, you've got to hand it to the Yanks; nobody does more to control the population than them.

Jim did not share his sheep like colleague's morbid glee at American teenagers being senselessly butchered and turned his gaze away from the huge screen, where it drifted up to his boss's office high up on the metal gantry. For all its illusion of corporate hierarchy, the office was merely a prefabricated hut, same as you would see on any building site. Functional rather than opulent. The only thing that denoted status about it was the two burly black suited armed men who stood either side of his employer's door.

The sound of rapid gunfire turned Jim's head towards one of the side corridors in the vast labyrinth of chambers in this subterranean bunker. Down that particular corridor was the gun range, where Jim and his co-workers can practice with the tools of their trade. The paradoxes being, although they are taught how to strip clean, reassemble and correctly shoot a gun... they are never given one until it was deemed necessary. These are controlled and owned only by the bunker's trusted zealots and guards. Although his employers praised the mass shootings of kids in Texas, they seriously didn't want the risk of Jim and his 39 conscripts turning their guns on them and escaping this nightmare.

Apart from a gun range, the bunker has computer technology sections dedicated to finding as much data about their targets as possible. Their weaknesses, their movements, hacking their bank accounts, medical records, looking for that vital piece of information that will render them vulnerable... before they pass it up the chain. The next section in an adjacent corridor to take this information from the tech boys are the murder squad detectives. These four ex C.I.D officers form part of the bunkers zealots who actually want to be here and were not recruited in the same press-ganged way Jim and his colleagues were. These retired bent coppers are in house advisors, they inform the Reapers of every flaw in their plans to butcher their target, that a trained serious crime squad officer would pick up on. Making sure that by the time the cops got to the corpse there would not be a single clue left for them.

Next up the chain running parallel to the murder squad detectives are the two pathologists on lucrative retainers, who lecture on evasive forensics so no Reaper's D.N.A is ever left near or around the scene of a killing. No fingerprints will ever be left. Assisting the pathologists is a ten strong mop up team who clean up and when necessary, cover up any botched assassinations by incompetent Reapers. They all worked in unison towards one common objective: 'Death by misadventure.'

Jim groaned inwardly, as even above the sound of echoing gunfire down the corridor he could hear that raucous sound that every day set his nerves on edge, the hyena laugh that heralded the arrival of Singen Lime. Jim's skin crawled as half a dozen of his co-workers slithered to

11

Slimey as if they were giggling schoolgirls at a boy band's stage door, shaking his hand, patting his back. Singen was the bunker's most prolific Reaper. A sadistic man who took to his recruitment with the same ease as a duck to water. The psychotic glee he took in executing people made Jim wonder that if Singen hadn't been recruited, would it have only been a matter of a time before he became a serial killer? This nauseating daily display by sycophantic invertebrates made Jim want to vomit up his own lungs as they worshipped and greeted him with the adulation only afforded to a premier league footballer. As much as Jim loathed him, when it came to his job, Slimey was premier league. Jim, at a push, was nearer to Sunday league for a council estate pub team.

After somehow fighting off his entourage, Slimey strode over to the big screen and stood legs wide apart with his hands on his hips, surveying the latest death toll. Nodding sagely, a monarch surveying his kingdom. He stood there in full pose for five minutes as his acolytes buzzed round him resembling bluebottles round shit. He then turned with a swish of his crumpled grey Macintosh coat with the theatrical grace of a supermodel on a catwalk and strode over to the desk next to Jim's. It was bad enough luck sharing a planet with Slimey and a terrible misfortune sharing a workplace environment with him, but to have a desk right next to his… oh God! It was really taking the piss. He must pay the almighty back on his way home by popping into church and pissing in the font. His nemesis removed the drab overcoat and draped it on his plush leather executive swivel chair. The only other person to have a chair like this was the head of section in his lofty Porto cabin office. Which just goes to show, back-stabbing pays much better than arse licking, especially in their line of work. Beneath Slimey's outer coat he wore an expensive handmade Italian black suit and a tailored shirt with silver cufflinks shaped like skulls. He was a walking caricature of a Hollywood hit man, and he absolutely loved it.

It is an unbreakable rule that all Reapers must look totally inconspicuous as they enter and leave the bunker. Never risking drawing attention to themselves or their work. They must be faceless in a crowd, like shadows, nobody sees them arrive, and no one witnesses them leave. Often, they leave the building several times a day in disguise to dispatch various targets and they are totally unrecognisable. To aid them on their quest, there is a full wardrobe and makeup department, along with a professional latex technician on hand to transform these unremarkable little men, so they are dressed to kill. And they are all men. According to bunker mythology, Chinese whispers and hushed office gossip, Jim had gleaned that in the department's infancy it had actually trialled a few women who were quite proficient at culling their male targets. However, these lethal ladies all had a crisis of conscience when it came to same sex gender genocide.

These Reaperettes were quickly eliminated and replaced with a more pliable workforce. Was this just an office urban myth started by a bored colleague, or black propaganda purposely dripped onto the grape vine by management to terrify the living daylights out of any would be conscientious objectors as a stark reminder of the price of betraying the department's secrecy and all important work? Either way, the unspoken threat was understood: If we can butcher a department full of our own female employees because they didn't come up with the goods, imagine what could be done do to you if you stepped out of line! Every successful business rules its staff with fear. There is no greater fear motivator than the fear of being murdered.

Singen slumped into his leather chair and put both his feet up on his desk, affording Jim a view of his hand made designer brogues. Slimey caught Jim's glance and bragged, "They cost £2,000."

"So, what do they do?" asked Jim. The other man frowned and removed his feet from the desk clearly annoyed.

"What the fuck do you mean "do?""

Jim glowed inwardly as this pompous prick had taken the bait beautifully.

"Well, for £2,000 do they make you walk faster? Can you now Morris dance whereas before you couldn't?" Slimey's flaring nostrils on his long angular nose were betraying his real feelings of simmering rage as he portrayed a thin false smile to counter Jim's disrespect for his overpriced footwear.

"I mean, I'm not being funny but, for £2,000 you could afford to pay a midget to pull you everywhere on roller-skates."

Singen inhaled deeply through those flaring nostrils that reminded Jim of a fish's gills, as it flapped about on the deck of a trawler. The senior Reaper then casually reached across his desk and started in motion his favourite desk toy. It was a disturbing version of Newton's cradle with their irritating click clacking metallic balls… but with a difference. The difference being that in place of the metallic orbs are chrome skulls. Whenever Slimey was not getting his own way or looked like he was close to losing an argument, he would subtly start the skulls clacking, all the while holding your gaze, knowing your train of thought had been broken as your eyes were hypnotically drawn towards the gleaming skulls that seem to look right at you as they smash into its neighbour. Singen leaned forward in his chair resting his elbows on his knees and gave Jim a cold emotionless smile.

"As you may be aware Jim, as the bunker's senior Reaper with an unblemished 100% kill record, I am being groomed to be the right-hand man to the Head of Section. The old man won't be around forever... then who knows?" He stood up and gripped Jim's shoulder and leaned close to the seated man's ear and whispered, "Biting the hand that feeds you... my, aren't we a clever little boy?"

The senior Reaper strode off and another colleague approached Jim waving books of small tickets in his face. It was that time of the week again... the staff lottery. If only it was a bowl of fruit or a bottle of glorified vinegar that passes for middle class nectar that was on offer as a prize. But this was no ordinary office, no this particular lottery was gambling to win the job of killing a minor hated B list celebrity. Apparently, this morbid game of chance was a staff morale booster as the computer "randomly" selected these poor wretches' names, whose only crime seemed to be that they were once loved by the public, now inevitably that love affair has turned sour. The very fickle nature of fame, one minute you're here, next you are gone... and this week's unsuspecting celeb's life was being auctioned for the price of a 50p raffle ticket. Jim bought two.

Chapter 4

The decaying poster on the snaking corridor tunnel wall advised the reader to "Keep Calm and Carry On". There were many of these well-meaning mantras, left over from a bygone era scattered throughout the bunker. Their employers obviously reckoned the sound bite support given to war time and cold war Britain's facing annihilation, applied to Jim and his fellow merry gang of murderers. The staff lottery ticket in Jim's pocket was seen as a perk of his job. Yet this wasn't the only perk a Reaper was given. In a bizarre twist, they enjoyed the same status as a diplomat, where the laws of the land did not apply to them. No matter what they did or who they killed for personal reasons, their employers would cover it up. After all, they couldn't have Hell's travel agents defecating into an overflowing steaming bucket in Wormwood scrubs, when there are monthly targets to be met. This sordid sweetener was used to soften the blow at being forced against your will into a life that was the stuff of nightmares. Most of Jim's colleagues took up this kind offer of butchering a couple of people from their past life. Old girlfriend, boss, that kid from your old school who used to wank into your towel in gym class just to watch your face as you used it. All wiped from the face of the Earth. But you could only have two free personal kills on the house. Although they would help you plan, execute and if necessary, cover up a botched attempt, any more than two personal kills was viewed as drawing attention to yourself. In the bunker, three strikes and you were out. Jim declined his employer's "kind" offer of exorcising two of his personal demons as he saw it for exactly what it was; him accepting his new life and committing murder of his own free volition that will trap him in the bunker forever. If he accepted, how could he ever be free? For Jim, unlike the majority of the sheep that surrounded him, wanted to be free. What would he tell the police if this nightmare ended?

"Oh yes officer, bad men made me kill innocent people against my will or they would've killed me. What? That lad who used to wank into my towel at school like a safari park chimp? Well, yes... I did sort of kill him for my own reasons. But, come on! He wanked into my towel for fuck sake... more than once!"

He passed various colleagues on his slow unhurried appointment. They gabbled inanely about kills they've come back from or ones they were planning to do. He pitied them, so accepting of their own fate. Not an independent thought in any of their vacuous skulls. Jim mused that this is what it must've been like at the backstage party at the Nuremberg rallies. Maybe it was a coping mechanism to block out the horror of what they do? Possibly the shock of being constantly threatened to be murdered if they didn't acquiesce? Or just good old-fashioned Stockholm syndrome, where the victim is brainwashed into loving their captors? Either way, Jim had very little to do with them. And like all sheep, they noticed the black one amongst their flock and avoided him. They gladly bought up handfuls of staff lottery tickets to show that not only was killing their job... it could be fun too. Jim was aware he was being watched. Aware he'd botched too many kills and shown up on C.C.T.V. at the scenes of his kills. The bunker's tech boys did their best to hack into these cameras and located and wiped most of the footage, but not all. And he froze yet again when it had come to killing a woman. He purchased the two staff lottery tickets to somehow take the spotlight off himself, blend in, to half-heartedly send out the message, "Hey, I'm just like you." He was clutching at straws, he may have bought a ticket, but they weren't buying his false enthusiasm. And that is why he was now being assigned a Mentor.

This Mentor would now oversee and accompany Jim while he visits and executes his targets. He had heard throughout the bunker about this retraining and the evil Mentors who watched you like a hawk, like taking a lethal driving test where the stakes were much higher. Some say these Mentors were seasoned ex M.I.6 assassins with hearts of stone and bollocks to match. These sentinels were only talked about in whispers because no one had actually met one... and come back from an assessment to talk about it. But to Jim, any merciless spook would be better than another day of being taunted by Slimey. As Jim approached the Mentor's door at the end of yet another endless corridor, he passed through the 4-inch-thick tungsten steel concrete filled blast doors that were strategically placed every 50 meters. The lighting in the corridors was all artificial and encased in wire frames, the overhead electrical cables, water pipes and air conditioning all were encased in bomb proof conduit. For a place that's sole purpose was to above all odds preserve life, it felt like a tomb. A tomb, that Jim and his fellow Reapers would leave on a daily basis to go out and kill the living. He hesitated to knock on the plain wooden door as he looked at the old green and red buzzer panel fixed to the wall beside it. His old headmaster had one of these antiquated wait and enter systems on his door. For in reality wasn't this exactly what this was, some psychological mindfuck to make him feel like a naughty little boy being summoned to his Headmaster's office? Jim hesitated to knock, suddenly a panic gripped him, and his heart pounded in his chest. He looked up at the small C.C.T.V. camera above the door.

These mini spies were all over the bunker, only the toilet afforded you any real privacy. Was his Mentor sizing him up right now? Enjoying the power kick? The loud buzzing and green light from the entry system brought him abruptly to the present as he gritted his teeth and entered the room.

The high-backed leather chair was facing the opposite wall for dramatic effect away from the bare wooden desk. Apart from three dusty filing cabinets there was nothing of interest on the windowless wall apart from another little gem from war time advising us that "Loose lips sink ships." This made Jim smile. Talking about your work may have given the enemy information to locate and sink your freighters during the second world war, for Jim to have loose lips; the penalty would result in being wrapped in plastic. Still, the chair faced the opposite wall, not a sound coming from it. A slow contempt welled from within Jim at this faceless prick playing "make him wait" petty mind games, that it soon engulfed any fear and trepidation he had initially felt. Jim's smile broadened as he confidently expected this inadequate bed wetter to be stroking a white cat as he slowly pirouetted into view. Jim's smile, along with any bravado disappeared as Slimey spun around and grinned manically.

"You're mine now!"

Chapter 5

Despite being a young fit man, Jim's thighs were burning whilst climbing the never-ending concrete stairwell that led from the bunker that lay at what seemed to him the very bowels of the Earth, to at least breathe fresh air that hadn't been recycled through mechanical filters. This thought brought a chuckle to his lips… "breathe fresh air." He was about to step out onto the streets of London. Where the hell did he think he would be snorting this crisp fresh oxygen, Mount Kilimanjaro? Out on these streets they'd kill a man for a giro.

At the top of the staircase lay a reception desk opposite the bunker's outer door. This portal separated the land of the living… and those who prey upon them. Both sides of this entrance door were guarded day and night. Inside was guarded by the bunker's head of security, ex S.A.S. captain Jeremy Naylor. The former soldier eyed the breathless Jim out the corner of his eye and picked up the phone and studied the security cameras on his three monitors. Under his desk were two loaded MP5 Heckler and Koch machine guns with 4 clips of spare ammunition, plus the Glock he always kept next to the computer's mouse. So, if anyone did breach the bunker's outer steel door, they would have to take the receptionist's word for it that, "we are not at home to visitors today."

"Hello, Naylor, delivery in two minutes, report status." He waited in silence for conformation from the C.I.D. officers in the observation post outside that the coast was clear.

"Affirmative." Placing the phone next to his Glock he activated the electronic door lock. Jim stepped outside into the narrow alleyway that was only four feet wide and waited for the door to close behind him with a heavy mechanical clunk.

The entrance to the bunker is a drab looking studded steel door, recessed at the end of a very narrow 50-foot-long alley way. There is litter and a couple of rubbish bins half full, but this is just window dressing. Camouflage, to make sure any casual passer by wouldn't give this place a second look. The location was chosen for its unremarkable façade by the original government department who built it in 1940. Because of the high-ranking calibre of the personnel who were to be given sanctuary down here from the Luftwaffe, its location was barred by the Ministry of defence from ever appearing on any map. Its very location was protected from scrutiny by the official secrets act and this level of secrecy regarding its existence only increased as the world entered the cold war. With each new level of national threat, the bunker had all its technology and facilities upgraded, but not the décor. A stark reminder you are not at The Hilton as you lay on your 1950s bunk bed gazing at faded wartime posters... be thankful you are still breathing. The cold war had thawed and successive government's appetites for funding and maintaining bunkers for non-existent wars were decreasing when there were funds needed to fight real wars... against the unions and the unemployed. So very quietly, these bunkers were sold off to the highest bidder. This particular facility had changed hands seven times since its original sale. With the covert nature of its sale, no official paperwork was ever filed. Plus, its location and everything to do with it is still protected by the highest levels of military secrecy on a rolling 30-year official secret's gagging order. So realistically, no government audit office would come searching for it, on paper or in person. For the Reapers needing a lair to operate from... It was perfect.

The entrance to the bunker was overseen by 25 high definition infra-red digital covert cameras, each only 10mm in circumference. These state-of-the-art surveillance lenses were counter sunk into the narrow alleyway's brick walls. The alleyway purposely had no street lighting, so even in daylight; the cameras were always in shadow. Day or night, nobody could walk up to this door and not be seen. That is if you even got that far. Opposite that alley way was a deserted back street, taken up completely with abandoned, boarded up offices. Every window was broken or boarded up... bar one. And this intact clean tinted window on the third floor was situated perfectly to view the entrance to the alleyway opposite. These offices were purchased by the Ministry of Defence over 70 years ago at the time of the bunker's conception. This precautionary purchase ensued that no new tenants would move in and casually view the movements of the occupants of the nuclear bunker, across the alleyway.

Behind this particular tinted window on the third floor, was a two-man surveillance team of the bunkers C.I.D. officers, who work in shifts to permanently provide outside security and Intel to captain Naylor back at the bunker. They report any unwanted visitors and via a digital scrambled radio link, let the Reapers know when the coast is clear. Their observation post has a well-stocked arsenal and as well as a video and binoculars set up on tripods... there is a silenced military sniper's rifle with 30 cyanide filled Kevlar tipped rounds, fitted with laser and thermo sight that can pick up a target's heat signature even through the side of a van. If all this failed... there was always Wolfgang.

Despite all these precautions, the only problem the bunker has had with intruders has not been with journalists or terrorists... but tramps. An advert must have been placed in "Incontinent and Unwashed fortnightly" depicting the bunker's secluded alley way and door entrance as a five-star vagrant bed and breakfast, with the bunker's outer door their en-suite toilet of choice. The meth tinged urine from these free spirits has done to the bunker's outer door what a bucket of Semtex could not. Not even the caustic blood from Geiger's cinematic alien would accelerate the natural rusting cycle of the outer door, like a full bladder of putrefied "Tramp's Tequila." Although not greatly loved by society, there is a common misconception about the homeless; mainly, nobody will miss them if they go missing. However, they are a community that, although existing on a different level of consciousness and personal hygiene, are a close-knit community no less. Next to taxi drivers, they are the eyes and the ears of any city. So, if one of their kind suddenly disappears, they will ramble on endlessly about it to anyone who will listen. For this reason, they are an indispensable source of information to investigative journalists... and extremely dangerous to the security of the Reapers.

Chapter 6

The early pub lunch was Slimey's idea of lightening the mood. A little bit of corporate team building. Yet another wonderful invention exported from America that Jim was grateful for. Treat your staff like shit... then buy them a pie. Because nothing induces amnesia and staves off industrial unrest like a pie. That great nation abolished slavery on its own shores, then repackaged and franchised the concept out to every other country on Earth. Today the pub on the outskirts of town was empty except for a pensioner wearing war medals on his jacket breast pocket and his Jack Russell terrier. Both seemed very uncomfortable at being within close proximity of the two Reapers. It is said that the elderly and animals are very perceptive when in the presence of evil spirits. Urban myth or not, after a few minutes of the dogs whining, the old guy left his full pint of Guinness and scurried out of the bar as fast as his replaced hip would take him. Jim shook his head and looked down at the floor. He felt embarrassed and somehow guilty that the old soldier, possibly a Falklands veteran had been subconsciously forced out of his local by him and Slimey. The look of fear on the old man's face on the way out the door made Jim feel cursed. Slimey viewed the pensioner's exit and Jim's body language and discomfort and hissed,

"Why the fuck are you concerned about that rotting old fossil? He'll be dead within a year... with or without our help."

"Have a bit of respect. That old guy probably fought for his country." protested Jim.

"Killed, you mean?" Retorted Slimey. "Murdered countless strangers in cold blood on the orders of his government... for the greater good." Satisfied he had made his point, he took his first sip of the wine he'd ordered. The taste soon wiped the smug look off his face. Against his better judgement it just wasn't in Jim to let his loathsome colleague's suggestions that the old soldier's valiant sacrifice in defence of his country, was in anyway the same as the disgusting line of work they were embroiled in. "He's nothing like us."

"Oh, so what would you do, Ghandi?!" Snarled his mentor. "Seven and a half billion and rising. Oooh!" He then looked at his watch for comic effect. "There's another 50,000 McDonalds customers being born! All going round your flat for tea, are they?! You going to make these rutting fuckers wear a condom, are you? Are you going to inform them that only vampires and members of the Royal family live forever? So... do you drop bombs on them to bring the numbers of these fucking locusts down to acceptable levels?" He took another sip of his wine and winced. "We've tried that... the voters don't like it."

Again, he scowled at the wine and clicked his fingers at the bar man. Jim groaned inwardly at this arrogant display of middle-class entitlement. Despite being financially starved into this thankless low paid job, this clearly riled the barman.

"Can I help you sir?"

A line he'd obviously practised in the faces of vomiting youths and Special Brew connoisseurs.

"This Fleurie is corked!"

The wine glass was held out at arms-length like a fresh hot shitty nappy. The fact that Slimey didn't even look at him, but expected the offending liquid to be taken away, sealed in a lead flask and dumped in the North Sea. Now this had really endeared himself to the now seriously pissed off employee, whose self-respect was worth more to him than the pittance he receives to entertain gobshites with delusions of being Alabama cotton plantation owners in the 1800s. The wine stayed at arm's length for what seemed like an eternity. Neither being handed over or taken. The uncomfortable impasse was broken by a nervous Jim who knew from past experiences with Singen, that the barman had already sealed his own fate.

"M... my wine's fine."

Slimey's eyes bored into Jim at this treachery. This wasn't about glorified grape juice anymore, it was a battle of wills... and one this jumped up little oik was going to lose. Like a ventriloquist's dummy, Slimey's head slowly turned to face the defiant barman. In a low tone devoid of all warmth he reiterated, "I said..." Pausing as he glared at the younger man. "...this Fleurie is corked."

After another agonising few seconds for Jim, the barman slowly took the glass from Slimey and held it up to the light. For theatrical effect he frowned as he studied the liquid in the light in the same manner a gypsy may scrutinise a crystal ball. He then sniffed at it with his eyes closed as if to ascertain the origins of the vineyard, or whether the peasant who trampled the grapes had a manky verruca or not. But for his big finale, he took a mouthful and sloshed it around his mouth like mouthwash whilst looking directly at Slimey... before spitting the lot back into the glass. Smiling right at Slimey, the barman coolly said, "You're right sir... it is corked. I'm sorry about that, let me get you another." Slimey returned his smile as the teenager lifted both Jim's and his glasses and walked off still smiling.

Two minutes later he was dead.

Emptying the contents of the wine into the slops tray the barman chuckled to himself at the little victory he'd gained over that piss poor life support machine for an arsehole, when all the hairs on the back of his neck stood up. He spun round quickly only to see Slimey's icy cold stare inches away from his face. Before he could scream, a banana was rammed deep into his mouth causing him to choke. Bent double, holding his throat, he felt Slimey's arms snaking round his neck... seconds before he snapped it with a sickening crunch. No sooner had the barman's body gone limp when Slimey opened the cellar trap door and dangled the corpse over the sheer drop by the ankle with one arm. With the other he carefully wiped the banana skin on the sole of the barman's shoe until the sticky wetness coated the sole and heel... before dropping the teenager 10 foot down onto the stone cellar floor below. Finally, he wiped a wet line of banana juice on the floor leading to the cellar trap door. He then dropped the incriminating banana skin for the staff to find before calmly going to the toilet to wash away his deed.

The car journey from the pub was a solemn one. Jim hadn't witnessed the killing, but sensed Slimey's sudden need for the toilet had a more sinister motive. It was Jim who broke the silence first. "And was he on the computer's list?"

Slimey just smiled whilst keeping his eyes on the road. "In this life, there are those who follow the lists... and those who write them."

Chapter 7

The student seemed totally oblivious to the red laser dot crawling up his body as he read his psychology textbook. The young man slouched on the park bench resembling an unkempt burst space hopper, sucking on his woodbine as if there was an Olympic medal riding on it. When the dot reached the bridge of his nose, he took a deep breath… possibly his last.

40 yards away, Slimey sat holding his laser pointer, concentrating his aim. Bored with the student, he levelled the crimson target on a couple of smooching teenagers playing tongue origami. Alternating the dot between the bag of rampaging acne with bum fluff to the sack of puss with blue eye shadow.

"Eeny, meeny, miney, mo…"

Slimey was clearly enjoying his morbid little game.

"Look at them… top of the food chain. They!" he gestured towards Romeo and Juliet, "…are our future! They have the vote; they outnumber us by a 1000 to 1… and they breed like fucking maggots!" Tiring of this misanthropy, Jim challenged his mentor.

"And you are better than them, are you?"

Sneering he replied, "Huh! Like you need to ask. We are the chosen." Jim groaned inwardly, surely a dum dum bullet to the back of the skull would be more preferable than the tidal wave of verbal diarrhoea that was fucking drowning him at the moment? Slimey jabbed an accusing finger towards the young couple.

"They are conceived up a shit littered back alley by inbred criminals and two-legged gonorrhoea factories, educated in council funded borstals and spend the rest of their lives welding their arses to a couch." Jim let him ramble on, the longer he did, the longer his targets had on this Earth. As if reading his thoughts, Slimey suddenly turned icy cold.

"Now… to business. Target…" pointing to notes on his digital phone. "…Albert Rickets, 43, lives alone." leaning towards Jim for comedy effect. "Lucky for you! He accessed "Latex Dinner Ladies" 184 times last month." Tutting now in mock disgust. "He has no telly licence, so that's our way in." Handing Jim a fake T.V. detector licence officer's badge with Jim's photo on it, from his black briefcase. Slimey could sense Jim's hesitation and fixed him with a thin cruel smile. "You can back out now if you want to Jim. But remember, it's him… or you!"

Chapter 8

From the corner of Albert's street, they sat in their grubby white Ford van. The same van they had slowly cruised the full length of the target's street only 5 minutes before. On that reconnaissance run Singen had pointed his hand-held scanner casually out of the van's window and scanned all the radio frequencies of the car alarms on Albert's neighbours' vehicles. Once these frequencies were stored, they drove off for 15 minutes. Many a cold calculating intelligent killer have been brought to justice, not by a superior police intellect, but by a fucking bored unemployed curtain twitcher. If only such pedantically vigilant nosey bleeders had been employed by M.I.6. during the cold war, then countless billions would've been saved on omnipresent voyeuristic satellites. Slimey glanced at his gold oyster Rolex.

"He'll be home in 15 minutes." Even though it was forbidden to have any outward display of wealth that could draw attention to the Reaper, Slimey couldn't help himself. It was as if he was untouchable. The fact that the bunker's whole ethos was never ever leave yourself open to scrutiny... you could tell he was bursting to shout from the roof tops that he was the number 1 assassin. Licence to kill. And there, the similarity with Ian Fleming's suave spy ended.

Slimey clicked the scanner onto setting number 2. The smooth black oblong box had two settings, the first would set off a single car alarm from a distance of up to 50 meters. Whereas the second setting would bounce the activated signal from the first car's recorded alarm combination code memory onto the next car to cause a domino effect, setting off up to 40 car alarms at the same time. That trademark cold smile snaked across Singen's gaunt face as he spotted three schoolboys kicking a football back and forth between them as they walked along Albert's road.

"Indeed, the Gods are smiling on us today, Jim."

Jim hated it when Slimey used his name in such a matey way. His name his Father so lovingly bestowed upon him, sounded dirty on this reptile's lips.

When the boys reached the first parked car, Slimey pointed the scanner out of the window of their parked van at the vehicle and clicked setting 2. Within seconds the whole street erupted in high pitched wailing, bleeping, blaring horns and flashing lights. This impromptu council estate rave resulted in dozens of neighbours rushing outside to join the party. British justice is renowned the world over for being blind. Unfortunately for the trio of schoolboys... shaven headed tattooed rat boys and obese taxi drivers are not. In the time it had taken the cream of MENSA to lumber down their paths, they had unanimously found the footballing children guilty of using their rusting chariots as goalposts, and promptly decided to complete these boy's further education by giving them a master class in Tourette's. In all the excitement and colourful language, not one of the irate neighbours spotted the two killers silently enter Albert's home to wait for their prey.

Chapter 9

The interior of Albert's house was eerily quiet, compared to the near riot going on outside in the street. His living room was cluttered: countless empty beer cans and days old take away trays lay next to one inside out sock. It needed a woman's touch... preferably one with a can of petrol and a box of matches. But with the overpowering reek of B.O., this place would go up like Hiroshima. The humongous plasma television took pride of place in the corner of his room, next to the brand-new latest edition laptop with all the usual must have, don't need, but I want it anyway bullshit gadgets you'll never use and don't know what the fuck they all do anyway nonsense. Now, there is only one way such cutting-edge technological opulence could coexist next to bachelor squalor... credit. Poor bastard thought Jim. Probably hocked up to his armpits to pay for these two "must have" toys. It would take him till he was 250 years old to pay for them... if he lived that long. Their very presence in his living room pulling on surgical gloves was testament to the fact that he wouldn't. Wasting no time Slimey quickly logged on to Albert's computer using the password supplied off his file. The bunker's hacker's ability to break any encryption code on anything was so chilling, it bordered on telepathy.

"Go look for a vacuum cleaner."

Jim dually complied and lamented at the dropping standards of basic manners in cold blooded assassins nowadays. He chuckled to himself, trying to cheer himself up at the same time feeling physically sick at the prospect of murdering a man in under ten minute's time. The irony wasn't lost on him. In all honesty he felt more like the condemned man, than the unsuspecting condemned man. Jim dug out the small vacuum with a long nozzle attachment from the under-stair's cupboard. It was ideal for what Slimey had in mind. Returning to the living room he saw his mentor delve into his briefcase and open a hinged secret compartment.

"This is for you." He said handing Jim a modified police stun gun... modified to increase the voltage ten-fold.

"And this... is for me." He beamed as he produced a black Beretta pistol with a silencer attached.

"Wh... where did you get that?" blurted out Jim.

"Oh, just a perk of the job." Smiling as he clicked back the top slide to chamber a bullet. "Fuck up this time Jim, and there won't be one body lying here... there'll be two." As his heart pounded in his chest, he heard Albert's key rattle in the lock.

Chapter 10

The balding portly Albert nearly dropped his six pack of cheap and nasty lager, as he saw the two smartly dressed strangers standing in his living room. His eyes darted to his beloved plasma telly to see if it was missing. Deducing the intruders weren't burglars, his fear turned to anger as he stepped towards them roaring,

"Who the fuck are you?! What are you doing in my gaff?!"

A cornered animal is the most dangerous of all. Totally unpredictable, there is no savage barbarism that it would not sink to defend itself. In situations like these, Slimey considered himself a matador. Utilising the beast's anger, he side stepped its lumbering charges with balletic grace. And, as a matador... he enjoyed playing with his prey before he slaughtered it. With the speed of a striking cobra, Slimey's hand shot out towards Albert's face causing him to snap his head back. It wasn't a weapon he held, but an I.D. badge.

"T.V. licence inspector!" Hissed the Reaper at Albert, whose legs visibly buckled briefly.

"According to our records, you haven't purchased a T.V. licence for that multiplex in the corner." Albert stuttered, his confused little mind racing, not noticing that both these "inspectors" had one hand behind their backs and a surgical glove on the other. "Mr Rickets let me save you some time, shall I? You have no dog, so he couldn't have eaten your licence. You drive a car, so you never left it on the bus." He smiled at Albert now. "A car consequently enough, you actually did find the energy to purchase a licence for. So, what is it? Do you fear the wrath of the boys at the Swindon car licensing authority, yet feel we at the T.V. licensing department can be ignored like a Big Issue seller?" All the while Slimey was clearly enjoying taunting Albert, Jim edged closer, knowing it would get very messy if he didn't get him first time. Albert interrupted Slimey'

"Oiy! Don't you usually knock? I mean… how did you get in…"

Before he could finish his sentence, Jim jabbed the stun gun into Albert's ribs and held down the button. There was a brief smell of singed hair as Albert momentarily danced on the spot before slumping unceremoniously to the floor. Slimey pushed past the stunned Jim and took Albert's pulse. Seconds later that vile smile flashed into view. "Who's a clever boy then?"

Police officers usually say that telling a relative that their loved one is dead is the hardest and most traumatic part of their job. Much more distressing than seeing the actual mangled cadaver. However, for Jim, slaughtering the innocent wasn't the end of his torment... but the beginning. For what he was required to do next took all his reserves of endurance.

"Get his undies off!" Barked Slimey, breaking Jim's train of thought. The dread overwhelmed Jim.

"L... look, he's dead. We've done our job. There's no need..." His mentor shot him that cruel smile.

"So what? Cholesterol made his heart go bang did it?" Holding up a dirty takeaway tray to illustrate his point.

"Well why not? He eats shit, drinks too much and..." Slimey jabbed his finger at their newest client on the floor.

"And?!... and a police officer can tell his arteries are like the M6 at 5 o'clock on a Friday night just by looking at him... CAN HE?!" Roaring the last sentence. He paused, his nostrils flaring as he tried to control his anger. Lowering his voice now to an insincere matey tone.

"Up till now, you've done well Jim. Don't fall at the last fence... horses that fall... often get shot." A braver man would not have murdered Albert. A braver man would have somehow got out of there and alerted the authorities. But Jim wasn't a brave man. Despite his wretched existence, he still wanted to live. So, he stripped the dead man, attached the vacuum cleaner to his penis and switched it on. Singen chose a suitable porn website on Albert's laptop, and then both of them left... with the man's life and his dignity.

Five miles down the road, Slimey broke the silence in the van.

"Open that case, Jim. Wait till you see this little beauty." Jim opened the silver metallic case and saw what appeared to be a standard screw together hit man's rifle. "Oh, a rifle." Jim replied emotionlessly.

"Ah, not just a rifle, a rifle that fires very special ammunition."

Then from the glove box he produced a jam jar... full of angry Brazilian honeybees.

Chapter 11

Cassandra's desk was situated at the far end of the newsroom. "Screws room" more like it. For the spiteful hand of fate had condemned her to work for a sub literate soft porn celebratory gossip rag. It wasn't always so. Once... oh, it seemed a lifetime away now... once, she was a real journalist. When she had a sniff of a big story that was it. No matter who you are, no matter how powerful you and your cronies were, once you had crossed the line... she'd take you down. And by Christ she did just that. Reports buried by the Department for Trade and Industry sub committees would be pulled out of her hat like a journalistic Paul Daniels. Submarine captain's logs whose very existence could bring down a newly elected government, would somehow find their way into her in tray. In her pursuit of the truth, she was fearless... and peerless. Let's face it; an honest journalist is about as plentiful on Fleet Street as rocking horse shit is on the Moon. Her scalps were many, and she took everything those wounded animals threw at her. Bankrupting liable actions? Yeah, right! See you in The Old Bailey your Lordship! Government gagging orders? Try it and the story will be all over the internet in three minutes flat. Then one day, she fucked with the wrong person… and her life turned to shit in three minutes flat.

She stopped tapping at her keyboard, the blood congealing in her brain as she was forced to write about the latest football "roasting," when her eyes drifted down to the closed drawer of her desk. Checking none of her colleagues were looking, she opened it surreptitiously and gazed at the photo of the man of her dreams. She had lost sleep over him, had fantasies of finally catching up with him. He was the only knight in shining armour who could take her away from all this… and he was a serial killer.

"Ere! I've bleedin' got it!"

The dulcet tones of her fat sweaty journalist colleague, Norman on the next desk snapped her back to reality, as she instinctively slammed shut her desk drawer a little too loudly. Did the panic show on her face? Surely, he must've noticed the slam. Her fears were unfounded as the B.O. factory adjacent regaled her with the cathedral of knowledge, he called his mind.

"Ere! You know that turd burglar of a panda in London zoo with the floppy dick?" Yee gods this was truly an epic dilemma of biblical proportions, surely Solomon himself would have to phone a friend on this one. On the one hand, pandering (she pardoned herself this mental pun... call it a work-related illness) to his inane gibbering as he opened his flabby arse extra wide to let the contents of his brain spill out, would distract him from her blatant attempt to hide the photo of perhaps the most prolific serial killer in British history. Then again... she did wonder about the serious effects of passive bullshitting. This scoop was too big to share with amoebas with learning difficulties, so for the greater good she blurted out,

"Erm, do you mean "Ming Ling," the Chinese giant panda on loan as part of the endangered species breeding program?"

"Yeah, that's the geezer. Eight bleeding months he's been over here and the only thing he's banged is his head on the cage door!" Waving the lack of procreational prowess the poor creature had aside; he gave her the classic forearm slap to indicate that successful copulation had at long last occurred.

"He's only gone and shagged two pandas in one sitting... in front of a busload of visiting boy scouts!" Slapping his notepad, she dreaded the pun laden headline he had created to accompany this story. Too late.

"Ming Ling in ging gang goolie gang bang!"

Holding up his headline to the light, his eyes beamed with dewy pride not seen outside the labour ward of a maternity hospital. Pointing at his masterpiece now, his mind racing ahead to when it would net him the Pulitzer prize, he informed her, "That crate of brown ale is as good as mine!" Rubbing the dull ache in her temples brought on by moronic osmosis, she lamented at working with Pavlov's dogs, who willingly come up with bad jokey rhyming headlines for arse achingly awful stories in return for bowel bludgeoning booze.

She gave Norman a big thumbs up and a false smile, as he waddled off towards the editor's office to claim his prize. She quickly locked her desk drawer, picked up her bag and darted for the lift in a desperate bid to breathe air she didn't have to share with the hard of thinking.

As the empty lift descended the 18 floors to freedom, Cassandra closed her eyes in a desperate bid to shake off the mask of banal compliance she has had to wear to survive in possibly the last job she will ever have. *No!* she reprimanded herself, her last shred of self-respect... not so much shouting these days, more of a hoarse whisper. Not giving in, remembering her potential... remembering...

Her head sagged as her forehead rested on the cold lift button panel. Tears started welling, *god no! That's what they want. Don't lose control... keep it together.* She threw her head back and took deep breaths, wiped her eyes... she focused on him. He'll make it better. She had two choices: Hunt down a soulless killer... or for the rest of her days work with the undead. The loud "ping!" of the lift doors opening made her mind up for her.

Chapter 12

Six hours into his shift, a vein started throbbing in his temple. Like an irritating snooze alarm slowly delaying the inevitable wake up call. His heart started beating faster as he noticed his hands were gripping the binoculars a little too tightly, for he would be along in a minute... his nemesis.

The older of the two surveillance officers sat at the bank of six digital screens all showing different angles in interchangeable frames from the 25 covert cameras that covered the entrance to the bunker. His age and his experience had taught him the coping skills to deal with impatient little gung-ho fuckers who think Dirty Harry is a real person. Unfortunately for him, these trigger-happy cannon fodder always seemed to be on a 12-hour shift with him. Without taking his eyes off the screens, he sighed as he spoke to the ball of nervous energy who had now swapped binoculars for the high-powered military rifle on the tripod.

"Darren... if you don't learn how to relax, you'll end up with an ulcer the size of a rhino's bollock." The younger man had other things on his mind as he slowly swivelled the rifle on its stand, the tip of its silencer only an inch away from the tinted window.

"Bang on time!" Darren licked his lips as the object of his burning petty obsession staggered into the street, carrying a plastic bag full of shag nasty lager. Closer and closer to the entrance to the bunker's alley way the tramp lumbered. Ten feet... five feet... The junior officer's thumb clicked off the safety catch off the gun as his index finger curled round the trigger. He felt the cold hard muzzle of the Browning high-power jab against the base of his skull.

"You pull your trigger lad... and I'll pull mine." The younger man's hand dropped away from the rifle, as he watched the tramp stagger down the alley towards the door to their secret kingdom.

Walking slowly back to his surveillance desk, the older officer tapped away at his keyboard and quickly brought up images of the stumbling tramp on all six monitors.

"Oh, that was fucking clever! That stinking heap of shit could be there all day now Mr Jenkins!" Still holding his side arm in one hand, the senior officer put on his headset and spoke into the microphone, ignoring his unstable colleague.

"Naylor, you have a visitor."

The guard at the bunker's entrance replied on speakerphone. "Armed?"

"Negative. Civilian. Homeless."

The guard paused whilst he assessed the security threat the old man posed to the bunker as he conferred with a second muffled voice in the background.

"We have a visual... he's been here before. We can suspend deliveries for 20 minutes while you deal with it."

A decision had been made.

Seven foot away from the guard, on the other side of the bunker's door stood Declan Hannah... pissing like a horse.

"Ahhh! Jaysus! Will ya just look at dat?" Pride welling up in his blood shot eyes. Wiggling his fat buttocks now in a figure of eight mimicking a grotesque belly dancer, he doused the bunker's outer door with enough urine to pickle a blue whale. He then opened another of his many cans of 'madman's soup' to refill his slowly emptying bladder.

Across the back street, he was being watched, on six digital screens. The older officer picked up his mobile phone and dialled. On the screen, Declan sat down in the doorway to the bunker, in his own fresh warm piss and drank heartily like a king on his throne.

The senior officer's call had connected.

"Hello Chris. I need you round here now with Wolfgang."

He saw Declan hurl the empty can across the alley way and open another.

"When was the last time he was fed? "The reply from the other end of the phone drew a thin cruel smile to the officer's face.

"Good."

Chapter 13

The third of Declan's empty cans was booted across the alleyway... watched by numerous high-resolution covert micro cameras.

"A... another goal for Best!" Opening up another can and tilting it in silent salute to his football idol, he slurred'

"Ah George... you could've been a star... b... but you never had my breaks!" This clearly tickled him as he giggled uncontrollably, the tears welling up in his eyes as he bent double. He laughed out loud until he inevitably broke into a coughing fit that only pensioners can perform, like a symphony of angry phlegm. When his marathon squelching death rattle had subsided, his bowed head looked up through his matted fringe... and saw the dog.

Wiping the tears from his eyes to be sure he really was seeing what appeared to be a horse with a wolf's head, he stammered,

"G... good dog... hey, who's a lovely fella, th... then?"

The huge Alsatian just stood there, silently. No growling, no barking... but with shoulders tensed.

Declan slowly straightened up, not wanting to startle this fucking hairy crocodile. His wild frightened eyes darted past the animal to the alleys entrance, in the vain hope of seeing an owner... anyone.

Then he heard the two short, whistled notes.

The Alsatian seemed to explode with rage as it leapt five foot through the air and sank its immensely powerful jaws into Declan's shoulder. For what seemed like the longest 20 seconds of his miserable life, the old tramp's body was ripped and torn by razor sharp teeth... until he heard those two whistled notes again.

The dog immediately stopped its savage onslaught and ran off... leaving Declan to black out next to pieces of himself.

The senior officer Jenkins watched the attack dog turn Declan into gory chunks until he felt a sufficient lesson had been learnt, before phoning the dog handler who was waiting out of sight at the alley's entrance on the backstreet.

Once the dog was recalled, in the van and away, he waited another 30 seconds until he was sure the tramp was unconscious before he gave the all clear.

"Naylor... he's down. bring a car round."

The younger surveillance officer Darren was delighted at the tramp's misfortune at meeting a beast that used him as a gruesome chew toy.

"Heh! Heh! That was fucking awesome! His piano playing days are well over!" Jenkins zoomed the camera in on Declan's fingers... which lay several feet away from his bloodied body.

"You're supposed to be watching the street!" The irritation telling in his voice.

The scolded junior duly complied and through binoculars saw a black car drive up at the side of the alley.

Two men emerged from the alley carrying the collapsed tramp and bundled him into the boot of the car.

Five minutes later, the men in the car radioed in that they had dumped him a couple of miles away and anonymously phoned for an ambulance.

They could have left Declan his fingers, there was still time for the doctors to save them... but they saved them for Wolfgang instead. After all, lessons needed to be learned. The alley way and bunker door were all furiously mopped and scrubbed of forensic evidence. From the moment Declan unfortunately staggered down the alley way, until the bunker door had opened up to let another reaper out... had taken less than 20 minutes.

Chapter 14

The young staff nurse checked Declan's nasal gastric tube and the drip going into his arm.

"I'm afraid we were unable to administer morphine to Mr Hannah, as he had considerable units of alcohol in his system when he arrived."

She was addressing the unkempt unshaven man with long greasy hair, pulled back in a ponytail with an elastic band. Even though he wore the uniform dirty long black coat of a meth connoisseur, she could tell he wasn't like the usual homeless people who would lumber through casualty. The way his eyes darted around the room checking everything, he had more adrenaline in his system than booze. Drugs? Speed perhaps, she wasn't sure. His pupils weren't dilatated, if anything they were clear and alert. He darted around Declan checking his stitches, his charts, but she felt she had to intervene when the scruffy lout touched the cardiograph.

"That's not a toy!" She reprimanded the visitor, asserting her authority.

"I know, love. I used to be a medic."

The staff nurse was taken a back. "Oh... a paramedic?"

Why not? She thought. She could name plenty who have lost their jobs whilst pissed on duty. Three in this hospital at least.

"No, I used to be a medic in the army. I was a sergeant in the Royal Green jackets."

For three hours, Robert Mcvie sat by his old pal Declan's bed. Declan was never what you might call a handsome man. But the poor sorry sight lying on the bed looked like he had been beaten to death with the ugly stick. The top of his head had been shaved, stitched and bandaged. His face was a mass of bruises and sutures. Declan's leg was bandaged to the toes and elevated in a sling on a ceiling mounted pulley. It would be very hit or miss whether his severed Achilles tendon would heal successfully. Only when the alcohol had left his system could they properly assess his chances of receiving surgery. With his heart problems, that was in the lap of the gods whether he would survive going under the anaesthetic. But it was his hands... or what was left of them. Bobby Mcvie prayed the alcohol would leave his system before he regained consciousness. Because when he saw his hands, he would need all the morphine they could give him to knock him out again.

Chapter 15

The legendary charm and sophistication that oozed from every pore had not deserted the badly mauled Declan, as he awoke and laid eyes on Bobby.

"What the feck are you grinning at yer feckin' gobshite?!"

Bobby smiled,

"I believe that poor dog's in the next ward with indigestion. Something it ate disagreed with him."

Hannah coughed a vile hocking sound and snarled through discoloured teeth,

"Dat was no feckin' dog! It was the hound of the Baskervilles big brother!"

The ex-soldier had known the old tramp for five years now and marvelled at how he was an old master at the blarney. For all his usual tall tales, the dog was probably a poodle. Then again, could a poodle have ripped the poor fucker to bits like this? Probably not.

The nurses had sat Declan up in bed, with both his hands elevated and tied by crepe bandages to two drip stands either side of him. With his two middle fingers severed and missing from each hand, it gave him the appearance of an aging rapper giving the "Horned salute." Bobby mused that with the old Irishman's volcanic vocabulary bordering on Tourette's, he'd make those bed wetting L.A. rappers blush. From the position where his heavily bandaged hands were strapped over his head, the vagrant couldn't see the aftermath of the dog attack. Bobby deduced that with his usual growling demeanour, that Declan had no idea yet just how horrific his injuries were. Which was a blessing for Bobby. He'd seen many men before blown to pieces in conflict, and the dawning realisation was always more traumatic when the soul-destroying screaming started.

"So old fella, what were you doing playing one man and his dog down by Blackfriars bridge at the side of the river?"

Snorting as best he could with an oxygen tube hanging out of his nose, he replied, "I was nowhere near the feckin' river! I was up a back alley two streets away from Bengal Booze when Zoltan feckin' pounced on me!"

Bobby's head snapped up. He knew this infamous 24 hour off licence, as did all of inner London's homeless community... and it was miles away from where the ambulance driver's found Declan.

"I should feckin' know where I escaped the jaws of Hell!" The younger man knew when to pour oil on troubled water. And Declan's imminent bout of colourful language could fill a swear box the size of a skip.

"I'm not saying I don't believe you old fella, it's just your Achilles tendon..." pointing at the half-chewed leg.

"Well... I probably crawled me way out of there. You know me; I'm not one to let a bit of a scratch get me down. I've got me second wind now; if it came back, I'd feckin' batter the shite out of it!"

Mcvie had sliced the Achilles tendons of seven different enemy soldiers in his ten year army career. If you wanted to totally debilitate a man without killing him, then severing the Achilles tendon would put that enemy out of action for a long time. Despite the bullshit Hollywood movies, once someone slices the base of your calf... You are going nowhere. That is why Declan didn't crawl twenty feet, never mind two miles... without being spotted... or run over.

"I thought I was a feckin' goner... until I heard dat whistle."

Bobby stopped looking at Declan's charts. "The what?"

"Da whistle! I heard it twice just before the fecker jumped on me, and two more whistles before it stopped and ran off."

Bobby was suddenly very alert. "Declan, did it growl or bark at you?"

The old Irishman went suddenly very pale at the memory.

"No, dat was the feckin' scariest thing about it... it never made a sound."

They are rigorously trained not to give their handlers positions away by barking. To attack the main arteries on the body for maximum damage. To savage quickly and without mercy and stop instantly the moment they hear the whistle. So, why would someone set a military attack dog on a harmless old tramp?

"Where exactly was this alley way Declan?"

Chapter 16

After so many killings you're supposed to be numb to it. Isn't that what the heroes in tinsel town blockbusters tell us? The stone-faced chisel jawed celluloid killers don't feel a thing for the lives they take. Oh, how Jim envied these imaginary people. He didn't just think about their deaths... he dreamt about their lives. Or the lives they would've had if they hadn't met him. Holidays they'll never have, grandkids they'll never meet, the endless possibilities taken away from them. It's not just their lives that tormented his dreams that he mourned for, he mourned for his own lost life. The oh so simple life he had, when he worked at that oh so dull job at the department for statistics.

Then one day, two visitors came into his office and his life as he knew it ended... five years ago. The buzz had gone around the department of statistics like wildfire, Jim had hit the jackpot! This was it, the big spooks at M.I.5. had opened up their books and chosen a new disciple. The last time this happened was two months before, when Jim's supervisor had asked where Simon Wilson was. After much searching, Jim found the "chosen one" smoking a crafty fag in the gents. Wilson looked like he had a coat hanger in his mouth, his smile was that wide when he heard he had got the call. As he went into the supervisor's office to face his destiny, he turned to Jim and handed him his fountain pen.

"Take it." Jim knew the sentimental value attached to that pen.

"Behave, your Mum gave you that the first day you came to work here. I can't take that." Simon smiled as he pressed the pen his late mother had given to him into Jim's hand.

"I know, but this is my big chance Jim. I want you to take this... maybe it'll bring you good luck and you'll be next." Like a green-eyed bridesmaid at a wedding catching a bouquet, Jim took the pen. Simon's mother had it engraved with his name. His best friend smiled that obscenely wide smile one last time that resembled a fridge showroom, before turning and walking off towards a bright future... and Jim never saw him again.

Two months later, Jim was summoned to the supervisor's office where two stern faced spooks requested that he come with them. And when he left the building, nobody ever saw him again.

In the car the two spooks became friendlier, informing Jim how lucky he was to have this great honour bestowed upon him. These imposing sentinels made Jim feel like Icarus soaring skywards.

Little did he realise it then, but he was about to share the same fate.

After 15 minutes the car pulled into an industrial estate and entered a huge empty factory unit via the back-sliding doors. The black car pulled up directly behind a black transit van with its rear doors opened.

The first spook spoke curtly to Jim, all traces of humour had vanished.

"You have to be hooded from here on. For your safety and our security, do you understand?" It was of course a rhetorical question, as the hood was roughly placed over his head by the second spook and Jim transferred to the back of the waiting van.

Twenty maybe thirty minutes they drove around, with Jim hooded and face down on the floor of the van. Two sets of hands held him down by his ankles and shoulders. "It's for your own safety. We don't want you falling and hurting yourself whilst hooded, do we?" Somehow, the soothing tones from the unseen organic seatbelt had the opposite effect. Instead of feeling safe, all Jim could think about was hostages. Oh fuck! He wasn't going to spend three years chained to a radiator, was he? He hadn't cancelled the milk! *Stop it!* He reprimanded his racing imagination. This was how they do things in the secret service. Cloak and dagger. He didn't mind the cloak. It was the dagger that he was worried about.

The van came to an abrupt halt. Whatever lay in wait for him, he was shortly to find out. Yet all he could think about was 700 bottles of milk lined up on his path.

Chapter 17

He could make out a heavy metallic clunk of a door, followed by an electronic buzzing noise. Then steps that seemed to go down forever, the air seemed stuffy and then they went through echo laden corridors. Suddenly lots of voices and the distant sound of gunshots that made him jump as he was unceremoniously dragged towards his destination. His head was spinning as the two spooks hurled him up steps now, only these ones sounded metal, through another door before he was finally plonked in a chair and he jumped nervously again as the door clicked shut behind him. Their footsteps made a curious rustling sound like a crisp packet being scrunched up as they walked here. Wherever "here" was. His own feet made the same curious sound as he moved them side to side. He was trying to control his breathing, totally disorientated and trying to work out where he was, and what the hell were those gun shots about?

"Take the hood off please Jim."

He nearly leapt out of his skin at the low well-spoken voice. He'd assumed he had been placed in a room all alone. Removing the hood slowly and blinking as his eyes adjusted to the light, he saw he was in a very sparse room. Sitting opposite him was a well-groomed grey-haired man in his fifties. He was sat at a flimsy looking wooden desk, not really befitting the rank his demeanour told Jim he held in this organisation. Apart from a filing cabinet that was it for furniture. Bare walls and not so much as a potted plant. Maybe this was the military way? If it doesn't have a function, it has no place in this room. On his plain desk there was an ultra slim cordless laptop, a desk tidy, cluttered with pens and various pieces of paper and a black open briefcase, facing away from Jim.

"Sorry about your journey. "He smiled trying to reassure Jim.

"But it's either the hood or tranquilisers I'm afraid. We're not called 'The Secret Service' for nothing, you know." Jim looked at the man's old school tie. What was it, Eton? Harrow? Certainly not the nasty violent comprehensive that churned Jim out, that's for sure.

"If you don't mind me asking... who are you? M.I5? M.I6?"

Oh, get a bloody grip lad! What's wrong with you? Stumbling over your words like a naughty schoolboy about to have his bare arse smacked in the headmaster's office! Jim roared inwardly at himself for subconsciously letting this stranger intimidate him.

"Neither dear boy. I'm the Head of Section at the Department of population downsizing."

Jim was confused. "I'm sorry, I don't understand. I... I applied for a job to work at M.I.5. not... what was it you said?"

"The Department of population downsizing." Replied the older man as he held up a silencing hand to Jim.

The intriguing stranger opposite Jim tapped away at his laptop and read out Jim's C.V. "Hmmm... left school at 16, with nine GCSEs. Impressive, seeing as the only certificates 98% of your peers left with were a letter from the nit nurse and an ASBO. Went on to university..." he continued talking about Jim like a newsreader trotting out a D list celebrity's obituary. "...gained a 2-1 in English... teacher training college... oh dear." Looking up from the screen rather condescendingly. "Dropped out after six months... drifted from one job to the next like a toxic leper ship... until you landed at the department of statistics." Sighing in a very disapproving manner he shook his head at Jim. "...and that was five years ago. I bet you are sick and tired of Bill Gates banging on your front door looking for an heir to his throne, aren't you?" Even though this grinning prick was Jim's future employer, high up in the secret service and held Jim's future in the palm of his hands... he was actively sitting there belittling him for his own petty amusement. And... against his better judgement, he couldn't help himself. It just slipped out. Ah, foolish pride.

"Well, we can't all be born with a silver spoon up our arses, can we?"

The moment the words left his lips, he immediately foresaw himself recanting this tale to a pensioner, in a post office queue... as he cashed his giro.

Yet instead of pointing Jim to the front door, he genuinely smiled.

"Untapped intelligence... underachiever... yet with fire in your belly... oh you're perfect."

The head of section had tea and biscuits brought in. The two sinister looking butlers fussed over the tea and hob nobs and then left. The last time Jim encountered these pair they were sat on him as he was hooded in a van. He concluded that they were his boss's personal bodyguards. Now he was really confused. He thought he had blown it with that outburst, but no. Here he was, having afternoon tea with the boss. Like a caricature from a period drama, the older man held his little finger out whilst he drank his tea.

"At the department of statistics, you must have noticed the correlated percentages of global births?"

Munching on a biscuit, Jim replied, "Yes."

Looking down at the interior of his briefcase on his desk now. "...and deaths?"

"Well, yeah. They are all part of the same cycle."

That smile again. "I'm so glad you agree." Linking his hands behind his head now. "Unfortunately, you must have repeatedly noticed through your work, that that the amount of people checking in... is disproportionate to the amount of people checking out?" Understanding the analogy, he replied,

"Well... advances in medicine, better diet, peace time. People today are just living longer."

The warm smile had dropped from his boss's face. "Aren't they just?"

Did he detect anger in the older man? Jim wondered where this was all going. Would that be part of his new role here, compiling the same boring statistics he had been doing for the last five years?

"There are 7.7 billion people on this tiny planet. In 80 years, there will be 9.5 billion. Quite frankly, the natural resources of planet Earth cannot keep up with the out of control population explosion that just will not stop."

Jim interrupted "Er... excuse me... but you say you are not M.I.5. So, what exactly is the work you do here?"

"Here... we are actively redressing the balance."

Sipping his tea, the head of section noticed the quizzical look on Jim's face.

"Jim... do you realise just how many times a day you cheat death?" Jim shifted uneasily on his seat, his feet making that curious rustling sound again that was bugging him.

"You may leave the house a little late for work and step off the kerb and meet the car that will kill you. A few minutes earlier and you'd miss it completely."

Jim frowned. "I'm sorry I don't..."

"Natural selection, dear boy. The reason some people live, whilst others die."

Sighing now,

"Tragically for us, natural selection just isn't moving fast enough. With the population rampaging through the food chain the way it is, there will be food shortages, that will escalate into global famines. Riots in every major city that can only be contained with martial law. The stock market will repeatedly crash as the oil, gas and coal are drained from the ground and the sea. And we will have multiple uncontrollable wars that will send us back to the stone age for a very long time. That cannot be allowed to happen." A nervous cough now. "So, a decision has been taken."

"What has all this got to do with this place?" asked Jim.

His boss's eyes yet again glanced into the open briefcase.

"Here... we cull the population."

Almost ten seconds of silence elapsed as the enormity of the situation dawned on Jim. His heart pounded in his chest, he heard that rustling again as he rose to his feet on shaking legs.

The head of section's hand darted into the briefcase and produced a Mauser pistol fitted with a silencer. Aiming it directly at Jim's head, he sternly spoke.

"Sit down!"

So, there they sat, staring at each like two star crossed lovers... except one of them was pointing a gun at the other. Out of fear, Jim automatically held his hands up over his head as he sat shaking in the universal pose of surrender in his chair.

"Put your hands down please, you're not under arrest." The gun was lowered from Jim's head to his chest. If this small gesture was supposed to put him at his ease, it wasn't working. His boss smiled again, which with the silenced pistol was quite a chilling sight.

"Take some deep breaths, Jim. I'm going to put the gun down. When I do, please don't do anything stupid like running for the door. The two gentlemen who brought you here, Tony and Gary are waiting outside, and they are both armed." Smiling again, "Besides... I'm a crack shot and you'd be dead before you reached the handle."

His voice rasping at first, Jim blurted out,

"Wh... what are you going to do with me?" Lowering the gun as promised, he placed it back into the open briefcase. When his hand reappeared from the case, he held a huge wad of bank notes tied with an elastic band, which he slapped onto the desk for dramatic effect.

"First... I'm going to brief you. Next, I'm going to train you. Then I'm going to provide you with a new identity and a place to live."

He found his voice again, "A... and then?"

"Then dear boy... I'm going to put you to work."

The nervous sweat just oozed out of Jim as he held out his hands, almost pleading. "Y... you've got the wrong man. Honestly, I couldn't kill anyone!"

Not taking his eyes off Jim, the older man's hand rested near to the open briefcase.

"Yes, you can. You just need the right motivation." It was Jim who smiled now. A false nervous mask that his boss saw through immediately.

"Look, you can trust me. I... I won't tell anybody about what's going on here..."

"You signed the official secrets act when you went to work at the department of statistics, so that will ensure your silence?" Said the older man. He was clearly playing with him.

Jim's eyes lit up. Seeing a way out. "T... that's right! The official secrets act. So, I couldn't tell anyone abou..."

His words were cut short as his boss yet again produced the gun from the case and laid it next to the huge wad of money.

"In a moment, I am going to make you a proposition. It will not be made to you twice." Jim swallowed hard as his legs started to shake again. His employer / executioner held up the gun in one hand and the money in the other.

"You can accept our offer... or you can refuse. Time to choose Jim... are you going to join us?"

His mind racing, no way out... and then he saw it... the reason his feet rustled on the floor of the office. Plastic sheeting that covered the whole office floor. The flimsy desk that could be moved quickly... when they wrapped his body up in the sinister floor covering. Like a thunderbolt, the question came to him as he blurted out,

"Simon Wilson! D...did he accept?"

His boss paused, "No... he refused."

Hanging his head in his hands and staring despondently at the floor his friend had died on, he replied in a low voice, "I accept."

Chapter 18

His boss stood up and almost bounded over to him as he heartily shook Jim's hand. "Gentlemen!"

On cue, the two guards came in and Jim was unsure as to whether he had failed the test and they were going to wrap him in plastic. The head of section announced like a proud father telling a packed pub his son had lost his virginity.

"Gary, Tony... we have a new Reaper!"

On hearing this, the pair of them shook his hand and slapped his back. In a moment... he'd wake up. That was it; he was still on the floor of the van on the way to his real job interview. Obviously, the lack of oxygen from being hooded on the van floor had caused him to hallucinate. What was it they called him?

A "Reaper"?

So, what was he expected to do? Wear a full monk's outfit and knock off old grannies with a scythe? No more gorgonzola for you at bedtime young man! Definitely a dream, oh yes. Without a shadow of a doubt.

"Jim?"

The voice brought him back to reality. He was dreaming, alas he was daydreaming in a state of denial that bordered on shock.

"Jim?"

That cultured voice again, only this time, there were visuals to accompany the audio, as the guards, his new boss and the room his friend was shot dead in loomed into view.

"I think we lost you there for a moment dear boy. Here, take your expenses."

He placed the telephone book thick wad of bank notes in the new recruit's hand. Taking a huge deep breath Jim spoke, aiming to keep on the right side of these upper-class assassins.

"So… do I get a gun?" Delving into his briefcase, his boss produced a D.V.D. compilation of home movie filmed accidents... and a banana.

"No, you get these."

Chapter 19

The D.V.D. his boss produced was loaded onto his laptop and all four of them sat down in the office that had a floor covering made of plastic sheeting. They drank tea and the experience although extremely surreal, wasn't entirely unpleasant. After watching the syndicated. D.V.D of amazingly bad home videos sent into the show's makers, each clip netting the sender £ 250. Jim felt like he should speak up. Instead he sat in nervous silence and watched a granny get her nose trapped in a moving escalator whilst the canned laughter soundtrack went ape shit.

In Victorian London, there was a mental asylum called "Bethlem Royal Hospital". Or as it was more notoriously known as "Bedlam." It was Europe's first and oldest mental institution. Bored aristocracy and the landed gentry would bribe the corrupt warders of this institution to let them look through the bars of the patient's cells. These pampered perverts would take sadistic delight at laughing at the misfortunes of tortured souls in pain and distress for their own petty amusement. But thanks to modern technology, you can do this from the comfort of your laptop. Progress indeed, as they sat and watched a chimpanzee try to drag a woman through the bars of its cage as she mistakenly tries to feed it a kebab. The canned laughter masked her screams. They had sat here and watched this disc for over two hours now and Jim could stay silent no longer.

"You told me that I am now a Reaper?" His boss sat beside him sipped daintily at his tea. "Correct."

"And that I am to kill members of the general public... whose names are picked out at random by your department's computer?"

Clinking his china cup gently onto his saucer, the head of section cleared his throat. "You are no doubt wondering why we are watching possibly the worst excuse for a T.V. program ever made? A program so bad, that if there ever was a Nuremberg trial equivalent for crimes against viewers... then the producers would be dragged kicking and screaming into the street by their hair... to be shot in the face in front of their ugly hairy chinned Mothers."

This tirade brought chuckles from the duo of hob nob munching guards sitting directly behind Jim. Before he could reply, his boss continued.

"That Jim is how we kill our targets."

"Wh... what? By filming them going arse over tit into a swimming pool?" This drew more chuckles from Tony and Gary behind him, which was seriously starting to grate his nerves now.

"Jim... what can you hear as you watch this drivel?"

Jim shook his head, bewildered as to what to say for the best.

"Er... I don't know, er... really crap one liners from an ex Aussie soap star hosting the show?"

"Yes, but in the background to each clip?" He gestured with a flick of the wrist.

With eyes looking skyward for inspiration, Jim replied "Laughter?"

Gripping Jim's shoulder tightly, he beamed, "Exactly! Their death knell... and our get out of jail free card!"

"If I was to put a gun to your head and blow your brains all over that wall, what would happen next?" This casual enquiry sent shivers through Jim as this same man was quite prepared to do exactly that, hours earlier... if Jim had given him the wrong answer.

"You'd have a big mess to clear up." replied Jim, bravado thinly masking his fear. He wasn't sure whether it was working. It turned out this answer delighted his boss. "That's right! You'd have a murder investigation, forensic teams sealing the area off whilst they rummage for D.N.A. like pigs snuffling for truffles. Witness statements, door to door enquiries... in short, bloody fuss!" Throwing his arms up incredulously at the petty inconvenience of the authority's audacity at interfering in their business. "But..." Jabbing his finger at the still playing D.V.D.

"...if I were to throw you down a flight of stairs, snapping your neck... and then dressed your twitching corpse up in a French maid's outfit... the public and the authorities will assume a transvestite had toppled off his nine-inch stilettos and pirouetted off this mortal coil."

Jim was aware his jaw had dropped open, and promptly closed it.

"You're serious?"

He gently sipped his tea. "I know all this is new, and a tad radical, but our methods are meticulous in the planning and evidence based. Do you remember a few years back when a famous comedian/ventriloquist was fixing the T.V. aerial on his roof during a football match and he slipped and fell to his death?" Jim acknowledged he remembered by nodding.

"Well seeing as that comedian was a renowned slapstick acrobatic comedian, what were your first thoughts when you heard how he'd died? Be honest, your initial thoughts? It's not a trick question."

Jim sighed, "I suppose like everyone else I thought it was a joke. Funny even. The type of thing he'd do in his act. Some of the lads at the office even said he had his ventriloquist dummy up there on the roof with him when he fell."

"Exactly. You thought it amusing. Trivial and comical. And your first reactions are what we want. We do not want any murder squad detective taking a second glance at our handy work. 'Death by misadventure' is our ultimate aim. The more ridiculous looking the death, the less chance of a murder investigation and an autopsy. You see Jim, any fool can kill someone. Barbarians have been doing it since the dawn of time. The real art, dear boy... is getting away with it."

Chapter 20

Cassandra trudged up the flights of stairs to her lonely flat. Most abodes welcomed you in with gentle wind chimes. The nearest she got was the customary three bottles of wine that clinked rhythmically together in the off-licence plastic bag she held as she climbed. She chided herself for her nightly purchase that the "de-stress" ritual from work was more like a cerebral sedative. Her old job investigating dictators and bent M.P's was stressful. Yet even with that relentless level of stress plus the Fleet Street's boozing culture, did she ever feel the need to systematically drink like this. And despite her rebuffing denial... it was a need.

Since her old life ended and the only work she was offered since nobody else would employ her, was on the "Daily Throbber", a fifth-rate red top tabloid. Up until she locked her self-respect away in a tightly sealed box and went to work for that rag, did she only ever fully understand the old saying to have "died from shame." For the first few months this once respected journalist's face was so red as she walked through the office doors, that everyone thought her sun bed was set to "Kentucky fry." Then she found a strategy for coping with it... and they clinked together noisily in the bag as she hauled herself up the stairs. No, her job wasn't stressful... it was a piece of piss. A monkey could do it. A monkey with learning difficulties and a brain that had been transplanted with an arse. Amongst the celebrity gossip, sport and brain-dead shite the paper churned out; there were still levels of tawdry tabloid tackiness that scraped right through the bottom of this diarrhoea filled barrel. And funnily enough, all these dregs ended up in Cassandra's in tray. No story was deemed too outrageous or not in the public interest. Since the Daily Throbber's ball scratching readership seemed to thrive on reading about Martians eating a man's giro or a woman who gave birth to a Welsh Elvis. The whole ethos of the paper seemed to be never let the facts get in the way of a good story. Eventually, faced with a stone wall, she stopped complaining, stopped caring... and started buying more wine.

It was only when she was given all the strange comical deaths to report on, that a glimmer of hope appeared in her dark and lonely world. She was usually given about four or six dubious demises a week. Because these were stories given to her to cover, the quality of the photos and facts were depressingly laughable. These unfortunate deaths of individuals usually happened under tragically comical circumstances. A man bungee jumping using a bungee made from his Mum's knicker elastic, a woman having sex with a horse, a stripper hiding in a big cake... as it was mistakenly put in an oven. Tragical and whimsical, their last real epitaph on this planet, reduced to making morons laugh. A couple of times as she had read the initial reports, she had found herself chuckling at the ridiculous nature of these people's demise, and then felt instantly ashamed of herself. Had working there made her so desensitised that she was beginning to think like them? As far-fetched and amusing as most of these people's exits from this world were... they were still human... and they had died. The shame bit deeper as this was no laughing matter.

Then, about a year ago as she was scanning the C.C.T.V. photos from three separate tragic deaths she noticed something odd. A face caught on camera in the background or reflected in a shop window opposite the deceased... it was the same face. At first, she put it down to a trick of the light. Then it turned up in another... and another. With a new journalistic zeal, she scoured all the new tragic deaths that landed on her desk with meticulous detail. Most were run of the mill, then he would pop up again. Always in the background, sometimes burred as the security cameras around the area weren't always the highest quality. She shared the photos with a hacker friend of hers, Marty, who had software to lighten shadows and make images clearer. When he did, the likeness was undoubtable... and his face had turned up around the scenes of 28 deaths. All officially explained away as 'Death by misadventure'.

Looking nervously over her shoulder to check none of her neighbours were about to walk onto the landing outside her flat, she gently opened the letter box on her front door. The taut fishing line was just visible pulled tight across the back of the door. Checking once again for nosy parkers, she turned the key in the cylinder and quickly shoved the door wide open. As she darted to the side of the frame, she felt the wind rush past her as the tungsten claw hammer missed her skull by an inch. She caught it expertly as it made its return journey into the flat, still supported by its fishing cat gut umbilical cord. Once inside she yet again checked the landing via her door spy glass and placed the hammer on a shelf next to the door. Ducking under the now flaccid fishing line trip wire, she checked her answering machine. It blinked and showed a digital red number one, she could guess who it was. These days the phone rarely rang. When you are cursed, why would it? Still, she had her protector. This though brought a rare smile to her lips as she gently patted the claw hammer as if it were a guard dog. The medieval anti burglar trap had served her well over the years. The calibre of scumbags she used to go hunting would send highly trained goons who could bypass the most sophisticated locks and alarms money could buy. Unfortunately, a 16 ounce claw hammer was neither sophisticated nor expensive. From time to time she would find the trap sprung and a trail of blood leading from her door down the stairs. All zest for ransacking and hacking suddenly evaporate when your teeth have been flossed by a claw hammer. She mused that she was in fact, doing these thugs a favour, effectively halving their toothpaste bill overnight. Chuckling to herself at this orthodontist fantasy, she pressed play on the answering machine and recognized the nasal tones of her favourite techno geek.

"Hold onto your hat, Cass, he's struck again... and this time I've got him on tape!"

Chapter 21

It only took her 35 minutes to get to Marty's by taxi. She could've driven, but if he offered her drink, which he usually did... she wasn't going to refuse. Jesus, at this stage of denial, would Alcoholics Anonymous even let her through the door? Paying the taxi driver, she approached the front door to Marty's lair. Any other adult human would reside in a flat, but her pet nerd lived in the realms of sci-fi, alien abductions and midget Orcs. If the council would let him have a moat and a draw bridge to his gaff, he would definitely have one. The rain was just starting its cycle of drizzle to village sweeping monsoon, when she spoke into his video door entry system. The crime rate in this area really wasn't that bad to warrant such a paranoid gadget... but this was Marty. A guy who bought a toothbrush on eBay that had a built in sat-nav for fuck sake!

"Were you followed?" The grainy spectacled face enquired on the three-inch green screen. The ice-cold rain that was chilled in the Arctic, blown thousands of miles across snow-capped mountains and fell three miles being pulled to Earth by the Moon's gravitational pull at twenty-two feet per second onto her head... really made being condescended by a bone-idle mummy's boy just that more bearable.

"Open the fucking door, my hair's starting to curl!"

Once inside the drab badly glossed blue front door she entered mission control at N.A.S.A. Well... if a nest of travelling gypsies ever set up camp at Cape Canaveral and decided to drop their standards and really let themselves go. His flat smelled of feet. The aftershave of many an unkempt bachelor. Alas, the term "bachelor" denoted choice.

Marty's very appearance relegated him into the beggar league, condemned to a life of frenzied masturbation that would put a chimp on Viagra to shame. If she so chose, she could cure him. She could fuck him once and release the poor bastard from his madness brought on by immense crippling loneliness and an insane addiction to women that he never asked for, and the cold turkey that was slowly killing him.

She knew Marty loved her. He chased after her, eager to please like a puppy. She had done nothing to encourage this, or so she argued with her chiding conscience. Yet, she couldn't deny, she had done nothing to discourage him either. Luckily for her, he had never pushed it further than unrequited devotion. His terror of her rejecting him outweighed any fantasy notion of her ever realistically being his. But she needed him... well, his skills anyway. He was the most gifted hacker she had ever met and had helped her break several of her biggest stories when she was once a real journalist. And when her career was murdered, and everybody deserted her... only Marty stayed loyal. So, as long as she kept visiting him in any capacity, he could delude himself that there may be hope. As warped a symbiotic relationship as this was, she always reconciled herself that it was a lot healthier and more honest than most marriages.

Even though the black and white C.C.T.V. footage wasn't of the highest quality, she held her breath as his face clearly flashed into view.

He wasn't tall, maybe five feet ten at the most. Thick black collar length hair... and that unmistakeable haunted look in his eyes. She had met killers in the flesh before. Mercenaries, gangsters and all of them had cold dead emotionless eyes, totally devoid of remorse. This man's eyes were different. She'd seen this look before... in a victim's eyes. In the gaze of a war zone survivor, someone who had witnessed horror.

"That's him." She said watching as Marty for the tenth time replayed the tape, he'd hacked from police data banks. The film showed a street scene at night. The time shown in the left-hand bottom corner of the screen showed 10.20pm. The dark-haired man enters a laundrette... he then exits and crosses the road at 10.47pm.

Cassandra looked up at Marty, incredulous that he had dragged her across town on a night wetter than a whale's arm pit for this.

"Yes, that's him... but washing his smalls is hardly going to get him a ringside seat at the Old Bailey, is it?"

Smiling the smile of the smug and the pedantic, the techno nerd rewound the footage yet again, only this time he started it at 10.05pm, when a very plain brunette in her late twenties entered the laundrette with a bag of washing. Sensing the reporter's notorious short fuse was about to blow, Marty explained,

"That's Lorraine Fuller."

Shrugging wildly, the hack was close to exploding now at Marty's obtrusiveness and blurted out, "And?!"

Reaching behind him, he slapped down on the table a frivolous tabloid story from a rival paper he'd stuck into his scrap book dated a week ago.

"Lorraine Fuller was found dead in a tumble dryer in that laundrette the night this was filmed."

Marty's espresso coffee machine gurgled noisily like an 80 a day woodbine smoking pensioner's lung, being drained by a suction pump. Even this vile sound could not detract her from the newspaper report in the hacker's scrap book.

SAUCEPOT SPINS IN FUMBLE DRYER

A 28-year-old woman was found dead yesterday in a London laundrette. Police have identified the deceased as Lorraine Fuller, who lived alone. Amazingly the police investigating the tragic death found a 12-inch vibrator next to the corpse inside the dryer. The sex toy was still switched on. Police are unsure whether the unmarried woman was trying to retrieve her "flexible friend" from the dryer after it had accidentally got mixed in with her washing, or if the years of lonely spinsterhood had driven her to seek bizarre sexual thrills... that ultimately ended in tragedy. We spoke to the makers of the "Bonkomatic 3000" and asked was it possible that their product could orgasm a woman to death? Their spokesman said, "It is tragic that this lady died. Although we cannot accept any responsibility for any misuse of our outstanding product, it cannot be denied that it will keep on working... even through a hot tumble dryer cycle. So, our customers can be reassured that the Bonkomatic 3000 is built to last."

Just below the newspaper report was a quarter page colour advert for the fearsome looking gusset gizmo. Her years in the merciless world of journalism had taught her that life was cheap. A young woman had been slaughtered... and nobody was looking for her killer.

Chapter 22

"We've got his face; we've got him at the scene of a murder…"

"Er…"tragic death" was the police verdict." butted in Marty pedantically.

She reared on him now, "Fuck you and your word games Marty! We know he murdered her! The police aren't even bothered looking for anyone, and if we don't stop him, he'll do it again!"

There was a tense uneasy silence.

He had pissed her off, like a precocious child always needing the last word. But this was his home. She had overstepped the mark. After she had bitten off more than she could chew on a big story a few years back and that powerful individual in question had chewed her up extremely viciously and spat her out… her career as a journalist was totally finished. Her colleagues and friends in the capital not so much shunned her, they ran for the hills terrified the angel of death would visit them with the unparalleled wrath that engulfed her, if they so much as spoke to her. All her sources seemed busy when she rang. Old favours to be called in were suddenly forgotten. Offers of work all dried up and the phone, like her future prospects... went dead.

Yet in the economic and social wilderness of big, lonely London, only one person stood by her... Marty.

There he stood now, in the uneasy silence looking down at his shuffling feet. Resembling a well smacked pup not wanting to upset its master anymore.

"I... I think I've found his lair."

One by one, C.C.T.V. images of street scenes flashed on Marty's flat screen digital monitor. The screen was split into four segments and different images of London streets whizzed by, at what appeared to be the speed of a rotating reel on a one-armed bandit. How he could view and dismiss the footage he didn't want, she'd never know. Her pet hacker could hack into the Metropolitan police's security cameras and view them at his leisure... then record anything he found intriguing.

"There!" He excitedly stopped the hacked footage and played it at half speed showing their murder suspect walking out of a side street. She looked confused.

"Marty, I don't..."

"Wait." He said, tapping wildly at his keyboard until another picture of an alley way flashed into view. "This is the other side of the alley way he has just walked out of, only six seconds earlier. "She frowned as she stared at the screen until the penny dropped. "Wh... where is he?"

"Exactly! "exclaimed Marty. "He has appeared twenty-four times out of this alleyway in the last nine days. Going in and out and not once has he appeared in the alleyway he has walked into?" Cassandra looked hard at the computer trying to figure it out.

"So, what... is he a fucking vampire? He can choose which cameras he appears on?" Like the cat that got the cream, he sat there tapping a biro on his goofy teeth. "I've also noticed other people appearing and disappearing at the entrance. But that's not the best bit..." He paused for his finale. "...there is a three second delay on the signals from the cameras surrounding that alley."

"So, what does that all mean?"

He replied, "It's a pre-recorded looped tape."

Chapter 23

Her old journalistic mind was going ballistic now. "So, one street he walks down all the cameras have been rigged?"

"No, four." he replied sardonically.

Her jaw dropped. "Four?"

"Yes." He said spreading an A to Z map of London across his cluttered coffee table. Pointing at various points on the map he elaborated.

"No cameras filming within one square mile of these four streets are recording and transmitting what is really going on there." This was too much for her cynical mind to take. She let out a weary sigh,

"Marty, this is the most digitally surveiled city on the face of the planet... and you're saying that somehow, one square mile of it has been blanked out under the noses of the police and the security services without their knowledge?"

He tapped one button on his keyboard.

"I can prove it."

Her jaw dropped as she saw the hacker at the entrance to each of those four streets, then strolling down them. The footage cuts to the alleyways seconds later showing people walking by... but with Marty nowhere to be seen.

"I did a series of recons over the last three days just to make sure, then hacked the footage later. I give a mean love bite... but I ain't no vampire."

She looked down at the square mile of streets that Marty had ringed in biro on the map. Within that circle was a vast labyrinth of streets and back alleys.

"He could be anywhere." she sounded deflated.

Again, they sat in silence before she spoke, "B... but I just can't believe he could hack into police surveillance cameras."

Staring back at the screen he replied, "Why not... I did."

Chapter 24

The cold baked beans tasted good straight from the tin as Bobbie Mcvie studied the unfolded A to Z of London by candlelight. The sound of the rain hammering down on his makeshift home of wooden pallets and plastic sheeting was deafening. Despite its dilapidated appearance, his "home" was extremely well constructed and completely dry. His old army survival training had taught him how to construct shelters in the most hostile and barren landscapes. So, constructing one under this railway arch was like a holiday camp by comparison. His floor was four wooden pallets square and two pallets high. Very important, to keep him off the icy ground... and away from the rats. When he first set up camp here, the rats came for him on mass every night. Then every morning his neighbours would find between ten to twenty decapitated rodents piled outside the new stranger's shack. This went on for over two weeks until the rats seriously took the hint. The heads were never found, his new neighbours never asked... a reputation was born.

"Oiy! Feckin' rat boy! You in there!"

The old silver-tongued smoothie himself, Declan was the very first person to talk to Bobby since he arrived here all those years ago. The only one with the balls to bang on the rat slayer's door... and ask to borrow a tenner. This same fearless Irishman now lay savagely mauled in a hospital bed by a military attack dog.

Every instinct told him to drop this. This wasn't a foreign theatre of operations. Whatever Declan had stumbled into had involved the military in this country. If he pursued his friend's attackers, he'd ultimately be up against his peers: men who were handpicked from every regiment of the British army, trained to the highest calibre and regarded as the most elite feared fighting force in the world. Bobby Mcvie took a deep breath. It had been five years since he was court martialled and thrown out of the S.A.S... and now here he was, contemplating dying at the hands of the men he served with.

Chapter 25

Jim found it increasingly difficult to comprehend exactly what he was seeing. Slimey sat cross legged in the back of the van slowly screwing together a hit man's rifle. Next, he picked up the glass jar containing buzzing bees and clicked onto the lid a clear plastic device that resembled a pub whiskey optic. The "optic" had two valves, which at the end had a dark grey plastic capsule. Sliding a small lever on the side of the jar, an opening the size of a five pence piece let one of the insects buzz angrily into the optic. This done, Singen closed off the tiny door and opened the first valve, letting the bee crawl this time as the tapered valve was only millimetres wider than it was. This procedure was repeated with the second valve until the bee was trapped inside the grey plastic coffin at the optic's exit. Slimey carefully decanted and loaded these grey buzzing bullets into the rifle, smiling at Jim as he released the safety catch.

"Tell me you are taking the piss?" exclaimed Jim as Singen carefully poked the silenced rifle's muzzle out of the van's side window.

Slimey grinned as he repeated the procedure and loaded another bee into the optic.

"Au contraire, Mon Ami."

Jim fucking despised the way people who were thick as pig shit, casually dropped into conversation a few French phrases when it was obvious, they couldn't speak the language, in a desperate bid to appear the very essence of civilised sophistication. Parrots can squawk out "Polly wants a cracker!" But this doesn't mean that the camp cousin of the budgie knows what it is saying does it? Mused Jim.

A third bee was quickly chambered into the gun and Slimey screwed a gas canister onto the stock of what Jim surmised was a converted paintball rifle... converted to kill. The muzzle was gently eased out of a small, tinted glass window at the side of the van. "For your information Jim, over 193 people die from bee stings every year." He said in a low calm voice as he squinted into the telescopic sight...seconds before pulling the trigger.

Chapter 26

Colin Hale was loading his daughter's brand new waterproof camera with film as the bee stung the back of his neck. "Jesus!" His hand went straight to the source of the pain, dropping his child's birthday present as he did so.

The second bee slammed into the side of his face, sending white hot needles of pain coursing through his cheek. He slumped against the kitchen table as his head pounded, and he started to feel dizzy. Looking down, he saw them; the dead insects lying on the floor like two soulless black eyes searching for their next victim.

"Get a grip!" He reprimanded himself, backing away from this hallucination... he was going to be alright.

The third bee begged to differ. It felt like it had burst his eyeball when its sting pierced his left eyelid. The sheer ferocity of heat and pain dropped him like a stone. He lay face down on the cold lino choking for oxygen, unable to breathe as the scalding hot heat tore at the muscles and nerves in his neck, cheek and slowly closing eyeball. Through the gasps and sobs he saw four men in suits stood in his kitchen. No, not four... it was two. The tears and double vision were blurring back and forth.

"H... h… help me!" Choked Colin, as one of the men opened a briefcase and produced a small eye drops bottle. His tears of pain turned to tears of joy, as this angel of mercy spoke,

"It's ok, I'm a doctor."

The suited man then filled the bottle's pipette while his silent colleague looked on.

"Open your mouth... this will help." The shivering Colin complied. His tongue held out... taking lethal communion... as Singen squeezed the pipette and coated Colin's tongue with concentrated venom from the Brazilian honeybee.

The extra concentrated venom in his system was sending Colin into anaphylactic shock. He could feel his windpipe swelling up as he found it increasingly hard to breathe. The sharp melodic rings from his phone concentrated his panicking mind, that was growing weaker by the second through lack of oxygen. When the answering machine kicked in, he heard his six-year-old daughter's voice.

"Daddy! I hope you haven't forgotten my birthday present? Mummy will be dropping me at your house at teatime. Love you!" With that, she was gone. His left eye was bloated and swollen shut, but through the other eye he could see that this "doctor" was grinning at him.

"That's one party you won't have to pay for."

The clarity of the situation hit Colin like a thunder bolt. These men in his kitchen were somehow responsible for his condition, and this "doctor" was fucking gloating over him after... after... poisoning him! That's it! The eye dropper! Since he had taken whatever came out of that eye dropper, he suddenly felt ten times worse.

He had to stop them... but how? He could barely breathe, losing consciousness... He knew he was dying. The flash of yellow caught his eye... his daughter's new yellow waterproof camera was right next to him. He'd take a photo... it was proof! They'd be caught! They wouldn't get away with it! A last desperate attempt from a dying man clutching at straws. With the last ounce of strength he possessed, his trembling hand grabbed the camera, aimed it at his killers and... in slow motion Colin's arm fell backwards smacking the camera into the oven's glass door as the flash went off. He gurgled his last breath before his windpipe closed forever.

Jim shuddered as Colin Hale's death rattle echoed round the small kitchen. It never got any easier, each time he killed... or was party to a kill. Whether half arsed or botched. Secretly he hoped they would dismiss him for being a crap assassin, but in reality, getting sacked in his line of work meant relocation to a nice little abode... six foot deep. The self-loathing was consuming Jim. He killed... so they would let him live. So, this was living was it? Slaughtering innocent strangers whilst dwelling in a netherworld. He hasn't existed on any computer data base in five years. No social security contributions, no tax bills and not even the subscriptions department of the Reader's Digest book of the month club could find him. He closed the open kitchen window the bees were fired through to mask their entry point and gazed at the surreal sight of Slimey dipping the corpse's fingers into a jar of honey he had taken out of his black briefcase. He then carefully holding Colin's wrist, used the dead man's hand to smear a crude glistening beard across his face.

"Trousers." ordered Slimey. Jim's self-loathing plumbed new depths as he complied and undressed the body. Slimey repeated the smearing... only this time on Mr Hale's genitals. Jim rigged up a noose of fishing line onto the jar of angry bees Slimey had shown him in the van. The jar was placed on the kitchen table and the line traced through the front door letter box. Singen produced a Guinness book of records book, put the corpse's honey smeared fingerprints on it and opened it at a suitable page. Once out of the door, his latex gloved hand reached through the letter box, yanked the fishing line and waited for the jar to smash.

Chapter 27

"Big Issue. Buy the Big Issue. "Bobby repeated in a half-arsed monotone. He had only sold three copies this morning; his usual sales patter wasn't cutting the mustard today. The huge tidal wave of apathy that had hit him was a result of his mind being on other things. Namely that morning's visit to see Declan in the hospital was draining. The full horror of the old Irishman's injuries, notably his hands, had sent him into hysteria. Bobby had to help the nurse hold him down whilst the doctor sedated him. As his service unit's medic, Sergeant Mcvie had held many a screaming soldier down as he tried to dig bullets out of them... without anaesthetic.

"Get a fucking job, you filthy scrounging bastard!"

His train of thought was broken by a wanky office worker in a nasty nylon suit. This low-level desk jockey was carrying a pint of overpriced trendy coffee in front of him like it was the Holy Grail itself. It never ceased to amaze Bobby in this "Fuck the poor, I want the bonus ball" society, how being seen in the street carrying coffee was regarded as a status symbol. So... these were the pitiful excuse for D.N.A. that Mcvie had over the years risked his life to protect? Any other day and Bobby would've let this flaccid little prick have his power kick for the day.

Very quickly Bobby thrust the magazine into the office clerk's face, simultaneously bumping into him. "Big Issue?"

The suit pushed Bobby away, sending him to the floor in the process.

"Fuck off you animal!" He roared at Bobby, who lay on the ground, his magazines scattered all around him. The clerk looked wildly around, as passers-by stared at the very modern analogy of modern capitalism: A man in a suit and tie knocking a tramp to the floor. It was such a perfect example that it almost looked like a logo for a multinational conglomerate. Yes, the passers-by did witness this, but they did not stop to help. They knew the unwritten official motto of this city off by heart:

"Don't get involved."

Panicking that his assault on a homeless person may be reported, he scuttled off at a hurried pace, spilling his precious coffee on him as he went. Slowly climbing to his feet, Bobby felt the office workers wallet in his coat pocket... and it felt good.

Chapter 28

The obnoxious office worker's credit card pushed back the latch after the third attempt. Bobby smiled at this pen pushing moron's complacency, he had a Chubb five lever dead lock with anti-pick curtain, and it wasn't locked. If he did, there is no way the irked Big Issue seller could have burgled his flat... using his own credit card. As well as the credit card, the man's wallet contained £94.00, a dry cleaning ticket, a receipt for his beloved status coffee and most importantly for Bobby, a business card... with the man's address on it.

Well, it would be rude not to burgle him, wouldn't it?

Controlling his breathing, he intently listened out for any occupants of the flat. Slowly dropping to his knees, he slid the bottom door bolt into its keep. A wise precaution against being disturbed by a key holder.

Once this was done, he went to work.

Rummaging under the sink he found a black bin bag. Moving swiftly through the bedroom he threw an iPod, laptop and various CD's (mostly rock ballad shit and lots of Dion Warwick... was his rotund benefactor so far in the closet that he would resurface in Narnia? Mused Bobby) into the bag. The electrical trinkets were just a smoke screen for what he really needed: a suit. After much searching, he found this at the back of the wardrobe... behind six multicoloured Hawaiian shirts. Oh, Narnia definitely beckons lard arse. If he had more time, Bobby was sure he'd find size 11 stilettos somewhere in there. The suit was a dark blue number. Trying it on, he sighed as it was swimming on his lean wiry frame. The office worker was a fat fucker, but Bobby could pass this off as a trendy loose fit... he would definitely need a belt though. The two paper napkins he'd picked up outside McDonalds served him well, as they acted as a buffer against everything the ex-soldier touched. In all of the Republican flats Sergeant Mcvie had burgled, not once did he leave a single fingerprint... he wasn't going to start now.

Passing a designer knife block, he slid out a gleaming razor-sharp knife, held the blade up to the light for inspection then slipped it into the deep inside pocket of his long black coat. He also took the sharpening steel for good measure. The obligatory ransack of the man's flat to cover his tracks, Bobby couldn't resist ringing a £10 a minute premium porn chat line using his host's credit card... and left the phone off the hook. When that creepy little pen pusher returns home tonight, he will wish he'd bought that Big Issue.

Chapter 29

Although her colleagues would go all the way to the village idiot semi-finals, she kept all her work on her serial killer story under wraps. They weren't cunning enough to steal her scoop and pass it off as their own. But they were petty and spiteful enough to get it spiked before it went to press. Unfortunately, Cassandra's chosen profession was riddled with rampant jealousy, that had seen some of the most ground-breaking and thought-provoking news stories of the 20th century killed stone dead... to placate the brittle fine bone China egos of a fellow journalist two desks away.

The result: Bingo, big tits and D-list celebrities gurning as they stagger in and out of rented limos. The world turns, the bombs drop, human rights are being eroded... and the elite smile like Cheshire cats; safe in the knowledge their sins will never be reported. Her fat sweaty colleague was not his usual jovial self today.

"Oh, fucking hell! Why me?!"

She casually enquired as to the source of his pain.

He replied, "I've been given the chance to do an exclusive on Mavis the Mammary Monster. And now they land this dead gobshite on me that was stung to death by bees in his own gaff. Bollocks! I can't do both, I'll lose me exclusive!" She shook her head solemnly at this poor man's dilemma, he was close to tears.

Although on the face of it, in journalistic terms, the story was trash... to her, this tragic death was exactly what she wanted to investigate.

"I'll take that story off you... if it'll help?" She held out her hand for the copy, trying not to look desperate... but inwardly, she was screaming at him to hand it over. He beamed and passed across the dead man's details.

"Cheers, Cass, I owe you one!"

On the contrary, she thought.

Chapter 30

The usual verbal sparring with the hospital trust's press officer was about as useful as an ash tray on a motor bike. The dead man's next of kin had been informed; he never died on their premises... so why did this P.R. bullshitter think she was outwitting an investigative journalist by deliberately withholding information on the deceased? Cassandra left this deluded smug little pen pusher to her self-important fantasy and went to the real source of information in any hospital... the porters.

Stanley Vaughn had been on a retainer from her for over ten years. Back in the days of her real high-flying career as a hard-nosed hack. In that time, he had supplied secretive information on E-coli and M.R.S.A. super bug cover ups. Then there was the covert Faustian pact between American pharmaceutical companies and hospital trust managers, who supplied harvested organs and stem cells from deceased infants without their parent's knowledge. Oh yes, this tubby 52-year-old porter was an invaluable fountain of classified data that the general public were never meant to see. As per their usual arrangement, she never met Stanley on hospital property, after all these right-wing privateering pirates weren't stupid. One whiff of Stanley's duplicity and they would mercilessly crucify him like countless conscientious whistle blowers before him. Within 30 minutes of meeting Stanley in a motorway service station, she had Colin Hale's hospital records, the coroner's report and his next of kin's address. All for the price of £100 and a bottle of Scotch.

Bargain.

Chapter 31

The desk sergeant on duty wasn't as miserable as the desk plod she had met in the past. Maybe it was his age. I mean, what was he, 12? She had knickers older than him! Cassandra made a mental note to herself: must get two knicker drawers, post millennium, top drawer. Pre millennium, bin. This spotty copper trotted out the unfortunate details of Mr Hale's death as if he were retelling a holiday camp comic's routine. "Heh! So, there he was, undies round his ankles with a pubic beard full of bees! We found a Guinness book of records next to him opened at a section where some crack pot yank had the world record for a beard of bees."

The reporter quickly jotted down all the details on her note A5 note pad. The boy in the police uniform continued,

"Heh! Heh! We even found a camera next to him. Can you imagine that photo of his honey covered sweaty goolies writhing in bees in next year's annual?"

Her head looked up sharply from her note pad.

"Camera? Did you examine the film?"

The policeman sighed "Listen love... (Oooh, that started her teeth off. She'd be able to grind diamonds between them if he called her "love" again) ...he wanted to get his mug in the Guinness book of records for having a beard of bees, and he wanted to up the stakes by going for a meat and two veg beard. Unluckily for him, the bees he chose were nasty little fuckers from Brazil. He played with fire... and the daft bastard got fried."

Wow, so this was the caring face of community policing that the government keep informing us about, she mused.

"What happened to the camera?" She casually asked, purposely not looking up from her notes. The last thing she wanted was for this cold-hearted bone head to actually wake up and do the job he was fucking paid to do properly.

"Oh, his daughter took that. It was a present for her birthday."

Chapter 32

"Mrs Hale?" Cassandra addressed the 40-year-old woman on the doorstep of the terraced house.

"Wh... who are you?"

"Er, I don't know whether I have the right address, but your husband bought a camera off me." The dark circles around the widow's eyes betrayed a week of crying. The puffiness of her lids was either swelling up or going down; it has hard to tell which. Delving into her handbag the journalist handed Mrs Hale a bulky white envelope.

"Er, I'm sorry to intrude at this time, but he accidentally dropped this at my house. I only saw it after he left. I didn't have the guarantee for the camera on me at the time, so I said I'd post it when I found it. He left me this address to send it to."

Gingerly, the bereaved took the white package and opened it. Inside was a card proclaiming, "Happy Birthday to my darling Daughter!" Inside were 6 ten-pound notes. Bewildered, she silently counted the cash and made the connection with the card. Within seconds she was in floods of tears again.

Cassandra wasn't proud of this deception. Pretty shitty, even by tabloid standards. But it worked. The poor crushed woman had lowered her guard and agreed to let the reporter use her toilet. She was inside the house... and nearer to the camera. She would say her Hail Marys later. For now, she had a story to write, a killer to catch... lives to save. Her own included. Wasn't that the real driving force behind her little crusade? She wanted her career back. She wanted to be a main player again and didn't know how much longer she could carry on working at that shag rag, that was sucking the life out of her like a cerebral vampire. Talking of vampires, here she now sat in a recently bereaved widow's living room; having deceived and lied to this tormented soul... as she spied the camera on the bookcase, she was planning to steal the memory card from. No, Cassandra wasn't proud, not proud at all.

When the latest bout of sobbing had subsided, Mrs Hale stared at the blank card and the money.

"He... he didn't get a chance to write it." She screwed her eyes tight shut in a bid to stem the tidal wave of salt tears that was now burning her cheeks. The journalist had gambled on the widow inviting her in as the subterfuge of trust being established after handing over the bogus birthday card, and the cash which although not lock picks, enabled her to gain entry to the woman's home. When Mrs Hale opened her eyes, she tried to compose herself and wiped her glistening eyes.

"I'm sorry... it's not like we were even close." She blew her nose. "We've been divorced for three years." She answered the unspoken question. "An affair." She saw the stranger shake her head at the dead man's deception. "No... mine. I was seeing someone at work. A lot younger than me, still wanted to see if I could still do it. Colin found us upstairs and..."

If Cassandra didn't act now, she would get dragged into an emotional quagmire that would keep her here for hours. Hysteria is totally unpredictable and even harder to control. She had to focus. She was here to do a job not play fucking agony aunt.

Jesus that was cold.

The desperation of the situation was sending her schizophrenic.

"Can I have a glass of water please, my throat's a little dry."

The widow jumped up. "Oh, how rude of me, would you like a coffee?"

No sooner was the click of the kettle heard when she pounced on the little yellow camera. Quickly turning it on she saw a digital number 1 had appeared on the tiny digital display panel on the camera's back panel. Only 1 photo taken. It was a long shot, her heart banged in her chest. The clinking of cups told her to hurry. Inside of 15 seconds she had the memory card in her purse and the camera back on the shelf.

When the widow reappeared with the coffees, in true journalistic traditions... she made her excuses and left.

Chapter 33

The stolen memory card was placed in Marty's digital camera. Both Cassandra and he scrunched up their eyes as they huddled round the small viewing screen on the back of the camera.

"I can't see a thing... maybe the flash never went off." Said Marty, plugging in a lead from his laptop into the camera. His fingers were a blur on the keyboard; the noise reminded her of Irish dancing... in clogs... on a corrugated iron roof. The blurry black monochrome image slowly appeared on his computer. This time the image was a bit clearer. In the centre of the screen there was a circular patch of white, with two blurry shapes just off to the right of it.

"No, the flash did go off... that's what this light is." Indicated Marty as he pointed at the screen. She fished out of her bag the photocopied coroner's report Stanley supplied to her and studied the details of where the body was found. Frowning now as she read from the report.

"It says here it was mid-afternoon when he died... so why with a flash on a high-resolution camera is this photo so dark?" They both sat in silence racking their brains. His mind raced as he wanted to solve this puzzle for her. To please her, oh god did he want to please her. For Cassandra, this maybe another piece of evidence linked to her killer that could crack this story... and save her long dead career. She sighed, as she was sweating desperation from every pore. Almost wishing every story that was thrown her way like scraps from the master's table would lead her to him.

The spark came to her as she studied the screen again and then scanned the hospital notes. She looked up at Marty.

"Colin Hale was found with his head next to the cooker."

It was Marty's turn to shrug bewilderingly. She jabbed the screen with her finger. "He did take a photo before he died... but of the cooker door."

This really threw the nerd as he looked more confused.

"This... is the glass door of the cooker. Most of them are tinted glass. And this... is the reflected image of the man who killed him."

Chapter 34

Whatever high-tech software Marty was using was filtering out layers of background gloom on the photo's image. The two shapes were still in dark monochrome, with one shape of a man was clearer than the one behind. Her breathing quickened.

"F... fuck... there's two of them!"

Tracing the image with the tip of a biro on screen, he replied. "Nah! The second one's a lot darker... probably just a shadow."

Yet again he tapped away at the keyboard manically as he ran the photo through successive levels of filters. With each one the image became less fuzzy and started to show the dark, but unmistakeable image of a man. If she squinted, she could barely make out the shape of his face. But not enough for a positive I.D. She didn't need a positive I.D. She knew every contour of that face.

"Hang on." Said Marty. "I'm going to cross match this face with the C.C.T.V. footage we have from the Lorraine Fuller murder." He chose his words very carefully this time. Last time he called it a "tragic death" she'd bitten his head off. The two images appeared side by side on a split screen on his laptop. One, a grainy black and white image of an unkempt man outside a laundrette, and the second a dark shadowy outline with an even darker shadow. Directly below the images was a digital counter that read 34 %, this number was very slowly rising.

"It's measuring the percentage of similarities in the shape of the head, bridge of nose, length of cranium to give us enough data for an accurate match. It's truly remarkable. Did you know, no two faces in the whole world are the same? Each one as individual as a fingerprint." She could see he was clearly getting off on this technological masturbation.

"This is the same software that Interpol use to scan passports and surveillance footage for terrorists."

Cassandra daren't ask the hacker how he came by this obviously illegal software... she was just grateful he had it.

Just then the laptop made a digital "ping" sound as the filter counter announced 100% match.

Chapter 35

Leaning back in his chair, Singen sat in his grim private office deep within the bowels of the bunker and addressed Jim.

"A poor start Jim... half arsed one might say..."

Oh, Jim could see he was enjoying this destructive dissection of his performance in front of his so-called Mentor.

"...yet, you did redeem yourself at the end. Alas, your lamentable truculent attitude of late has brought you to this unfortunate point in time."

Jim gritted his teeth and clenched his fists behind his back. If this was it, he was going out fighting. He'd dive on Slimey before he could draw his gun, beat the shit out of him and use his pistol to kill anyone who came running through that door. He was dead already, he had nothing to lose. The one consolation... Slimey would die first. His mentor's hand delved into the open briefcase on his desk as Jim brought his hands out from behind his back ready to jump... when a huge wad of bank notes was tossed onto the table. Jim froze. His breathing harsh, his nostrils flaring. Was this a diversionary tactic? Jim looked wildly behind him in case a silenced pistol was inches from the back of his skull.

"Wh... what the fuck is going on?" blurted out Jim.

Slimey sat back in his chair in the spartan room with his hands interlocked behind his head. "Relax Jim... you've passed your assessment. Not with flying colours, but a pass no less." The senior Reaper smiled as he eyed the money on the desk.

"Take your expenses Jim, you've earned it. You've got two days off. Go out, get laid, get drunk and come back ready to fight the good fight." He gave Jim a mocking grin now. "Welcome back into the fold."

Jim picked up the money and left. It felt heavy in his pocket... like a burden. So, this is how Judas felt on pay day. He hung his head low as he skulked out of the bunker... his shame stalking him like a hungry dog.

Chapter 36

Slimey sipped the twelve-year-old malt as he sat in the head of section's office. His boss stood, looking through the venetian blinds at his nest of Reapers all busy at their desks. Singen glanced at his boss's desk and mused it won't be long before he is sitting there... won't be long at all. His envious eyes drifted over to his boss who stood with his back to him. The arrogance of Caesar... he turned his back on Brutus as well... tick... tock, old man.

"We have a breach in security." said the older man, walking back to his desk.

"The old tramp?" replied Slimey.

His superior waved the suggestion away with some annoyance. "No, not him! He's been dealt with. No, this is someone hacking into our looped signals we are feeding into the parameter's C.C.T.V. cameras."

Slimey sat up and put down his whiskey. "Only our people have access to that type of equipment surely?"

His boss opened an A4 cardboard file on his desk and handed Singen a sheet of details and a photo. The younger man studied the picture of a dark curly haired looking geek with big thick glasses and black frames.

"One of our tech boys noticed regular signals tapping into the perimeters cameras and traced them back to its source. As far as we know, he's not M.I.5, but when it comes to the security of this facility, I can't afford to take that chance. So, go armed to the teeth." Slimey had never seen his boss this rattled before. almost showing a vulnerable chink in that impenetrable armour of his. Just enough for a dagger to slip through. He snapped out of this wonderful daydream to his boss's stern voice.

"I want everything he has on us. Take a sweeper team with you and take his flat to pieces." Slimey held up Marty's photo.

"And him?"

His boss stared blankly at his computer. "Bring him back here… and we'll take him to pieces."

Chapter 37

It is a commonly known fact that everywhere Her Majesty the Queen visits; there is the fresh smell of paint. The same can be said of Mavis Davis the Mammary Monster, the highest paid glamour model on Fleet Street. Everywhere she goes, she can smell male drool. The unspoken power she has over the male species is truly awesome. From Nobel peace prize winners, to eminent scientists and philosophers, from the moment she jiggles into the room they all turn into zombies with hard-ons. It is eagerly touted about that her enormous bra was constructed by the same engineering firm that designed the Golden Gate suspension bridge in San Francisco. Urban myth or not, The Daily Throbber's readership loved it. And this marvel of human science fiction sat one desk away from the paper's only lady journalist.

"So, Mave, er... I can call you Mave, can't I?" Enquired Norman, fawning over the most famous sperm bank in London. The freshly salted slug that lay dormant in his Y fronts suddenly doubling in size.

"Yeah, whatever." Said Mave looking bored or vacant... or both.

Yee gods, it can speak, mused Cassandra as she gazed at Dr Frankenstein's blow up doll. Who sat trying to contain half of Silicone valley in a tiny red P.V.C. mini dress?

"How many blokes did you bang in your latest D.V.D. Mave?" Norman's eyes fixated six inches lower than Mave's.

"48 I think... or was it 50? I don't know, I know one of the fluffers is off sick now with repetitive strain injury and dislocated knuckles."

As much as Cassandra wanted to block out and ignore this inane interview one desk away, Mavis possessed the same hypnotic qualities as a mute television in a pub... namely you couldn't stop looking at it. For the men, the attraction was obvious, for the women, it was Mave's phenomenal denseness. They say a fool can ask more questions than a genius can answer. Her infantile stupidity bordered on absolute genius that could tie a philosopher's mind up in knots and fold it into an origami animal. Then Cassandra spotted it, the thing that had bothered her about Norman as he interviewed the model. There was something different about his appearance... oh sweet Jesus!... He was wearing a wig! Wow... the power of this porn star. She had made him sell his self-respect and used the money to buy dodgy syrup made from the arse hair of a gyppo's donkey!

Cassandra covered her mouth with her hand to stifle a smile. She bit her lip, but the tidal wave of sarcastic Tourette's overwhelmed her.

"Er, excuse me Mave, but what is your film called? You see I'm going to the Cannes film festival this year and I must look out for it."

Norman looked vexed at his colleague at this intrusion into his exclusive interview.

Sticking out her zeppelin like bosoms with pride, Mave replied, "It's called "The Ship of the Desert." This threw the journalist.

"Oh, is it a nautical tale?"

Mave replied, "Nah, stupid! It's called "The Ship of the Desert" coz I'm full of Arab semen."

Cassandra turned her back on "Mave the Rave", as her tabloid colleagues loved to call her, and jotted quickly on her note pad. Looking up every few seconds to check no one could see her work. Well, as opposed to the bullshit sex, gossip and brain dead "work" she was supposed to be doing. Her killer was an expert hacker who could bypass the Metropolitan police's surveillance cameras.

That could mean:

A, He's in the I.T. industry. Fuck... that's half of London!

B, He works for a security company. Either on maintenance or setting up the systems for top companies with council and government contracts.

C, He works in the control rooms, where he would be able to change and alter the tapes at the source. *Holy fuck... he could be a copper! Whoah! Hold them horses there girl, you've got no proof. Stick to the facts. Christ for all she knew he could just be a techno nerd like... Marty.*

No, now she really was letting her imagination run...

A cold chill ran up her spine. All the proof she had on tape, the photos, the film footage... all came from Marty. He was an expert on computers. She shook her head trying to dismiss this notion. Ah, but no, that first photo she had of her killer supplied from a security camera still frame didn't come from her... *friend.*

117

The word sounded really creepy as she said it in her head. She shuddered. Yet, she did leave that original photo with Marty for a while... and ever since, that face has been popping up on tape and film after every so called 'Death by misadventure.' What was it they call it in Hollywood? Digital mapping. The technological know-how where they can scan a photo and animate it on computer. Used to great acclaim in the Tolkien cinematic trilogy. The film footage supplied by Marty wasn't worthy of an Oscar... but good enough to fool a desperate hack who was chasing a killer, who only existed on tape. When inches away from the monitor whilst she was given these grisly slide-shows... sat a man who regarded her as prey.

Chapter 38

The door to her editor's office swung open and there the pot-bellied pig of porn stood... Mervin Foster. The very essence of Australian manhood let out a gurgling mangled cry,

"Oiy! Sheila!"

He was looking directly at Cassandra. Seeing as she was the only female in the newsroom, bar the pouting plastic porn star of course, she could hardly look over her shoulder to sarcastically look for the brain-dead antipodean scrubber he was so obviously addressing. Instead, she went without question when summoned in such a respectful way. She swore if she listened carefully, she could hear Emily Pankhurst spinning in her grave like a pea in a whistle. Her only act of defiance was to lock her notes in her desk before entering the Daily Throbber's mission control room.

"Park ya bum girl!" Ordered Mervin the Midas of the faeces world. He could turn "shit into gold." His words, not hers... and yes, he did have this printed in gold on a frame on his office wall. He stared out his office window at Mave the rave, who was miming a scene from her latest film for poor flustered Norman. Although Foster couldn't hear what Mave was saying... the mime indicated she was choking on something... repeatedly... at speed.

"Strewth! She's a farrkin' goldmine!" Drooled Foster, unashamedly yanking at his groin in a manner that would make a safari park chimp blush, as he got his giblets in a half nelson, Cassandra yet again groaned inwardly at her workplace purgatory. She said a silent prayer to a god she doesn't believe in to get her out of there. To make a deal with this imaginary agony aunt that if she had been bad in a former life, then give her a face full of warts... or a Brummie accent. Anything, but this torment. Stifling a sigh, she knew she would have to engage this multimillionaire retard who had a financial strangle hold over her.

"Don't you think she's a bit of a one trick pony?"

As soon as the words left her lips, she cursed her sarcastic Tourette's.

Oh, you dozy mare, that fucking mouth of yours! Here you sit in the high church of the latter-day perverts, with the high priest of porn... and you have just taken the piss out of the Holy Mother of Mammaries.

Bizarrely, instead of exploding at her, he seemed genuinely pleased.

"My thoughts exactly girl! That's why I want you to do a big interview with her new bloke."

Cassandra sat stunned with a deep sense of dread and foreboding about this new assignment and she couldn't quite fathom out why. Until it suddenly dawned on her who Mave the rave's latest boyfriend was... infamous self-styled chirpy chainsaw celebrity gangster... Mickey Mullet.

Holding up his hands skywards, Mervin Foster resembled a gospel preacher spreading his vision. Which indeed was exactly what he was about to do.

"Mave and Mickey! They are going to be the king and queen of Fleet Street. Never bleedin' mind yer lah-dee darr snooty Posh 'n' Becks, Mave the rave and geezer Mickey Mullet are gonna be the next big thing!" Incredible. Only a kangaroo shagging alcoholic like Merve the perve could possibly think Mr Beckham and his limpet wife are members of the British aristocracy.

She sat dumfounded. "I... I'm sorry, but..."

"Look girl, this pair have it all in a celeb couple... sex and violence! Think about it girl..." (yee gods was he calling her this just to wind her up?) "...I can fill this rag to the brim eight days a week; the sales will go through the roof!" Silently she applauded his insight into admitting his paper was a rag, dismayed at getting the ratio of days in a week wrong to the tune of one... and seriously doubted his circulation forecasts based on parading pond life... to pond life.

She squirmed in her seat as she dared to ask,

"But, isn't Norman already doing an exclusive with Mave? So why don't you let him do an exclusive on them both?"

Mervin lit a cigarette. "Very noble of you girl. But Norman's thinking with his smelly fella! He'd only concentrate on Mave's tits!" He then cupped imaginary breasts in mid-air to illustrate his point.

"That's why you'll be going around to Mickey's mansion this afternoon." He opened his office door by way of bringing their meeting to a close. As she walked past him, he uttered a word of caution as he blew cigarette smoke in her face.

"Take a notebook only, no tape recorders. If he even thinks you are a copper's nark he'll carve you from ear to ear!"

He drew his index finger slowly across his throat.

Chapter 39

The immense gates to Mickey Mullet's mansion swung silently open as she drove in, watched by numerous C.C.T.V. cameras. The high walls surrounding the house were peaked with four interlocking coils of razor wire to give it that cosy touch. Had Mullet's decade inside various prisons totally institutionalised him to the point where he has to live in a gilded version of his cell in Wormwood Scrubs?

She parked her battered Renault next to his vehicle, a huge American Humvie jeep. Someone should tell him that instead of looking macho, he just looks like the endless array of bone-idle ladies who do lunch on a school run in their oversized monster trucks. Someone should... only not her. Mickey was a great believer in "Bitch slapping," as many an ex toothless girlfriend could tell you. Well, the ones whose jaws aren't held together by pins and plates anyway. Cassandra didn't delude herself that her press badge would offer her any protection against an unstable man who could violently take offence at anything you did or said, depending whether he got his fix that day. His fix wasn't drugs. Not on moral grounds, oh no. He would gladly sell them to your kids and watch you on News at Ten crying at their funeral, knowing he had secured their membership to the six foot of soil club.

Mickey's drug was his ego.

As vast as the known universe and ever expanding. Einstein could have drawn up an equation to explain Mickey's papyrus thin ego: Feed Mullet's ego on a regular basis or paranoia sets in quickly. Followed by uncontrollable violence until feelings of adequacy are restored... as he repeatedly stamps on your neck.

As the obligatory rottweilers strained at their chains, which were staked to the ground a foot from the mansion's huge oak double doors, she smiled at the tinted windows on his Humvie. It just screamed out, "I'm a drug dealer and this is my heroin ice cream van!" This was topped off with the personalised number plate: A.C.A.B. Oh dear oh deary me, she mused, the piss poor acronym: All Coppers Are Bastards. That legendary tattoo of the illiterate unwashed excuse for Mafioso, seen on countless knuckles of insufferable little gobshites everywhere.

Once inside, her bag was checked by Cro-Magnon man, the missing link in a suit. On the wall in the hallway opposite an immense dark oak staircase hung a huge oil painting of her host. The composition consisted of Mickey as a hang man... pulling the lever on the judge who put him away.

"That's farhhkin' lahhverly, init?" Nobody could mistake the soothing tones of celebrity extortionist, Mickey Mullet. Despite his ill-gotten multi millions, he was, possibly the ugliest man she had ever met. It wasn't so much the smashed in boxer's nose... although this did look like something that had been agonisingly squeezed out of a Jack Russell's ring-piece. This was eclipsed by his fat blubbery lips and deep set piggy eyes. And finally, to set him apart from every other gangster on the planet and give him a totally unique look... he shaved his head bald.

"That pic-chahh cost me five grahhhhhnd."

The tiny anvil shaped bone in Cassandra's ear drum oscillated like a manic pin ball round her skull at the shrill, over exaggerated Chas'n'Dave cockney rhyming bollocks accent of his. Nails raked across a blackboard didn't come close.

Mullet thrust a book into her face.

"Ere, girl! You 'ere to plug me new Christmas cookbook?"

Now this did throw her. A violent criminal writing recipes?

"Er, well, I suppose I could, what's it called?"

That hideous face beamed with pride "Carving up the Christmas nonce!"

All the while he spoke, Mullet munched on handfuls of multicoloured sweets from a gold champagne bucket beside his ridiculously ornate armchair. Mickey offered her a handful of sweets which coincidentally bore his initials.

"Ere, want some sweeties' girl? I even have my sweeties monogrammed, don't I?" She let the moot point go, that the confectioner's creators came up with the double initial brand name long before this testicle with teeth purloined credit for their name, as she was here to do a job. Opening her notebook, she asked,

"So, Mr Mullet, how did you go from being the most feared and respected..." (Beautiful touch, she silently commended herself. The "R" word was like heroin to this inadequate prick) "... man in the East end, to a best-selling author?" Leaning back in the antique, bordering on priceless Queen Ann chair, she wondered did the late monarch envisage a prison rapist parking his arse on her furniture. Those hideously bloated cod lips replied,

"Well… it all started with mah old man. He was…"

What?! A dustman? Did he wear a dustman's hat? Did he wear gor blimey trousers and his son is a flat nosed twat?

Cassandra blinked rapidly and bit her tongue. That one nearly slipped out.

"… a mug! Worked all his bleedin' life and died without a pot to piss in! We had fahhhk all! So, I had to duck and dive."

Ah yes, that wonderful East End euphemism for demanding money with extreme menaces. Just then Mickey's mobile rang.

"Hang on treacle, I need to take this." His voice slipped down a few notches of nastiness.

"Gor blimey! Well cut the other one off and see if that jogs his memory! If I've gotta come dahhrn there, I'll dig his granny up and feed her to my fahhhkin' rottweilers!" Throwing his head back in exasperation as he ended the call, he sighed heavily as he addressed the journalist.

"Yer can't get the fahhhkin' staff darlin'. Now… where were we?"

"You were about to tell me that you were a reformed character." She replied.

For the next hour, this aging rat boy regaled her with his "mischievous" career in the underworld. He loved dropping in cute childish phrases to downplay and describe sickening acts of brutal violence. It was all so scripted, that a tabloid journalist could have written it for him. This thought brought on a wave of shame as here she sat, a tabloid journalist… doing just that. Even his description of H.M.P.

Wormwood scrubs, or "Butlins" as he liked to rename it was like recalling a fond childhood family holiday. Some years earlier, on an unrelated story into prostitution and human trafficking, Cassandra investigated Mickey and spoke to some ex-convicts who were on the same wing as him. They told her that Mullet's taste for anal sex wasn't a latter-day avant-garde attitude... but an acquired taste he developed in the shower block taking young lads by extreme force. Off the record that day, Mave had told Norman her colleague that Mickey would only ever,

"Do me up the wrong'un."

Would this possibly explain his pathological hatred of "nonces"? A trained psychiatrist could retire on the book he'd write on this basket case. All this talk of killers and psychos drew her attention back to her own killer. To hunt him, she would need to know what made him tick. She suddenly looked up from her note pad as she had the answer... right in front of her. Maybe this afternoon wasn't going to be a total waste of time after all. She halted him mid moronic monologue.

"What's it like to kill someone Mickey?"

Those piggy eyes bore straight through her.

"You farrrkin' wearin' a wire?! Coz if you are, your friends are gonna hear your farrrkin' nose being sliced off!"

Calmer than she actually felt, she replied,

"No, I'm not... I just wanted to know how, after you've killed someone, how you can function. Carry on with your normal day? Knowing you've destroyed a life and if you are caught... that you'll be imprisoned for the rest of your life. Tell me, when you are alone with your thoughts and you close your eyes... do you still see the last look on their faces?"

Chapter 40

Marty used the back of his sleeve to wipe the tomato puree from his chin; he had yet again dribbled from his microwave pizza. Some of this had dripped onto his pride and joy, his Union Jack print jeans. Or as he liked to delude himself, his "pulling" jeans. Unfortunately, not once had having his arse wrapped in the Union flag has ever turned the opposite sex into lust filled nymphomaniacs. For the eighth time he had run the blurry stolen digital photo through numerous computer imaging programs in the vain hope of getting a clearer picture. Sighing angrily, he stood up and started rummaging through piles of computer discs covered in dust and empty crisp packets, knocking over teetering towers of technological data as he went. This frantic search went on for over ten minutes until he mimicked the Arthurian legend of the lady of the lake holding aloft Excalibur, as he triumphantly waved the disc he had been searching for. He blew off the dust as he hadn't used this software since he had tried to filter out shadows from the grassy knoll opposite the Kennedy assassination tape. He didn't find any gunmen that time. Well, how could he? After the F.B.I. had snipped out seven crucial frames from the original Abraham Zapruder film? Marty inhaled deeply and stopped himself... if he let his mind drift down that particular road, he would be off on a two-hour tangent that would see him seething more than when the sci fi channel stopped showing the original series of Star Trek.

The software was kicking in now. The grainy figure was clearing to reveal a man in his thirties. It was our guy alright. The one that had showed up on numerous C.C.T.V. footage around the numerous strange deaths Cassandra had been investigating.

"Holy fuck! "gasped Marty as the shadow behind the killer became lighter, more defined. She was right... it wasn't a shadow. It was a second man... and this one was smiling.

The cleaned-up photo of the two murder suspects was quickly uploaded to Marty's "ghost" trio of memory bank websites in cyberspace. To safeguard against hacking, his files were automatically sent on to the next website after fifteen seconds and an encrypted firewall slammed shut behind it. So, every fifteen seconds all files were shifted between all three sites with the speed of a magician shuffling cards, so no hacker could break in, browse and download his memory. If, any hacker did penetrate the codes for any of the sites, the program automatically sends all the data on to a safe chosen web address of Marty's choice. Two seconds later, all three sites crash down behind each other like dominoes and a nasty virus is dispatched back down the line to the hacker to destroy his computer's software and mangle the hard drive.

Information like this is pure gold dust to the security services, bent politicians and elite cabals that pull global leaders puppet strings. He could have had the final destination for all this incriminating data end up on conspiracy theorist societies websites on the internet. Instead, he chose someone he knew... a certain female journalist. Was it because she was a fearless old school reporter, who could be trusted to use his secret files to bring the bad guys to justice? Or, deep down, was it because he loved her with his heart and his soul and was leaving her his life's work in his will? For in all truth, that's exactly what this was. If his unrequited love ever received these files in her inbox, then the subjects of those files had finally caught up with him... and took him for a ride in the boot of a car.

Sadly, for Marty, his paranoid little prophesy was chillingly closer than he ever predicted.

Chapter 41

The gentle pressure behind his eyes indicated the strong Belgium lager was taking effect. Jim lay sprawled on his huge mahogany coloured sofa, can of beer on his chest and remote control in his hand. Between him and the expensive flat screen plasma telly, was a huge wad of bank notes resting on his coffee table. He took another huge swig of beer trying desperately to get drunk and obliterate his miserable waking existence. Alas, his digestive system would only allow for one more can, before it objected to the alcoholic abuse and violently vomited Belgium's finest export all over his shag pile carpet. His inability to drink more than five pints of alcohol had brought him much derision from his peers in his teens. A time when drinking was about competing, establishing yourself on the social pecking order and plucking up enough courage to face rejection on the night club dance floor. Upon mature reflection he mused, his digestive system was actually doing him a favour. Better to be a part time social drinker than have a nose like Father Christmas's favourite reindeer.

His flat was extremely plush, on the outskirts of town. He was well paid and had a harem of hookers at his disposal that his employers supplied to all Reapers. His bosses preferred they use prostitutes rather than form a relationship with an unsympathetic woman, who would object to you butchering strangers. Jim had to admit, the sex was good, but when the sex worker left... his loneliness engulfed him, and he wept.

A real selfish part of him wished his late friend Simon Wilson had accepted his Reaper's post. At least then, he'd have someone to share his pain with. Yet Simon was honest and decent with strong moral values... and that is what had resulted in him being shot dead in cold blood. Now here he stood in his expensive bachelor pad, pockets bulging with money... so, what did that make him? The large gulp of beer didn't wash away his thoughts as he walked barefoot out onto his balcony. He rested his elbows on the balcony's gleaming chrome bar that was attached to his gilded cage.

"I could run away..." he said out loud. Living alone, he rarely got to hear the sound of his own voice. Shouting at daytime T.V. chefs didn't count.

Then he remembered last November when a new Reaper, Thomas Ludlow ran away. It took the bunker's zealots nine days to catch him, on the Scottish Isle of Mull of all places. When they eventually frog marched him through the bunker, he was unshaven and looked like he'd been sleeping rough. Briefly his eyes caught Jim's gaze as they led him up the gantry stairs and into the infamous interview room. That wide-eyed pleading look of a man who knew he was about to die, slapped away any foolish thoughts Jim had of running away. When Thomas Ludlow next emerged from the interview room, he was being dragged out... wrapped in plastic.

The cold night breeze ruffled his unkempt hair as he drained the last of his can on the balcony. Wasn't this what he and Simon always dreamed of? Bags of cash, expensive man cave and a secretive important job with the security services? Never mind the arse achingly boring pen pushing jobs poor saps ended up doing who were recruited by M.I.5. Snooping on peace protesters and anti-motorway pressure groups, their job was pure M.I.6. James Bond style. They even had a licence to kill. Jim sighed deeply. At least Mr Bond gets other duties like spying and espionage... all they did was kill. Day in, day out.

Secretly, he was stashing money away. Not here, he daren't. His flat was randomly searched by the sweeper teams for any sign of escape or behaviour that would compromise their operation. One Reaper had a scrunched up piece of paper in his bathroom waste bin with a scrawled phone number on it. Turned out to be a direct line to the news desk of the Daily Mail. That Reaper was soon given a plastic overcoat and was never seen again. The sweeper team would always deliberately move ornaments, unplug toasters, upturn mugs in a subtle reminder, you are always being watched... and they can come for you at any time. Every couple of days the silver fountain pen given to him by his late friend Simon was moved from one end of the table to the other, just to let him know they have visited. No, Jim's secret stash was in a train station locker, he hid the key in a coffee jar buried beneath a gaudy coloured gnome in his communal back garden. As he looked out over the balcony, he could just about see the gnome's red hat and it gave him comfort knowing this little guardian was safeguarding his future. Ludlow's mistake was to just panic and run like a headless chicken. No planning no thought of the consequences. Jim would need a fake passport, a home, a surgically reconstructed face... and a gun. If they ever did somehow catch up with him, there was no fucking way he was going to be wrapped up in plastic. If they showed up on his doorstep, they had better be prepared to die. The anger of his stolen self-respect and slaughtered friend was boiling into molten rage. He would channel all that rage one way and when he was ready... his lacklustre attitude towards killing would disappear completely. His mood was lifting; he could see a way out. Financially, it would take him a year to achieve his goal. He would use that time constructively, learning everything he could about his organisation and use their skills against them. Jim felt uplifted, felt like celebrating. He picked up one of the many call girls' cards from his coffee table and dialled.

Chapter 42

Bobby Mcvie's drunken stagger was worthy of an academy nomination. He wasn't drunk but needed the watching eyes to think he was absolutely one pint short of shitting his trousers. Every few steps he would take a hearty gulp from his cider can... that was filled with water, to reinforce the inebriated caricature. Using the directions given to him from Declan, he found the back street opposite the infamous off-licence frequented by half of the capital's homeless community. The back street that would lead to the alleyway where Declan was savagely mauled by a military attack dog. Through his long fringe he spied all the windows on this back street were boarded up, caked in years of grime or had security wire running through them. All... except one.

This particular window stood out like a sore thumb. It was three stories high and was directly opposite a narrow side alley. It had a single pane of tinted glass that was dark yet its shiny surface reflected sunlight. Every other window in this street was covered in thick layers of filth and baked on pigeon shit... yet this solitary window had been cleaned. This was an observation post. From that point you could scan the street, keep an eye on the entrance to the narrow alley way, and co-ordinate a dog attack on an old tramp that unfortunately just happened to be in the wrong place at the wrong time.

As Bobby lumbered across the road, he passed a doorway directly below the tinted window three stories above; he noticed a brand-new shiny night latch had been fitted to the grime coated door. No mortise lock. He smiled under his veil of fringe, and staggered past and out the other end of the street. Only when he was two streets away did he drop the drunk routine, throw away the can of water and tie his hair back in its customary ponytail. Before he could go down that alleyway, he'd have to deal with the dog lovers in that observation point. When he did, he'd make sure he sent them Declan's regards.

Chapter 43

The ingredients Bobby would need for his incendiary device could easily be picked up from around his "cardboard estate", but he couldn't risk buying the lighter fluid. The first places detectives hit when they investigate arson incidents are D.I.Y. shops and ironmongers to see if any dodgy looking people had been purchasing flammable liquids. Methylated spirits, however, that's another matter. Nobody bats an eyelid when a tramp buys meths. The buying of toiletries: shaving kit, shampoo, soap and deodorant did bring incredulous looks from various office workers in the chemist's queue. Not a word was actually spoken, but Bobby could feel their collective revulsion at his very presence. It wasn't so much their bigoted stereotypical dislike of his way of life that made them feel such unease. It was something much more primal... fear. For each and every one of the briefcase brigade was up to their pretentious arses in spiralling debt. Desperately trying to live a middle class lifestyle on a working class wage packet. With every passing year it gets harder to pay that inflated mortgage. The trophy car that just eats every pound you earn and gives you nothing in return like a spiteful ex-wife. Then there are the credit cards... so seductive... so destructive. The vultures are circling and waiting to pick at the carcass of this doomed fiscal fantasy. How will it end?

They know exactly how it will end. And, like the ghost of Christmas future, there he stood... next to them in the chemist queue.

Chapter 44

If she was excited at the prospect of catching one serial killer, imagine how she'd feel about a pair of predators? Cassandra had been hanging around him quite a bit since the angel of death had been looming. Morbidly, he was relishing this golden opportunity that had thrown him, temporarily together with the girl of his disturbed dreams. A wave of guilt shook him to his core, causing him to shudder involuntary. He knew this one-way romance would fade away, the moment she nails this duo of killers. The dark thoughts at the back of his mind scared him.

She'd be the toast of Fleet Street. No more crap tabloid job. No more living on past glories... no more Marty.

The unpalatable truth left a sour bile taste in his mouth. By helping her in her quest, he was like a turkey looking forward to Christmas. He would never see her again. Secretly, he knew she was using him as a steppingstone to get her career back. He put his troubled lonely head in his hands. Why else would she continue to come here? Those dark thoughts turned even darker.

What if... if... I held back on the newly cleaned up photos? It would delay the killers' incarceration. She would still visit me for help.

Sighing heavily now, he ran his trembling hands through his curly locks.

How fucking desperate was he?!

He reprimanded himself as he realistically considered letting innocent people be butchered by these sick bastards, just so he could drool over a woman who couldn't give a shit about him. Marty stood up quickly, a new determination filling him as his long-exiled self-respect returned like the prodigal son. As he turned around a black silenced pistol was inches away from his eyes, held by the smiling killer in the photo.

Chapter 45

"Congratulations! You've just found out all those internet bogeymen are real!"

The digital killer made flesh echoed the same smile he gave his last victim as he levelled the gun at Marty's head. Behind the immaculately dressed gun toting killer stood five stern faced men in black boiler suits and surgical gloves. Marty started to hyperventilate. Holy fuck, they were going to chop him up! One of the men plonked himself down at Marty's computer and then looked over expectantly.

"Well?" Said the gunman.

Bewildered and frightened, the most Marty could muster was "Eh?"

"Well, we could start chopping off your toes until you reluctantly gave us your password... or you could save us some time, plus your tap-dancing career."

The threat clearly understood, he complied, "E... enterprise."

The grinning gunman nodded to his lackey who duly accessed Marty's files.

"Star Trek fan are we?"

Bizarre beyond belief, he was being quizzed on his cult T.V viewing by a serial killer who employed his own staff!

"In a moment, you are going to be hooded, cuffed and taken away for questioning. If you comply... you'll be back inside your flat within 24 hours. If you resist..." The tip of the silencer was placed directly against Marty's forehead.

"...I will kill you right here and now."

Marty blurted out "I...I won't resist."

"Good boy." Said the killer.

Then the lights went out for Marty.

Chapter 46

The acne factory on the till, at the Municipal swimming baths, gave the 35-year old tramp with the black bin bag a disgusted look as he took his money. An hour later, the same surly youth politely bid farewell to a clean-shaven pony tailed yuppie in a smart baggy suit... carrying a black bin bag.

It had been a long time since Bobby Mcvie had worn a suit. Let alone a stolen one from a fat fucker. If his neighbours could see him now after using tramp's Kryptonite (soap) they would unceremoniously banish him from their aromatic kingdom forever. His normal clothes lay in the public baths' locker, where he would retrieve them later. He only planned to be gone for two hours... if he was still alive.

Fifteen minutes later, he was stood on the corner of the street he had done a reconnaissance on earlier that day. Carefully, he walked down the street then dropped the plastic bag he had been carrying which was open. Taking two cigarettes from a packet, he lit one and placed it face down inside the packet. He then dropped the packet into the open bin bag on the pavement and casually crossed the street towards the observation point. Bobby had timed his journey down the street on his first visit and cut the fuse to his incendiary device accordingly. By the time he reached the observation point's front door, the firebomb should go off... hopefully. The snapped cigarette he had placed face down in the packet burned slowly towards the heads of the matches he had crammed in. This rested on a pile of methylated spirits-soaked rags and four old bicycle inner tubes.

A minute later, the street started to fill with smoke.

Chapter 47

"Fuckin' yuppie prick!" Darren hissed as he looked through the high-powered binoculars in the observation point, his nostrils flaring in anger. His superior was daydreaming about "accidentally" shooting the younger man and how he would report the regrettable demise of a much valued colleague to his governor.

"I mean, who the fuck does he think is gonna pick that bin bag up, eh? Probably wipes his arse on fuckin' doilies the stuck-up prick!" Clearly, the young pup had a bone, and he wasn't letting go.

Letting out a weary sigh, the senior officer said, "Have you ever thought about broadening your horizons, lad?"

He looked over at his boss. "Wh…what? What are you talking about Mr Jenkins?"

Sipping his coffee, he replied, "Well, surveillance, not really your cup of tea is it? Young fella like yourself should be out there in the thick of it. Not stuck here with an old fart like me."

"What? Do you mean, be a Reaper?"

"No, lad. Don't talk daft. You know we can't be Reapers. They are specifically chosen to fit a certain psychological profile... and they are dispensable. We are not. Without us, they couldn't do their jobs. But you've heard the rumours of the Yanks wanting us to expand our operations over there. Big opportunities for the right candidates. And all those Yank birds love a British accent. I mean, you'd be like Hugh Grant... only with a broken nose."

His junior replied "Yeah, well, Hugh Grant would have a broken nose too if he went to our school." He could see the ego was being duly massaged and cut to the chase.

"Er, I could, if you want... put in a word for you? You know, help you with the transfer forms." The rusted cogs turned. "'Ere! You're not trying to get rid of me are you?" With mock hurt in his voice the older man replied,

"Me? No! Bloody hell lad you're one of the best I've ever seen. But as much as it pains me to see you go, I can't stand by and see such talent go to waste." The inflated pride was glazing the young man's eyes, a silly smile played on his lips. Which dropped quickly as something caught the corner of his eye and he darted back to his binoculars. Jenkins suddenly switched on, his hand hovering over his handgun on his desk.

"What's wrong? What's going on out there?"

His junior was too preoccupied, so he left his desk and darted to the window. There he saw a black plume of smoke coming from a small fire at the end of the street.

Three stories below, Bobbie Mcvie had bypassed the lock and had silently slipped into the building unnoticed.

Chapter 48

Bobby dropped to his knees behind the closed door. He controlled his breathing and let his eyes slowly adjust to the darkened hallway. The only source of light came from a skylight at the top of the building that shone directly down the centre of the spiralling staircase. This place smelled of neglect. Every wall had discoloured peeling paint and damp was everywhere. Whatever this place was, the twenty first century hadn't touched it yet. Dust mites floated lazily in the central shaft of light from above. He waited for thirty seconds before he gently padded up the stairs. If they were coming for him, they would be here by now. Off to his left was a half-opened door to an empty office. He paid this no heed as the office he was interested in was three floors up and occupied. Bobby only used the sides of each stair in case one stray creak of a protesting floorboard gave him away to his killers. Only one elbow touched the wall for support. There was no way he was going to leave fingerprints on the balustrade that was caked in decades of dust.

The razor-sharp kitchen knife stuck down the back of his trousers was starting to dig in him as he climbed each step. The blade would remain hidden until needed. He had no way of knowing if covert infra-red cameras weren't watching his ascent. Better that they see him unarmed and threaten him with a pistol, than see him tooled up and come out all guns blazing. Nearly on the Third floor now where the observation post was, he controlled his breathing further and moved much slower. He could see a bright horizontal shaft of light under the door on the third landing he was looking for. This light was momentarily broken by shadow, then clear again.

Movement.

Bobby was crawling on all fours now and slowly brought out the knife. He inched very slowly towards the door; his eye drawn to the keyhole like a moth to a flame. Would he too share its fate? He held his breath. Only when the ex-soldier spied through the keyhole, did he realise that his old pal Declan had upset some very serious people indeed.

Chapter 49

Mcvie's descent down the dirty staircase was much swifter than when he had climbed in silent trepidation. His heart was beating like a hammer now. This was always the time when the shit hit the fan. It wasn't the stealthy entrance; it wasn't the vigilant reconnaissance; it was always the hasty retreat. Over the years he had seen members of his units die in Belfast, Iraq and Sierra Leone. All covert black ops, all went tits up in the last five minutes.

Bobby had reached the front door... and he wasn't dead. He must buy a lottery ticket on the way home tonight, he mused. Tucking the blade back into the back of his trousers, he gently edged open the door a fraction to check the street. He felt sure his mini smoke bomb will had filled the back street with enough dark smoke to mask his escape.

He was about to slip out the door when he froze as a black transit van screeched to a halt at the entrance to the narrow alley way. Both back doors flew open and two men in black boiler suits jumped out. Then, they dragged out a handcuffed figure with a black hood on his head. Bobby noticed he had very bright Union Jack print jeans and baseball boots covered with yellow dots. No, not dots, smiley faces. Mcvie's old training had taught him the utmost importance of noticing detail; it helped to pick a suspect target out of a busy crowd. Lives could depend on it. And in the past, they have. As the trussed figure was dragged down the alleyway, something small and black fell from under his hood and onto the street. The passenger side door to the van opened and a third man, well dressed in a dark suit and long winter coat climbed out and picked up the black object and held it up for inspection. Bobby could see that the man with the long angular nose was holding a pair of black framed spectacles. Seconds later he disappeared down the narrow alley way as the van sped off. Bobby waited a full minute before darting out into the empty smoke-filled street and stayed close to the building to avoid surveillance, he made his escape.

Chapter 50

The black cloth hood was yanked off Marty's head unceremoniously. Blinking wildly, he could just make out two fuzzy shapes sitting in front of him.

"These are yours, I believe." Said an eerily familiar voice. Once his spectacles were handed to him and adjusted, he could see two well-dressed men in suits sat at a plain wooden desk. One was in his late fifties, looked ex-military with slicked back grey hair. The other was the creepy bastard who brought him here by gun point.

This was no police station.

Marty decided to take the bull by the horns. "I have a right to make a phone call."

Both men looked at each other, then his abductor replied,

"Who are you going to call... Ghostbusters?" Marty was clearly irked as both men chuckled away.

"I have my rights!"

This angry outburst brought the chuckling to a stop. The older man with the icy cold eyes suddenly cleared his throat and spoke in an upper-class accent.

"Can you guess why the floor of this office is covered in plastic sheeting?"

Marty suddenly looked down. His blood ran cold. Instantly, images of horrific torture and death filled his mind. The grey-haired man slowly opened an ultra slim laptop on his desk and continued,

"I'll narrow it down for you, shall I? It's not because we don't have a departmental budget for carpets."

Marty was visibly shaking now, all bravado drained as his fight or flight reflex was kicking in. And the flight reflex was off on its toes, leaving fight to take the kicking. They were going to connect his bollocks to the mains. Oh Christ! He had no pain threshold whatsoever and they weren't going to show him any mercy at all. He was finding it hard to breath. "Wh…why am I…"

The older man flashed the trembling hacker a frosty smile.

"It's only just dawned on you Marty, hasn't it? That you are in the biggest trouble of your miserable little life. Your pitiful excuse for wit won't talk your way out of this one and not even the Lord God Almighty's personal solicitor can save you from what is about to happen to you." His head was spinning. They knew everything about him. Birth, school, who he last voted for, phone calls and as for the internet...

The grey-haired man, who Marty had deduced was in charge, had refreshments brought in by two huge black suited goons, who had Glocks clearly on show in their shoulder holsters. The older man sipped his tea quite delicately and then looked up from his laptop.

"You've been hacking into police C.C.T.V. cameras around the capital, accessing and downloading their footage... why?"

Marty stammered "I... I'm curious."

His accuser placed down his cup. "No... a child playing with matches is curious. A cat taunting a pit bull is curious. YOU!" The word jabbed loudly at him, made Marty jump. "YOU! Have accessed government websites. You've been monitoring C.C.T.V. cameras and you have the textbook psychological profile of a member of an active terrorist cell who is planning to bomb London."

The prospect of being whisked off to an American military concentration camp in Cuba loosened Marty's tongue. "No! Y... you've got it all wrong. Look, I'm not a terrorist!"

They knew he wasn't a terrorist.

They couldn't give a shit if he planned to blow up a bus full of nuns... as long as it didn't interfere with the work they were doing here. Unfortunately for this nosey little bastard, that's precisely what he was doing. The younger of the two with the long angular nose leaned over and whispered something into his boss's ear. He then stood up and slowly walked round the desk towards Marty. He leaned in close to Marty's ear and said in a low emotionless voice,

"Would you say you were very observant, Marty?"

The hacker didn't answer; he just trembled at this invasion of his personal space. He continued, "Do you know what you need to be a good eyewitness, Marty?" The answer was hoarse, "A... a good m...memory?"

Bringing out a razor-sharp surgeon's scalpel and tapping the blade against the glass lens of his spectacles, he hissed,

"No... EYES!"

Chapter 51

The prostitute had only been gone ten minutes, but Jim could still feel her warmth in the big empty bed. He now occupied her vacant space like a thermal vampire, imagining what it would be like to wake up next to someone who wasn't waiting for a tip. A very strict rule that all Reapers must obey, is to totally walk away from your former life. Your local pub, the corner shop you bought your newspaper in, even your friends. All of them... gone. His new employers provided him with a new home and a new life. He had officially disappeared from the face of the Earth. If, for any reason a colleague or friend from a former life did accidentally bump into him in the street, he was instructed to completely ignore them and flee as quickly as possible. He must then report the security threat to his superiors who would deal with it swiftly. The moment anyone was classified as a "security threat" their chances of making their next birthday were very slim indeed. The bunker had no concerns of Jim's family being a threat, as he didn't have any. Jim was an orphan, no siblings, no one...like all the Reapers. Jim wondered if Simon Wilson's Mother had lived for just one more year, would the Reapers have passed him over for recruitment? With no family coming looking for them, the Reapers could just vanish into thin air. Invisible, unremarkable, bland little nobodies able to blend into a crowd without drawing a second glance.

The perfect assassins.

This made Jim very jittery in public. Although he had no family, he had ex work colleagues and casual drinking buddies from university who he didn't want dead. To actually set eyes on him was to sign an old friend's death warrant. He had considered lying about any chance meetings with anyone he once knew, but that would then put his life in danger. He wouldn't realistically be saving them, more like swapping their head on the block for his. To his department, security and secrecy were everything. His employers pointed out in no uncertain terms that if an ex friend were allowed to talk to anyone about a chance meeting, then it was that Reaper's very existence that was seen as a threat. That Reaper would be dead that very day.

Jim had little worries about the safety of lives of old friends. He only had one close friend... and his employers blew his brains out when he refused to work for them.

Chapter 52

The smiling killer returned into the sparse office which instantly sent Marty's heart pounding against the huge smiley badge on the front of his long-sleeved shirt. The earlier threat of having his eyes burst with a scalpel nearly tipped him over the edge. He had always had a squeamish phobia about anything hurting or touching his eyes. So much so that it had precluded him wearing contact lens in his teens. A time of rampaging hormones and merciless acne that turned his face into crimson bubble wrap. At that point in his life he really didn't need anything else on his face that would repel the girls he was so desperately chasing. Yet, faced with touching his naked eyeball and sliding a contact lens under his eyelid, he opted to take the lesser of two evils and be called "Four eyes!"

Clearly, his tormentor was not happy with our techno-nerd. After yet again whispering to his older boss, he turned to face Marty.

"Our I.T. boys have accessed all but one file on your computer... unfortunately, they had a bit of trouble." Marty swallowed hard.

"That little virus you left for us has destroyed all our hacker's software. In fact, his whole computer and four others that were helping him open your files have contracted what they call in nerd speak "Cyber Syphilis.""

Marty was shaking again, giving his huge smiley badge on his chest the illusion of chuckling. This was a stark contrast to the terror on Marty's face.

It was the turn of the older man to speak now. "What was on that file?"

His answer was already thought out, because he had been waiting for that question ever since he had been brought here. His answer had to be convincing.

"Porn."

A smile grew on both their lips. Marty acted his socks off as an embarrassed porn addict.

"A... a mate of mine took his computer in to get fixed and they found his stash of fat lass kebab porn. Have you heard of the website "BOBFOC?" Bemused, the older man replied, "I, er, can't say that I have."

Marty extrapolated, "It's an acronym: Body Off Baywatch Face Off Crime watch." They both smiled at each other as Marty saw a way out of this. "Anyway, when they found my mate's lard porn the police were called, and he was nicked. The virus was for the cops, not you. I'm just a lad who doesn't want the coppers to find my wank stash!" To overemphasise his disgust at state oppression curtailing the rights of a lad to choke his chicken over morbidly obese dinner ladies in Grimsby, he shook his head in disgust.

They chuckled now; he may just get out of here alive. Better they thought him a pervert than a threat. Perverts get laughed at... threats get murdered.

Marty couldn't believe his luck. Here he was, wherever the fuck "here" was, in a government interrogation room... and he had just bullshitted two intelligence officers! They actually swallowed all that shit and he was off the hook.

Not quite.

The older man pushed an A4 sheet of paper across the desk for Marty's perusal. He picked it up, and quickly realised it was a printout of itemised phone calls he had made and received in the last two months. A few of the calls were illuminated in florescent highlighter pen. Even though he was looking only at the printout, he could feel the scalpel twirling; Psycho's eyes boring right through him. His voice made Marty jump. He cursed himself inwardly for this outward display of weakness. Oh, what was it his wise old Mother used to say? "Never show a bully you are frightened." Well gee whiz! Thanks Mum. Those pearls of wisdom were like a suit of chain mail when he got the shit smashed out of him every day at school.

The repeated question snapped him abruptly back to reality.

"I said, whose is the phone number we've highlighted?"

He'd gambled and won once today... time to play his ace.

"A woman."

He dramatically sighed in the deadliest game of poker he had played in his entire life. Marty was no knight in shining armour. But in a miniscule nod to chivalry, he felt the need to protect Cassandra from the enemy. And in times of turmoil and terror, this was how Marty dealt with pain; he retreated deep within the realms of a Dungeons and Dragons fantasy. And here he was, the dashing knight, protecting his princess from the forces of darkness. Not with a sword... with his lies.

158

"A woman I want to sleep with... who couldn't give a shit about me. I help fix her computer and update her anti-virus software in the vain hope she'll see past this." He said pointing pathetically to his face.

And with that last card, Marty had pulled off a full house.

"I don't think we need detain you any longer. It's just a formality, but we need a sample of your handwriting before you leave. If you could just write down exactly what we dictate to you, you'll be home in twenty minutes."

The grey-haired man then handed Marty a pen… and a valentine's card.

Chapter 53

In his sparse Porto cabin office, the head of section had been sifting through print outs of all the data the I.T. boys had extracted from Marty's computer, before the cyber syphilis had turned their state of the art lap tops into extremely expensive paper weights. There were stacks of bog-standard government conspiracy fodder. From J.F.K's last car ride, Elvis hiding on the moon, to the cure for breast cancer being found in fresh male sperm. This last one brought out a chuckle, as he himself had used this as a chat up line in the 1950's to a girl from Barnsley. Oh, how he wished he had all this technological data and dubious home office reports to show her back then, she may have reconsidered her decision for the good of her future health. More files contained wholesale takeover of countries by multi-national global corporations. He sighed; tell us something we don't know. Was this curly haired geek studying for a Master's degree in the bleeding obvious? All very mediocre indeed, yet not a trace of the C.C.T.V. recordings that the interfering little rodent had been hacking into. The sweeper team took his flat meticulously to pieces and put it back exactly how it was. They found nothing.

The virus Marty had lovingly left for them, his furious hackers informed him, was to protect the site or final email address these damming files were sent onto.

Torture was an option. He could let Singen off his leash. Although not a skilled medical torturer like the ones he had met in the army in Belfast, his right-hand man was a rabidly enthusiastic sadist. A military doctor could bring you to the point of death and revive you countless times, making you last for weeks, as the victim begs for death. He feared Singen's desire to see an individual scream would just take Marty to the point of death, then push him straight over the edge.

But all that was academic now.

A recurring phone number was flagged up on Marty's phone bill. Ten minutes later, the bunker's I.T. boys had the person's name, address and photo in a neat A4 file on his desk. When the head of section saw who it was, Marty's sell by date had just expired.

A sharp rap at the door announced Singen's entrance. He removed his heavy winters coat and sat down.

"Did you flush that little turd?" Said the older man.

"I ran him a bath, if that's what you mean?"

They both smiled.

Singen nodded towards the open file on his superior's desk. "How bad is it?"

Clearing his throat, he replied "Very." Pointing with a hard-jabbing motion at the photo in the file. "Five years ago, this nosey little bitch nearly destroyed our glorious benefactor. At that time, he was the party's blue-eyed boy and word was, he was being groomed to be P.M. I offered to kill her then personally, but... he had other plans for her."

Shaking his head now he picked up his scrambled mobile and used a secure untraceable line to dial out.

"So, what are you going to do?" Enquired Singen, leaning forward with his elbows on his knees. His boss said quietly, "I'm going to ruin his day."

Chapter 54

The fat man was straining against the metal handcuffs that held him securely, as he was struck again. He gritted his teeth in anticipation of the next one, each blow increasingly harder than the last... and he was loving every minute of it. The high-class call girl who was spanking his colossal buttocks was an expert in inflicting pain without leaving too many marks. This lady clearly missed her calling, as a career in the metropolitan police force surely beckoned. As per her distinguished client's usual instructions, she was dressed up as nursery rhymes most careless shepherdess Little Beau Peep.

"Where's my sheep?" She roared in a crisp debutante's accent. Going through her rehearsed lines like an upper-class pantomime dame.

"I... I... shan't tell! Do you hear? I shan't!" The moment these incendiary words left his blubbery lips, her silk gloved palm sent shudders of pain through his now glowing arse. The last blow shook him so much that his ears were ringing. Yet, the ringing continued. Through the floppy brim of his oversized baby's bonnet he was wearing he could see the lights pulsating on his mobile phone.

Letting out an exasperated sigh, he turned to face the £600 an hour dominatrix.

"Er, could you get that for me, my dear? It might be the chief whip."

She wiggled over to the phone and cooed "But I thought I was your chief whip?"

He leered as sexily as he could. Well, as sexy as an 18 stone naked Lord could be whilst wearing a baby's hat.

"Oh, but of course you are my dear."

She knew when to role play and when to be serious. Very quickly she unshackled him, handed him the phone and dutifully stayed silent.

His playful smile dropped. He clearly did not want to speak to whoever was on the other end of that phone.

"This had better be..." The blood seemed to drain out of his face as he spoke. The call girl had never seen the right honourable member look so worried before. His voice was almost croaky now as he replied to the caller. "I... I'll meet you at the usual place in about fifteen minutes."

Chapter 55

Sir Hugo Montgomery sat on the green moss-covered bench opposite a stone angel in the empty graveyard. Normally there was no way he would ever sully his £3000 cashmere coat on a seat guaranteed to net him a £200 dry cleaning bill. But today, moss stains were the least of his worries and he really felt the need to sit down. For everything he had built, all the backs he had so savagely stabbed to claw his way up to this point in his career, all of it would have been in vain if this bitch got lucky a second time.

Looking up at the lichen and pigeon shit covered stone angel, he thought her open armed pose seemed more condescending than compassionate. Almost as she towered over him, she was somehow judging him for the life he has led and the countless lives that the merchandise he sells have destroyed.

An angel... looking down on a demon.

This thought brought a smile to his blubbery lips as he quietly uttered to the statue. "That's right bitch, a demon... with a Bentley."

The crunching on the gravel path heralded the harbinger of doom walking towards him, carrying the customary bouquet of white lilies. The head of section sat down next to him. Moss stains held no fear for this seasoned killer. After an uneasy silence Sir Hugo Spoke,

"So, she's got C.C.T.V. footage of the Reapers?"

"We don't know for sure. Her boyfriend did all the hacking and sent encoded files onto an unknown email address. His close association with her narrows it down considerably."

The Lord lit a cigar. "What about political affiliations? His peer groups? Any subversive links to extremist groups?"

Looking surreptitiously around, checking the graveyard for prying eyes, he replied,

"Nothing to concern us, loner, no friends... only her."

The mere mention of her made Sir Hugo's face contort with anger.

Clearing his throat, he continued, "Marty is your classic cyber conspiracy nut. Two a penny."

Looking straight ahead, avoiding the agent's gaze, he quietly said "And?"

The head of section gave a wry smile. He knew full well the implication of the purposely vague question, left hanging there. He waited a full ten seconds, enjoying seeing this man sweat in this cold graveyard.

"He now has two pennies on his eyes."

"Well? The clock is ticking. Marty sent that last file on thirteen hours and..." Checking his watch. "...forty-two minutes ago. Whether she has seen it, copied it, passed it on... you need to make a decision now."

The peer stood up and nervously paced back and forth on the gravel path.

The head of section stood up now agitated at Hugo's procrastination.

"What is there to think about? If you didn't tie my hands five years ago, we wouldn't be standing here now surrounded by our customers!" Sir Hugo's eyes blazed at the impertinence of his employee's tone.

"You're forgetting your place aren't you?! You fucking work for me and you do as you are fucking told!" He stepped closer to the head Reaper now. "You need reminding of where you stand in the Master servant relationship. IF, she has something on us and she is killed, it will be political suicide for me." Not once did the grey-haired Reaper subserviently avert his gaze. Instead, he stepped uncomfortably close to the peer and without blinking hissed,

"If the good people of this country ever find out what we've been doing... then suicide is your only fucking option."

Hugo swallowed hard. He was staring into the ice-cold eyes of a man who every working day killed total strangers without mercy. And here he was, totally alone with this man in an empty graveyard. Suddenly he felt very vulnerable and very cold. Shivering almost... or trembling.

"J... just give me two hours to close all her outlets to this story on Fleet Street…"

The head Reaper cut him short. "You don't control the internet."

Hugo sighed. "Y… yes. you're right."

The head of section put a placating hand on the Lord's shoulder.

"Okay Hugo, you've got your two hours... then we'll put Pandora back in her box... permanently."

Chapter 56

Some clubs are relatively easy to get into. The Mickey Mouse club, if you have the subscription fee. The golf club, if you have the dress sense of a blind pimp. And the pudding club, if you happen to be in a Doncaster pub toilet when Darren is feeling randy. However, there are some clubs that are so exclusive that Jesus would be refused entry on account of their strict "No sandals" policy. One such establishment is Sir Hugo's private gentleman's drinking club where good breeding and inbreeding are almost a prerequisite of entry. Normally a place of sanctuary and nefarious business deals for the peer, today his visit was neither business nor pleasure. Today he was here to meet Mervin Foster, who he had summoned as a matter of utmost urgency.

A twelve-year-old Scottish malt should be savoured on the pallet, like caressing a lover's tongue... not swilled down the gullet like mouthwash.

"Oooh! That's like an angel pissing on yer tongue!"

Sir Hugo forced a smile back at the tabloid editor. "Yes, quite. Glad you are enjoying it Mervin. Now Mervin, you know I didn't invite you here to my private club just to get drunk, don't you?"

Clunking his heavy crystal glass down on the antique wooden coffee table drew looks of disapproval from privileged pensioners' two tables away.

"Righto! Well they say there is no such thing as a free scoop, so what can I do for yer cobber?"

Hugo winced at this buffoon's strangled cat accent. He didn't much care for Australians. The way they were so fearlessly proud of never mentally evolving in over 200 years from the alcoholic sheep molesting criminals they were descended from.

"How's your lady reporter coming along Mervin?"

"She's alright I suppose. "He sighed and leaned forward, elbows on his knees. "I mean, she's not a team player. She's just not suited for the work we do at our paper."

He looked around checking for any eves droppers as he lowered his voice. "Between you and me Hugo, I think she's one of those carpet munching lezzas!"

Brushing aside Mervin's ill-informed bigotry, Sir Hugo got to the point as subtlety would not work on this uncouth little oik.

"Mervin... what is she working on at the moment?" Hearing this, the editor's eyes lit up. "Oh! She's working on possibly the biggest story this paper has ever seen!"

Hugo's blood ran cold as he felt the earth opening beneath his feet to swallow him up. He gulped down his whiskey, desiring its anaesthetising qualities rather than savouring its rich Celtic heritage. As the architect of his downfall sat directly opposite him. "Mervin..." The Lord forced an insincere smile through gritted teeth,

"...you can't run that story."

170

The tabloid editor's mouth dropped.

"You what?! You pulling my plonker, Hugo? This farrkin' story will blow Fleet Street apart. It'll be worth millions when it is syndicated worldwide." He shook his head disgusted that Hugo could even suggest such a reprehensible course of action.

The knight of the realm's breathing quickened at the treachery of a paid lapdog that so viciously dared to bite its master. Both men fell silent. One very confused the other contemplating merciless revenge. Despite the odd hocking cough of a rich O.A.P. and the loud mechanical ticking of the club's grandfather clock, there was an eerie silence. Hugo leaned in close to Mervin, who in turn mirrored the peer's posture.

Hugo's voice was low, almost a whisper.

"I want you to know Mervin, despite our years of friendship, I wouldn't hesitate in having you murdered if you seriously thought of running the story she is working on." Foster's eyes opened wide with shock, he tried to speak but Hugo held up a silencing hand.

"Your children will be kidnapped from their schools, your wife snatched from your home." His voice full of menace now.

"All three will be found decapitated floating down the Thames." Mervin tried to stand, but Hugo's vice like grip on his shoulder held him firmly in his seat.

"And as for you... you will be expertly tortured by military professionals who will make you last for a week... before you join your wife and kids. You will fucking learn that the sword is, and always will be mightier than the pen!"

A shell-shocked Mervin sat stunned looking at an old friend, who had just threatened to annihilate his entire family. "H… Hugo, Jesus… I mean, if it means that much to you, I'll spike the Mickey and Mave story."

Hugo blurted out "What? What the fuck are you talking about?!"

Wiping beads of sweat from his brow, Mervin replied,

"Mickey Mullet the East end celebrity gangster and glamour porn star Mave the rave. They're the next big thing. That's the story that Cassandra has been working on."

Hugo sat there totally stunned. His turn to be slack jawed now, as Mervin continued, trying to placate his powerful friend.

"I mean, it's a great scoop. If they marry, it will go mental. But to threaten my kids! Jesus Hugo…"

Closing his eyes, trying to make sense of the situation, Hugo slowly said,

"I… is that it?…the big story?"

"Well yeah. Biggest one we've had in years."

The peer gulped at his whiskey. His mind a cocktail of emotions: fear, rage and slow simmering embarrassment. His hand covered his eyes, a glimmer of relief spreading through him.

"Is there anything else, Mervin? Something she's been keeping to herself? Anything?" Mervin's cogs turned as he looked skyward for the answer.

"Only a hotel spit roast by a couple of Chelsea players and a girl off the bacon counter at Tescos."

Whether it was the sheer weight being lifted from his shoulders, or the naive diseased ramblings of a mucky magazine editor, Hugo found himself collapsing into uncontrollable hysterical laughter. As the tears rolled down his fat jowls, a very irate Mervin stood up and left the mad man to his manic cackling, which still rang in his ears as he stormed out of the club.

Chapter 57

The newsroom was a hive of activity. Reporters babbling excitedly on phones and tapping away manically at their laptops. Every desk a whirring spinning cog in Mervin Foster's porn empire. Every desk... bar one.

From his glass fronted office, Mervin could not take his eyes off that desk. Her desk. The thorn in his side. The fucking cuckoo who had been forced to live in his nest, by the old "friend, "who only an hour ago had turned into a terrifying enemy. Five years ago, a shit storm was brewing on Fleet Street. She was the epicentre of that scandal. Even though he had never met her back then, he was well aware of her and very wary of her. She was the worst kind of journalist... she couldn't be bought. And she waged a personal vendetta against Sir Hugo over his legitimate munitions company... and the people who he secretly sold arms to.

Mervin cosied up to Hugo back then as it was almost a cert this dynamic well connected M.P. was being fast tracked to 10 Downing Street. Mervin's papers paved that path and let his readership know who they were expected to vote for. Over the years, Foster had collected many bent politicians to add to his trophy room... now it looked like he'd complete his set and have a Prime Minister in his back pocket. But she fucked all that up with her in depth expose of the war crimes committed by Hugo's customers... then British soldiers slaughtered by the products from Montgomery munitions. No other paper was interested in taking down a future P.M., no hack stupid enough to try. All except for one. Like a dog with a bone, she wouldn't let go. Despite all advice, he wouldn't have that mad dog put down.

The damage was done; he for the sake of his party agreed to a foreign posting that quietly enabled him to concentrate on the supply chains for every military conflict across four continents. Making him one of the world's most powerful arms dealers now the spotlight was off him. He found himself in a unique position to broker arms deals for British companies through his old buddies at the home office. The billions in export licences he brought to the U.K. inevitably earned him a knighthood and a seat in the House of Lords, where he returned from exile a conquering hero. But before he left Britain to the smoke and mirrors public exile there was the little matter of the person who ended his dreams of becoming P.M. He used all his power and influence to blacklist her from every avenue of journalism. Every road closed off to her... or so she thought. A week later she was working for Mervin.

The very same private members club Mervin's life was threatened an hour ago, Sir Hugo met him and made him a very bizarre offer he couldn't refuse, five years ago. Since then, they would meet annually at his club and the Lord would hand Mervin two envelopes: one containing a substantial bribe for Foster's back pocket, and the other,

Cassandra's whole wage packet for the entire year. In short, she was working for Mervin's paper for free. More than that, unbeknown to her, she was on the payroll of the man she sought to destroy. Did the knight of the realm get a kick out of being his nemesis's puppet master? Who knew what went on in these pommie ponce's deviant little minds? Brooded Mervin. Whatever it was that she had on Hugo had got him so rattled, that he was prepared to kill the editor's wife and children to protect that secret.

Chapter 58

Even though the hours worked by a journalist are flexible (usually depending on the temper tantrums of their editors) Cassandra had decided that her daily quota of gathering "exclusives" for the drooling unwashed to read had been filled. The bottles of Merlot clinked together in the bag for life. She had acquired six of these bags now, almost making her immortal. The wine was squashing her instant microwave meal for one. Meal for one...booze for eight. She quickly by passed her brutal burglar alarm and placed the claw hammer on the shelf beside the front door. Glancing at the answering machine, no calls. Nobody loved her today... or any other day. She sighed heavily as she slammed her tea in the microwave. Before her dismal excuse for haute cuisine had spun twice in the microwave she had drained one glass of red wine. Was there an ocean of vino deep enough to drown her sorrows? She doubted it. Cassandra used to worry that she was drinking too often. Using it as medicine, killing brain cells. This thought made her laugh out loud. What the fuck did she need brain cells for in her job? The metallic "ping! "announced that dinner was served.

She looked up from her glass and saw it. There on the front door mat... a red envelope. In her rush to get in and open the wine she had failed to notice it there. As she picked it up she could feel the hard object inside the envelope. The contents felt stiffer than paper, a card? But again, the solid object she could feel through the card started her heart racing. She flipped the card over and saw her name and address and a London post mark. It had gone through the postal system. As there were no communal letterboxes downstairs, a neighbour had probably popped it through her front door as a kindness. It had by passed her locks and burglar alarm. It had reached her inner sanctum where she felt totally safe. The words screamed in her skull loud and clear...

LETTER BOMB

And she was holding it in her trembling hands.

The suspect envelope lay in her bathtub, held down by one corner by a heavy metal award she had received for journalism many years ago. The prestigious award mocked her now as an unwilling disciple of tabloid tittle tattle. Her lack of investigative integrity was put on the back burner for the moment as the pressing matter of the letter bomb in her flat took precedence. She turned off the cold water tap as the bath was half full, then closed the door and went to finish her second glass of wine. After all, no need to turn a drama into a crisis.

Of course, she could've phoned the bomb squad. Then everybody who lived within a square mile of her flat would have to be evacuated. Every business shut down and disrupted. Public transport into the area suspended, all gas and electricity

178

supplies shut off, same with the water. Her flat stripped and doors removed to allow the bulky remote-controlled military robot access to the suspect device. Police officers would be dragged off other duties just to handle crowd control. And, for the agonising two hours it would take the robot to defuse, remove or detonate... her flat would be on every radio, T.V., satellite and social media network watched and listened to by half the planet.

Fuck that!

What if it was just a card? Cassandra's real journalistic career ended five years ago, and every day that she had worked at that titty newspaper eroded all the good work she had done in the past. Sinking another glass of Merlot, she lamented that soon... all that people would remember her for was the work she did now, rather than the champion of social justice she used to be. So, phoning in a false bomb threat would be the final nail in the coffin of her ailing career. Too many people wanted to see her crash and burn, and she wasn't about to offer herself up on a plate for them. Faced with this stark choice, she'd rather take a chance and be blown to smithereens.

Through her association with Marty and his obsession with the murkier elements of the internet, she had learned some bizarre statistics and facts. Most of the time she just let him ramble on until he gave her the solid data she needed, on whatever bent bastard she was hunting that week. But it was Marty's expertise in anti-terrorism that led to her drowning her letter bomb in the bath. According to her pet nerd and his internet buddies, the circuits, detonator and explosive would all be rendered useless after an hour in cold water. Whether this was urban myth or urban warfare bomb maker's bible tips, she really didn't know. But she was running out of options and since she'd rung Marty five times with no answer, submerged the card and hoped for the best. Then another of Marty's little gems popped into her head to counter this technique... what if it was made by a professional, not a piss poor amateur? The hacker had once told her that the components used by Special Forces can blow open the hulls of ships docked in St. Petersburg days after being planted.

She hoped the bomb maker was a half-wit.

The sharp bread knife she had Sellotaped to a mop handle edged under the bath water and gingerly eased open the soaked card. Her body halfway out of the doorway, prepared to run. What was the speed of combustion? Was it slower than sound? As long as it was slower than a half-pissed reporter could stumble out the door, she couldn't give a shit. She held her breath as the envelope's flap opened and a solitary bubble escaped from the card within and seemed to take an age to slowly rise to pop on the surface. Nudging the hard object from within the card, she laughed out loud when she saw it was a teaspoon. Satisfied now that no postal assassin had plotted her demise, she delved in and fished out the envelope and spoon by hand. Inside was a card... a valentine's card. With the sleeves of her blouse soaking wet, she read the sodden sonnet.

"Come round to my flat at 8pm, I've got something sweet for you. P.S... bring the spoon. XXX"

"I'll fucking kill him!" She roared as she jabbed at the telephone. The water from her elbows dripped onto her feet soaking her tights really darkening her mood. No answer. No answering machine. Fucking nerd and his practical jokes! She slammed the phone into its cradle and quickly slipped on her shoes. Without thinking she reset her claw hammer alarm and stormed out the door.

Chapter 59

"Jim's back tomorrow, isn't he? "Asked the head of section. Singen looked bored perusing a printout of that week's departmental confirmed kills.

"What? Oh, yes."

"So, has he come back to us?"

Putting the page of statistics down, he replied,

"Yes, reluctantly. I mean, he has fought so long against his position that I realistically don't think we can trust him. We have plenty of willing Reapers who have taken to their calling like ducks to water. So why are we unnecessarily investing so much time and effort into someone who shouldn't have made it past the interview?" His boss noted the barely concealed conceit. The head of section gave a warming smile.

"Come now Singen, I know you and Jim haven't hit it off, but we have great plans for that young man."

Singen turned to face him. "We?"

He sensed the younger man's annoyance.

"You are aware of our impending American expansion?" His junior suddenly took notice. He continued, "Well our Senator is very impressed with our operation and has given a green light to expand stateside" He looked thoughtfully at his laptop.

"The deal, however, needs to be sweetened by taking care of a little problem for the Senator. Call it a test, if you will."

"I'll do it." Blurted out Singen, knowing full well the implication of what was being asked. His boss stood up and put a hand on the younger man's shoulder.

"Not this time, old boy. The Senator has asked for someone who fits a specific psychological profile to assassinate this unique target."

Incredulous, Singen asked "Huh! And Jim fits that profile?"

"Oh yes… he's the perfect Oswald."

Chapter 60

Eventually she flagged down a taxi. She wouldn't risk driving on four glasses of wine. A drunk falling out of a kebab shop thought of arguing with her as to who hailed the cab first, then saw the rage in her eyes... and thought again. Cassandra delved into her handbag until she felt the comb in her hand. It was a hairdresser's comb, a specific one that had a five-inch long metal spike for a handle. Used to part hair in a salon. An ex-boyfriend who happened to be a policeman advised her to carry this "weapon" for self-defence. In the event of her having to use it, a court would deem it the first thing she reached for in her bag. Whereas a serrated edged lock knife would net her some serious prison time.

If Marty was the serial killer as she had just recently suspected, then why the fuck was she racing across town to see if her shroud fits? Surely a crap practical joke with a valentine's card didn't warrant this journey? So, what was it, curiosity? Journalistic instinct? Or the raging desires to put the final piece in place in this macabre jigsaw puzzle? Yet what good would her reinstated career be if this sick fucker carved her to pieces with a jig saw? She shivered at this thought as the taxi's worn brakes announced their final destination.

As the red taillights of her cab disappeared into the night she approached the intercom. Her hand stopped an inch from the buzzer when she noticed the front door had been wedged open with a phone book. For a man as paranoid about government conspiracies as Marty, this was totally out of character. In his hobbit driven world, his home literally was his castle... and here he'd left the drawbridge down.

Will you walk into my parlour? Said the spider to the fly.

Stop it! She was scaring herself now. Gripping her spiked comb in her hand, she stepped over the threshold mustering up all the bravery she had left.

Glancing up the gloomy staircase she saw soft light flickering from Marty's half open flat door.

Apart from the sound of blood pounding in her ears, Marty's darkened flat was eerily silent. The prongs from her spiked comb dug sharply into the palm of her hand as she gripped her one chance of fighting off a killer, a little too tightly. His ramshackle domicile was lit only by dozens of tall red candles dotted around the room, on piles of computer discs and unwashed mugs. The flickering flames caused dark shadows to loom threateningly towards her, instinctively she lashed out, thrusting the vicious spike aimlessly into empty space. With her other hand she slapped the wall to the left of the door frame until she found the light switch.

Nothing. She clicked it up and down repeatedly, no lights came on. She then lumbered towards his desk lamp, knocking over a teetering pile of discs and comics. Again, she repeatedly clicked the button on the base of the lamp… nothing.

From her vantage point in the centre of the room she could see all the bulbs in the room were in place.

He'd cut the power…

She was finding it hard to breath. Her legs were beginning to tremble. The open front door seemed a very long way away from her now.

RUN! YOU STUPID BITCH!

The words roared in her skull. She was playing Russian roulette with her life and the odds were getting slimmer by the second. All those cheesy horror films she had scoffed at where the girl walks into a darkened room... were all now coming back to haunt her. In a voice full of bravado, laced with crippling fear she called out, "Marty? Are you there, Marty?"

Oh, that's right... if he couldn't find you in the dark; the sound of your voice will draw him towards you like the vibrations of a struggling bluebottle in a spider's web.

Silence.

Then, she noticed it. A pattern. All the candles were lined up... leading to the open bathroom door. There seemed to be more candles in there as the red flickering light was brighter. The smell of hot wax, and something else filled the flat.

"M…Marty! This isn't fucking funny anymore!"

She swished at the shadows again with her impromptu weapon. The only sound, her short panicking breaths. The all-consuming fear that was engulfing her, was momentarily forgotten as she squinted in the candlelight at the palm of her hand. Only when Cassandra saw blood did she realise that her tight panicked grip had forced the comb through

186

the skin in her hand. She welcomed the pain. It helped her to focus. It brought a much-needed shot of adrenaline that pushed her fear to one side.

There were two doors open.

One was bathed in white light that led to the stairway and freedom. The other... shimmered in flickering crimson like the gateway to Hades.

Should she stay, or should she go?

This fucker had terrified her. Ensnared her in this darkened room... and now she was bleeding because of this little shit! Fear now turned to rage as she swapped hands with her weapon and barged into the bathroom prepared to meet her maker... or send Marty to his.

Marty was waiting for her in the bathroom.

In the bath, be precise. Completely naked and staring wildly at her. She dropped her makeshift weapon on the tiled bathroom where its clatter echoed around the tiny bathroom. There was no need for protection anymore, seeing as her bogey man lay under the bathwater... quite dead.

She edged closer to the submerged computer geek tentatively; almost afraid he would erupt from the water like an avenging leviathan. At the side of his chest lay a retro radio cassette player, its power cable trailing over the side of the bath and into an extension lead that snaked back into the flat. The water appeared deep red in the spooky glow of the numerous scattered candles, like he was bathed in his own blood. A quick glance of his up turned wrists told her this was not the cause of his demise. The electrical appliance in the bath was nearer to the mark. She smelled that odd smell that was bothering her again, only stronger in here. A sickly-sweet smell... strawberries.

The journalist felt quite drained. The cocktail of emotions she had gone through from horror to anger and now shock. And... sorrow? No, strangely not a sense of loss, but numbness. She reached out to touch her... friend? The word seemed empty in her mind as she knew she'd really regarded the late Marty as nothing more than a journalistic source. She recoiled her hand in horror as the bathwater she touched was solid and felt rubbery to the touch. Curiously, she prodded the surface again and scooped a handful of the sticky red substance up and sniffed it. Only when she licked her finger did she realise that Marty's dead body was encased in strawberry jelly.

Chapter 61

As a little girl, her mother had taught her that when you are in someone else's house, you abided by their rules and mind your manners. When she'd brought the head C.E.O. of a price fixing pharmaceutical cartel down, she ignored her Mum's advice. Her parent's teachings were pushed to one side when an arms-dealing M.P. withered under her relentless questioning during a Commons select committee hearing.

So why the fuck should she listen to her Mummy now, a zealous half-wit detective with delusions of joining the Sweeney was trying to fit her up for Marty's murder?

"We'll start again Miss, shall we?" Droned the detective as his older colleague paced back and forth behind her for dramatic effect.

"Why were you in Marty's flat?" This relentless broken record had gone on for six and a half hours. From the moment she had made the call after finding Marty, the circus had snowballed at breakneck speed. The initial sympathetic W.P.C. who took her statement before she was handed over to these two pricks who read her rights and drove her away as an army of S.O.C.O. moved into measure, photograph take samples and put her late hacker in a rubber bag.

The older officer never gave up eye contact, in a piss poor attempt at psychological intimidation. Denying her nicotine breaks wasn't an option for them once they learned she didn't smoke. She knew all the tricks. She'd studied mental torture techniques extensively and could predict these amateurs next move. She refused all drinks as they would use access to the toilet as yet another pressure point.

They fucking bored her now

"So, Miss, what is it, kinky bonk and thrash sex games gone wrong?" The journalist knew the score. It was their training. They were instructed to wind her up until she snapped. An unresponsive suspect was supposed to blurt out incriminating evidence in the face of such a relentless barrage of manipulative abuse. Training that's all, nothing personal. The older detective behind her gave a low muffled chuckle,

"So, on top of all that jelly, was it gonna be whipped cream before the whipped arse?"

Oh... it was fucking personal now.

Her head snapped round and glared at the older officer.

"I'll make this very simple for you, shall I monkey boy? I don't fear you, understand?! So, you can stop pacing up and down behind me in your piss poor attempt at intimidating me or go ahead and give me the beating your hard-on suggests your fantasising about!"

The seated detective sensed the balance of power had shifted in the confined interview room. "Look Miss, if you could just answer the..."

Her hand slammed hard into the table, making him jump and cutting him mid-sentence. Through gritted teeth she snarled at him, leaning over the table, he backed away for fear of being head butted.

"I made a statement hours ago. YOU! Wrote it down." She jabbed the statement in front of him.

"If you have Alzheimer's, then get your fucking carer to read it out to you until it sinks in! If you can't read, then why not retrain as a traffic warden?!"

The older officer behind her spoke again, this time the cockiness had departed from his voice.

" Madam, we're only trying to ascertain the facts..."

She reared round on him.

"I told you dumbass!" Spittle shot out of her mouth and hit his shirt. "Either beat the shit out of me..." She was nose to nose with him now. "...charge me or let me fuck go!"

Fifteen minutes later, she was back on the street.

Chapter 62

"There he is! I fuckin' love this fella!" Desmond Shanks, or Desi as he liked to be called, pumped Jim's hand to the point where he felt his shoulder click. The 54-year-old sweeper squad supervisor was in charge of nine man support team, whose whole career is based around mopping up after Reapers who botch up their kills. Seeing as Jim botched up more than most, and the sweeper teams were paid double time to erase his mess, he was very popular with these lads.

"Here lad, take this, I baked it especially for yer." Desi handed Jim yet another homemade cake lovingly baked as a thank you for the new kitchen Jim's incompetence paid for. The reluctant Reaper weakly smiled and accepted the chocolate cake from Desi, blushing slightly as his fellow Reapers smirked and nudged each other at this ritual. Like a simple kid at school who gets prizes off the teachers for being thick as pig shit. Desi waddled off as Jim plonked himself down heavily into his seat and turned on his computer.

So, who would it be today? A doctor? A banker? A mother of three? God no, not a woman! He really didn't think he could take killing a woman. He knew he couldn't. Not after Lorraine Fuller. He shuddered at his desk at the vivid memory. That was the only one person who he actually bought an evening paper for. To morbidly acknowledge his progress? To see if he had gotten clean away with it? Or... to somehow posthumously gets to know the woman who died only because she ended up on Jim's job sheet? Except... Jim didn't kill her, Singen did. When he froze on the spot in the laundrette Slimey pounced on her. She never stood a chance; never saw him coming as his disguise as an old lady totally threw the young woman, before he physically threw her into the huge dryer. Bile rose in his throat and Jim raised a hand to his mouth for fear of vomiting. The dull thudding of his heart in his chest, mimicked the horrific memory of the woman desperately kicking out at the glass door of the dryer as the drum started to turn. The angry Slimey, clearly pissed off at Jim's cowardice ordered him to return to the bunker as he sat calmly and was obviously enjoying the show.

Jim snapped open his eyes to try and block out the memory and saw the green raffle ticket stapled to an office memo on his desk. Picking it up the words he dreaded ever since he had come to work here: "Congratulations! You have won the staff lottery!"

Today a celebrity would die.

Chapter 63

She had considered saving up all her urine every time she went to the toilet. Once she had swilled the news pack on her doorstep with piss, their priorities between hounding her and running home for a shower would change. The golden rule of journalism had been broken; report the story, don't become the story.

Cassandra was the toast of Fleet Street. For all the wrong reasons.

Marty's death... and her links to him had seen all her colleagues past and present come calling. She closed her eyes, and then suddenly snapped them back open. The stark picture of Marty entombed in crimson jelly. Although the official coroner's report wouldn't hit the streets for another two days, she still had contacts within the force. That is how she had a full copy of that report on her lap right now.

Marty's heart had stopped after a large electrical current had passed through it. The close proximity of the old cassette player that had fallen into the bath was probably the source of that current. The bathwater helped to conduct the electricity that quite possibly either rendered Marty unconscious or delivered a fatal wattage. The junction box circuit breakers had only blown and tripped after a sufficient charge had travelled to the cassette player. Marty's lungs were full of congealed strawberry jelly. His head was submerged beneath the water resulting in drowning. A romantic compilation tape of love songs was found in the cassette player. With the number of candles placed around the flat and valentine's card and spoon sent to a woman, the verdict is: 'Death by misadventure'. A romantic gesture gone wrong.

Case closed.

Slammed shut... fucking key thrown away. Something wasn't right. Cassandra quickly scanned through the coroner's report again until she found it. Her heart pounded in her chest as it stared back up at her from the page... Marty had been murdered.

Chapter 64

"I could lose me pension doing this, y'know?" Moaned Stanley Vaughn as he tried to manoeuvre his Rubenesque rump in the tight confines of the late Marty's electrical cupboard.

"Well, the sooner you get on with it, the sooner you get your Scotch and two hundred quid."

Vaughn poked his head out of the cupboard. His face eerily illuminated from the torch he held in the darkened flat. "Two hundred and fifty quid we said. I'm not risking prison for being caught in a dead man's flat for less than two fifty." Cassandra smiled sweetly at the moonlighting hospital porter to reassure him before he haggled for strike pay and luncheon vouchers.

"Thank you for correcting me, Stanley, two hundred and fifty and the Scotch it is. Now, at the risk of being rude... we are here on business."

"Oh, right you are." He replied ducking back into the cupboard. Long before he worked at the local hospital, Stanley was a time served electrician. It was this string to his bow that she now needed to confirm her darkest fears. They had entered the apartment with a spare set of keys Marty had given her a long time ago. She reluctantly accepted them but never used them for fear it may be sending out mixed messages and wanted to retain a professional distance. The keys remained in an old bowl on top of her kitchen cupboards along with dead batteries, loose change and a champagne cork. Never been used, until tonight they were helping her commit a crime, breaking and entering, plus tampering with a murder scene.

In the gloom of the flat she could just detect the aroma of wax... and strawberries. She gripped the door to the electric cupboard for support as the image of Marty dead in the bath filled her mind. His face frozen in a silent scream. Marty's face changed became fuller, aging rapidly.

"You okay girl?" She blinked hard as Stanley stood right in front of her.

"I thought you were gonna pass out, there." He pointed his torch at a burnt-out fuse and then at the large red trip switch.

"If the cassette player did fall into the bath, this red switch would've tripped. But for this fuse to have blown like this, someone must have physically stood here and held it up to prevent it tripping. Once the fuse blew, no more power would go to the cassette player. Certainly not enough to kill a man."

"So, the only reason this red trip switch was held up was to purposely burn out and blow this fuse?" She said pointing to the charred half melted fuse on the circuit breaker board.

"Oh aye, a bloody apprentice spark would've spotted that." Confirmed the porter. She screwed her face up in confusion.

Chapter 65

Jim sat down in the head of section's office as Slimey closed the door behind him. Instead of taking a seat, he remained behind Jim leaning against the door. Was this for psychological effect, or blocking Jim's escape?

"So…" Beamed the grey-haired head Reaper "…are you all refreshed from your time off?" This threw Jim. The last time they spoke he was being screamed at by his boss for incompetence, who then had Slimey mentor him… now here he was, nice as pie. Jim wasn't buying it and his head snapped round to check what the snake behind him was up to. When he turned back to face his boss, an A4 sheet of paper with a photo stapled to one corner was pushed slowly across the desk to him. Jim's stomach started to knot; his breathing quickened.

It was a photo of a woman.

"She's going to send us all to prison. All our homes, our money, all our valuable work… gone." The older man leaned back in his chair.

"The amount of prison time we are talking about is thirty years minimum. No parole, banged up twenty-three hours a day with only an overflowing shit bucket and an amorous cell mate for company."

Shock turned to panic as Jim blurted out "Wh…what are we going to do?"

Delighted the head of section addressed Slimey. "See that?" Pointing at Jim in mock pantomime pose. "Always thinking! Always proactive in ways to help the department. Well done Jim. Well done!"

He couldn't see, but he could feel Slimey's evil grin behind him as he enjoyed his boss's little act.

"There you go, Jim" The older man handed Jim the page of details and photo.

"I need her dead by close of business today."

A refusal wouldn't just offend… it would be suicide.

"We needed her dead yesterday, but with the media sniffing round her, we couldn't get close. But she's yesterday's chip paper now, so you should have a clear shot at her, so to speak." He said with such a serene smile on his face.

Jim was clutching at straws, and he felt the raffle ticket in his coat pocket. He brought it out and showed it to his employer.

"But…I've just won the staff lottery."

His mock hurt acting had to be convincing… this woman's life depended on it. His boss frowned. "As much of a staff morale booster that culling pleb celebs is Jim, our very security depends on that bitch going in the ground tonight." His unexpected salvation was delivered by a low voice behind him.

"I'll do it."

Slimey walked slowly over to the desk whilst his superior gave a disapproving look at this impertinent suggestion.

Slimey answered his superior's unspoken question. "We need it done quickly; we need it done right." He turned to face Jim with mock concern in his eyes. "No offence."

"None taken." Replied Jim.

What the fuck was he up to and why was he helping him out like this? Mused Jim.

Sighing as he handed the journalist's details to Slimey. "I suppose you are right." He suddenly fixed Singen with an icy stare. "It has been specifically requested that this one's demise be as utterly humiliating as possible. It has to totally eclipse her infamous career and absolutely destroy in people's minds any shred of credibility she once ever had."

"It'll be my pleasure." Grinned Slimey, scanning the photo.

Even though his inner voice screamed NO! The burning curiosity bubbled out of Jim's mouth before he could stop himself.

"Requested?"

"Sorry…" Said his boss.

"Y…you said, "specifically requested"…by whom?"

Slimey and his boss glanced at each other before the older man replied, "Need to know basis, dear boy."

"But I thought the computer randomly picked…"

Slimey cut him short. "Jim! All you need to know is that she made the "in" tray. She will be processed in due course. Now…" That insincere smile again "…let me be the first to congratulate you on winning the staff lottery."

He picked up a celebrity paparazzi magazine from the top of the filing cabinet and started flicking through… until something, or someone caught his attention. He smiled and showed the head of selection the object of his amusement, who just shrugged and said, "I suppose, why not?"

200

The open magazine was thrust into Jim's hands by a beaming Slimey. Amongst all the Hollywood film stars, the alphabet of fame quickly shot up until amongst a pond life of fame one face stood out amongst the catwalk models and soap stars for its sheer hideousness. Jim looked up open mouthed at Slimey.

"Th... that's drug baron Mickey Mullet! I... I mean, he's... he's a..."

"Celebrity." Said Singen. "...Apparently, he's written a few books of his exploits and now he's gone from infamous to famous... and very soon to be posthumous." He put a congratulatory hand on Jim's shoulder.

"Enjoy your prize Jim."

Chapter 66

Which would kill him first? The dum dum bullet from his disgruntled employer at his next contract appraisal, or the passive smoking he'd received from 25 minutes in the company of a bent ex C.I.D. officer's company. This duplicitous machine for turning oxygen into nicotine napalm was putting the finishing touches, the final pages of Mickey Mullet's life story. Not so much a biography... more of an obituary. Every detail that a murder squad detective would pick up on, every tell-tale trace of D.N.A. that forensics would incarcerate Jim with, would be side stepped with pedantic precision. Anyway... if he fucked up, there was always Desi Shanks and his mop up squad with the van revved up, grateful of any overtime Jim could throw their way. The briefing at an end, Jim wafted his hand back and forth to indicate his lungs colour was never meant to be brown.

"Do you know it's no smoking in the bunker?"

Without blinking the officer said with a fag dangling from his lips,

"No... but I do know all the words to "Agadoo.""

On the way to the costume department to have his disguise fitted he overheard a trio of Reapers gossiping by the coffee machine. From what he heard as he passed, the officers in the observation point set an attack dog on a tramp that was blocking the bunker's entrance. Jim wanted to ask did he die but thought better of it. He knew the other Reapers saw him as not one of them and kept him at arms-length. The feeling was mutual; he wouldn't want to be one of them... fucking sheep!

Twenty minutes later he was in the makeup chair having his false rabbi's beard and curly wig fitted. As he was having the bulbous latex nose glued on he wondered how the hell a makeup special effects technician ended up aiding and abetting assassins. Jim had never really exchanged small talk with this guy before. Usually he had other things on his mind, like the imminent death of a stranger.

"It's Julian, isn't it?" The slightly built man with a floppy long fringe and nose ring meekly nodded.

"How did you get into this line of work then?" Julian seemed genuinely surprised that a Reaper had honoured him with conversation. There were cliques and a pecking order in the bunker. The crazy Zealots at the top, Reapers, support staff, mop up squads... right down to the dog handler. Even Wolfgang was above Julian... at least they all remembered the mutt's name.

"Oh, well... I've always had an interest in Hollywood and theatrical makeup." Elaborated the slightly camp technician.

"No, I mean working here." Clarified Jim.

The young man's gaze dropped and so did his usual cheery demeanour. Sighing he replied. "I... was recruited... the same as you. Thought initially that it was a dream job,

203

working for M.I.5…" His voice quivered. "Th… then I saw the gun… and the plastic sheeting… I… I'm not afraid to say, I shit myself."

Jim reached out a comforting hand. "Me too mate, I was scared."

Julian looked straight at Jim. "No, literally. Good job the plastic sheeting was there."

Chapter 67

Shuffling past the tech boys in his long black orthodox rabbi's coat and tall black hat, Jim was slapped on the back by a computer nerd and congratulated for winning the celeb lottery. After the lung busting stair climb he reached the bunker's entrance and caught his breath. Captain Naylor at the reception desk stifled a giggle when he saw Jim's outfit.

"Bless me father, for I have sinned."

"Wrong religion." Snorted Jim, unamused.

Talking into his headset now,

"It's Naylor, delivery in two minutes confirm status."

He looked Jim up and down with a grin, as the two surveillance officers in the observation point outside checked that the coast was clear. "Affirmative." He removed the headset and placed it next to his Glock handgun.

"Okay Jim, you're clear to go forth and spread the word." Instead of telling him to go fuck himself, the heavily disguised Reaper just grunted and waited for the electronic door lock to buzz open.

"Say hello to your girlfriend for me will you Jim. She's waiting for you in a blue Ford Focus 100 yards from the main road parked in front of a white van."

Jim stopped in his tracks at the opened outer door. "Wh...wha..."

Naylor cut him short. "She's giving you a lift to Mullet's place. You're a jammy bastard. She's got a cracking pair of tits on her!" He cupped both hands in front of him to illustrate his point. Confused, Jim stepped back through the half open bunker door. "On your way Jim!" Snarled Naylor. "This door can only stay open for 20 seconds at a time."

As the electronic lock buzzed shut behind him, he scurried out of the alleyway and melted into the London rush hour traffic... to meet the unknown female driver of a blue Ford Focus.

Chapter 68

The car was parked exactly where Naylor said it would be. Approaching from the rear he could see someone was in the driver's seat. Someone with blonde curly hair. Ten yards from the car and the woman leaned across and opened the passenger door. Obviously watching out for his approach in the rear-view mirror. Jim checked the street to see he wasn't being watched, and, not knowing quite what to do next, got into the car and closed the door.

"Glad you could make it Jim." Said the eerily familiar voice.

Could Jim's day get any fucking worse? There, in all his glory, sat Slimey... in full drag. Julian had done a very good job, Singen resembled a tarty divorcee out on the pull... down the docks. With gangs of unwashed sailors.

The car turned into traffic and sped through town as fast as the bone-idle yummy mummies in the monster trucks would allow them.

Slimey caught Jim's incredulous gaze at his appearance.

"Admit it Jim, after a few pints... you would, wouldn't you?" He cooed, blowing Jim a kiss.

"Only if it was fucking chloroform on draught!"

His Amazonian driver slapped the steering wheel and laughed, as he turned left at the roundabout and headed for the motorway. Three miles up the motorway Jim cocked his thumb over his shoulder.

"Mickey Mullet's mansion is back that way." The patent leather stiletto pressed harder on the accelerator.

"I know. We're taking a little detour." Jim's eyes widened. Slimey sensed his passenger's disquiet and tried to sound reassuring. "Calm yourself Jim. If I was going to kill you, I wouldn't have bothered having my legs waxed, would I?" Jim shuddered at this revolting thought.

"No, my dear Jim, this whole outfit was not for you. You are certainly not worth all this effort." Strangely enough, Jim felt a mixture of hurt and relief. Slimey continued, "That fucking bitch reporter however... SHE definitely is worth it!"

He hurriedly checked his pink wristwatch. "Better get a move on. Don't worry Jim, you'll keep your appointment with Mullet."

They turned off the motorway and were soon racing down country lanes... a rabbi... and a tart. Jim felt there was a joke in this somewhere. After another twenty minutes Jim felt compelled to break the silence.

"Look, where are we going?"

Slimey pulled the car over at the brow of a hill. He then silently pointed to a parked-up police patrol car a mile down the road in a lay by.

"We're here to kill him."

Chapter 69

Slimey stared through the windscreen with his mini binoculars at the police car in the distance. If he squinted, Jim could just about make out a figure standing next to the car. Slimey passed the binoculars to Jim.

"That's our boy. The one holding the radar gun." Jim focused on the young traffic cop. What was he? Twenty-three? Twenty-four? His bored colleague in the driver's seat looked slightly older. Jim handed the binoculars back to Slimey.

"So, are you gonna use your wasp gun on him?"

Singen chuckled at his minion's jibe. "It was a bee actually, as you well know. And no... I think we can do a lot better than a bee. Something with a bigger sting." He glanced at his lurid wristwatch. "I don't mind telling you Jim, that I am quite proud of this one…" His voice trailed off tantalisingly and daring his audience of one to beg for details with drooling anticipation.

"Oh." Mumbled Jim, bursting his ego balloon with apathetic glee.

Slimey's nostrils flared at this little bastard who refused to worship at the altar of his greatness.

"For over a month now…" He continued, trying to hide the dent in his ego… and failing miserably. "…we've been phoning in bogus speeding offences to P.C. Davis's station. Dogs nearly killed, paper boys knocked off their bikes by joy riders and two horses narrowly missed being mown down by townies using this country lane as a racetrack. Eventually, they had to send a car to set up a speed trap."

Jim suddenly looked up at the hideous drag queen.

"Er… how could you be sure they'd send him? I mean, I'm sure there are loads of coppers they could've sent. The odds on him being on duty here today at this, the spot of your choosing is astronomical."

Slimey again checked his wristwatch.

"Not if you stack the odds in your favour. You see Jim, at the same time we phoned in all these boy racer reports tearing up this stretch of road; we dealt with his co-workers."

"Dealt?"

He smiled. "Not in that way, Jim." He peered through his binoculars again. "One by one, we either mildly poisoned his colleagues or engineered trivial crises of anyone on his shift pattern. The only ones who never phoned in sick this week were him and his partner. Very easy to introduce a nasty waterborne virus into someone's water supply through the mains… you don't even have to enter the house."

Jim stared down the road, then back at Slimey. "What about his partner in the car? Is he on the list?"

"Alas… no. Casualty of war I'm afraid. What is it our colonial cousins call it when they kill innocent civilians and want to get away with it?"

In the distance, a small dot appeared in the sky preceded by a huge thunderclap.

"Friendly fire." Answered Jim.

"That's it! Friendly fire. "His gaze followed the advancing jet as it roared overhead.

"You have to hand it to the Yanks, Jim. They could slaughter fifty women and babies with the whole world watching, and then they just shrug and use the ultimate get out of jail free card: friendly fire."

Jim glanced upwards as the jet made a second pass.

Looking at his watch Slimey said, "And in five minutes... you are going to get a practical demonstration."

Chapter 70

Slimey's eyes darted from the low flying jet, to the stationary police car as he spoke. "John F Kennedy was killed by a sniper's bullet. George W Bush nearly choked to death on a pretzel. The world and his great aunt Fanny have been hunting for Kennedy's killer none stop for over fifty years. So much so, that a whole industry has grown up around it... nobody is looking for Bush's would be assassin."

Jim stared out the windscreen of the car as the Harrier made another low pass.

"So, we fucked up on that assignment did we?"

A low chuckle, then Singen replied, "No, although it bore all our hallmarks, we weren't asked to assist in that particular euthanasia. The would-be assassin... was the pretzel."

"The brain's dead only the body doesn't know it yet." added Jim.

"Quite. Any way you can rest assured that if we were involved, he wouldn't have been draping his war crimes in the flag... he'd be riding down Capitol Hill on a gun carriage draped in it."

Jim spied the young policeman standing next to his car, only minutes from death and tired of Slimey's eulogising.

"Ah, gallows humour, eh?" Looking mockingly at his hated superior now. "...possibly even lower on the comedy ladder than sarcasm, wouldn't you think?"

Singen held Jim's gaze coldly.

"There is a deluded mis preconception about gallows humour, Jim. The general populace perceives gallows humour to be a coping mechanism to prevent executioners from going insane. In our case, it is the humour itself that masks our executions in the first place!"

Chapter 71

P.C. Neil Davis held the yellow portable radar scanner out in front of him with both hands as the Mini Metro drove past. His seated partner in the squad car's driver's seat chuckled at his friend's gunslinger's stance. Davis dragged his feet as he ambled back to the car. Checking the digital read out.

"31 miles an hour... fucking Sunday drivers!"

"Oh, cheer up Neil! It's a fucking doss, is this. No smack heads trying to carve you up with a sharpened screwdriver. No pissed-up sprogs spewing up all over your back seat and we're out of Braveheart's way for the day. Result in my book, lad." Placing the radar scanner on the car's bonnet, P.C. Davis had to reluctantly agree with his colleague on the last point. Their ferocious Scottish sergeant McCrery was positively puce with rage that for the fourth day in a row, over half his station's day shift had rung in sick with diarrhoea. With another officer taking time off when all the electrics and boiler blew up in his flat. That only left Davis and his partner Billy Duggan to cover for traffic duty on this stretch of road.

Duggan looked up as the jet roared overhead. "I texted Nobby before. Apparently, he's got an arse like a fresh bullet wound."

Davis grinned and leaned into the open car window.

"How many's that, now?"

"Nine. Braveheart's going fucking mental. He's threatening to haul them all back into work and make them wear nappies!"

Neil looked back up at the passing jet.

"Had they all been out for a curry together?"

"Nah, I asked Nobby that very same question. Heh! He swears blind he was all alone when Niagara Falls shot out of his arse."

Davis had to step away from the car to peer up at the low flying Harrier as their car was purposely hidden under a canopy of trees and hedgerow, so no speeding cars could see them until the last moment. The young constable picked up the radar gun and pretended to shoot crows out of the trees with it. Well, the ones that weren't terrified by the bigger faster bird made of metal tearing up the treetops. Duggan couldn't contain himself at his friend's western mime.

"How's your transfer to the armed response unit coming along?"

"Bastards turned me down. Said I didn't score high enough in the exams."

"How many times is that now?"

Davis sighed, "Three."

Duggan jumped as the Harrier's latest low pass took him by surprise as the air was filled with swirling leaves blown from the trees in its wake.

"It's a well sought-after post, mate. They practice most of the time, get called in to do jobs as and when... and as for the dosh! Fucking hell! I'm afraid its dead man's shoes if you want a slice of that glory, mate."

His sullen partner suddenly spied a car in the distance coming towards them. From their training they could tell when a car was speeding, even at this distance. P.C. Davis cleared the digital display and held out the radar gun at the approaching car. Even without his partner's imaginary gun, Duggan could see the car was tearing down the road towards them. "Hey up fella! I think we may have a punter!

Davis didn't seem to be listening as he levelled the radar gun at the speeding car now only 100 yards away. The policeman stepped out of the bushes thinking his very presence would slow down the car... it didn't.

He felt the ground shake as the car roared past him, just as the jet thundered precariously close to the treetops. P.C. Davis noticed the ugly female driver was smiling right at him.

Chapter 72

Singen turned on the engine and pressed his size ten stiletto down until the noise of the accelerator was deafening. Jim said something to Slimey which was lost in the noise. The red stiletto eased up on the pedal so that Jim could reiterate his question.

"I said, are we just going to mow him down in the car?"

The hideous pantomime dame pointed to the swooping jet.

"We're not going to kill him... he is."

Jim stared hard at the war plane, then back at Slimey.

"When I was planning this one, I couldn't believe my luck when I learnt that the R.A.F. uses this area for their aerial manoeuvres."

Jim blurted out. "Th... the pilot! Is he one of us? Is he a Reaper?" Singen glanced at his watch this time, then back at the jet. All the while he constantly revved the engine.

"That's the beauty you see Jim. He's just an innocent pawn in my game. The pilot is only a weapon... we just have to point him in the right direction."

The driver's breathing quickened, his eyes burning into the Harrier. All at once Jim heard the metallic click of the hand break and his head snapped back into the head rest nearly toppling the rabbi's hat from his head. Above the screech of tyres, the gearbox wailed in protest until it was slammed into the next gear. Slimey's blood red painted fingernails were a blur as he ploughed through the gears, propelling the Ford Focus down the road towards the waiting policeman.

Jim's hands shook as he tried for the third time to put on his seatbelt. He let out an exasperated sigh when he eventually heard the click.

The young policeman stood out from his hiding space in the bushes, aiming the yellow radar gun at the speeding car. The digital speedometer read 85mph when they roared past the patrol car. Jim struggled to turn in his seat, squinting trying to view the quickly diminishing P.C. in the swirling leaves and dirt thrown up by the car. His neck jolted again as Slimey slammed on the brakes and sent the car skidding across a T junction. The drystone wall loomed into view and Jim held his hands up to shield himself from the imminent impact.

No sooner had the nightmare car journey started, and then it ended. The car shuddered to a halt with the driver's wing mirror inches from the drystone wall.

Singen, totally unfazed by the near-death car crash, quickly unbuckled his seat belt and leaned across Jim's seat, frantically winding the window down. His normal aloof demeanour deserted him as he drooled like a dog at the unfolding carnage that was about to happen.

"Look! Isn't it fucking beautiful?!"

Chapter 73

Lieutenant Alan Sichetti banked sharply in his Harrier jump jet as he eyed the wildly spinning compass on the jet's dashboard. The lush green hills and woods below meant nothing to him. He hated Britain and its shitty romanticised landscapes. Give him the Grand Canyon to fly down any day. Every time he came to this fucking lousy barren backwater was like the worst school reunion in history. All through school, being systematically brainwashed about the very cradle of civilization not being Mesopotamia... but Great Britain.

How much of a kick in the teeth was that? Five years old, no hairs on your balls, trying to find a sense of identity, a sense of belonging as you stand in front of and pledge allegiance to... the flag. Home of the brave, land of the free.

Doesn't have the word "Great" in the title though, does it?

What the fuck were our forefathers thinking of? Mused the pilot, his helmet pinned to the back of his seat as the jet hit Mach 1. *"Awesome America" yeah, that's it. Who needs to be United when you can be Awesome?* As this thought germinated in his skull, he felt elated and pushed the throttle further until his stomach danced like a stranger at the end of a hillbilly's rope.

Not much of interest on this training exercise, apart from a tiny blue car racing down these pathetic excuses for roads. So, this was the land of Shakespeare, huh? Sichetti smiled at the thought of his huge 4x4 Humvie back in Alabama getting stuck in these limp Limey lanes.

The missile lock warning light and buzzer on his cock pit's dashboard soon wiped the smile from his face. His head snapped back and forth... no jet. Sky clear across the horizon. Threat must be from below. Nothing in sight... hidden.

Think, Alan! Think! He roared inwardly, trying to control his emotions.

He felt the unmistakeable mechanical clunk as his onboard computer automatically uncoupled the safety brackets that were in place to stop the misfiring of ordinance.

The safety catches were off.

Another light and buzzer told the Lieutenant that the onboard weapons guidance system had locked on to the original radar signal that had a missile lock on him and was awaiting his orders. The FIRE button glowed blood red. Pulsating... almost keeping time with his heart. Alan didn't need to think. The automatic weapons system had done all the thinking for him.

All he had to do was act.

His training had taught him that the moment an air to air, or in this case, a handheld surface to air missile had locked onto your aircraft... you have less than 30 seconds to eliminate the threat, or, be eliminated.

Through gritted teeth he hissed,

"I didn't survive Iraq so a Limey terrorist could fucking kill me!"

He jabbed at the fire button... and down below him two unsuspecting policemen were about to have their pensions cancelled.

Chapter 74

"Cheeky fucker! He's not going to stop!"

Even after all the years on the force P.C. Neil Davis wore his naivety around his neck like a yolk. Even though countless mangy rat boys have tried to run him over after fleeing ram raids on off-licences, he still clung onto the child like notion that the mere sight of his uniform could stop a rampaging joy rider. He squinted as the Ford Focus shot past him, throwing up a mini whirlwind of leaves and dirt.

The noise from the jet above was deafening.

Wiping the grime from his face, the policeman stormed back to the car.

"Come on Billy, I'm having that cunt!" Billy Duggan held up a calming hand to his gung-ho colleague.

"We've got his registration number, relax. He'll get points on his licence and a nice little fine in the post. Now leave it... you'll give yourself an ulcer the way you're carrying on." P.C. Davis's nostrils were flaring with rage as he looked on at the fleeing car.

"What speed was he doing anyway?" Asked Duggan in a bid to defuse his irate friend. Davis took his eyes off the car and then read the digital radar scanner. His brow furrowed as something seemed to trouble him. He jabbed at the buttons and then smacked it with the heel of his hand.

"What's up lad?"

"Th… that can't be right…" Said Neil, again, jabbing wildly at the radar gun again.

P.C. Duggan was beginning to get irritated at his colleague's obtuseness.

"What the fuck's wrong Neil?"

P.C. Davis stared open mouthed at the scanner's screen.

"I… it says 730 miles per hour!"

Billy looked at Neil… then skywards at the Harrier that was banking sharply to make a return pass. He then broke into uncontrollable laughter and covered his eyes.

"What?!" Neil was already pissed off at Freddy Kruger's twin sister nearly wheel spinning on his face without his drinking buddy rubbing his nose in it.

"Th… the jet!" Said Billy in between laughing.

Neil looked sharply at Billy, then up at the spiralling fighter plane. The dawning realisation brought a slow smile to Neil's face.

"Heh! Yeah, right! Like a poxy Ford Focus could do 730 miles an hour!" Neil gave a silent salute to the oncoming jet.

Wiping his eyes Billy quipped, "Do you want to pull him over lad?"

Neil cleared the read out. "Why not, I'll get a tow truck down here and we'll have it crushed." Both policemen smiled and looked up at the vehicle that broke all Metropolitan police speed ticket records.

Their smiles turned to jaw dropping horror as two plumes of smoke streaked out from beneath the jet's wings, only to cross each other mid-air… and plummet towards their patrol car.

Chapter 75

"Look! Isn't it fucking beautiful?!" Both Reapers eyes were fixated on the Harrier in the sky. More importantly, the two Sidewinder missiles fired from the jet. Both of them crossed each other in the sky and then gathered speed as they rocketed down... and blew the police car to kingdom come.

Jim watched impotent in a state of shock as out of the huge fire ball he saw the squad car torn in half and then land in different fields. The glowing Singen calmly put the car in gear and drove them back towards the motorway.

Jim tried to control his shaking. Partly because he didn't want Slimey to have even more ammunition against him. Singen was positively elated at his latest kills and was brimming with smugness. Jim didn't have to wait long for that creaking dam of smugness to burst.

"Admit it, Jim... was that not the most exhilarating thing you have ever experienced?"

Jim reached for the dials of the car's stereo. Slimey, without taking his eyes off the road was way ahead of his jittery junior.

"No need Jim. It's only been twenty minutes. We won't get a decent news report for another couple of hours yet." Adjusting his false breast under his silk blouse he continued, "I usually wait until I catch the ten o'clock news with a single malt to congratulate myself on a job well done."

Jim could just picture him at home in a silk dressing gown, whooping and a hollering in true Ku Klux Klan style watching a victim's eyes bulge as the noose tightened.

"Tape them, do you?" Jim was aware there was a sneer in his voice and instantly knew he would be made to pay for it.

"Of course, I don't!" The false eyelashes did little to mask the fury in his eyes.

"You know the rules as well as I do, Jim. Our apartments can be searched day or night without warning. Any evidence whatsoever of our employment that could incriminate us, or the bunker will be seen as a threat." Staring blankly out of the windscreen, Jim replied emotionlessly,

"And we all know what happens to threats."

Slimey smiled. Seeing this upstart momentarily crushed improved his day even further. "I'm glad you understand the delicate balance of things and the precarious tightrope we walk daily." Jim knew he had struck a nerve. Of course, Slimey taped these news reports of his kills. His ego wouldn't allow him not to. Only he was too cunning to keep this damming batch of evidence against him in his flat. Jim mused that if he could find his secret stash... then he would own Slimey and aid his own escape from this nefarious netherworld he was trapped in. This thought lifted his spirit. The light at the end of the tunnel was becoming brighter day by day. The car lurched to a halt and Jim's light was snuffed out.

"End of the road for you I'm afraid." Jim looked up at Slimey's painted fingernails, which were reassuringly curled around the steering wheel... and not a silenced pistol. Slimey nodded with an unnerving lipstick grin towards Jim's passenger side window. There it stood, in its entire grotesque monstrosity... Mickey Mullet's mansion.

Stepping from the car, Jim couldn't help feeling that he had jumped out of the frying pan and into the fire.

"Remember Jim, he's only the most prolific drug lord this country has ever produced. Who uses sulphuric acid and meat cleavers on anyone who crosses him. But if you really piss him off, there are rumours of him feeding his enemies to his packs of rottweilers... some of them take hours to die."

With that, he drove off laughing.

Chapter 76

Even though he lived in a squalid tramp camp Bobby Mcvie kept himself and his makeshift dwelling scrupulously clean. His army training had taught him to ignore bacteria and infection at your peril. He hadn't survived countless fire fights to be slain by botulism or food poisoning. A ridiculous way for a warrior or ex-warrior to die. Oh, he did smear ash from wood fires on his skin and clothes for appearance sake. After all, he had to fit in. Call it camouflage if you will. For this homeless community had taken him in, quietly accepted him, but most importantly given him the one thing he needed most... anonymity.

Like Alice stepping through the looking glass, he had stepped outside of normal organised society to go live amongst the mad hatters. That didn't stop the ex-Special Forces soldier keeping an eye on the other side of the mirror. The one perk of being homeless was the abundance of used newspapers that came your way. Okay, so by the time you got to read them they were two days old, creased and stained with bin juice... but they were competitively priced.

Bobby read everything.

The stock market reports in the financial times he cross referenced with war reports and coups in the Guardian. With his trained eye, he could easily join the dots between global financiers and third world dictator. And yes, he did read the tabloids as well. Well, it got lonely at nights and they were the nearest he'd got to seeing a woman in years. It was while he was perusing one of these intelligentsia manuals of onanism that a story made him sit bolt upright in his sleeping bag. The publication was The Daily Throbber and the headline read:

STRAWBERRY FRUITCAKE TRIFELLED WITH MY AFFECTIONS.

It wasn't so much the story that gripped his attention... but the photo.

Apparently, a man had drowned in a bathtub full of strawberry jelly in a love gesture gone tragically wrong. The deceased photo showed him as a curly haired 30-year-old with thick black framed spectacles... and Union Jack printed jeans with smiley badges all over his baseball boots. What were the odds on two men dressed like that? Although he was hooded, the man being bundled out of the black transit van where Declan was mauled was wearing the exact same clothes. Then there was the smartly dressed man who got out of the van and picked up a similar pair of black rimmed spectacles that had fallen out of the captor's hood. Bobby clenched the article tightly in both fists as he read on. The dead man's demise was a romantic act to impress the newspaper's only female lady reporter. Bobby carefully tore out her photo and studied it. She was in her mid-forties and looked more like a copper than a journalist. Well, if you could call the shit throwing chimps who work for this soft porn rag journalists.

She certainly stood out from the rest of the women in this publication. For one thing, she was fully clothed. He flicked back to page 2 were he found the address of the newspaper and again, gingerly tore it from the page. Within minutes he had found the address in his London A to Z and was frantically lacing up his boots. This woman's lover was dragged down the same alley way that Declan was savaged in. According to the date of the article he was found dead the day after Bobby last saw him. Despite the jokey overtones of the piece, the lovelorn lothario didn't look in the mood for love as he was dragged away. Hooded and cuffed.

Classic execution style.

Declan had stumbled into somewhere that was being observed by a heavily armed observation point with a mounted military sniper's rifle. But the woman's lover? The paper had said he was a computer expert. Then again, she was a journalist. Was he slain for what he knew, or as a warning to her? Either way, it was she who could shed some light on why his old friend had been torn to pieces by a military attack dog. Bobby checked the entrance to his decrepit domain was clear of people before he slid swiftly and silently out onto the streets of London.

Chapter 77

Bobby strode into the reception of Mervin Foster's newspaper and slapped a padded brown A4 envelope on the receptionist's desk. It bore the lady reporter's name and the newspapers. Also, for authenticity in big letters:

URGENT. DELIVER BY HAND

The security guard looked Bobby up and down with all the disdain a man on £2.50p an hour and a crimplene jumper could muster.

"It's urgent she gets this delivered to her home address as she requested. We've arranged for a cab to courier it to her if you could give the cabby the address when he arrives." Before the kebab addict could question Bobby, the soldier handed the guard a ten-pound note.

"That's for your trouble." He also handed him a smaller envelope with £30 TAXI FARE written on it.

"That's for the cab." All disdain was banished by a crooked smile as the guard pocketed his tenner and politely bid the stranger farewell as he walked through the automatic doors.

Mcvie crossed the road to a public phone and dialled a local taxi firm whose cards nestled amongst the prostitutes advertised rates. He ordered a cab to courier a package to an address that the guard on reception will give them. He then crossed the road again to sit in the back of a rival cab company's car he had waiting for over ten minutes. The Latvian driver was given £20 up front to wait and not ask questions. His illegal status guaranteed his pledge.

After fifteen minutes, the second taxi arrived, the driver emerged from the newspaper's reception shortly after with package and his fee in his hands.

"Just like the movies mate... follow that cab."

Twenty minutes of snail like London traffic and his courier cab pulled up outside a Georgian terrace. Like a good boy, Bobby's Latvian cabby stopped 50 yards behind the first cab and parked behind a van. With such well-versed anti-surveillance driving skills, Bobby wondered was his driver ex-military or ex criminal. Nah, he reeked... he was ex criminal. The courier cabby got no answer at the door... he looked shiftily left and right then pushed the parcel through the letter box. Once he had driven off Bobby tipped his driver and watched him drive off. He waited 5 minutes before crossing the road to the lady journalist's address.

He scanned the glowing entry buttons for any names... none. Fuck! fourteen flats, which one was hers? So near yet...

Wasting no time, he brought out the fat office worker's credit card and swiftly bypassed the doors electric strike the exact same way. Bobby smiled, the fat office worker's wallet helped to pay for cab fares and bribes too. Once in, he picked up the package addressed to the lady journalist lying on the mat. He scanned the address, but there was no flat number written on it. Even so, the packet had cost him £80.

The packet that contained only ripped up newspaper. But a valuable package no less.

The vigilant security guard who had earned £10 from this package and never gave away the lady hack's address. The courier cabby who delivered it and inadvertently given Bobby her location earned £30 from it. And the dodgy Latvian, whose no questions asked tail of the courier, netted him £20 plus a £20 tip.

For the price of £80 this worthless package had given him the reporter's address without any suspicion whatsoever.

Chapter 78

There is no way Mcvie could take the chance of hiding behind overgrown bushes in the garden outside or opposite the reporter's flat. One nosy neighbour and he would be arrested. So, he would have to hide within her building's lobby instead. The communal bin store was also too risky, used too often. So that only left one option, the electricity cupboard at the foot of the stairs. He easily slipped the night latch and slipped into the cupboard which was waist high and three feet deep. Bobby sat cross legged and made himself comfortable, careful not to knock any of the flats electric circuit breakers. The last thing he needed was a tenant opening the small cupboard to see why their shitty lava lamp had been deprived of power. He held onto the back of the lock case to keep the door closed, with only a tiny crack for him to view the bottom of the staircase. Apart from the luminous dial on his army wristwatch and the thin shaft of light from the door's jamb, he was enveloped in total darkness.

For the next five hours Bobby had only the gentle whirr of the electricity meter and the numerous spiders crawling all over him for company. He didn't mind spiders, mainly because he fucking hated flies. Dirty bastards who started their life as a maggot then evolved into a shit eating monster who river danced their crap coated feet all over your pie and mash. Repeatedly! So, any insect that could hunt, torture and bite the head off these vile little fuckers is a good friend of Bobby Mcvie.

Unless you were a black widow or funnel web of course, then they would be unfriended on Facebook. During this time in the electric cupboard many people came and went. The cramped cupboard was musty smelling, but at least he was dry. Several years before, Sergeant Mcvie had been buried inside a stinking compost heap in the pissing down rain in South Armagh waiting for a provisional I.R.A. active service unit to retrieve three Armalite rifles from an arms dump on a remote farm. So, the little hiding place he now found himself in was heaven by comparison. His thoughts snapped suddenly away from that particular ambush when the sharp sounds of stilettos filled the lobby.

Chapter 79

The sound of high heels echoed up the stairwell towards the journalist's flat. The constant rhythmic clicking relentlessly gaining momentum like an eerie metronome. The clicking grew louder now as the stilettos climbed the last set of stairs leading to the top flat. Singen stopped on the landing; he could see the bitch's front door. Only ten steps separated him from his prey. He waited, listening for any sounds on the stairwell. Slowly and deliberately, he climbed the last set of stairs his high heels barely making a sound. A skill he had practiced in these heels over and over in his flat alone. He justified it to himself that one day he would have to silently creep up on someone whilst sporting stilettos. The fact he had a pair in his wardrobe his exact size just showed he was a conscientious employee that took pride in his work... nothing more. Scanning the other flats on her floor for any open doors or signs of life, he approached her door which lay directly opposite the stairs. Perfect for a quick getaway. The senior Reaper took out the lipstick from his handbag and smeared it on the door's tiny glass door viewer. If she was in, there was no way she was going to see him coming. He'd use wet wipes to remove this later as he prided himself that no jumped-up forensic scientist had ever detected his prescience... and never fucking will. The bulky handbag held many items: the thick veiny rubber dildo that he was going to insert in her corpse. The cocaine and lesbian porn he was going to scatter all around her bedroom... and the syringe filled with a special cocktail that he was going to kill her with.

He loved the ritual. Pulling on his surgical gloves, only he wasn't here to save a life… just end one. Checking the landing was clear once more, he got to work on the lock with his picks. The first three pins in the cylinder clicked up into place beautifully, but the last two were trying his patience. He tried again for another couple of minutes, the tiny tension bar in the cylinder's keyway bending with frustration. The last two pins refusing to line up and stay in place. Anti-pick pins? Some higher-grade security cylinders had them to thwart lock picks. It wasn't impossible... it just took more time. Singen didn't have time and was never known for his patience. Sighing and trying to control his urge to break the world record for the loudest roared profanity, he took a couple of deep breaths and checked no neighbours had entered the landing. Singen abandoned the picks to his handbag and brought out five ultra-thin strips of mica.

They are made of the exact same material that is used in the manufacture of kitchen work tops, Formica. These flexible thin strips of plastic type material were used to bypass the latch. The first piece was slid between the door and the frame at the same height of the cylinder, in line with the latch on the other side of the door. Singen stated to relax when he felt the door was quite loose in the frame and this would allow more strips of mica and greater chance of success at popping the latch. As he pressed the door gently with his knee, he wiggled the mica strips up and down, always maintaining forward pressure on the latch. Then he inhaled deeply as that sweet music filled his ears... the gentle click as the mica was forcing movement of the latch back into the lock case. The door moved inwards slightly. Foreplay over, Singen slid another strip in under the first two and with one more wiggle and gentle rattle of the door... the latch clicked completely out of its keep... and the door swung wide open. Almost as wide as Slimey's own smile.

He didn't see the claw hammer.

But he vaguely heard it cut the air... a second before it smashed into his nose. If anything, the sheer excruciating pain in his nose took his mind off the pain in his head, back and legs as he was catapulted backwards down the staircase.

He lay there for what seemed like an eternity, but in reality, was only 30 seconds. Blood gushed out of his nose and soaked his white silk blouse. He was concussed, not sure what had happened. Had he been attacked? he glanced up at the opened doorway, no assailant was waiting with a baseball bat to finish him. But there was a claw hammer gently floating to and fro. No, not floating, he squinted and saw it was held by a twine of sorts. Whether there was anyone up there, an angry boyfriend they didn't know about, Singen knew no good would come of going back up there now. His flight reflex was screaming at him and he listened. Limping up the stairs with ripped tights and his wig almost hanging off, he hurriedly collected his belongings and staggered out of the building as fast as he could.

In all the excitement of having his face rearranged, he failed to notice... he'd left something behind.

Chapter 80

A noise suddenly made Bobby switch on in the tight confines of the cramped electricity cupboard. The sound of stilettos. He edged closer to the narrow opening of the barely closed door and got his eye as close as he'd dare.

Somehow, she looked different from her photo.

Bobby watched the blonde tartly dressed woman walk to the stairs. Walk? or amble? There was something about the gait, the jaw line... the hands. Bobby smiled in the darkness as the transvestite climbed the stairs. You're fooling no one, mate, mused Bobby. Still, some drunk is going to be in for a nasty shock when he slides his hand up that skirt after the last slow dance.

Talking of drunks, it had been two days since he last visited Declan in hospital. He must go tonight and try to cheer up the poor old bastard. He really wasn't looking forward to that. Then again, wasn't that why he was here, cross-legged in an electric cupboard, for Declan? Or was it the buzz he missed of being on active duty? Having a mission, a goal, a purpose? Or just to relieve the crippling boredom he felt from his life on the run? Hiding amongst the homeless from the teams of hired killers sent by a vengeful billionaire with a long memory and very deep pockets.

His train of thought was broken when he heard a thudding sound followed by the clatter of high heels on the stairs. It came from above and got louder as the transvestite from minutes earlier came staggering down the last six stairs and collapsing onto his knees with a loud thud.

His appearance was even more noticeable than before. His nose was pouring with blood which had turned his white silk blouse into a visceral splattered Paisley design. The blonde curly wig hung halfway off the back of the of his head revealing his own brown hair beneath. It was as he looked up from the crumpled position at the foot of the stairs that Bobby recognised the face.

It was covered in blood, badly smeared makeup, the long angular nose... but Bobby had seen this man before. He was the one who was immaculately dressed getting out of the same van as the journalist's dead lover was hauled out of, hooded and cuffed. Bobby's heart was banging now. This man was now disguised as a woman in the lady journalist's building, covered in blood. The transvestite staggered to his feet like a new-born deer and all but fell through the front door and out into the street.

Bobby was about to dart out after him when an old lady came out from the ground floor flat to see what all the commotion was about. The situation would not have been made better by a tramp leaping out of the electric cupboard. The old lady had missed the transvestite. But she would certainly have a description of Bobby to give to the police. So, he stayed put and gnashed his teeth, willing the nosy old busy body to get back to her knitting. By the time the pensioner eventually returned to her flat and Bobby emerged... the killer was long gone.

Chapter 81

She gave as sincere a smile as she could walking through the newsroom amongst the cheering and the clapping. All hail the conquering hero.

Conquering what exactly? Her only friend and ally was drowned in a bath of strawberry jelly and she was now on the receiving end of Fleet Street's dogs of phwoar. There on her desk were two cream and jelly puddings in glass dishes.

Don't bite girl! They're watching you. Don't bite. If you take the bait and explode, you'll be their whipping boy for months. Her fat sweaty colleague, Norman could barely contain himself. Cassandra could see he was virtually chewing lumps out of his tongue in a bid to stop himself from laughing. Out of her peripheral vision she could see the Cro-Magnon clique all straining their necks her way like a sea of monobrowed meerkats. She slowly swivelled her chair to face her bland inquisitor.

"Something on your mind, Norman?"

Quick as a flash he whipped out a printed front page of the Daily Throbber that bore his puny paw prints all over it.

STRAWBERRY FRUITCAKE TRIFLED WITH MY AFFECTIONS!

She dutifully smiled and gave a few gentle claps. The newsroom erupted in cheers. Several well-wishers slapped Norman's back and shook his hand. A couple even pointed to the trifles on her desk and then at the headline to hopefully hammer home the finer rudimentary points of investigative journalism. Again, she smiled at the two-day-old headline that she was seeing for the first time. Her besieged flat from the rampaging media after Marty's death was devoid of newspapers, even the shit excuse for one she worked for. The cheering was dying down now and amongst the carnival of cretins she failed to notice the flickering envelope icon on her computer screen that announced:

You've got mail!

She turned to face her console but was distracted by the phone ringing on her desk. It was an internal call. She picked it up and noticed her inbox had a new message. She reached out to open her mail when a voice from the phone stopped her in her tracks.

"Get your arse in here now!"

Cassandra sensed the tension in the air as Mervin Foster paced the length of the huge office with a printout of her latest copy. The heart-warming piece about two Chelsea footballers spit roasting a girl who worked at the bacon counter at Tesco's. No doubt Norman's expertise will be called upon to draw a link somehow between spit roast and bacon. By now she was a past master at appeasing vacuous puppet editors with whatever third rate, ill-informed bigotry their readership were hopelessly addicted to. They were worse than drug dealers. At least with crack cocaine you could get help to kick your habit. Alas, there is no Betty Ford clinic equivalent to wean you off being fucking proud to be stupid. It served a purpose. She supplied the drivel, the editor's peddled it to the readers and she could hunt for her serial killer in peace. The hunt was tinged with sadness. Her mind drifted towards Marty. Poor lonely Marty. And to think, she actually thought he was the killer. The wave of guilt made her feel nauseous. The guilt opened a gate deep within her and something icy and searing bubbled to the surface to erupt in a cascade of self-loathing.

You used him.

I...I didn't! We were working together... she pleaded in her mind.

Used him as bait. Staked him out, a lamb to the slaughter. While you waited for the killer to show himself. Gamble didn't pay off though, did it? Marty got butchered and the killer got away... and so did your illustrious career. So... who's next to be sacrificed at the altar of your ambition?

At this moment in time Cassandra needed this self-righteous internal sermon to stop resonating in her skull. She needed to think straight and have her wits about her. She was acutely aware in a bid to block out the internal taunting's of her subconscious that was rampaging forth into her conscious mind; she had screwed her eyes tightly shut.

When she opened them, a stern-faced editor was glaring back at her.

"How do you feel about working from home?"

It took her a few seconds to take this in. "Am I being fired Mr Foster?"

"No, you're being promoted."

He had to make this convincing. After all, this was no page three bimbo who was squatting in his newsroom. This was an intelligent independent woman. She was Kryptonite to his Superman. The very thing he hated more than the unions. The women he was used to working with were gorgeous, voluptuous and had about as much need for a brain as the rest of us had for an appendix. Bitter experience had taught him not to ever turn his back on a Sheila with a brain. A cornered rabid dingo would show you more mercy. He had to speak her lingo.

Appeal to her ego.

"I want to take this paper upmarket."

Cassandra's eyebrows made an escape bid through the top of her skull.

He continued, "I want to offer my readers a bit more than just something to squirt their dirty man fat at." Her jaw dropped. Not a road to Damascus conversion, surely? Pornography was in this man's blood. Kiss and tell tabloid tarts had made this Aussie parasite a millionaire many times over. Yet here he was, proposing that they drag this wank rag out of the quagmire and elevate it to Olympian heights.

She didn't buy this bullshit for one minute.

But… he did mention working from home. Every day she passed through the doors of this mausoleum of masturbators chiselled away at any credibility she had left. She had seen her ex colleagues at the national newspapers trying to stifle sneering grins as she passed them in the street. They were off to change the world. As far as they were concerned, her duties were on par with changing the loo roll in the bogs. She was worth twenty of them, yet it was her that was left the leper of Fleet Street.

And here was her editor, offering her a way out.

A drowning man will grasp at a shit smeared stick if offered.

"I want you to use your expertise to produce hard hitting stories that will give us a serious political clout" He lit up a cigar. "

These farrrkin politicians are shit scared of real journalists." Watching her reactions all the time, Mervin could see that this ruse was starting to work. He pointed the cigar at her. "You are my secret weapon." He waved his arm around the room as if pointing out culprits.

"Them barrrrstards in Whitehall will sit up and take notice when you squeeze their balls!"

Her eyes opened wide. "Metaphorically, of course?"

He blew smoke in her direction. "Yeah, of course."

She nodded to herself... a way out, at last.

Mervin smiled. Oh, the hook was right through her lip... time to reel this bass in.

"So... if you could just clear your desk and I'll have the boys drop all your files and computer round your gaff." He walked over to the door and opened it for her.

When she was gone, Mervin drew the blind and picked up his children's smiling photo. He was aware his hands were shaking.

She felt like she has just been dismissed. Only she hadn't. Foster had assured her that she would retain full pay plus expenses. On top of that, she would never have to mix with the disciples of the dense ever again. Technically, she would be freelance for Mervin's paper. Close enough to collect a wage, but with enough distance to try and claw back a shred of dignity that she could at least look a sewer worker in the eye. It didn't take her long to empty the drawers to her desk of anything sensitive or important from prying eyes. She always travelled light. Her note pad and I pad were both encrypted with a personal shorthand that both Egyptian hieroglyphic translators and enigma code deciphers would dislocate their frontal lobes trying to crack. The rest of her files were all connected with Mervin's wank rag and caused her little concern should Foster's lackeys go rummaging through them. Cassandra quickly picked up the photo of her serial killer and buried it at the bottom of her bag. Her colleague Norman was too engrossed in trying to eat a kebab and talk to a D list celebrity on the phone at the same time to notice.

She was about to stand up and float out of this intellectual desert for the last time when she saw an email blinking away in a desperate bid to gain her attention.

She clicked the mouse, unaware that her world was going to collapse all around her.

The e-mail's heading set the tone.

MARTY'S LAST WILL AND TESTAMENT

There was a PDF file attached. With some trepidation, she opened it.

Well hi there! I'll be brief. If you are looking at this file, then I am dead. Contained within these files are incriminating evidence on every low life government agency, secret society and corporate conspirator that I have been hunting for over the last 10 years. One of them has, as you are aware, had me assassinated. I entrust all these files to you as you are the only one on this lonely planet who I trust.

Also, if these enemies of truth and freedom come to my flat, then they will have been filmed on high resolution hidden cameras that will automatically send the footage onto a ghost website, and then, to you.

You have within these files the means to avenge my death. Blast them all over the internet, it is the only way you'll be safe. These jackals hunt in darkness. It is time for you to shine some light on them.

I know it's too late now, but ultimately; I have nothing left to lose. Where I am, rejection cannot torture me. I just wanted to say that I have always loved you with my heart and my soul and, in death, I have finally found the courage to say what I was too cowardly to utter in life.

Marty xxx

Chapter 82

Jim entered the kingdom of tat. A cross between a rag and bone man's workplace and a colour-blind pimp's bedroom. Indeed, if gypsies ever lived in Buckingham Palace, this is what it would look like. Instantly, Jim recognised Mullet's vomit inducing face on an immense garish oil painting on the wall. But before he could truly appreciate the finer nuances of the composition, a poster boy for homemade steroids ambled towards him with hands so big that they could spank God's arse with.

"Arms up father."

Jim pondered as to correcting the chemically enhanced brain donor as to his outfit's non-Catholic denomination... then he saw the snub nosed 38 Smith & Wesson poking out the waist band of his trousers. Jim used all his imaginary telekinetic powers to move the trigger and blow this shaven headed steroid abuser's shrivelled cock off. But, yet again his mental superpowers had failed him. If the thug proceeded to search him, he'd find the syringe. Explain that one away my quick-witted friend. Which would move faster in this gunslinger's duel? Jim's silver tongue and sparkling wit running intellectual rings around the missing link's retarded sibling? Or... the clubbing fists and speeding bullets?

Jim tensed and waited to be turned into pate.

"Oiy! Get your fucking manky hands off him you stupid tit! 'He's a holy man, ain't he?!'"

He'd seen photos of her in newspapers. well, quite hard not to really as every tabloid and even most of the snooty broadsheets had succumbed to her circulation enhancing assets and printed at least two images of her every day. Jim tensed his jaw and nearly grinded his teeth in an overcompensating measure to stop his chin dropping and cracking the tiled floor. Mavis Davis, AKA Mave the Rave stood before him, in 6-inch-high, blood red patent leather stilettos, a skimpy black satin French maid's outfit and shimmering fully fashioned seamed nylon stockings. Her heels clacked loudly on the black onyx marble tiled floor as she stomped over towards Jim. The huge thug looked genuinely worried as the porn star admonished him further. "You can't fucking touch him! He's a man of God! Do yer want his guvner to ram a thunderbolt right up yer jacksie?!"

The man mountain imitated his own dick and visibly shrivelled under this tirade and almost whispered. "N... no, Mave."

"Then go do something bleeding useful! Go get the bag!"

The scolded pup dutifully lumbered off as Mave linked Jim's arm and led him towards a seven-seater red leather sofa in the vast living room.

Then a moment he will relive many times in his dreams as this infamous porn star pouted through crimson wet glossed lips,

"Now... what have I got to do to persuade you to marry me?"

Despite his employers being despicable cold-hearted killers, they nevertheless begrudgingly impressed the hell out of Jim with their research into their prospective victims. This coupled with excruciating meticulous planning, resulted in all the odds being stacked in the Reaper's favour. Whereas Mullet's criminal army planned crimes, the Reapers zealously planned to get away with the crime first to such a precise art, that the actual act of committing the murder was a mere trivial formality. Their research had told them that celebrity junkies Mave the porn star and drug dealing "author" Mullet planned to marry. Both had a burning hunger to be famous and within their own careers, they were. Yet, a big lavish showbiz wedding would nudge them one rung up the ladder of fame shame from D list to at least a C.

Every year, these pitiful wannabes would gurn out the pages of paparazzi pamphlets and tie the knot in ever more extreme publicity grasping ways.

"I wannabe a Jewish princess!"

Gushed Mave as her massive mammaries tried to make a jail break from her low-cut French maids' outfit.

Mave had fallen in love with the ostentatious weddings she had seen on lifestyle programs of young Jewish New Yorkers, all living the fairy-tale dream. Alas, Catholics cannot be Jewish princesses. For the past week Jim's employers have been monitoring every synagogue across London, they all politely declined Mave's pleas to convert to Judaism. After all, no self-respecting religion would risk admitting a one-woman porn empire and her rabid boyfriend who broke every commandment on a daily basis...

and then went and had his breakfast. Surely two people could not possibly bring down a whole religion that has outlasted wars and thousands of years of persecution? No… but they weren't stupid enough to take that chance.

Mave was despondent. Her dream was floating away, and Mullet's mutant rat boy army were totally powerless to do anything about it. After all, how could he threaten his way into Heaven? Threats of, and the use of violence were the tools of his trade. Take them away and Mickey was nothing. An embarrassing sub literate prison rapist with all the social skills of a shit throwing masturbating chimp. Realistically, this was possibly the only time in their entire lives when either of them had not got their own way. Mave always used her body. Mickey always used his fists… or Stanley knives and claw hammers. Faced with the prospect of a brand-new emotional experience… disappointment, the pair of them were as helpless as little children. The Reapers knew a wounded gazelle when they saw one.

They contacted Mave and informed her that they were an Orthodox synagogue on the outskirts of London who were very sympathetic to the couple's plight. In fact, they would send a rabbi round to discuss the finer nuances of religious conversion the very next day. So there Jim sat, dressed as a holy man listening to Mave bang on about him making her a Jewish bride, while he was planning on making her a widow.

Jim realised that although Mave was no nuclear physicist, she had enough street smarts to sniff out a bullshitter. This wouldn't have bothered Jim so much if the three-armed gangsters weren't standing less than 15 feet away. So, he had to make it look convincing. After all, every respectable synagogue in the capital had shown her the door. So, to just hand her the fantasy dream wedding on a plate would definitely set alarm bells ringing in that empty husk of a skull of hers.

"Mavis" Said Jim in a soothing tone he envisaged a man of god would talk in.

"Call me Mave, all the boys do."

"Okay, Mave. How do you feel that the colourful alternative lifestyle that you and your boyfriend lead would conflict with the peaceful teachings and path of righteousness that our faith abides by?"

He had come on too strong. Used too many syllables. Mave's head looked like a toaster that someone had poured water into. He swore he could see sparks pissing out of her ears as both her frontal lobes of her brain did back flips in an attempt to understand one-word Jim said. He had to dumb it down to a level lower than a snake's armpit. He smiled benevolently. Well, as benevolently as he could under a 5lb hairy false beard.

"Do you feel your lifestyle would cause our faith any bad publicity?"

Her face lit up and she beamed a smile that was responsible for half of Britain's adolescents having a five o'clock shadow on the palms of their hands.

"Publicity! Now yer talking! When something bad happens and it gets on the news, they always say you can't buy that type of publicity."

It was Jim's turn to be totally lost now. Then, without warning, Mave's shrill voice echoed off the walls of the mansion.

"RICKY!"

The Reaper swore that one screeched name would give him tinnitus for hours to come. A familiar shape of Jim's would be frisker loomed into view carrying a sports bag which he plonked down on the expensive glass coffee table in front of Jim, much to the disgust of the evidently house proud Mave. She smiled and pouted at him as she seductively crossed her stocking clad legs. The nylon making a slight scratching sound as both thighs rubbed together. She stretched one leg out and smoothed out the slight wrinkles in the nylon, holding his gaze all the time. He felt totally entranced.

"Open it." She nodded towards the bulky sports bag. Jim tried twice to prise himself out of the huge deep sofa and on the third attempt rocked foreword and unzipped the bulging bag. His eyes went wide as every fifty-pound note on the face of the planet seemed to be staring right back at him. Mave smiled again and rubbed her hand slowly up and down her thigh. The scratching sound of the nylon distracting Jim as his eyes darted back and forth from the cash to her legs like windscreen wipers. What a combination: a flirting porn star and god's wage packet in a sports bag.

"Call it a donation, shall we?"

Oh fuck! He was getting a hard on! Jim was going to kill her future husband in cold blood dressed as a religious leader and he was getting a full-on erection at the thought of fucking his widow. How would he be able to sleep at night? As he eyed the cash, he reconciled he would sleep a lot better once he'd stuffed his mattress with that little lot. Despite this over endowered gangster's dick ornament sending Jim's gonads into an epileptic fit, it was all that money that held his attention. He could walk out of here with that bag and be well on his way to a new life. Freedom.

Before that could happen, there was still the small matter of filling Mickey Mullet's coffin first.

Jim beamed a smile and announced,

"Welcome to the Jewish faith, my child!"

Mave exploded with excitement and jumped on Jim's lap, kissing him repeatedly. His wiry beard was now matted with red lip gloss. In her dizzy hysteria she bounced up and down on his lap... and his now painfully throbbing erection.

"Oh, thank you! Thank you! Thank..."

Any other time and Jim would have been delighted at a stocking clad porn star in a French maid's outfit using his gland as a trampoline; only he was here on business. He was saved by the bell... or in this case the pounding of fists on the front door.

"Open up! It's the police!"

They both jumped up. Jim reached to cover his erection which stuck out prominently from his rabbis' robes, Mave reached for her mobile phone and hit speed dial.

Trapped.

This day was always going to come. A lifetime behind bars. He was torn in two between sheer horror... and rapturous relief. The fight or flight response can totally consume a person in times of life-threatening stress. "It separates the men from the boys" bragged booze riddled pub heroes who have never realistically been put in that position where their bravery was put to the test. All that posturing manipulative horse shit didn't bother Jim. He was ready to run like a six-legged man with his arse hole on fire. Only he was locked in a gangster's house surrounded by the police. He wouldn't get very far before the front door was lying in bits in the hall under a copper's boot.

Despite his holy attire, there was no invisible omnipotent being coming to rescue Jim from spending his eightieth birthday squatting on a prison bucket whilst his cell mate fills his arm full of heroin.

No god perhaps, but an angel...

Mave put the chain on the front door and thrust the mobile phone through the gap and into the awaiting detective's face.

"Talk to the phone coz the face ain't listening!"

With her hand still held out of the half open door, she turned to Jim and gave him a saucy wink. She then gazed down at his erection... and winked at him again. Under the heavy makeup, latex prosthetics and huge beard, the Reaper could feel his face flushing red. Jim could just about see the irate detective talking on Mave's phone as uniformed officers peered in through the huge patio windows, to get a glimpse of Britain's most famous porn star. The detective's voice was tinged with anger as he spoke to the caller.

"No... well, no we haven't... but we can soon get one."

The detective sighed wearily and handed the phone back to Mave's outstretched hand, which had stayed in the door's gap throughout the policeman's short conversation. Summoning up his last shred of self-respect, the detective issued the obligatory threat, "We'll be ba..." Only to be cut short by the solid oak door slamming shut inches from his nose.

While Mave was occupied at the front door, Jim eyed the solid gold champagne bucket half full of Mullet's favourite monogrammed sweets. He reached inside his robes and felt the top of the plastic syringe. Then the sight of Mickey's three monster black suited skin heads loitering either side of the front door stopped him in his tracks. They too had delved their hands inside their jackets. Although these titanic trio were more preoccupied with the police at the door, he was in no doubt that if they were to casually cast a glance his way and caught him in the act, it wouldn't be pleasantries they would be swapping... it would be lead. Jim let go of the syringe and watched Mave clip clop back across the tiled marble floor in her 6-inch, blood red, patent leather stilettos towards him. This image did little to calm the unstable erection that thrashed violently beneath his bogus cassock.

"That brief's worth his weight in gold!" Crowed Mave.

He feared his heavily makeup covered face would melt as the nervous sweat seemed to be pouring out of his forehead. Mave did little to calm his nerves or bring down his temperature in her current attire. She caught him admiring her outfit and felt the need to explain.

"I don't normally dress like this father. Not what I usually wear round the gaff, just that I'm in the middle of making a movie upstairs when you called. It's all very tasteful and it's just me and thirty geezers and a Welsh midget covered in Bovril who is hung like a gyppo's donk…"

Jim held up a silencing hand, "No need to explain Mave."

The glorious sight of Mave in her French maid's outfit and sheer shimmering nylon stockings explaining the plot of her latest man milking movie was a pleasant momentary distraction from the deep dark hole Jim was in. Oh, what a tortured crossroads he was stranded at. He was faced with killing a sadistic East end gangster without being murdered by his prey. Yet if he failed in this trifle task, his employers would send him off to slaughter a woman journalist instead.

Fail in this task and his big toe will be sporting an identity tag before bedtime. Oh yes... nearly forgot, there was always serving eight life sentences in a maximum-security psycho factory if the authorities ever caught up with him.

And his old headmaster once said he would never amount to anything.

Well fuck you Mr Hargrieves! How many ex pupils can you name who have had a porn star bounce on their engorged member and then go on to kill one of Britain's most notorious gangsters?

And there it was... the shaft of golden sunlight that burst through the clouds. For the first time since Jim was first press ganged into becoming a Reaper, he actually felt a pang of job satisfaction. His mind became focussed. In the past he had agonised over the innocents he had been forced to kill. Now here he was with a chance to rid the world of a six-foot cockroach who wore Old Spice.

Jim felt quite confident he could outwit Mave as he slowly shuffled on the sofa edging nearer to Mullet's stash of sweeties. Yet the three tooled up monsters who hovered over them, although they might be candidates for "DENSA," they would not just stand idly by when Jim whipped out the syringe. A gorilla may not win many Pulitzer prizes... but it can still rip your arms off and bitch slap you with them. Jim cleared his throat and made his pitch to get the goons out of the room.

"My dear, the conversion to Judaism is a sacred oath."

"Yeah, I know." Said Mave, not really knowing what all those word type things were that were tumbling out of the rabbi's beardy face. Jim continued with his ad libbed plan.

"The knowledge I am about to bestow upon you is for your ears only."

She looked at him blankly as tumble weed rolled slowly behind her pupils.

Jim nodded towards the trio of thugs.

"I cannot reveal the sacred text to unbelievers." More tumble weed followed the first lot. Jesus wept! Jim despaired as her one brain cell must be yodelling all day in the vain hope of finding a mate on the next mountain range. He gripped her hand gently.

"Mave, these gentlemen are not converting to Judaism like you wish to... so they cannot listen to the rest of our private conversation."

Ping! Light bulb went on. Penny dropped. Grating voice erupted,

"Oiy! You three fuck off! Go on! Me and the rabbi want to talk about me wedding!"

The way these three attack dogs skulked off towards the kitchen told Jim they were truly responding to their master's voice. Jim's knowledge of the Jewish faith was quite lamentable. Yet for the purpose of this particular assassination, all he needed to know was two or more phrases than Mave knew.

"Now my dear..." *oh dear* chastised Jim's inner voice, *who do you think you are impersonating... Ron Moody in the film version of Oliver?*

"...I want you to swear on this bible." Jim produced a small black book and placed it in Mave's hand. She held the bible in her left hand and instinctively held up her right hand.

"I solemnly swear."

Jim bit his lip as a smile threatened to rampage across his heavily disguised face. How many times had she solemnly sworn like that on a bible for Mullet?

258

"What? Chopped up a club owner with a meat cleaver? Oh no, he couldn't have... we were watching the Antiques Road show at the time, your Honour. Set fire to a nun and beat her to death with a Jack Russel terrier? Surely not, we were both at our Morris dancing class at the time."

Stifling the grin, he continued, "Now close your eyes Mave and pray to almighty God that your faith is pure..." Jim's inner voice piped up and questioned just where the fuck he was dredging all this up from? He'll be spouting Halleluiahs next!

"... now keep them closed as you experience god's love."

Mave's eyes scrunched up tight as his hand shot into his robes and in one deft movement, produced the syringe and aimed the clear jet of liquid at the multicoloured sweets in Mullet's champagne bucket. The syringe was swiftly back in its hiding place and the glistening liquid had started to dry on the now deadly candy. Mave closed her eyes a blushing bride and opened them a widow.

There was a violent vibrating in Jim's groin, only it wasn't his painfully throbbing erection. His mobile phone had a text message for him. It was from the bunker.

GET BACK HERE NOW.

Reapers were never contacted whilst out on kills. Something was wrong. *No shit Sherlock! Your Father wanted you to be an English teacher and here you are, head gardener in the fucking graveyard!* And as quick as it came, it went... that pang of job satisfaction was truly horsewhipped out of town. Mave saw the concern on his face as her stared at the text.

"Something wrong, father?"

Jim stood up and headed for the door.

"N... no, it's, er... an emergency circumcision... Rabbi Goldberg can't do it, er... because he's got hiccups." He then threw up his arms in mock exaggerated stress.

"Oy vey!"

Even Jim could see he was becoming more pantomime by the minute. If he didn't tone it down he would be mistaken for an Aussie soap star and offered a summer season doing Aladdin on Hull pier! He was at the door when he was stopped dead.

"You don't get away that easy!"

Jim froze. This was it, rumbled. He closed his eyes and waited for her thugs Curly Larry and Moe to be joined by Glock, Heckler and Koch. He slowly turned to face her, waiting for the inevitable.

"You forgot yer bag... Look I know you're a proud man, but your church could always do with sprucing up a bit." Letting out a huge sigh of relief he went back for the bag and grunted as the sheer weight of all the bank notes made the shoulder strap dig into him as he lifted it. At the door he addressed the porn star.

"Mave, promise me one thing."

She pouted, "Anything for you father."

"Promise me you won't eat any more of those sweets in the champagne bucket. Very fattening. You have a wedding dress to get into..."

"I promise father."

"Good. Bless you my child, I'll be in touch."

Despite the weight of the bag, he virtually floated out the door.

Chapter 83

Despite hauling a box of her heavy files up four flights of stairs to her flat, Cassandra felt quite chipper. Working from home. No more titty rag. No more shameful glances off ex colleagues as they see her enter the temple of Judastic journalism. Her beaming smile dropped when she spotted the blood trail on the second landing. Just spots at first… then small pools. Ending in quite a big puddle on the next to one landing below her flat. As she tried to sidestep the crimson liquid a familiar voice called from above.

"I think you've had one of your little visitors again, dear."

Her elderly nosey neighbour Mrs Bennet stood mopping up blood outside Cassandra's open front door. There in the doorway silently hanging by fishing line was her ever vigilant claw hammer. Another intruder seen off. It had tasted more claret than Dracula having a stay behind in a blood bank. Putting down the box she ran up the last flight of stairs as Mrs Bennet squeezed and twisted the mop into her bucket, turning the detergent diluted water dark red.

"I mean, far be it for me to pry, dear, but..." Cassandra knew that this was just a precursor for an avalanche of prying that would put the Spanish Inquisition to shame.

"... have you ever thought of buying a Rottweiler? If you want, I can give our Neville a call. He's got a couple of Rottweilers he's looking to get shot of. Well, he has to really, after Kong took a chunk out of the postman's arse." Cassandra mock tutted at poor misunderstood Kong's dilemma. Ah, if only the misery ended there.

"I mean, how's our Neville supposed to get his giro now, eh?"

As much of an insurmountable human rights issue as this was, the small matter of her freshly attempted burgled flat took precedence over a bone-idle sack of shit's giro cheque and a homeless psychotic vampire mutt who is a connoisseur of arse flesh. She looked over her flat's threshold. No sound. If they were in there... they were quiet. The mop bucket full of blood told her no one was in her flat. In casualty maybe. The pensioner's cigarette bobbed up and down in her lips as she spoke.

"Mrs Braintree on the ground floor said she saw a woman stagger down the stairs with her face covered in blood." Cassandra's head snapped round to meet the old neighbour's gaze.

"A woman?" Mrs Bennet sloshed her mop up and down the red streaked landing. "Aye, a woman." She then delved into her voluminous cardigan.

"And she dropped this outside your front door."

The 12-inch black veiny dildo looked like a baseball bat in the pensioner's frail arms. This was getting too weird, even by her usual opponent's standards.

"L… look Mrs Bennet, thanks for cleaning up… again. But I really should go check everything's okay inside." The elderly lady took her hint and picked up her mop bucket and walked back into her own flat. Only when the journalist had locked her flat door did she realise that the pensioner had taken the fearsome looking vibrator home with her.

Chapter 84

Sir Hugo gulped at his single malt whiskey out the back of the cliff top restaurant. He was glad of the bright sunshine, so he could wear his sunglasses. The eyes are the mirrors of the soul... and his were betraying the fact that he was shitting himself. He shot to his feet in the deserted restaurant when he saw the unmistakable figure of Joshua Goodchild walk into reception with his trademark white linen suit... and six black suited armed mercenaries. The maître d' didn't have much trouble directing the American senator to Hugo's table; after all, they had hired the entire restaurant for the whole afternoon. One pumped up mercenary pulled out Goodchild's chair for him then retreated to a respectful distance, covering all the exits with his five other associates and leaving the waiting staff in no doubt as to keep their distance from the far terrace table. The right-wing Southern Baptist broke the ice.

"That commie abortionist loving mother fucker will be coming to London this week. How's my David? Is he ready to slay Goliath?"

"Oh, he's ready, it's as good as done." Hugo's insincere smile failed to impress the 70-year-old politician. Joshua poured water from the crystal jug and gently sipped from his glass in the glorious Jersey sunshine.

Goodchild didn't drink alcohol. He didn't do drugs or fornicate with anything. Joshua was pure. His body was a temple. And non-worshippers were burned as heretics. No, Joshua didn't drink. But he did personally hang garrotte and burn alive 36 Afro Caribbean males when he was climbing the ranks of the Ku Klux Clan.

And ordered the murders of 82 more. He used the funds from his church to kill 52 doctors at abortion clinics and used all his political influence to deny medical treatment for gay H.I.V. sufferers. Add onto this his private mercenary army that he would hire out to any third world torturing despot and you had your all-American-god-fearing messiah. One who would gladly crucify anyone joining a trade union.

"Hugo, the fact I've flown two thousand miles to Limey land should tell you just how serious this belated abortion is."

"It's the Channel Islands, actually."

The elderly brow buckled under an avalanche of barely concealed rage.

"Don't you fucking correct me, boy! I was gutting pinkos when your Momma was sucking gangs of stinking Dockers cocks!" Breathing harshly, he looked down at the table trying to regain composure. Joshua looked directly at Hugo and flashed him a wall of enamel as false as his personality.

"I want your personal guarantee that rabid little Judas will not be getting on the return flight back to Washington."

"I… I guarantee it."

Goodchild took out an expensive monogrammed pen and one of his personal business cards and proceeded to

265

write on the back of it. He then put away his pen and handed it to the Peer as his eyes bore into him as he read it.

"To Hugo, swear to god... and hope to die. Joshua"

Hugo swallowed hard.

The immaculately dressed American gave that unnerving smile again.

"Hugo, I like you. And there are not many men around today that I'd say that to." Hugo nodded genially; in the same way a school child would to placate a relentless playground bully. He glanced at the thinly veiled threat on the back of the business card that lay on the table.

"I have built up a vast army of warriors of Christ, ready to smite down the heathen hordes that are the evil legions of Satan himself."

Ah yes, the "warriors of Christ," mused Hugo. Typical American concept of rebranding. These saintly warriors were a totally privatised army made up of every low life cutthroat mercenary who had ever butchered their way across the Congo in the last 20 years. Every war crime that made the news in the last two decades in the third world... these angels were there. Not one of them had a single religious inkling in their ice-cold black hearts. Yet to these veterans, a drill sergeant barking orders or an evangelical psychopath delivering sermons, it was all the same to them. God paid better.

The church that Joshua founded in the sixties had grown so big and powerful, that he was rumoured to be capable of buying presidential candidates. Yet if he funded you on your path to the Oval office, he expected a substantial return on his investment once you got there. His church maybe for tax purposes be a charity... but Joshua certainly wasn't. So as much as Joshua's church was rumoured amongst political journalists to be capable of buying presidents, it remained rumoured, because such nefarious deals were never done in public. His vast covert donations to the last three administrations had secured his personal army extremely lucrative contracts, in numerous theatres of operations, all over the profitable parts of the globe. His military muscle was in such demand that when the joint chiefs of staff were discussing foreign policies, Joshua's fee and band of merry men were always factored into the costings.

As much as a saviour for the free world as Goodchild purported to be, his army was only for hire to the highest bidder. Impoverished wretches being tortured in third world countries didn't fall under his remit. So, the highest bidder tended to be…

The White House.

There is nothing in this world that really spoils eating a slice of wholesome Mom's apple pie, like live T.V. coverage of hundreds of U.S. troops coming home in coffins draped in the flag. It really makes it quite difficult for the Commander in Chief to deliver a press conference and explain to the inhabitants of the only superpower on Earth, why their sons were wearing shrouds instead of medals; just so a few greedy billionaires could steal oil from brown people. The trouble is… the brown people fight back. After all, nobody likes a thief.

Joshua's boys however weren't officially classified as soldiers. No, their media manipulating misnomer was "contractors." Doesn't have the same gut-wrenching news bulletin appeal does it?

"Today, 18 contractors were killed in Fallujah."

In trailer parks across the mid-west, shit kicking hillbillies wouldn't even spit out their chewing tobacco at the mention of a contractor's death. What would that mean to them? 18 plumbers or carpenters had kicked the bucket. Little did these web-toed patriots realise it, but these plumbers carried Heckler & Koch MP5 SMG's with armour piercing rounds. And it was this simple smoke and mirrors rebranding that this private army could be so dispensable, as no one in the media would give their deaths a second look, that made them so attractive to the President. So, while this administration was using Joshua to pursue its own sinister agenda, he was doing exactly the same thing to them.

Goodchild sipped his water and continued,

"My warriors' number 20,000, did you know that, Hugo?"

Hugo didn't. He'd suspected the number of troops to be around 8,000 at the most. But if he was telling the truth, then this old man was much more dangerous than Hugo ever imagined. He could realistically destabilise a whole country with that amount of manpower.

"And I'm seconding 5,000 of them to work solely on the U.S. Reaper project." Hugo was taken aback. He knew Goodchild had resources, but he hadn't expected anything of this magnitude. Joshua smiled to himself. He secretly enjoyed seeing men who thought they were his equal, suddenly realise that they were hopelessly out of their depth.

"I'll need your head of section to fly over and train my boys. I want the Holy Warriors of Christ cutting down the satanic army in their thousands within two months."

Hugo stuttered "Y… yes, of course. I'll brief him immedi…"

Goodchild suddenly grabbed the peer of the Realm's hand.

"Hugo, if all goes to plan, we will expand into Europe in three years."

The peer beamed a huge smile, totally overwhelmed by the speed and magnitude of Goodchild's offer. The smile was soon wiped off his flabby face.

"The whole deal however hangs upon your boy putting Congressman Daniel O'Brian out of my misery. If he is allowed to return to Washington, he is going to chair a commission that is investigating my private army. I have been reliably informed by my friends on Capitol Hill, that they cannot step in and protect me if that treacherous bastard opens his can of worms!"

He was clearly rattled. Did Hugo detect a flicker of fear behind those piercing vulture's eyes? Goodchild looked out to sea, lost in thought then quietly said, "This is the last roll of the dice for both of us, Hugo."

The peer suddenly looked up sharply. "Both?"

"Hugo... if I touch him in the States, his death will stick to me like shit to an army blanket. Yet, there is nothing to link his demise in the U.K. to me. It has to happen here. You see Hugo, if your boy fails, then I'll have nothing left to lose. And your part in my downfall will not go unpunished."

Hugo ordered another whisky even though he knew this would be construed as weakness in the eyes of the teetotal, billionaire psychopath. Joshua gazed at the tiny sail boats bobbing gently out at sea from the cliff top restaurant.

"Dark forces are rising, my friend. I have seen my once proud nation being poisoned from within. The rotting cancer ravenously gnawing at the very fabric of American family life. Feminists, communists, trade unionists, civil rights activists now all have more power over the minds, hearts and souls of our young than the church!" His elderly eyes were wild with anger. "Can you believe that, Hugo?"

Yes, Hugo could believe that.

All of the people on Joshua's hate list showed more biblical qualities of love and compassion, than Goodchild's toxic religious doctrine of control and destroy. Yet Hugo was faced with a man who would have every other book other than the bible burned... along with their authors. In Goodchild's eyes, a library was more sinful than a brothel. An enquiring mind is a sinful mind. The peer didn't swallow any of this horseshit. No matter what the denomination, no matter what name they gave their particular invisible war mongering deity... they all pissed in the same pot.

They all used their religions to seize power and control vast swathes of the population…and it was a slice of that power that Sir Hugo wanted. After all, who wanted to be a big fish in a small pond when you could be a killer whale in an ocean?

So, he let the religious fanatic vomit his bigoted bile, for this particular lunatic was going to make his Reaper project a global reality. Goodchild's Southern drawl lowered slightly into a conspiratorial tone,

"These diseased elements in our society need to be purged from the Earth."

Hugo felt his flabby stomach tighten at this Arian view of the future. When he created the Reaper project, his vision of controlling populations was always a fiscal decision: workers live, shirkers die. Nothing personal, just business.

Joshua however would string up an I.T. entrepreneur and stock market genius if his skin was brown... and his god was Allah.

Hugo's best chance of realising his worldwide dream of restoring population control, would involve getting into bed with this unpredictable zealot. That would seriously leave the peer wide open to being brutally, gang fucked in that bed. But, before that marriage could be consummated, a certain congressman who has been investigating Joshua's private army would have to be cut down by one of Hugo's Reapers.

A Reaper named Jim.

Chapter 85

Mickey Mullet wasn't having a good time. The bottom had just fallen out of his world. Or, to be precise, the world had just fallen out of his bottom. Sweat poured from his tortured brow as boiling hot soup poured from his scalded arse. For the past thirty minutes, Britain's most ruthless gangster had been stuck on the lavatory... terrified to move. Every few minutes he would rock backwards and forewords for fear that the heat generated by his anal avalanche would weld his buttocks to the solid gold toilet seat that now resembled the last days of Pompeii.

"Oooh, farrrkin 'ell!!" Mickey nearly snapped the toilet roll holder off the wall as he feebly tried to brace himself for a fresh onslaught, as his contorted bowels pumped unfeasibly large amounts of liquid through his blistered anus at frightening velocity.

The vile rectal gargling symphony sounded like several ducks being drowned in a vat of custard as it echoed around the enclosed room. Mullet yet again hit the toilet flush and wiped the tears from his eyes. For the fifth time, Mickey had racked his brain as to why he had found himself in this undignified predicament. He hadn't eaten curry in over a week. No kebabs last night or booze for that matter. Just a couple of lines of cocaine, but no way would that give him the galloping shits.

No, but his private stash of chocolate candy covered sweets would. Especially, if a Reaper had been anywhere near them. The syringe that Jim had emptied into Mickey's champagne bucket full of sweeties contained a very special cocktail that the Reapers are quite proud of. The Reapers standard cocktail mixed in the bunker's chemistry laboratory, is a clear odourless chemical toxin that produces a massive heart attack in the victim and is virtually impossible to detect in a quickly decomposing corpse. By the time the body reaches the autopsy lab, all traces of the drug have disappeared completely. The drug is an old favourite of the C.I.A. who have been using it for over forty years, but the Reapers have tweaked it by adding a very powerful diuretic to the mixture.

Thus, ensuing Mickey's final moments before his heart exploded were as humiliating as possible. The shooting pains down Mickey's left arm told him something was seriously wrong. His grey-haired old mum smiled back at him from the photo frame on the window ledge. Her smile held no comfort for him now as his chest tightened up and his breaths were coming in short sharp gasps.

"M.... Mave!" His weakened voice couldn't be heard by his starlet fiancée, who was on the last leg of filming a gang bang with a Welsh midget with a penis the size of a giraffe's neck. In a panic, he stood up and, in the process, knocked his mother's photo to the floor as he staggered for the door. Diarrhoea gushed out the back of him in foot long jets, hitting his mum's photo. The irony was lost on him as he had been doing this to her all his life, so only fitting he should finish their relationship the same way. He grabbed hold of the toilet door handle as his £3,000 silk trousers round his ankles were repeatedly splattered with hot faeces. He twisted the handle just as a sledgehammer seemed to smash through his rib cage. He gasped and threw his head back and staggered backwards only to slump back onto his throne with a squelch.

Mickey always wanted to die like his cinematic gangster hero Jimmy Cagney, going out in a hail of bullets. Alas, he went out like Elvis, not with a bang... but with a loud wet fart.

Chapter 86

After quickly searching her flat for intruders, Cassandra double locked the mortice lock and reset "old faithful" her claw hammer burglar alarm. She smiled as she thought she really should carve notches on old faithful's handle. How many times had it shed blood to protect her? It must be nearly nine by now. It should be sponsored by Colgate with the number of teeth it has caressed. The teeth and puddles of blood were always found in the hall and adjacent staircase... never her flat. Her claw hammer sentinel relentlessly protecting the threshold of her inner sanctum and asking nothing in return. The journalist sighed as she yet again opened a bottle of Merlot, if only she could find a man to do that for her. She frowned at this frivolous thought that had burgled her mind more successfully than her would be intruder. Thoughts like this were happening more and more lately. It had been a couple of years since her last relationship and the need for company was starting to bite deep. She sat down at her computer and smiled to herself again.

The need for company.

Even in her mind she couldn't allow the word "lonely" to rear up like a mad relative locked away in the loft.

"I'm not lonely... I just like my own company ".

She said out loud. To no one. In her empty flat. Cassandra let out a humourless laugh and necked her glass of vino, before refilling it to the brim. Opening her purse, she took out and loaded the pen drive she had downloaded Marty's emailed files onto before leaving her office. Again, she gulped half the glass as she waited for the files to load. She glanced at the half empty glass.

Dutch courage? What are you scared of finding? The conspiracy stuff would be a doddle compared to the last few lines of Marty's introduction to his last will and testament. Jesus, she felt suddenly very low. Not like her at all. Usually, she was hard as nails... had to be. But a man who knew his death was imminent had left her his life's work and then declared his undying love from beyond the grave.

Well, well… wasn't fate a twisted and spiteful little bastard then?

The very qualities she longed for in a man and Marty had them all, but she didn't want him. She deluded herself that it wasn't about his nerdy looks. After all, she wasn't that shallow. No…it was about what was inside that counts. Only men are that shallow. That cold stabbing voice from the back of her mind chided her.

Why didn't you fuck him then? Like Al Jolson, Marty would've walked a million miles for one of your smiles... and you wouldn't piss on him if he was on fire.

She screwed up her eyes and took a deep breath. When she opened them, Marty's legacy was laid out before her on her flat screen laptop.

The meticulous menus alone were breath-taking.

She gulped the Merlot and clicked the computer mouse attached to her P.C. and scanned down through endless headings on corporate conspiracies, misuse of secret service power and then she halted. The name on the screen sent her heart pounding.

Lorraine Fuller.

Lorraine Fuller, the young woman who the sick fucker she was hunting had put her into a laundrette tumble dryer. Her snapped neck, scalded flesh and burst lungs through suffocation set he reporter's teeth grinding with anger. The scanned in frivolous newspaper report and C.C.T.V. footage of her killer going into the laundrette and leaving shortly after. Cassandra's nostrils flared and she drained her glass, filling it again without thinking. She clicked down the menu, moving on. If she dwelled on the Fuller murder, then nothing else would get done.

Next, she clicked on the late failed Guinness record breaker Colin Hale. The photo retrieved from his memory card looked totally different from the last time she had viewed it at Marty's flat. An involuntary shudder went through her. Somehow the reflective image from the cooker's glass door showed not just one killer... but a second killer standing behind him. She edged closer to the computer screen and studied the face of the second figure who she had dismissed as being a shadow on the initial gloomy image. Unlike the troubled face of her serial killer, this man looked extremely delighted with himself. His cruel eyes seemed to shine with a murderous glint that made her back away from the screen. She shook her head at her own jitteriness. Cassandra looked over her shoulder and saw the front door was still locked, and her silent tungsten steel claw hammer hung high above the door in the hall... waiting.

Two killers.

Was this why he had never been caught? This "shadow" was covering his back, looking out for him like a malevolent guardian angel. Her head was feeling fuzzy. The wine perhaps? Or the revelation that this murderous fucker now outnumbered her by two to one? She let out a long sigh. Since Marty had died, she was hunting a pair of killers totally alone. She could hand what she had over to the police. Then what? Grainy photos and autopsy reports all obtained illegally, breaking and entering into a dead man's flat... guess who's going in the cells girl? She glanced quickly at the locked door once more. She drained the last of her glass and poured the remaining inch of Merlot into her glass.

"My, the evaporation rates of these French vinos are quite remarkable." That old line was wearing extremely thin these days. Okay, so she didn't reek of piss or live under a railway arch, does that mean she wasn't an alcoholic?

She pushed these tired old nagging thoughts to one side as she clicked further down the menus on the late hacker's files. Cassandra stopped at the next section of headings.

C.C.T.V. MARTY'S FLAT

This section had arrived separately from the bulk of the files on the email as each sub file was dated. Opening the most recent file she gasped at the film footage. She recognized the two figures instantly.

It had been quite some time since she had last seen herself on T.V. Back in the day when she had a career she could be proud of. When she was a journalist instead of saying, "I used to be." Oh, how she hated hearing that debilitating phrase apologetically dribbling out of her lips. Draining yet more self-confidence every time her old job cropped up in conversation.

The last time she was on television, she had brought down a rising star in the Tory party... Sir Hugo Montgomery. An ambitious M.P. earmarked for a top cabinet post and all insiders said he was being groomed to be the next Prime minister. Pity he was an arms dealer doing covert embargo breaking deals with a South East Asian version of Hitler. A tyrant who collected skulls in the same way a dog collects fleas. Oh, and the British soldiers killed with weapons illegally sold to our enemies on three continents... oh dear.

Cassandra's meticulous expose of Montgomery's dirty deals and her evidence presented on live television at a cross party selection committee was like a torpedo that sank his political career without trace. The Tories shipped him off to a foreign posting for a few years and when he returned all tanned and twice as fat, they gave him a peerage and put him out of harm's way to snooze in the House of Lords. Cassandra however, found herself jobless and her world collapsed like a house of cards. Hugo made some calls and got his revenge.

There is no such thing in journalism as an unfair dismissal tribunal. Hacks are no different to football managers; you can be just sacked for the flimsiest of excuses and you are powerless to do a thing about it.

That was the last time she was on T.V.

This time she was not alone.

She squinted as she watched herself and the portly porter Stanley Vaughn creep about Marty's empty flat. She was intrigued to see the image change on screen as she entered a different room and another camera picked up where the last one left off. She surmised that Marty must've rigged up motion sensors to the cameras in each room so they could track anyone who entered the flat. For a paranoid conspiracy nerd like Marty, why was she surprised? On screen, she and Stanley hovered around the electricity cupboard, scrutinising the dubious burnt out fuse out of the fuse box then leaving silently. There was no audio on the footage, and it was all in infra-red.

She clicked the next file dated 4 days before. Her heart raced as she watched a room full of white forensic suited S.O.C.O. teams dusting her ex friend's flat for prints. She put her hand over her mouth as the image changed and showed the officers dragging Marty's naked corpse out of the bath full of set jelly, before he disappeared beneath the zip of a body bag. These images were very clear and not in infra-red. Obviously these cameras must be self-adjusting and linked to a light sensor.

The arrow on her computer screen hovered over the next date.

The date she found Marty dead.

Did she really want to relive this nightmare again, even if it was only on a computer screen? Not without a drink in her, she didn't. The second bottle was quickly opened, and a brimming glass brought back to her laptop, which she suddenly spilt some on the keyboard. "Shit!" The relentless dabbing with kitchen role seemed to take forever, or was it a stalling tactic at not wanting to open the next file?

Gulping half the glass, she gritted her teeth and clicked the mouse twice.

The salt tears burned her cheeks as she watched herself enter Marty's bathroom and lay eyes on Marty for the last time. She closed the file and sobbed, her shoulders shaking uncontrollably. Standing up she staggered towards the bathroom feeling stunned to rinse her face with cold water.

With the tap running wildly, she clumsily splashed her face and soaked the front of her blouse but was feeling too pissed to care. Looking at her bloodshot mascara smeared eyes in the bathroom mirror, her soaked fringe hung down like rats' tails. As beautiful a vision as this was to dwell upon, she would rather stay here using the sink as a drunken crutch, rather than go back and view the last file on the computer.

The file dated five hours before she entered Marty's flat.

Cassandra needed to clear her head. The wine was about to untether her jangled nerves and leave her in emotional meltdown. She plunged her face into the cold water in the overflowing sink. All senses dulled. No sound. No sight. Peaceful almost. Was this how Marty felt just before he drowned?

Like a phoenix rising from the ashes her head snapped back as she straightened up, showering her bathroom with water. Through gritted teeth she stared at her reflection, water shooting out of her mouth and splashing the mirror as she roared,

"He didn't fucking drown! He was fucking murdered!"

She rubbed her face vigorously with a bath towel and then wrapped her head tightly in a turban with it. On a mission now, she gulped down three pints of water and boiled a pot of coffee. Cassandra pulled out a large, serrated knife from her utensil drawer and swiped it back and forth, satisfied as she heard it audibly cut the air before her. By the time the coffee had boiled she had checked her door viewer six times, manically pacing the flat. All the while the weapon held tight in her fist, her knuckles bulging and white.

Whoever had their face pulverised outside her flat had smeared what looked like lipstick on her door viewer that she had to clean off. Old Mrs Bennet had said a neighbour on the ground floor had seen a woman soaked in blood darting out the building.

A woman assassin.

My, sexual equality at last. This drew a humourless smile to her lips. Yet again she checked her door viewer was clear, with only the distorted goldfish bowl image of her hallway and staircase staring back at her. Forcing the hot black coffee down, she winced and put the knife down next to her computer. The last file was clicked open and she held her breath.

For the second time she had set eyes on the other grinning killer. This time in bright light. He was immaculately dressed in a dark suit and tie and had a distinctive large angular nose. He was also holding a gun fitted with a silencer to Marty's head. The hacker was visibly shaking as he stripped naked before the killer, who then reached into his coat and produced a black object the size of a mobile phone. Only when he jabbed this into Marty's ribs did she realise it was no phone. Marty jerked violently on the spot before falling to the floor. Again, the footage had no audio. He lay motionless on the floor as the killer kneeled over Marty and appeared to be taking his pulse on his neck.

He then stood up... and smiled

The killer moved at breakneck speed through Marty's flat. Cassandra watched impotent with her hand over her mouth, barely blinking as the horror before her compelled her to watch as Marty's naked body was dragged into the bathroom and unceremoniously dumped into the bath. The suited killed then took several small boxes of powder out of his briefcase and poured the powdered contents onto Marty and then run the bath taps. She guessed these boxes of powder were the strawberry jelly mix. Her eyes started to fill up as the bathwater reached Marty's chest and the killer forced the hacker's curly head under the gelatine filled water. From his open case the next images showed the killer setting up and lighting dozens of candles around the cluttered flat. An extension lead and a small cassette player were produced from a larger, black sports bag along with more candles. Cassandra's breath was coming in short gasps now, the anger building in her as she wiped her tears.

Everything seemed to then happen in slow motion. The tape player being dropped into the bath onto of the submerged body. The lights going out as the water in the cassette play activated the circuit breaker. The infra-red on the cameras automatically switching over allowing her to see the grinning killer turn off the taps and turning on his own small torch. The candlelight flickering and the small torch caused the infra-red footage to fluctuate, distorting the image slightly. The small flat in candlelight now resembled a chapel of rest. A bottle of champagne was left beside Marty's bed, along with two fluted glasses. The last act this evil grinning bastard did before he left was to lean into the electricity cupboard and with a brief flash of light, blow the fuse. Just as Stanley Vaughn had said it was done. Collecting the rest of his belongings, he left Marty's home without closing the front door.

So, there it was, in glorious high definition... Marty's swansong.

Cassandra slumped back in her chair and glanced at the knife beside her keyboard. After what she has just witnessed, some sort of stun device that can kill upon touching the chest and a silenced handgun, that serrated fish knife didn't seem to offer her the same feeling of protection as it did before. Her hand reached for the mouse to replay the footage... then hesitated.

Her eyes darted towards the wine bottle. No! She had just found out her chances of being slain had doubled. If she got pissed out of her skull, they would quadruple.

Think girl! Think!

She had both these fuckers photographed at the scene of Colin Hale's death in his kitchen. She had C.C.T.V. footage of her original killer coming out of the laundrette Lorraine Fuller was killed at. And most damming of all, the murder and covering up of Marty's death by the second killer. She grabbed for the phone and dialled 999; she didn't have to fight this battle alone.

"Hello emergency services, which services do you require?"

She gulped down the rest of her coffee.

"Emergency services, which service do you require?"

No... if the police get involved; this story will start a feeding frenzy on Fleet Street. She wouldn't get near this story; it would be taken from her.

She ended the call

"No... they're mine! "

Chapter 87

Bobby Mcvie drank the weak sweet tea out of politeness, rather than comfort. It was such an English thing, in times of shock, trauma or bereavement, the cure was always the same... sweet tea. If he was in America, he would've been handed Valium. Stiff upper lip you see. If the Martians ever landed on mass in London, you'd be deafened by the sound of whistling kettles.

"I'm so sorry... he died at 2.20am this morning." Said the pretty young nurse with dark circles around her eyes. For one so young, she too had seen more death that was conducive with a happy carefree outlook on life.

"That's okay... the old fella had a good innings." She gave a nervous smile, grateful that he was making it easy for her. Some relatives howled the hospital down. Others became extremely violent. So, this unkempt rugged stranger, with his quiet dignified composure, was much appreciated by the overworked nurse.

"His injuries were quite severe... and his heart was very weak towards the end. We had to double his dose of morphine, so he felt very little pain in his last moments." Bobby sipped the sweet tea thoughtfully.

"We couldn't find any relatives of Mr Hannah's to call…"

"There are none. He's all alone."

It sounded a lot colder than Bobby had meant it to come out. He looked up from his tea and gave the young staff nurse a reassuring smile. She seemed relieved to see this and smiled back.

"I was with him when he passed away peacefully in his sleep." Bobby smiled broadly,

"The second-best way to die." He handed her the cup and started to walk away. Her voice stopped him in his tracks. "And the first?"

He turned to face her and then winked.

She smiled back and her face visibly blushed. Bobby spun on his heels and strode through the automatic doors out of the ward. He smiled to himself. It had been a long time since a woman had flirted with him. He chuckled to himself and said out loud. "It would never work... my career would get in the way."

It only took the former Green jacket sergeant fifteen minutes to run across town. Dodging foul mouthed taxi drivers and randy pissed up hen parties. His fitness had always been good. When his meths guzzling neighbours would be marinating their livers in industrial paint stripper, Bobby would slip out of the tramp camp and do a five-mile run. He knew if his fitness went, he was finished. There would be no difference between him and the broken souls who inhabited this human scrap yard. He would always end his run with an hour of martial arts training under a disused railway arch the other side of town.

He had stuffed an old army kit bag with rags and strung it up from the arches rusting metal studded beams. Each night he would hammer this homemade punch bag in controlled bursts of fury in bouts of three-minute rounds. Bobby had weighted the bottom foot of the kit bag with sand he had purloined from a local building site. The sand gave this bag a rigidity that helped with its swing and it also toughened up his shins as he repeatedly round house kicked it whilst gritting his teeth and ignoring the pain. He bounced around on the balls of his feet stripped to the waist as he checked his watch, waiting for the thirty second break to elapse before he exploded at the bag once more. A cloud of dirt masked his dancing feet on the uneven soil floor, as his front kick sent the bag lurching far away from Bobby. The rope securing it from the beam above groaned under the strain masking his panting breaths. The heavy bag made its return, with a momentum hell bent on revenge. Bobby's knees dipped momentarily, and he sprang up into the air. His head spun first, then his taut upper torso jerked round as hard as he could, almost feeling like he was twisting himself in two. The bag was almost upon him when the bottom half of this coiled spring whipped round and sent a shin smashing into the bag stopping its flight in mid-air with a loud whack. Sweat dripped down his bare scarred chest as he panted. A thin smile through gritted teeth showed his satisfaction with today's workout. The bag swung pitifully away at a slower pace; all venomous momentum kicked out of it. Spirit truly broken. Still smiling, he pointed at the gently swinging bag and said,

"This town ain't big enough for both of us, bollocks."

That was fifteen minutes ago. Although his shins, elbows and knuckles still throbbed from his workout, his mind was focused on other things.

The razor-sharp kitchen knife down the back of his jeans for one... and the lady journalist's flat for another. He crossed the road opposite her abode and this time he was determined to pay her a visit.

Chapter 88

The bunker's makeup technician, Julian, dabbed nervously at Singen's swollen nose, trying to remove the makeup without incurring the head Reaper's wrath. He wasn't succeeding.

"Y… you should really go to a hospital to get tha…"

No sooner had Julian uttered those words when the volcano erupted.

"And say what exactly?! Oooh! Sister, could you help rebuild my poor old hooter? I appear to have inhaled a claw hammer whilst trying to murder a woman! What? The women's clothing? Best not to ask."

The verbal onslaught had started a fresh trickle of blood from his bloated nostrils. The makeup artist was close to tears, until the head of section stepped in and saved him.

"That will be all, Julian."

A rare compassionate smile crawled across his usually stony face.

"Go get yourself a coffee." Julian saw his escape route and took it as fast as he could.

Singen dabbed at the blood, some of which had dropped onto his bare chest. Well, bare except for a well stuffed low-cut black lace push up bra. He hadn't had time to remove his skirt, or his torn black tights. But the blonde wig was lashed into the corner of the room like a scolded pup. The older man held two glasses of whiskey and handed one of them to his second in command. He sipped his single malt and considered how to handle his junior. Both Singen's eyes were bruised black, with the whites going more blood shot by the moment. But his nose... looked like it had been chewed up and shat out. The only thing that kept the pain at bay was his rage. Singen was handed two white tablets by his boss.

"They are powerful painkillers."

The younger man held them up to his mouth then hesitated. When you kill people every day, paranoia is a side effect.

His boss sighed wearily,

"Naylor was a medic in the special forces. He told me he wants you drugged up to the eyeballs when he comes down later to reset your nose." Singen suddenly looked worried. His boss put a comforting hand on the younger man's shoulder.

"You said it yourself, a hospital visit is out of the question." Singen nodded and gulped the pills down with the single malt. He winced at the pain in his nose.

"I...I want to go back out there tonight and finish it. Take the gun an..."

"No!" His boss held his gaze. Up to now he had danced on eggshells around his minion's temper tantrums, but this was a place of business. Emotions were a luxury this facility could not afford.

"You had your chance." He sipped his whiskey before making Singen's day even gloomier. "I'm sending Jim." Singen's eyes widened, but his boss firmly cut him short.

"Put your bruised ego away! You were probably seen as you left your fucking D.N.A. all over her building." He jabbed his index finger very close to that smashed nose, causing the younger man to involuntary jerk his head back out of the way. This pleased the older man who had noticed the arrogance of his junior slowly blossom into unconcealed contempt over the last few months. Did this little boy really think he was big enough now to kick Daddy's arse? Taking down a peg or two just wasn't enough. Strangling with the washing line was much nearer the mark.

"When Congressman O'Brien visits London this week he will be murdered by a loner who disappeared off the radar 5 years ago. A deluded fool who has left a trail of circumstantial evidence of his killing spree for all to find. And who finally butchered the heroic female journalist who tried to stop him."

Singen grinned and clinked his whiskey glass against his boss's, sounding the journalist's death knell.

When all the makeup and any traces of femininity were removed, Singen donned a black dressing gown and the two men had relocated from the makeup technician's section to his boss's office. Once alone, the door was locked. The two huge guards outside with orders they weren't to be disturbed.

"I know you and young Jim haven't quite hit it off."

"He's a gutless little prick!"

"Quite." His boss walked around his desk and sat down. He cleared his throat and continued. "But he is vital to the future of this facility… and the whole worldwide Reaper project." Singen brooded deeply. This was shit he did not want to hear.

The head of section exhaled deeply, growing weary of his tempestuous junior.

"You are aware that when I am seconded to Nevada to train the American Reapers, you will be head of section here." Singen took a gulp of his whiskey and smiled. His superior continued. "Also, Sir Hugo informs me that if all goes well in the States, then they'll need a head of section to train up all of the Reapers in Europe… in only three years' time." His boss deliberately paused, allowing the enormity to sink in.

"Think about it Singen. America is mine… Europe is yours." Singen looked into space, lost in the moment. His bloodshot blackened eyes danced as the next ten years unfurled in front of him in a wonderful kaleidoscope of ambition unimagined, until now. His boss poured them both another whiskey.

"So, you see, dear boy, as much as you may loath young Jim… he does hold both our futures in the palm of his hand." Singen looked into the golden liquid in his glass and then slowly looked up at his boss. "And when he's killed the congressman, what will Jim be doing?" His boss tilted his glass in a silent salute.

"That depends, dear boy… on how you want to kill him."

Chapter 89

Mervin Foster sat at an antique desk and scrolled down the files on his ultra slim black laptop. The files his pet hacker dredged from the bowels of his lady reporter's computer. 98% of it was the staple diet of his moronic readership: porn, celebs and brain donors in football shorts. It was the latest 2% she had just recently received in a couple of emails, that sent blood rampaging through Mervin's lard clogged arteries. The hacker was a true professional. In the past he had invaded the mobile phones of adulterous Royals and cottaging M. Ps alike. Discretion was this cyber thief's middle name. Not even a boot in the bollocks off the C.I.D. had loosened his tongue. Not once had he disclosed to the authorities that Foster was his paymaster. The stakes were higher than a mere cocaine snorting grandchild of the Queen this time. Foster had quadrupled his fee and as he bid him farewell, informed the lad he'd pay ten times that amount to put a contract out on him if any details on the lady journalist's files ever left his office. The hacker left with his fee... and a brown stain on his gusset.

This was Mervin's private penthouse office on the top floor of his filth factory. The only people who usually got to see this floor are bent politicians, corrupt coppers, moronic celebs or fledgling porn stars who want to work on his paper. He paid extremely well and expected more than a gurn into a camera lens for the King's ransom these girls get. It was for this reason that the criteria for gainful employment within his glamour industry could be encapsulated in his nick name:

"Blow job-No job."

Little did his readership know as they drooled over these outrageously sexy vixens, was that Mervin had done everything to these girls that they had only fantasised about... and secretly filmed it. After all, Foster was no fool. After turning these unwashed council estate trash, into super stars, a few had seriously developed delusions of grandeur and stopped taking his calls altogether. This truculence and ingratitude was foretold by Foster right from the start. After all, what's the point in placing a choker chain round a mutt's neck if you're not prepared to yank it? Once a copy of the starlet's blow job audition footage along with a date such carnal viewing will be available for download on the internet was sent to her, the lost sheep came scurrying back to the flock... for a fuck.

There was no sex in the penthouse office today... only death.

Well, on his laptop anyway. He had watched the C.C.T.V. footage from Marty's flat over and over for most of the afternoon. Furiously writing notes and gulping black coffee. The lights on his switchboard phone on his desk blinked like an epileptic Dalek, as his minions 20 stories below were trying to reach him. Celebrity gangster Mickey

Mullet had died, and Mervin's disciples needed guidance on how to surf the tidal wave of media madness, that would engulf all of London within the next 3 hours. In his paper's terms, this was the biggest thing to hit the capital since the Luftwaffe last visited. An East End gangster's funeral was like striking circulatory gold.

Foster couldn't give a flying fuck.

His mind was on other things. His world had suddenly just got smaller. Sir Hugo, the bent arms dealing Pom of the Realm, had threatened the only things precious to

Mervin... his kids. Okay, his Missus was threatened as well. But the gold-digging bitch was cancer to his wallet, so this could be his silver lining.

Realistically, the only way he could take on and beat an arms dealer of Hugo's magnitude was to wield an even bigger weapon. Such a weapon was in his female reporter's possession... now it was within his.

Chapter 90

Jim wasted no time on his way back to the bunker, dropping the huge sports bag full of cash off at his secret train station locker. Checking all the while he wasn't being followed. As he entered the taxi, the locker key felt good in his hand. Such a small dull insignificant object, but too him, it was the most beautiful thing in the world. It was his key to freedom.

An hour later, with all latex prosthetics, makeup and disguise removed, he sat opposite the Head of Section, deep within the bunker.

"Congratulations Jim! That machine for turning jellied eels into shit has written his last criminal confession." He sat back in his seat, beaming a smile at Jim that conveyed a father's pride at graduation. Little did Jim realise it, but he had just graduated and was about to move up to a higher league altogether. Going from gang land hit, to full political assassination in one fell swoop. The head of section poured Jim a whiskey and then one for himself. Jim sipped the foul burning liquid that flambéed his oesophagus all the way down to his stomach. There wasn't even a potted plant near to dump Scotland's finest export into.

So, Jim drank to celebrate his part in ending a drug baron's reign of terror. Was it the whiskey or did this specific killing feel good because morally he could justify it to his gnawing conscience?

"We are at a very special period in our Reaper project, Jim."

Oh goody. Mused Jim. He's using corporate bullshit to sanitise murdering innocent people for a bogus cause.

"How would you feel if I said you were only two killings away from retirement?" He sat back in silence and let it sink in, but in the uneasy silence, Jim wasn't biting. What the fuck was all this leading to? After Jim plants two stiffs, he joins them in the ground shortly after? His heart started its bid to erupt through his ribcage. The older man sensed Jim's disquiet and held up a placating hand.

"Relax Jim, this is a promotion, not a dismissal." The cold cheerless smile did little to rid Jim's skin of the billion or so of goose bumps that had erupted in the past 5 seconds. Despite the cold image of Thomas Ludlow, the Reaper who ran, being dragged out of this very office in plastic sheeting filled Jim's mind. Yet, his boss did say "promotion." Only the living got promoted. That dark sarcastic schizophrenic voice from deep within his psyche begged to differ.

Not if you are martyred for your cause. Then, death would naturally lead to promotion. Whereas this life was seen as your shit digging holes in the pissing down rain job, the afterlife is a rollercoaster Hollywood movie star non-stop fuck-a-thon. His boss interrupted his troubled thoughts.

"The whole world will soon be yielding to the control of the Reapers who will restore order to the natural balance of things." The older man sipped at his whiskey, while Jim just stared blankly into his.

"We are very soon to be expanding into America." His eyes darted downwards.

"But, before that can happen, you must cut down a certain American congressman named Daniel O'Brian." The uneasy silence sat there between them like a vile rancid fart dropped in a confined lift, poisoning the very atmosphere that they breathed. It was Jim who broke the silence.

"Y… you said, 'two killings'...who's the first?" His boss regarded him coldly.

"The woman journalist."

His luck had just run out. "I'm afraid there was a bit of a hiccup with our lady journalist. Our top man fluffed the ball, so I'm handing you back your original kill." Jim opened his mouth to speak but was cut short.

"Don't worry Jim, you won't be alone on this one."

Jim flinched as he heard the door handle click behind him and in walked Singen dressed immaculately in a sleek tailored black suit, crisp white shirt and black tie. Jim did a double take when he saw Slimey's nose was twice the size it was the last time he saw him. His face was also plastered in foundation makeup and he wore opaque sunglasses. He perched himself on the corner of the older man's desk, folded his arms and faced Jim. When he spoke, his voice was icy with venom.

"It seems like our girl likes to play games. Now, normally I don't mind a gal playing hard to get, but she is taking the teasing a bit too far." Slimey slowly removed his sunglasses and revealed two swollen eyes. The makeup obviously masking severe bruising. The whites of his eyes were replaced by deep red making them look almost demonic. His pupils, a pair of onyx islands floating in crimson lava.

"Jesus! Did she do that to you?"

Slimey replaced his sunglasses.

"Booby trap I'm afraid." Said the Head of Section. "But it won't happen to you, forewarned is forearmed." The older man gave a nervous cough. "Er... could you give us a moment?"

Slimey stood up, took his cue and opened the door.

"I'll be waiting for you in the car." His voice cold with impatience.

Once they were alone, the older man smiled. "The work we do here is vital for the survival of the whole human species. Earth is, to use an analogy, a Garden of Eden.

And like a garden, it can tolerate only so many weeds. If these weeds are left to grow out of control, they can choke all life in, and eventually kill the whole garden."

So, there it was, the contempt human life is held in... fucking weeds.

His boss continued, "We Reapers have to prune back the weeds in order for the rest of the garden to survive. Whether morally acceptable or not, realistically it is the one and only solution to the doomsday course that mankind has set itself on."

Jim opened his mouth, but his boss held up a silencing hand.

"Hear me out Jim." He leaned back in his chair and interlocked his fingers. "They say the kids of today have never had it so well, with their iPads, smartphones and internet..." He suddenly frowned. "...bullshit! My generation..." He thumbed his chest. "...we had it all! Baby boomers we were called on account of all the procreation that war weary Britain's got up to in 1945, and the economic rewards we reaped. How many times Jim, have you had a smug bastard from my era ram it down your throat, that he could walk in and out of three to five jobs in a week and never have to claim unemployment benefit?" Jim nodded in agreement, not quite sure where all this was going.

"We had jobs coming out of our ears and more money than our parents had seen in their entire lifetime. We got the jobs, the prosperity, a guaranteed future, and when you left school Jim... the party sadly ended. What was your inheritance eh? Mass unemployment, strikes, inner city riots and a cold war that was realistically going to go nuclear. Oh, I nearly forgot... a global A.I.D.S plague. So, tell me Jim, how do we go from mass unemployment, social upheaval and soup kitchens of the 1930s to milk and honey in the 50s and 60s... then, go full circle with your generation having the same nightmare ride through society as your grandparents? Was it because my baby boomer generation were the hardest working entrepreneurial go getters in history and the 30s and 80s generations were bone idle lazy bastards?"

"No! Allow me to let you into a little secret that no baby boomer ever wants to admit to. That the reason why we went from bust in the 30s to boom in the 50s was that between 1939 and 1945 millions of men went away... and millions of men never came back. So, you see Jim, all our success is off the backs of dead heroes. Ever wondered how all those valiant heroes who paved the road to prosperity that my generation have rode, ended up dead... hmmm?"

"Hitler." Was Jim's bored reply.

His boss waved the suggestion away with his hand. "He was one man, but the actions of him alone didn't change the world. He was just a domino in a long chain... a chain that goes all the way back to the First World War. That very first domino was toppled by Gavrilo Princip."

Jim furrowed his brow. This clearly amused the older man.

"Come now Jim, you an ex teacher not heard of the man who shaped the 21st century?"

"I must've been off that day. What did he invent, condoms?"

A wide smile preceded the reply. "No Jim, he didn't stop life forming, he took life. He was an assassin."

The head of section tapped his pen in mild annoyance on his desk to hammer home his point. "Lee Harvey Oswald and John Wilkes Booth both killed American presidents. Did nations crumble and empires fall because Kennedy and Lincoln were slain? Alas, as much as America thinks the world revolves around them, the world carried on as normal once their glorious Commanders in Chief were cold in the ground." He let out a self-satisfactory sigh. "No, the world exploded into world war one, that created dissent in Germany, which ultimately led to world war two. All because of the actions of one man. Pol Pot slaughtered thirty million. Stalin buried twenty million... but the one bullet from Gavrilo Princip's gun cost in human life across two world wars over fifty million people."

Jim sat there in stunned silence as the doomsday sermon continued.

"One man can make a difference. So, you see Jim, compared to Gavrilo Princip, Herr Hitler was a fucking amateur by comparison."

"On the 28th June 1914, the heir to the throne of Austria-Hungary, Archduke Franz Ferdinand and his wife Sofia paid a state visit to Sarajevo the principle capital of

Bosnia. Princip was a member of the infamous Black Hand gang intelligence department in the Serbian army."

"Look what's all this…"

"Patience Jim…" Said the older man in a calming voice. "The bullet that Gavrilo Princip fired into Franz Ferdinand's neck that day changed the world forever… a lot like the way the world will change again, when you kill the American congressman Daniel O'Brien."

The hairs on Jim's neck were standing on end.

"When you kill him… Gavrilo's legacy of 50 million will be nothing once we expand into America." Jim was aware his nostrils were flaring, and his breathing was reaching panicking levels. The situation was snowballing out of all proportions. He had to try and wrestle back some control. "Wh… who is in control of the Reaper program here? A… and why is this congressman's death so important to us expanding into America?"

His boss sat there for the best part of 10 seconds in serene silence before replying.

"Need to know basis dear boy."

His boss had played this card too many times for Jim's liking, but now the balance of power had shifted in the room. Jim took a big breath.

"So… you want me to murder an American congressman during a rabid hysterical 'war on terror' and I'm not allowed to know who I'm doing this for? Both here and stateside? I know the threat of death is constantly hanging over my head like the fucking sword of Damocles… but stop insulting my intelligence by thinking I'm an unquestioning sheep with the brains of a fucking rubber duck!"

The trademark briefcase was open on his boss's desk. The sheets of clear plastic still lined the floor of the office.

302

A quick flick of the wrist and the silenced Mauser pistol would be produced and end the living torment that was Jim's every waking day.

It never came.

A line was crossed. Nobody came back from that line. His late friend Simon Wilson crossed it and now... so had Jim.

In those brief moments as he waited to be shot through the skull, he almost found a tranquillity and inner peace he had not found in the last five years. Almost an acceptance of his fate. No more worry. No more pain. No more killing. He closed his eyes and tilted his head back inhaling possibly his last breath. He didn't get a bullet... he got a smile.

"Oh Jim, it was never our intention to keep you in the dark, only the security of the bunker is paramount".

"So, who am I working and killing for? Or am I just a mushroom?"

His boss finished the quip for him. "Kept in the dark and fed on shit? Okay Jim, you win." He then delved into his case and produced a small business card. He handed this to Jim. It read "Joshua Goodchild CCO Warriors for Christ." Jim flipped it over and there was a handwritten note: "To Hugo, swear to God... and hope to die. Joshua ".

Jim looked confused as he handed the card back to his boss who nonchalantly placed it in his desk tidy along with various desk clutter. He smiled at Jim.

"Our American benefactor gave that card to our British benefactor... who in turn, gave it to me. So, you see, we are well connected. I suppose since after you've killed that bitch journalist and the yank politician, you'll be management, so to speak. You deserve to be privy to the company's secrets." Jim's eyes went wide.

"Yes Jim, you will be in charge here at the bunker. Your days of killing and getting your hands bloody are nearly at an end."

This really stunned Jim. It was the last thing he was expecting.

"Wh... what about Singen? I thought he would..."

"He will initially be head of section until he has trained you up... and then he is off to be head of section in Europe." He smiled again.

"As for me, I'll serve out my retirement training the American Reapers. So, you see Jim, your future is looking bright."

Chapter 91

The bunker's electronic lock buzzed shut behind Jim as he turned up the collar on his drab winter coat and made his way to his rendezvous. He cast a quick glance skywards at the tinted window three stories up opposite the bunker's alleyway. He was being watched by omnipotent eyes and he fucking hated it. At least God had a day off... these fuckers never slept. Yet the constant surveillance was secondary in his mind as he was still reeling from the aftershock of being finally told his employer's true identity.

Sir Hugo Montgomery, the disgraced ex Tory minister and international arms broker. Jim smiled at this sanitised description of soulless merchants of death. Jim wondered when would do gooding pop stars wake up and realise hunger isn't keeping Africa in the unenviable position of being perpetually bottom of the third world. No, it is gun running bastards like Hugo who sell warring factions the means to blow each other back to the Stone Age on a daily basis. If you lived in a war-torn African hell hole what would speak loudest to you: the rumbling of your stomach? Or the rumbling of one of Sir Hugo's newly purchased Apache helicopter gunships blowing your village to smithereens?

Not content with slaughtering the innocents of the third world, he now focused his sights on the first. Hugo's visions for the Reaper project as revealed by the Head of section were very much akin to the cutthroat ways he ran all his other businesses. Namely, if your company was overstaffed, you laid people off. Unfortunately for the inhabitants of planet Earth who found themselves on the list, this had more sinister connotations. Sir Hugo used part of his vast fortune to fund the Reaper project which would explain the endless supply of money. Money that paid for all their bonuses, money that paid for all the weaponry, gadgets and resources for each execution... and money that would pay for Jim's new promotion.

Promotion.

Here he was, constantly plotting his escape from this conscripted nightmare and he was soon to be in charge of the whole operation, with forty killers under his command.

His chances of escape were growing slimmer by the minute.

As Jim walked through the busy litter and shit strewn streets near Piccadilly to meet Slimey he considered his immediate future. Well, his C.V. would certainly need updating when he slaughtered the U.S. Congressman. Jim had heard of this man from media news bulletins. He was known as a man who wanted to clean up politics in Washington. A man of integrity. A man who couldn't be bought... and Jim was going to kill him. That dark cloud over Jim's head just grew blacker. Another good man dies so a bad man can prosper. His thoughts drifted to his murdered friend Simon Wilson.

So, who was the bad man here?

The U.S. backer of the Reaper project, Joshua Goodchild, a right-wing evangelical Senator who owned the biggest private army on the planet. A man who vehemently believed that the biblical end of the world prophesies were soon to come to fruition. And this religious maniac was doing everything in his considerable power to make this rabid rapture a reality. This was the despicable being that Jim was going to protect by culling the one man who could stop Goodchild's genocidal crusade. His boss had called Jim the 21st century Gavrilo Princip.

Jim was always adamant as a young fresh-faced boy with a head full of dreams that he was going to change the world. That old phrase reverberated round his skull like an angry trapped wasp… be careful what you wish for.

Chapter 92

Bobbie Mcvie didn't know how much time he had left to save the lady reporter, or for that matter if he was too late at all. In desperation he took a chance and decided to knock on all fourteen flat doors until he found her. He need not have bothered as he hit the jackpot on his very first knock. The old age pensioner on the ground floor, opposite the electricity cupboard he recently used as an observation point, she pointed him in the direction of the top floor flat. With the aid of Bobby's charm and a skip full of bullshit... "Long lost sister."

He raced up the staircase 3 steps at a time without breaking a sweat and rang her doorbell twice... nothing. Was he going to find her with her throat cut if he had to break in? The walls decorated in a kaleidoscope of her bodily fluids? The image snapped out of her mind as the door opened sharply a couple of inches, held by a stout door chain.

Despite the dark circles round her eyes, he recognised her instantly from her newspaper photo he'd torn from the tabloid. Her eyes were wild and scared... the 12-inch serrated blade she held threateningly in the gap in the door only compounded her deranged demeanour.

"I know who killed your friend... and I know where they took him before he died."

She looked unconvinced and was about to slam the door when he jammed his foot in the door. "Look love! If I was the one who was going to kill you, do you think that poxy chain or that bread knife would stop me?" It was harsh, but she had to listen, and he didn't have time to indulge her mounting hysteria. He softened his voice now.

"My name is Bobby Mcvie. I used to be a soldier and the same people who butchered your friend, killed my friend Declan Hannah."

She found her voice. "The same two?"

"There's more than two. I counted five in black boiler suits and one guy dressed like a stockbroker. I think he was in charge." His head snapped back and forth scanning the corridor. He lowered his voice to almost a whisper.

"I know the one who was in charge come here today dressed as a woman... and left with his face smashed in." He smiled at her. "Fair play to you love... but he'll be back with reinforcements. You won't get lucky twice." The door closed slightly after checking the soldier's foot wasn't there, and then she hesitated.

"Wh... what is it you want?"

"The same as you... the bastards who killed my friend. Look, I know you're scared. But like I said, if I was here to kill you... that chain wouldn't stop me."

The door slowly closed. The chain rattled and then swung wide open.

Once he was inside, she put the chain on again… but still nervously held onto the serrated blade in her hand. She cleared her throat and addressed the stranger.

"You said there were six of them. And If they do come back, what can you do?"

Bobby replied, "Like I said, I was a soldier… I used to kill people for a living."

Chapter 93

Singen slowly applied the handbrake and switched off the engine. The short car journey across the city to the female journalist's flat had been a silent one. Jim lost in thoughts of dread at killing a woman… and Singen almost drooling for sadistic bloody revenge.

"So, Jim how does it feel to be almost management?"

Despite the gloomy night-time interior of the car and the dark sunglasses, Jim felt those evil bloodshot eyes were mocking him.

"I… I'm lost for words."

It brought back countless encounters of being cornered by a pub snarler. Nothing you could say could stop what was about to happen to you… so you say nothing. That fucking cocky smile again. Slimey's black mood was lifting. Then again, he always did get like this before a kill. He had got the scent of blood in his nostrils.

"Not like you, Jim. Not like you at all. Oh, tell me you are not still squeamish about culling a female are you?" Jim closed his eyes in a vain hope of blocking out this nightmare. That creepy low chuckle snapped them back open.

"Oh, what is it? Some chivalrous romantic notion that men are the life takers and women are the life givers?" Singen reached foreword and clicked the release catch on the glove compartment. The heavy object within caused the drawer to open with a thud. The automatic light illuminated the object. It was a silenced semi-automatic Glock handgun. Slimey reached in and brought out the gun's separate magazine and held it up for Jim's inspection.

"These dear Jim, are the next evolution in killing people." A silly little smile played on his lips as if he were a child setting eyes on his first bike at Christmas. He continued,

"A.P.L.P's... or Armour Piercing Limited Penetration rounds. These little beauties are created using what the arms manufacturers call "A blended metal process.""

"Oh... dum dum bullets." Said an unimpressed Jim.

"Oh hardly... these are the Rolls Royce of dum dum bullets. They will bore through steel like a knife through butter, but they will not pass right through the human body. Instead, they are designed to shatter just inside the entry wound and destroy everything, tissue, bone and organs, leaving totally untreatable wounds. It is the equivalent of being hit by a mini exploding round."

Jim jumped as Singen slammed the magazine into the handle of the Glock and quickly clicked back the top slide, chambering the first round.

He pointed the gun at Jim.

"And if you aren't out of her flat within twenty minutes with good news for me, then I'm going up there to empty this whole fucking magazine into her."

He lowered the gun and passed Jim a small canvas bag. "Give her my love."

Jim stepped out of the car, his legs starting to shake as he crossed the road. He nervously looked at his watch. He had just twenty minutes to save the woman journalist's life... and his own.

Chapter 94

Cassandra re-set her claw hammer burglar alarm. "Old Faithful" had a 100% success rate and had brought her more comfort and peace of mind than the homeless soldier hiding in her hot water tank cupboard, clutching a razor-sharp carving knife. It wasn't her cutlery; his dishevelled Boy Scout had brought his own. Despite his repeated reassurances, she really did think she was about to die when he produced it from the back of his jeans.

She sipped at her coffee and her eyes flickered from the front door to the cushion beside her on the couch. Her own serrated carving knife lay underneath and within quick reach. If push came to shove, could she really plunge this blade deep into another human? She'd nearly lost a finger chopping carrots with this blade, so the assailant had a 50/50 chance. The gentle ticking of the gold carriage clock on her coffee table was the only sound in the room. She had never noticed the ticking before. It was getting on her fucking nerves now. Like a ghoulish time-bomb counting down the seconds till the killer arrived and ended her torment. It was going in the bin on Monday. A man at the front door and a spare in the cupboard. A murderer and a hero. But which one was in her cupboard? Typical! She hadn't had a man in two years and now she had two fighting over her body. Again, she looked over to the door of her hot water tank cupboard. It was open a hair's breadth so he could view the killer before he struck. The gaudy clock told her he had been in there for an hour and a half... she hoped he wasn't wanking.

Apart from shadow boxing, it was the only exercise most of these tramps get.

Sitting in silence had heightened her senses as she heard the unmistakable sound of her letterbox opening. She clamped a hand over her mouth to stifle a scream as she saw the fingers poke through the black brush strip on the back of her door. Like huge fat swollen maggots these probing digits wriggled around searching... until they touched the fishing line trip wire pulled taut across the door. "Old Faithful "twitched in anticipation of cutting the toothpaste bill in half of the intruder on the other side of that door. The fingers disappeared. Seconds later a long pair of scissors poked through the letterbox and after several snapping attempts, snipped the fishing line. Hyperventilating now, she resisted the urge to grab for the carving knife; the soldier had told her to let him get into the flat and leave her mortice lock unlocked. And here she was, staked out like a lamb for the slaughter... *just like Marty*.

Was this going to end in some sick poetic justice for her slain friend?

A new noise drew her attention now. Her front door night latch shot back into the lock case with a metallic click. Slowly her impenetrable front door swung open and there he stood... the man of her dreams. Their eyes met and he softly spoke.

"Don't scream."

Chapter 95

He had closed the door slowly behind him and took a couple of steps towards her as she flinched. He stopped and dropped the small black bag he was carrying and held up his palms in a placating gesture.

"Please... I'm not going to hurt you. Y... you are in terrible danger. You have to get out of this flat now."

Her hand was under the cushion and curled around the knife's handle. She shot a glance at the cupboard door. Had her Rambo fallen asleep? Possibly. A hot water tank cupboard would be like a penthouse suite at the Hilton to a soap dodger. Either way, if she didn't protect herself, this fucker would gut her here and now. The intruder reached into his crumpled baggy winter's coat and the material bulged under the armpit as he pulled the object free.

"I've got something for you."

Cassandra shot to her feet and brandished the knife before he could draw his gun. There was a flash of black behind him as the soldier burst out of the cupboard and pinned his knife across the killer's throat.

"Drop it or I'll cut your fucking head off!"

She saw blood start to drip from beneath the blade. It

was obvious now that this tramp was not lying about his former career. The killer frozen in time, terrified to move, dropped the object. When she looked down, she saw it wasn't a gun. It was money… a lot of money.

She walked forward and picked up the four-inch bundle of twenty-pound notes.

"Killers don't usually tip their victims."

He replied as best he could, his Adam's apple touching the serrated blade as he tried to speak. His voice a mixture of fear and desperation.

"I'm not here to… to kill you. I'm here to save you. Take the money… th… there's five grand… get out of London… n… now."

She ran the blade along the edge of the bundle causing it to whirr like a mini fan.

"And if I don't?"

She felt a lot more defiant with her unwashed guardian holding this serial killer at knife point. He spoke again,

"Th… the man w… who came here today to kill you. The one whose nose you smashed in. H… he's downstairs in a car with a gun. I… if I don't tell him you're dead in fifteen minutes, he's coming up here to finish you off."

The soldier still held the stranger at knife point and used his free hand to vigorously search him. "He's unarmed."

"Why are you helping me?" She lowered her knife; the soldier did no such thing.

His eyes, still understandably frightened, darted to the soldier then back to her.

"B… because you are the only one who can save me. They've killed thousands… and when they expand into America and Europe… millions will die."

She stepped closer to him. "They? Who the fuck are "they?"

He hoarsely replied, "Reapers."

Chapter 96

The twenty minutes were up. The soldier and the journalist peered through the bushes at the side of her block of flats. The pair of them saw the stranger named Jim furtively approach a car parked opposite her front communal door entrance and lean in towards the open vehicle's window. Seconds later, the smartly dressed killer leapt out of the car and slammed shut the door. They both recognized him even in the dim streetlight, despite his facial injuries and swollen nose. He strode across the road to her building, tucking a black long object into his coat as he went. Jim followed meekly behind him.

They waited in silence for a full 10 seconds, and then Bobbie Mcvie all but dragged her at breakneck pace through various back gardens until they emerged into an alleyway. They hailed a taxi and were soon speeding through London's busy streets, Bobbie constantly looking through the taxi's back window for the entire journey. Cassandra just stared at the three bulging bin bags that Bobbie had hastily packed for her. One contained warm clothing, her laptop and Marty's files on disc, another, tinned food and basic toiletries, the third a sleeping bag. A sleeping bag! Where the fuck was he taking her? As she contemplated her nocturnal sleeping arrangements, Bobby abruptly halted the cab 10 minutes into the journey. She paid the driver and his red taillights diminished into the distance leaving them alone in the dark beside derelict boarded up buildings in a litter strewn street.

"We walk from here."

It was an order, not a request. For two miles they yomped (for the ex-soldier only seemed to go at that pace) over the wrecks of former factories and burnt out cars until quite breathlessly, she stopped next to large graffitied corrugated iron fence.

"W… wait!" She gasped, adjusting the strap on her shoulder bag that was now digging into her.

"I'm not going any further until you tell me where we're going. I'm exhausted." He took a step closer to her.

"I'm taking you to my place." Bobbie then nodded his head towards a gap in the metal fence.

Despite the poor light she could see the tramp's cardboard makeshift shanty town spread out beneath the motorway flyover. The inhabitants of the warm dry cars travelling over it blissfully unaware of the sea of human misery and despair beneath them. Cassandra squinted to focus on the small dots of flickering light that illuminated these broken wretches huddled round their flickering warmth like foul smelling satellites. Wide eyed, she snapped her head back in his direction.

"You have got to be fucking joking?! I… I can't live…"

He cut her short.

"Would you rather die?" His face stern as he spoke to her. "You heard what that guy at the flat said. They can hack into C.C.T.V. cameras, bank cash machines and track phone signals. If you spend money, make a mobile phone call or are seen on camera… they can find you." He nodded again towards his home.

"Technology hasn't touched this place." He gently gripped her shoulder to reassure her. "You'll be safe here." Sighing heavily, she stepped through the gap in the fence and left civilization behind.

Chapter 97

"I understand the importance, but we can't kill her if we can't find her, can we?" The Head of section had been at this repetitive merry go round conversation with Sir Hugo for over half an hour now. The phone almost melting his ear as he rolled his eyes skywards for the umpteenth time. Jim and Singen sat opposite him in his office in the bunker and watched in silence. Slimey was inwardly enjoying seeing the older man take a verbal pummelling off the Peer of the Realm. Jim's stomach was turning cartwheels, trying to control his body language in case his duplicity was unearthed. The phone call was abruptly ended. The Head of section gently cradled the receiver with the final expletive still jangling round his aching ear drum. Their boss closed his eyes and gently massaged the bridge of his nose between his thumb and forefingers. When he opened them, he spoke wearily. "So, you definitely think she's skipped town?"

Slimey cleared his throat and replied,

"Clothing was missing from her wardrobe, but her suitcases and sports bags are still there." His boss suddenly looked up.

"She didn't have time to pack?" He stood up now and paced back and forth on the plastic sheeting that lined his office floor.

"A woman running through the streets of London with an arm full of dresses will show up on a camera somewhere…"

Singen interrupted, "Our tech boys have hacked the C.CT.V. Cameras and memory banks of every mounted public camera within a five-mile radius of her flat within the last three hours. Her credit card pin numbers are all flagged and will give us her location the moment she taps them into a terminal."

His boss chipped in, "And her phone? "

"She's not used it yet, but the moment she does, we'll have her. Our boys are also dissecting her hard drive to see if she has received, or viewed the missing files that

Marty no doubt had sent on to her." The older man still paced, angry and frustrated that realistically, everything that could be done to find her, was being done.

Jim cringed in silence. It shocked him to actually be privy to the mechanics of how they tracked their prey.

The phone rang. It was an internal call.

"They are? Thank you, Derek."

He walked around the desk and opened the door. The two Reapers took their cue and walked dutifully through it past the pair of ever present black suited guards. All five of them stood on the metal gantry overlooking the 39 Reapers sat at their desks. As all eyes looked up towards their boss, Desi Shanks and his crew of mop up squad had placed a small black attaché case next to each Reaper on their desks.

"Gentlemen…" The Head of section addressed the Reapers below.

"All operations will cease effective immediately. Until further notice you will all have the same single target." He paused. "Open the cases on your desks please." The air was filled with the sound of metallic clicks as each attaché case was unlocked as they reached in and found a file of their latest kill... it was a woman. Each case also contained a silenced Glock high power pistol and 3 magazines of Sir Hugo's designer dum dum bullets packed in memory foam.

"Gentlemen... the time for subtlety is over."

Chapter 98

Bobby's ramshackle, makeshift home stood at the far end of the overhead motorway flyover, almost hidden by the piles of unwanted fridges and television sets. This is how the consumer society dream ended when you ate too much cheese before bedtime. The various tramps the pair of them passed barely gave them a second glance. Well, in their pickled condition, the double vision would've seriously distorted their perspective on life.

Bobby drew the vicious blade from the back of his jeans and darted into the dark plastic opening of his home. Cassandra heard matches being struck and the inside was suddenly illuminated with shimmering yellow.

Flickering candles…

Her heart beat faster and the urge to run was unbelievable. The last time she saw flickering candlelight, she witnessed Marty dead, in a bath of strawberry jelly.

Bobby's head popped through the flap of plastic sheeting and took the decision out of her hands.

"Get in! "He hissed. Against her better judgement she crouched down and entered Bobby's shack. Blinking as her eyes adjusted to the candlelight, she was pleasantly surprised at how comfortable it was. In the yellow flickering tea lights, she saw the ex-soldier light his makeshift stove. This heater/cooker comprised of a foot-high empty metal coffee can with holes punched through it. This mini furnace sat upon two house bricks with a metal tea tray beneath to catch any hot ash. At the top of the tin a metal petrol pump funnel was gaffer taped on and a length of garden hose secured to the tapered end in the same fashion and was threaded through the top of his plastic shack to act as a chimney. Within minutes the mixture of small pieces of wood and strips of linoleum fed into the two-inch square cut opening in the stove, resulted in a mini inferno that made Cassandra's fear of camping out diminish by the moment. Bobby rolled up her bags of clothing to make a mattress and lay her sleeping bag upon them.

"Make yourself comfy, I'll be back in a couple of hours."

Her eyes went wide.

"I'm coming with you! We agreed to meet him together." In the flickering yellow candlelight his smile looked demonic.

"There are some very determined men out there, who have already murdered your friend. They've been to your flat and picked your locks... twice." He held up a palm to silence her interruption.

"They know what you look like and according to our nervous little hit man with the huge wallet; you are the one person who can destroy their nasty organisation." She placed her laptop bag down on her makeshift bed and slipped off her shoes. Frantically rummaging through one of the bin bags of clothes he had packed for her, she proceeded to pull on a pair of jeans whilst lying on her back.

"Do I fucking look like a stay at home wife?!"

She fastened her jeans and discarded her skirt. Bobby shook his head and chuckled "No, no you don't. Not with that mouth anyway. Okay, you win. Dress warm, it's going to be a long night."

Chapter 99

Jim cursed as he slipped on rubble in the dark. He rubbed the damp soil from his hands but sniffed it anyway just to make sure. The dogs in London seem to track his every move by some sort of canine telepathy and placed copious amount of their arse porridge in his path wherever he roamed. So much so, that he no longer wore his beloved all-weather Timberland boots. The sheer misery of decanting a mongrel's bowel movement from the corrugated soles with a wooden ice lolly stick like a foul smelling Toblerone just wasn't worth it anymore. He squinted at the inky blackness of the disused railway arch.

Every instinct told him that no good would come from entering that dark foreboding abyss. Feeling very vulnerable, he kept looking over his shoulder expecting to be attacked at any moment. He gingerly edged foreword, pulling the collar of his heavy puffer jacket up to shield him against the cold night air. Or was it harking back to his childhood, pulling the blankets up to ward off the omnipresent Bogey Man? After all those fortuitous nights of fending off that infamous night-time demon, Jim feared tonight would be the night he would finally have to pay the piper. In times of crisis and fear, it is natural for a mind to drift back to a safer time, and for Jim that was always with his Dad. Jim's Mother had died during his birth, so not only was his Father his soul parent, his protector and provider, he was also his hero. Those were dark times, but the old man supported and nurtured him as a boy and took him out for his very first pint when he was a man. He supported Jim through teacher training college and did his best to hide his disappointment when Jim dropped out and drifted aimlessly. He had a dry, razor sharp wit, which he passed onto his only son. And one which he kept right up to his dying day in hospital. Jim received the phone call whilst he was working at the department of statistics; at least he went in his sleep. Two weeks later, Jim was in another job… this job.

He stood there in silence under the decaying railway arch and very slowly, his eyes started to adjust to the darkness. He could just make out shapes of discarded consumer goods. Fridges missing their doors, televisions missing their screens and a burnt-out Mercedes missing its MOT certificate. It was then that a sudden break in the clouds suddenly bathed everything in pale blue moonlight. Despite being alone, his nerves started to calm as the welcome Luna light show illuminated his surroundings.

His jaw dropped when he saw the figure hanging from a rope suspended from a metal beam that bisected the archway. The eerie figure was in silhouette against the contrasting moonlight coming from the opposite side of the railway arch. Jim had seen a lot of death…some of it he had caused, yet to be in close proximity to a hanging corpse was enough to make his legs involuntarily shake. Panicking, he delved into his coat pocket and produced a brass Zippo lighter with an engraved cartoon picture of Elvis Presley eating his final cheeseburger on the toilet. It was a veritable Faberge egg... for people devoid of taste. Jim let out an exasperated laugh when in the flickering glow of his petrol lighter; he saw the swinging dead body... was a makeshift canvas punch bag.

"Shut that fucking lighter now!"

Jim spun round and in the yellow light saw the soldier who had held him at knife point in the reporter's flat earlier that night.

"I said shut that lighter!" The threat was hissed in a low voice. A metallic click rendered the arch way in darkness once more. In the ten seconds silence that had elapsed, well apart from his heart banging in his chest, his eyes adjusted to the gloom once more. Jim let out a startled gasp as the soldier roughly frisked him with one hand and held the serrated blade with the other. Even in the poor light, the mere sight of this knife brought Jim to involuntarily touch the small wound on his neck it had inflicted on their earlier encounter.

"Your clothes, are they new?" It wasn't a casual enquiry about fashion between one man and another. This Rambo tramp was somehow extremely proficient in anti-surveillance techniques and knew not only would Jim's flat be bugged, but every item of clothing he possessed would've had micro transmitters surreptitiously planted so that he would light up his employer's radar like a Christmas tree. After all, no one wants their dog to slip its lead.

"Y... yeah, I bought them all new at a supermarket, underwear and all, just like you told me."

Another voice spun Jim's head in the opposite direction, a woman's voice.

331

"You said I'm the only one that can save you. Well, if you want salvation... you'd better start talking."

Chapter 100

All the while Jim unburdened himself, Bobby Mcvie's head twitched and darted left and right, searching for the ambush that wasn't there. The secret cabal of ex Special Forces, ex coppers, pathologists, and intelligence officers who had crafted a mini genocide squad was shocking enough. Even the imminent assassination on British soil of an American congressman was itself the story of the decade, but to Cassandra, the identity of the man behind it all totally stunned her:

Sir Hugo Montgomery.

The bloated, blue blooded bastard who was responsible for her languishing in perverts publishing purgatory. The man whose revenge for her journalistic diligence left her the ostracised leper of Fleet Street. After the initial shock, she finally found her voice.

"Why is he doing this? His stock and trade was arms dealing. Killing random strangers yields no profit for him. Why the hell would he risk everything when there is no benefit to himself? It makes no sense."

Jim sighed wearily. This last roll of the dice confession was mentally draining him. "Maybe not to you, but to them it's almost a religion. What you have to understand is, they are playing the long game. Boom and bust economies, stock market crashes and global wars all have one major factor that drives them: overpopulation."

"Bullshit! The world's not that black and white." She snarled.

Jim held up his palms.

"Hey! It's not my philosophy, I was just conscripted... at gun point." Cassandra shook her head incredulously.

"They actually believe this shit? And then, force you and your colleagues to go out and kill for them?"

"Yes, they do believe this, without question. In the old days a war could be engineered and prolonged until the population was brought down to acceptable stock market quotas... then Vietnam changed all that."

She stepped towards him in darkness. "What do you mean?"

He continued his voice slightly croaky, a mixture of this intense interrogation and nerves.

"The masses were usually taken from the soup kitchens and dole queues and then dumped into the trenches to await their imminent slaughter. It was in a sense a human abattoir that you were never realistically expected to return from. They weren't sent to fight; they were sent to die. As Sir Hugo's bank manager will tell you, nothing makes money more than war." Bobby looked over at Jim now intrigued.

He continued, "With Vietnam, it was as if whole populations of countries suddenly woke up. What was the zeitgeist chant of the era?" It was a rhetorical question.

"Hell no, we won't go." Bobby answered it for him.

Jim smiled at the unexpected reply.

"That's right, "Hell no, we won't go.""

The Reaper looked up from beneath the railway arch which was once again bathed in pale Moon light through the shifting clouds and nervously ran his hands through his tousled dark hair. "You see, at that point in time after Vietnam, no young man, with his life ahead of him was going to throw it all away to protect rabid greed of a select few. In short, "Fuck your wars, I'm going surfing!""

Cassandra could hold her tongue no longer, though the urge to step in and tear apart his explanation had been overwhelming, the journalist in her told her she needed him to talk.

"So... the cure for famine, pestilence and global war is a group of underachieving office clerks, press ganged into secretly culling the population?" The cold sarcasm dripped from every syllable as she spoke. Apologetically Jim blurted out,

"Look, I... I know you find it hard to believe..."

"I don't." Said Bobby. "I've seen this all before."

Cassandra looked quizzical at Bobby as he spoke.

"Boy soldiers in Angola and Sierra Leone, some as young as twelve are kidnapped by local war lords and taken out into the bush. They are trained to use machetes and AK47s and are given a very stark choice: kill or be killed."

Jim was nodding silently in the shadows, almost overwhelmed with emotion, here was another soul who actually understood his nightmare situation and the hopeless trap he was in. Bobby paced as he spoke,

"It's amazing really, those boys' spindly little arms heaving a huge machete. Carving up grown men like they were slicing bread."

She screwed up her face at this gruesome recollection.

"Boys with their toys, eh?"

The reporter instantly regretted this infamous feminist jibe.

Bobby jabbed a finger close to her face.

"They don't fucking do it to be macho! They do it because they'll end up dead if they don't!" He saw the fear in her eyes at this outburst and softened his tone.

"But you are right, they are boys... they just want to live long enough to become men."

Jim's smile was soon wiped from his face as Bobby reared on him.

"And you! You're going to give me the full lay out of that bunker and observation post across the alleyway. I want the full number of armed personnel, the location of the armoury, calibre of weapons, alarm systems, and I want the bastard in charge of that facility. You know the one... the fucking one who orders dog attacks."

Blinking rapidly at Bobby's onslaught, Jim stammered,

"A... and then what are you going to do?" In the pale Moonlight, Bobby's tight smile sent shivers through Jim.

"I'm gonna make those fuckers scared of the dark!"

Cassandra gently stamped her feet to vainly ward off the cold gnawing its way through the soles of her boots. It wasn't working. She prided herself that as a journalist, she was a master of extracting information from uncooperative sources. Yet this ex-soldier was like a surgeon, meticulously extracting what he needed from Jim's skull and discarding anything that did not suit his purpose. The Reaper looked visibly punch drunk as his cranium was drained like a used tea bag, until the soldier was satisfied Jim was holding nothing back or had anything more useful to offer.

Then, very coldly, this mental rapist took a step closer to Jim.

"Thank you, you've been very helpful. Go home; go back to work as normal…" He then gently grabbed the collar of Jim's bubble jacket. "…and dump these clothes."

"What about the congressman? I'm supposed to kill him in two days-time."

Bobby replied as he adjusted the collar on his own long coat against the wind. "Then for two days they won't let you out of their sight. They'll be watching you…" He thumbed his hand over his shoulder towards the reporter.

"…they'll be hunting her… and seeing as they don't know I exist… they'll never know what hit them!"

Chapter 101

Mervin Foster could no longer buck his obligations. He had spent his whole day coordinating his hack pack on the biggest story in his newspaper's lurid history: Mickey Mullet's imminent funeral. He needed to keep the grieving porn star widow sweet, so the whole tone of his rag's coverage needed to be a puff piece. Local boy done good. Self-made man who loved his Mother. Mervin smiled to himself at this thought as he travelled to his penthouse via his private lift. Mickey Mullet, Mummy's boy. Mervin loathed the Poms with their fucking inbred antiquated class system. Even with his own self-made millions and over generous donations/bribes to successive Pommie governments, they would never accept him.

The outsider.

Despite his open vocal hatred of their parasitical Royal family, he secretly yearned for a knighthood. This exiled antipodean orphan was aching for his adopted stepmother to bestow some praise upon him. Yet the establishment's sneering snobbery at his country's penal colony ancestry sickened him to his very core.

Land of Hope and Glory?

Not if you were an Aussie it's fucking not!

And it was this nation that is now about to give a Pommie criminal a state funeral that would make Gandhi's... look like Eleanor Rigby's.

The lift doors whirred open and he saw Sir Hugo sat at his desk.

"What the fuck?"

It wasn't so much the fact that his penthouse security had been breached by a Peer of the Realm that had stopped Foster in his tracks; it was his hacker bleeding from the mouth, on his knees with a silenced gun pointed at his head. The gunman was immaculately dressed in a sharp black suit and opaque sunglasses. The gunman spoke. "Don't even think about stepping back into that lift."

Mervin jumped as the decision was made for him as the lift doors closed behind his back cutting off any escape. Still sat defiantly at Foster's desk, Sir Hugo beckoned the publisher forward with a genial smile. The kneeling hacker shook uncontrollably with the silencer firmly against his temple.

"Mervin dear boy, your little rat here has told us that you have some files on your laptop that we have been looking for."

Foster's slim black laptop was open facing Sir Hugo. The mere presence of his private hacker bleeding profusely from the mouth told Mervin that any denials were futile. He straitened his back and tried to compose himself, take charge of the situation. "Look here Hugo, what the fu..."

The unmistakable "Phutt!" sound preceded the hacker's head yanking violently to one side as a section of his frontal lobe erupted in a crimson shower splattering Mervin's cream carpet. The gentle swirling cloud of cordite emanated from the silencer's muzzle as the hacker slumped to the floor.

The whiskey glass shook in Mervin Foster's hand. Alcohol was the last thing on his mind, but Sir Hugo had insisted on it. The Australian, in his murky career had paid for people to be killed, in his early days of the cutthroat world of publishing. But this was the first time he had seen one actually executed in front of him. The lumps of grey glistening brain lay like remote islands in a sea of crimson. The bile rising in his throat told Mervin that he may just add some more stains himself to this gory shag pile.

Hugo could see the effect the late hacker was having on his publisher friend and clicked his fingers at his lethal lackey.

"Cover that up, would you."

The smartly dressed gunman disappeared into Mervin's en-suite bathroom and reappeared with an armful of towels, which he proceeded to drape over what was left of the hacker's head.

"It's always a shame to let good staff go." Hugo's tone was mocking. The morbid silence broken, Mervin met Hugo's gaze. His hacker's killer stood vigilantly, one hand resting casually over the one that held the silenced Glock. He smiled as he spoke. "Did you enjoy seeing my little home movie? "Mervin gulped hard as the guessed the gunman meant the covert CCTV footage of Marty's murder on the files they retrieved.

Then it dawned on Mervin as he looked at this killer that he was the same one who had murdered Marty on the files.

That icy smile again. "He was a hacker as well."

Hugo stood up and waddled his humungous frame around the desk and stepped gingerly over the fresh corpse.

340

"Will you just look at the mess that little bitch has caused." Mervin's eyes flicked nervously to the slain hacker, then back to the Peer.

"Has she contacted you?"

Foster sighed "No. No she hasn't. H... have you tried her flat?"

"Of course, we've tried her fucking fl..." Hugo held up a silencing hand to his volatile minion.

"Come now, be nice to Mr Foster. After all, he's one of us now."

The publisher arched his eyebrows. "Eh?"

"A line has been crossed dear boy." He waved casually at the corpse. "How many years do you seriously think you could do in HMP Belmarsh? I'd say when the murder squad get here; your infamous legal team will be waving the white flag. Life... no parole, you will die inside I can guarantee it. But... I can make all this go away, like it never happened. All you have to do is set that little bitch up for us." He walked over to the lift and pressed the call button. His lackey with the sunglasses picked up Mervin's laptop and dutifully joined his Master by the lift. The doors whirred open and both men walked in. Mervin put down his glass and stood up.

"Set her up? H... how? I honestly don't know where she is? She could've skipped the country." Hugo straightened his silk tie and stopped the lift doors closing with his hand.

"We have people watching the airports and ferry terminals. Trust me, she's still here. In two day's time, a drug Baron will have a vomit inducing funeral. She did an interview with the deceased and has met the widow. She will contact you, and when she does, I want you to get her to cover the funeral. Offer her armed protection, lots of money, even the editor's job if you have to. But get her there!"

The lift doors started to close. "Oh, and don't worry dear boy, my cleaners are downstairs and they'll take care of that nasty little stain on your carpet for you."

Chapter 102

Bobbie Mcvie had ignited his mini stove and turned his gloomy hovel into an oasis of warmth, on a bitterly cold night. She watched as he drew floor plans on scraps of paper with a chewed bookmaker's pen, of the Reaper's bunker and the manned observation post that protected it.

"You have me at a bit of a disadvantage, Bobby."

He looked up from his map in the flickering yellow candlelight.

"What?" was his puzzled reply.

"I mean, I know why I am here, hiding in a homeless makeshift..." she paused and looked around, searching for an adjective that would not offend her host. After all, it was this kind offer of a safe house that was prolonging her life.

"Shithole?" was Bobbie's emotionless reply. Cassandra suddenly went on the defensive "N... no! no, I wasn't going to say that. I... I meant makeshift..."

His face broke into a wide grin.

"Hello magazine are coming around to do a photo shoot next week."

She let out a little laugh, all tension broken now she realised that he was just teasing her. Smiling now, she continued,

"Anyway, I'm here in your sumptuous palace... (he grinned again, a charming smile) ...because crazy bastards are trying to kill me. But you don't seem crazy, alcoholic or one of life's losers. So, how did a trained soldier end up here?"

"Officially, I was a medic in the Royal Green Jackets. I went on to become a sniper. The Royal Green Jackets are the finest riflemen in her Majesties armed forces, their proud lineage dates back to Napoleonic times." He paused..." But unofficially, I was a sergeant in Air Troop of the SAS."

She looked up at him sharply.

He smiled again, "I know exactly what you are thinking; every shaven headed piss artist in every boozer up and down this land all lays claim to being in the Special Air Services." His eyes lowered now, deep in thought, lost almost in another moment in time. "But, for a time I was. Whether you believe me or not, it's not important."

"No, no, I believe you..." (not really sure or not whether she did or not, but this is the most conversation that she had got out of this enigmatic stranger since they were first thrown together) "...it's just you told me you were in the Royal Green Jackets and now..."

"The Royal Green Jackets were my parent regiment. The moment you pass selection for the SAS, you are informed to not tell anybody. So, as far as your family and friends are concerned, you are just a medic in the regular army."

Cassandra furrowed her brow "If your membership is such a closely guarded secret... how come you can tell me now?"

Bobby gave a weak smile.

"Because I'm not in the Regiment anymore... or the army. I'm... I'm nothing. I'm a "used to be.""

That phrase haunted her. *Used to be.*

These two lost souls had now found common ground in those three little words. He broke the uncomfortable silence by continuing.

"Plausible deniability" it's called. If you are killed during black ops behind enemy lines, your next of kin and the media will be informed that you died in action with your parent regiment."

She shook her head.

"So, the SAS just wash their hands of you? Pretend you never existed?"

He looked up and sighed,

"You have to understand, to an enemy, capturing and parading our tortured carcases on TV, would be like winning the World Cup. The secrecy isn't just for our government's embarrassment; it's for our very survival." The ex-soldier softened his tone now. "Anyway, they do give you a place in SAS history… they engrave your name on the clock tower in the parade ground in Hereford. It's symbolic"

She frowned again.

He answered the unspoken question.

"It's symbolic that you didn't beat the clock." She took a swig from a can of lemonade from one of the bin bags Bobby had quickly packed for her.

"Well you did, otherwise we wouldn't be enjoying this 5-star hotel now with hot and cold running piss."

He laughed now, she was softening him up, a skill she had honed on many a journalistic source over the years. His laugh slowed to a chuckle.

"I know what you want... but it's not a nice story, and it doesn't have a happy ending."

Cassandra wasn't sure whether she was overstepping the mark, but she reached out and touched his cheek.

"Bobby, I'm a journalist... if you cut me in half, the words "Nosey Bastard" would run right through me like a stick of Blackpool rock."

His head sagged slightly and in a low voice replied, "Okay."

The plastic sheeting that made up the walls and roof of Bobby's domain undulated in the rising winds. Yet despite the mini gales vain attempt to recreate the opening scenes from the Wizard of Oz, the warmth from the stove made it quite cosy inside.

"I was seconded to provide intelligence to an American Delta Force unit in Afghanistan, hunting insurgents who had obtained laser guided shoulder launched surface to air missiles. They had taken out four Black Hawk helicopters with these and the Yanks were baying for blood. The Delta Force are supposed to be the American equivalent of the SAS, but they still stampede into any theatre of operations like John Wayne with piles." She smiled as he continued.

"Anyway, the leader of this particular unit was a nasty little bully called Sheldon Cates."

"Sheldon?" lemonade shot out of her mouth as she laughed.

"I know, it explains a lot, maybe that Johnny Cash song "A boy named Sue" was more prophetic than we ever imagined? Well, after three weeks of hunting for shadows in the mountains and getting nowhere, we came across this little village and Lieutenant Cates ordered his men to round up every male within the vicinity at gun point." He looked broodingly into the flames of his mini stove.

"That's when the beatings started."

Cassandra felt her stomach tighten.

"In the heat of battle, information is power. The speed you get that information can determine whether your men live or die... basically, it's them or you."

She shifted uncomfortably now. "You mean torture?" He nodded.

"Sheldon got hold of this Afghan kid. Couldn't be no more than 16 and started to beat the living shit out of him. As far as Cates was concerned, they must know who is taking out their helicopters and where they were hiding. I told him that the boy knew nothing, but he just smiled and smacked the kid again. I mean, I'm no angel. I've done similar things... but to men, trained soldiers, not boys. So, I grabbed his arm to save the boy more pain... and Cates backhanded me across the face, split my lip." He let out a sigh and smiled.

"Then he laughed at me... unfortunately for lieutenant Cates, I have been training in Thai boxing since I was seventeen years of age. I have won nineteen of my twenty-two bouts, sixteen of them by knock outs." He then gave a thin cruel smile.

"That day ended rather badly for Mr Cates. I kicked that fucker all over the village square. I'm used to fighting barefoot, so my steel toe cap combat boots gave that

347

Southern hillbilly a severe makeover. He was big and strong, but his clumsy haymaking punches could've been seen by Stevie Wonder on a foggy day." He stared back into the flickering stove again as he recanted the memory.

"I seriously think that was the first time that poor little Sheldon had come second in anything."

"Character building." she said.

"Er... not really, you see getting his arse kicked in front of his men by a Limey slightly dented his gung-ho pride... so he pulled a knife and tried to stab me. Now a fist fight is one thing, but a knife is an attempt on my life. So, I did something very unprofessional."

Cassandra's eyes opened wide "Y... you killed him?"

"Wh... what? no, I didn't kill him... but he lost an eye. During the struggle to get the serrated blade off him we rolled on the floor and I made it look like an accident."

She felt quite unnerved at this cold admission.

"I popped his eye with his own blade, and the moment the knife went in, my soldiering career went pop too."

An uneasy silence hung in the air.

"He shouldn't have laughed. Within an hour he was medivaced out of there and I was under armed escort on my way to a military tribunal. The yanks don't take too kindly to one of their boys being turned into a Cyclops by a Limey. They wanted me extradited to face trial in the States, but the officers in Hereford said it was a regimental internal matter and over their fucking dead bodies would they hand me over. I was quite touched actually." He threw his hands skywards in the small confines of the shack.

"Then the politicians got involved!" She suddenly sat up at the mention of government involvement.

"What do you mean?"

"It turns out that poor little one-eyed Sheldon's Daddy is one of the Republican Party's biggest financial donors. A regular visitor to private functions at the White House. He pointed a finger at her.

"I made a very powerful enemy that day in Afghanistan. With his friends on Capitol Hill and our pussy whipped government doing everything to appease them, it was threatening to blow up into a full-scale diplomatic incident if I wasn't hog tied and put on the next plane to Washington. So, the Regiment did the only thing they could to protect me... they court marshalled me and kicked me out of the SAS and the army. My commanding officer warned me that Cates senior was apoplectic with rage and was rushing through my extradition warrant within the next 24 hours. He advised me to disappear. I moved from town to town and held down various menial jobs in the vain hope Daddy Cates would soon forget about me."

"And did he?" She enquired.

"Alas, no. The first of Cates's contract killers caught up with me as I finished my night shift at a supermarket in Leeds."

"Did you kill him? "She tentatively asked, not sure whether she really wanted to hear what came next.

"No, but if he ever came up behind me again, I'd hear the squeak of his wheelchair. He sent two more contenders, Columbians, real nasty bastards to my bed-sit in Glasgow five months later. Don't know how they found me, but Cates senior has a lot of contacts and resources. I decided to make an example of these two and cut their Achilles tendons so they could pass back the message I wasn't someone to be fucked with. The nearest they came was when the next guy narrowly missed me with a 38 Smith and

Wesson in Newcastle. It was then I realised Cates was fighting a war of attrition He knew my luck would run out one day... and so did I. So, I disappeared... dropped right off the radar. Where no private investigator or security camera could hunt me."

The journalist gestured around his humble abode. "You came here."

"Yes and no one has found me in nearly five years."

Chapter 103

Jim had a scheduled briefing about his imminent assassination of the American Congressman in fifteen minutes. He spent that time in the company of Julian, the bunker's makeup artist.

"You happy in your work Julian?" Was Jim's opening gambit. Time was short. He was taking a huge gamble and if it backfired and he had somehow misread Julian, then the only way he would leave this building would be through a severe case of lead poisoning. Julian's haunted eyes nervously darted to the Reaper, then back to the huge latex nose he was moulding on his work bench.

"Y… yeah, it's very interesting work." He beamed in a flamboyant way. But his usual upbeat demeanour seemed rather deflated today.

"A new challenge every day. I am a creator of chameleons."

Jim quickly glanced at his watch. As pleasant as this exchange of social pleasantries was, he needed to know where Julian's loyalties lay. Jim stepped closer to the younger man and surreptitiously glanced over his shoulder for prying eyes at the doorway to Julian's workshop.

"If you had a chance to leave your present employment and get your old life back, would you take it?"

Julian looked even more nervous now and looked away from Jim, almost cowering under his gaze.

"I… I'm very happy here… a… and the money is fabulous, I…"

Jim grabbed the makeup artist by the shoulder and spun him around.

"Julian! I'm not trying to trick you. This is not a test. On a daily basis, you disguise us Reapers so we can go out and anonymously murder people in cold blood. Innocent strangers…" Julian's frightened eyes started to moisten.

"… but we can only get clean away with it because of how good you are at your job. We are dressed to kill… by you"

His breathing was panicked, and his hands shook as he replied,

"I… I don't want to end up like Thomas Ludlow."

His reference to the errant Reaper, who deserted, sent a fresh shiver through Jim. Checking over his shoulder once more, Jim lowered his voice down to a whisper.

"I told you this is a private conversation." He removed his hand from Julian's shoulder. Julian screwed his eyes tight and then sharply opened them again.

"Okay… yes! If I could leave, and no one would come hunting for me with guns… then yes! I'd fucking run for the hills and never come back!"

Jim gave Julian a warm smile, and then walked towards the door.

"Me too." replied Jim before walking off.

Did Julian just unburden himself… or sign his own death warrant? He didn't know. Shaking now he buried his head

352

in his hands and waited for the footsteps along the corridor of the firing squad.

Chapter 104

Desi Shanks, head of the bunker's mop up squad was supervising a group of Reapers who were lined up at the underground gun range. Despite all the Glocks being fitted with suppressors, all the Reapers wore ear protectors.

As Jim passed the gun range's open door, he noticed there were very few crack shots amongst this conscripted crew. He smiled as he watched, musing that more damage would be done if they threw the dum dum bullets at the paper targets. This new thought tickled him further: dum dums firing dum dums.

The smile was soon wiped off his face when he turned away from the incompetent display of marksmanship and suddenly saw Slimey stood inches away from his face. Jim didn't even hear him approach. How long had that fucker been standing there? "Impressed?" was his opening gambit. Still, he wore his opaque sunglasses to mask the damage done by the lady reporter and her claw hammer door alarm.

"Oh yeah, best pacifist army I ever saw, Gandhi would approve."

Singen craned his neck to look over Jim's shoulder at the piss poor sharp shooting and Desi Shank's imminent nervous breakdown.

"For fuck sake lad! Aim the fucking thing! Jesus are you like this when you go for a piss?!" He then snatched the smoking pistol off the embarrassed Reaper and quickly grouped 4 rounds, millimetres from the bullseye on the paper target.

"See?" He pointed to his temple.

"Imagine there's a sweaty Gyppo at yer front door trying to sell you some lucky heather and you've only got one chance to shoot the fucker before he puts a Gyppo's curse on yer!" The admonished Reaper looked unsure.

"Is that what yer want? Coz that's what'll happen!"

Slimey put his hand on Jim's shoulder indicating that they should move on.

"Quite the motivational speaker, isn't he Jim"

"Oh yeah, it's right up there with "We shall fight them on the beaches.""

Chuckling now, as he straightened his black tie, they passed a group of tech boys feverously hunting for one particular phone signal on their scanning software.

"Don't be too harsh on them Jim, they don't need to be top marksmen." Together they climbed the gantry steps to their boss's office. He continued,

"With all 39 of them having three magazines, each containing twelve rounds of Sir Hugo's APLP ammunition, well... that's one tidal wave of hot lead she'll find it hard to surf."

The ever present black suited guards genially nodded as they entered the office.

Three Scotch's were poured and Jim surreptitiously glanced at his watch. Alas, not surreptitiously enough for Singen.

"Going somewhere? Hmmm?"

Jim, aware two suspicious pair of eyes were on him replied,

"Just counting down my date with destiny."

Chapter 105

On the Head of Section's desk lay a large detailed map of the graveyard where Mickey Mullet's carcass would serve eternity as a council estate for maggots, who, given the late gangster's diet of Lard and jellied whelks, would soon themselves die of heartburn.

"So, our chaps will all be dressed as grave diggers and take up positions around the funeral in sector D here." Pointed out his boss with the tip of his silver pen. He continued,

"Once our target is identified, all of our boys will cut her... and anyone else in our way down. Given the identity of the vermin in the casket, naturally it will be put down to a gang land slaying in which the female reporter "unfortunately" was caught in the crossfire."

All the while he talked; all Jim could focus on was that small object casually sitting in his boss's cluttered stationary holder. Almost hidden under post it notes, scraps of paper, receipts and paper clips. Jim thanked his lucky stars for this idiosyncratic desk clutter, that was so out of character for such a cold, clinical killer as his employer was. The clutter would mask the object's absence, when Jim stole it. From the very first time his boss first showed him it and then casually tossed it into his stationary tray; he surreptitiously checked its location hadn't moved, every time he visited this office.

Yet again, these two imposing psychopaths had robbed him of his manhood, as he regressed to being four years old again and raised his hand for permission to speak.

Singen and his boss both looked at each other, then at Jim.

"Yes?"

"Erm… just one question really..." said Jim.

"Once the shooting starts, in broad daylight... how are our boys going to escape? I mean, a gangster like Mullet is going to attract half of London's underworld to pay their respects."

"Go on..." Encouraged the older man, curious as to where this was leading.

"Well..." continued Jim nervously, "…naturally the bulk of the Metropolitan police are going to turn up to film or arrest the crème de la crème of Britain's underworld. There'll be armed response units, CID, serious crime squad, helicopters not to mention the local and international press and TV coverage... I mean, how can they possibly get away?"

Had he gone too far? After all, it takes a big man to admit he's wrong. It takes a fucking big idiot to get men with loaded guns to ever admit they are wrong.

His question was answered by the slamming down on the desk of a black metallic object the size of a tin of beans. The cylindrical object had a ring dangling from the top of it.

"Explosives?" Gasped Jim.

Slimey chuckled and tossed the object to Jim, who fumbled it as it clattered to the plastic sheeting covered floor. He shut his eyes tight and waited for his bollocks to be blown into orbit.

The two men's laughter opened his eyes.

"Oh Jim, you're fucking priceless!" Goaded Slimey, picking up the object.

"These are army surplus smoke grenades, used in war games training exercises at Aldershot. Courteous of our arms dealer and benefactor, Sir Hugo." Explained the Head of Section.

"Each one of these little beauties is capable of covering an area of a quarter of a mile in dense red smoke. When all 39 of our chaps drop the two canisters we give them, helicopters and spy satellites won't be able to spot our Reapers as they file out in an orderly fashion, dressed in the policemen's uniforms they will be wearing under their grave digger's overalls."

He then held up a florescent glow stick.

"Before the shooting starts, each man will casually snap one of these and drop them in the grass from their transport, in a line to the kill zone. In day light, they won't be seen. But in the impenetrable crimson mist... they will have a glowing runway that will lead them to freedom. These and the military issue night vision goggles each Reaper will be supplied with, will help them to kill any witnesses they bump into along the way of course."

Slimey chipped in,

"And to the two waiting coaches filled with extra ammunition and members of the mop up squad to help out if need be."

Both men smiled... like two smug toddlers who had just taken their very first big boys' shit in a potty, to a rousing family's applause.

"I've just spotted a flaw in your plan." said Jim.

Slimey removed his opaque sunglasses and cleaned the lenses with a tissue. All the while those red bloated eyes mocked him.

"Well, I for one am open to constructive criticism, aren't you?" He enquired theatrically to the older man who was warming to this game.

"Oh... oh I agree, yes! Er... carry on dear boy, I'm all ears."

The threats on his life he could handle... it was being the butt of their piss poor Laurel and Hardy routine that was gnawing away at his very soul.

Slimey's sunglasses now shielded the most hateful part of his face, as he and his boss were grinning in anticipation of whatever pointless drivel would emanate from Jim's mouth with all the eloquence of a wet fart.

"Well, isn't it a bit suspicious, all our Reapers dressed as grave diggers?"

His superiors glanced at each other, and then scowled at the young upstart.

"Grave diggers... work in graveyards. The clue dear boy is in the name." The Head of Section smiled now, clearly enjoying himself.

"What would you have us dress them as, pantomime horses?"

Jim wiped the smile off their faces.

"When was the last time you ever saw more than one, possibly two grave diggers working in your life? I bet the

Metropolitan police with all their experience, have never come across 39... in one graveyard, at any one time."

They both looked at the floor... Jim looked directly at the object on his boss's desk as he slowly edged nearer to it.

The colour was draining from their faces. As beautiful a moment as this was, watching these two public school ponces being mentally fucked over by a reject from the comprehensive system, Jim had to focus. Lives depended on it.

His own included.

"Rabbis."

They both spoke as one. "What?"

"Rabbis." Reiterated Jim, casually pacing the office in mock nonchalance, getting ever closer to the object on the desk.

"Think about it. Mavis, Mullet's grieving widow wanted a Jewish wedding." Jim smiled at the unconvinced Slimey.

"So, we give her the next best thing... a Jewish funeral."

Slimey's jaw dropped open "You've got to be fucking jo..."

"Hear me out!" Interrupted Jim. "Mavis trusts me. Well, the Rabbi I was dressed up as anyway, when I met her. So, if I contact her and say as a mark of respect in her newfound faith, we will send a party of holy Rabbis to attend Mickey's funeral... I'm sure she'd go for it. No coppers are going to frisk holy men at a funeral with the media watching."

The old man smiled, taking the bait.

"Let's face facts; you could hide a fair old arsenal of weapons under those respectable robes. And, amongst the crowds, they would be able to get very close to the lady reporter."

Singen eyed him with suspicion.

"You've changed your tune suddenly, haven't you?. Since you've come here, you've pissed yourself at the mere thought of killing a woman. We've mopped up your mess countless times and had to finish the job because you get stage fright when it comes to culling anything with tits... now all of a sudden you're Jack the Ripper?"

Jim was ready for this answer. He'd practiced the line of reasoning as he knew it had to be convincing as these men were no fools.

"I was informed after the lady reporter is dead... then the Yank Congressman, our Head of Section will go to America to train the Reapers there. You will go to Europe and train the Reapers there. And I, was promised the position of Head of Section here. It will make me rich, and I intend to thrive here. But I can't do that... until she is dead."

There was silence.

Then the Head of Section erupted,

"My god! Did you just see what he did?" He gushed, addressing Slimey.

"He just snatched victory out of the jaws of defeat!"

Slimey had a whiskey tumbler thrust into his hand, his eyes on the amber liquid being clumsily poured by the older man for fear it may spill over and stain his suit.

That was all the distraction Jim needed to snatch Joshua Goodchild's business card from the stationary tray on the desk and stash it in his pocket.

He was one step closer to freedom... he just needed to make a phone call first.

Chapter 106

The sight of an unkempt tramp boarding a London bus with an attractive woman, drew quite a few discerning looks. It wasn't some collective unspoken prejudice about the homeless finding true love that made the passengers do a Mexican wave of rubber necking. No, it was the fact that the aforementioned female didn't reek of rancid piss and wasn't in the semi-finals of the world's Tourette's championships. The odd couple retreated to the back of the top deck and awaited an important call. Cassandra produced her mobile phone from her pocket and was about to switch it on.

"No!" Hissed Bobbie Mcvie. "It's only five minutes to four... he said he'd ring us at four." His eyes darted to the minute hand on his army wristwatch.

She kept her voice low. After all, the top deck was quite full and even though there was a steady chatter of background noise, she didn't want to draw any more attention to herself than she had to. Yet his curt tone was grating her nerves.

"For fuck sake, it's only five minutes; I haven't switched this thing on since you made me turn it off three days ago.

I don't even know if the battery's dead or not. It's not like I could've charged it at your place is it?"

Bobby checked his watch once more and grabbed her wrist, a little too tightly. His voice was stern and lower than hers. All the while he spoke, his eyes darted around the bus looking for the nearest hint that their covert conversation was being eavesdropped.

"They have guns. They have transport, they can hack into Metropolitan police CCTV cameras. Once that phone is turned on, we're like a struggling bluebottle in a spider's web. Every second that phone is transmitting our position to them. I hope you can run... because once we end that call and we switch it back off you're gonna run till you puke."

She sat back in her seat, rubbing her wrist as the blood returned to her hand. Even more pissed off at being spoken to so abruptly. It was quite a new experience for her, taking her own medicine.

"I've been on better dates Bobby."

The bus ride wasn't exactly a gondola drifting down the sun kissed canals of Venice, but it would slow down the hunt somewhat. Bobbie knew the sophisticated GPS tracking system could easily pinpoint them to that phone as a stationary target. A moving target, however, would cause them some problems. Although a trained radar operator would deduce from the speed of the moving signal that they were in a vehicle, in rush hour traffic... which one? It was this minor counter surveillance technique that would buy them a few life-saving minutes. Well... that was the plan anyhow.

When Bobbie had interrogated the Reaper named Jim under that dark railway arch, he extracted from Jim the details of his clandestine organisation, its strengths and particularly for Bobbie's interests... its weaknesses. He instructed this nervous Reaper to call him today at 4pm exactly, with their exact plans to hunt her down and how many armed personnel would be left to defend their bunker.

It was 4pm; Bobby checked his timepiece and nodded to her.

No sooner had her pin number been entered, when the mobile rang.

"Hello? Cassandra is that you? Please don't hang up!"

The unmistakeable Australian accent of Mervyn Foster echoed out of her phone.

Chapter 107

Cassandra sat stunned on the top deck of the moving bus as Bobbie leaned in closer to her phone to listen in on the call.

"Listen girl I know who's trying to kill you... he's threatened to kill my kids as well!"

Bobby mouthed silently "Hang up!"

But she hesitant to do so, there was something in his voice she had never heard before... genuine fear. Her finger hovered over the red button to end this unwarranted call when Foster blurted out,

"I know Sir Hugo is sending men to kill you at Mickey Mullet's funeral. He's asked me to make sure you're there... or he'll have my kids murdered!"

Bobby jabbed at the face of his watch and scowled.

"Look Mervyn, I can't talk. I'm expecting anoth..."

"Okay! But I'll text you a number. Ring me from a public pay phone tonight at 10 o'clock."

"Okay, bye! "She ended the call as Bobby stared out of the back window searching for chasing cars, when the phone rang again.

She recognized Jim's voice instantly.

"Yes, look I'm sorry, there was another call! I'm here now, be quick!"

Covering her free ear with a cupped hand to drown out the surrounding bus chatter, she listened intently to what the Reaper had to say. Her face contorted in concentration, nodding intermittently. Her phone beeped telling her Foster's text had arrived.

Bobby checked his watch and instantly froze when he saw the two hooded figures looming towards them. They were white, early 20's, both 6 foot and very broad.

No escape.

She finished her call and instantly turned off the mobile. When she looked up, she saw two glaring faces towering above her.

Bobby did a quick threat assessment; their hands were visible and empty, no bulges in their hooded tops concealing weapons.

These men were not professionals.

It was only when they spoke in fake Jamaican accents was this confirmed to Bobby.

"Hey bitch! We want your phones and wallets! Don't have us smash you up or we'll cut you as well!"

Cassandra didn't see him move... only the carnage that followed.

The ex-soldier's size 10 steel toe cap boot slammed up into the testicles of the first pretend Yardie with his left leg, and then jumping up, smashed his right knee into the future eunuch's face sending him sprawling back down the bus aisle.

The second assailant's clubbing right hook was deflected quickly, and Bobby brought his right elbow up into a sweeping arch past his ear and connected with a sickening crunch on the younger man's eye socket. It exploded in a shower of crimson, as Bobby's left elbow struck the thug's temple... he was unconscious before he crashed to the floor. Taking no chances, he stamped twice on each prone man's testicles for good measure and dragged Cassandra out of her seat and over the two bloodied heaps. Seconds later they were off the bus and sprinting down litter strewn back alleyways. Bobby hadn't lied to her... they did run till she puked.

Chapter 108

The ex-Marine pounded the car horn again in frustration. The calmer Congressman seated in the back smiled.

"Ronnie, as much as I admire your enthusiasm, I scarcely think that your drum solo on the horn will make this traffic go any faster, will it?"

The bull necked driver conceded. "No Sir."

Congressman Daniel O'Brien turned to his bi-spectacled advisor/secretary Miles, who sat typing away on a laptop on his knee. Miles was constantly checking news feeds from back home, if it happened in Washington, Miles would know about it.

O'Brien looked skywards out of the Daimler's bullet proof tinted windows, at the three hovering police helicopters close to London Bridge. On every street corner there seemed to be police officers talking into radios, most of them sported Heckler and Koch machine pistols and body armour.

"Erm... tell me Miles, is all this for my benefit, or is it for the soccer hooligans that this country is so proud of?"

Miles didn't look up. Miles didn't need to. He didn't graduate from Harvard with the highest grades that institute had seen in its illustrious history, without learning a thing or two. Next to Miles, the three wise men looked like Curly, Larry and Moe.

"It's for a local hood that's getting buried tomorrow."

O'Brien saw four huge police vans and three sets of dog handlers on the street. "Who the fuck was this guy, head of the Gambino family?"

Miles looked at his boss now.

"Nah! Not in our league. If he wanted to kill a cop he'd only use a piece, the fucking peasant."

He smiled and looked back at his laptop.

"Not the same as a couple of Sidewinder missiles, is it?" Congressman O'Brien rolled his eyes skywards and let out an exasperated sigh.

"What is the situation with lieutenant Sichetti?" referring to the U.S. air force pilot who fired two air to air missiles from his Harrier jet and killed a couple of British traffic police, whilst on manoeuvres only days ago.

"Confined to base under arrest, pending a full military investigation. The press and the anti-war lobby are having multiple orgasms, demanding our bases are removed from the U.K. citing we are trigger happy mother fuckers who shouldn't be trusted with a pea shooter. Our London Embassy now resembles Custer's last stand. I'm surprised the Met could spare any cops for this thug's funeral and protect our diplomats at the same time. Still… we're lucky this isn't Paris. Our embassy over there gets pelted with petrol bombs." He smiled again. "Over here… it's eggs."

O'Brien furrowed his brow and replied,

"I… I should go over there to the embassy, show some moral support."

"No!" Myles's tone was sharp.

The traffic started moving again.

Before his boss could protest he said, "You're going to need all your strength for the congressional hearings when we get back to Washington, if we are going to nail Goodchild." He handed O'Brien the A4 glossy catalogue of the permanent Salvador Dali exhibition on the banks of the Thames.

"Yeah, you're right Miles. Surreal monsters first, before we get Stateside… and deal with the real ones."

Congressman Daniel O'Brien idolised the late Spanish surrealist artist Salvador Dali, in much the same way as devoted fans loved The Beatles.

O'Brien's world revolved around facts, figures, statistics and very strict parameters that trussed his mind up in a mental straight jacket.

Dali's mind soared through the known universe and beyond, rampaging through the second, third and even fourth dimensions. His paintings were an optical orgasm that predated holograms, 3D cinematography or even hallucinogenic drugs.

When O'Brien immersed himself in a Dali painting, his bureaucratic shackles disappeared, and he was free. The stringent rules that governed his every day waking world ceased to be. He felt elated. It lifted him into a better place.

With some Congressmen, it was whores and cocaine. With Daniel, it was Dali. His love of the Spanish genius had taken him all over the world. From Amsterdam, Florida, private galleries in Czechoslovakia and Japan, on to the pilgrimage last year to see the Dali museum in the artist's

371

birthplace in Figures in Spain. Daniel would travel anywhere to worship at the altar of Dali's genius.

This was the reason for the Congressman's two-day trip to London, to view the recently unveiled sculpture of Dali's most controversial long-lost sketch:

"The Abortion of Damocles."

Dali's infamous black and white pencil sketch was drawn whilst the artist was living in Paris in 1939. The drawing depicts a huge cherub with bat wings hovering over his parents. The cherub along with grotesque bat wings has a huge corkscrew umbilical cord hanging down, tapering to a razor point. The umbilical cord mimics Michelangelo's God and Adam touching fingers sparking creation, as it accusingly points down at the parents who denied it life. The disproportionate size of the cherub symbolises the enormity of the burden that will hang over them for the rest of their lives. The double-edged Freudian symbolism of the razor-sharp tip of the umbilical cord hovering inches from the top of the parents bowed heads, threatening to skewer its killers. Also, paradoxically, reaching out for the safety of the womb where it was once safe. It's journey into our world the very reversal of birth itself: It left the womb to die.

Even for the bohemian galleries in 1930s Paris, this one sketch was too hot to handle. So much so that Dali feared for his life if he ever dared turn it into a painting. Sneers from art critics and broken gallery windows didn't scare Dali at all.

The invasion of the Nazis in 1939 was a totally different matter altogether. Via Spain, Dali fled to America and kept his troublesome sketch firmly under lock and key. Not wanting to upset the puritanical sensibilities of his American benefactors, Dali let no one see the drawing.

The artist was the toast of New York and tried to forget all about "The Abortion of Damocles." Unfortunately, the drawing's very existence scandalised the Vatican who denounced Dali with the unbridled fury of a witch's curse. The Christian far right saw the creation of such a blasphemous sketch as proof that Dali was pro-abortion and demanded this heretic's immediate deportation. Their rabid drooling crusade snow-balled and Senator Joe McCarthy also had Dali in his sights when his witch hunt for communists and undesirables started in the 1950s.

Yet, through his charm, genius and subsequent religious paintings, the vexatious right-wing religious witch hunt against him faded away... as his persecutors looked for other innocents to prey upon. The sketch was locked in a box and sent to his home in Figures, where it lay dormant until Dali's death in 1989. Some say the sketch was stolen and sold to a private dealer. Some say it was a myth and never existed as no one who last saw it in 1939 is alive to verify its existence.

Its whereabouts unknown.

However, in 2016, copies of "The Abortion of Damocles" appeared on the internet and social media. The mystery person who put the images on their web page claimed to be the owner of the sketch. A gardener at Dali's home, who claimed the artist gave him the sketch before he died for his loyal service over the years. The sketch's new owner agreed to let members of the art establishment and forensic scientists authenticate the artwork at a secret location... with a view to sell.

The sketch was declared genuine.

The art world went apeshit. It sold privately for £89,000,000

Two years later, controversial London artist, Crispin Fry, was commissioned to sculpt and cast in bronze, Dali's infamous hidden masterpiece. The new private owners of the sketch allowed Fry access to the artwork to recreate and bring to life for new generations, a drawing that was Dali's secret curse.

Fry was chosen for the project because of his outrageous, attention seeking pieces that rendered him box office gold. Who could forget his notorious exhibition, where he pickled twenty dwarfs in a 3,000 gallon Perspex box, filled with actual human mucus... called "Midget Phlegm's?"

Crispin's statue of the cherub was eight feet long and weighed five tonnes. The demonic looking foetus was suspended from a girder in the London exhibition's gallery. The parents in the sketch were dispensed with. Instead, Fry painted a four-foot diameter white circle on the floor directly below the razor-sharp umbilical cord. Visitors to the exhibit are told to stand in this circle and look up, giving them the same view as the aborted baby's doomed parents. Thus, bringing the viewer into the sketch and interacting with it. The anti-abortion Christians screamed blue murder. Alas, their screams about the offence caused to their invisible mate, were drowned out by the ringing cash registers of the gallery's ticket office, as crowds queued round the block in all weathers, for weeks to see the statue. The crowds subsequently had died down now as O'Brien was driven across London to indulge in his passion. The seasoned politician in him warned that visiting this infamous sculpture tomorrow would fuel the fire for his

374

enemies stateside, who condemned his support for a woman's right to choose to terminate a pregnancy. But the art lover in him said, "Fuck 'em!"

He fully intended to bask in the dull bronzed beauty and stand directly beneath that suspended, five tonne aborted cherub and gaze up at its razor tipped umbilical cord.

Unfortunately for him... the Reapers were well aware of his intentions.

Chapter 109

Grief is a very personal thing. It affects individuals in many different ways. To some, it can be totally debilitating and totally destroy the surviving partner's life. The never-ending injustice that plagues your every waking moment as you try to come to terms with your loss that was nobody's fault, nobody to blame.

But what if it was some body's fault? What if you knew exactly who to blame for your loved one's death? What if you received a very detailed phone call, telling you not only who murdered your partner... but exactly where they intended to be at your loved one's funeral?

In such an instance, piss poor Karma will be told to sit in the corner with his coloured soft crayons, whilst Revenge sharpened his machete.

The tears had not so much dried... as turned to ice. Mavis Davis applied yet another layer of wet look lip gloss to her bloated collagen filled lips. The dark smoky eye makeup gave her the demeanour of a 1950s Hollywood movie star. She stood up from her dressing table and smoothed down the black silk, knee length pencil skirt on her £4,000 Versace suit with matching silk gloves. She had gone through the ritual of dressing in this outfit every day since Mickey's death. Her six inch black stilettos announced to everyone downstairs that the mistress of the house would be downstairs shortly, and you had better stand to attention, one way or another.

Gliding gracefully down the immense, mahogany staircase she passed framed photos of her and Mickey on the walls. Two smiling faces enjoying themselves on every continent. It was almost as if she were voyeuristically peering through windows at two contented souls, as they peered pitifully back at this barren vessel before them.

She had never understood the demons that drove Mickey when he was consumed by his murderous rages. How she would plead with him not to go out late at night and exact bloody retribution on someone who had slated him. She never understood how he would risk losing everything they owned, just to get revenge.

She didn't before... but she did now.

For revenge is all she wants. The house, the diamonds, the cars... all meaningless to her. The threat of incarceration, not so much a threat, but a price she was gladly willing to pay. She could see it all now. The threats of reprisals were what keeps everybody in line. That is how order is kept. Without it, you could hurt, or kill whoever you want. You were free.

That was the mindset that Mickey lived by: an eye for an eye.

As she walked into the living room filled with 80 huge black suited armed thugs...this was to be her new mindset also.

All were silent as Mave addressed them.

"Your Guvner and my Mickey was murdered. I have been informed that the firm who did this, are planning on turning up to Mickey's funeral... tooled up." She paused and waited for the general murmuring and expletives of the pumped-up gangsters to die down. On her expensive glass coffee table sat three Spas 12 shotguns and five boxes of cartridges. Normally this would piss off the house-proud Mavis, but today she would let it slide. Even the 500 black golfing umbrellas dumped unceremoniously in the hallway failed to irritate her. For they will be needed at the service. Mavis carefully placed on her black silk fedora and lifted the net veil off her face to rest on the hat's brim.

"Ricky, what have we got?"

The man mountain cleared his throat. "Well Mave, we've got Spas-12 military shotguns, Glock pistols, 38 Smith and Wesson's, nineteen Uzis, fifty-six MP5 machine guns, thirty-one Desert Eagles, enough lead to resurface every church roof in London and... two of these beauties."

The wall of meat heads parted as Ricky stepped over to a large canvas on the floor and with a grunt; he picked up one of the huge weapons.

"This, Mave, is a M134 mini gun. You may've seen them on films mounted to the side of helicopters in Vietnam. It is belt fed and can fire out of its Gatling gun revolving barrels 6,000 rounds a minute. One of these alone will cut down anyone's firm in London in minutes... we've got two."

Mavis stepped forward and gently stroked the barrel slowly of the fearsome weapon. Using all the powers of seduction that she had been blessed with or had surgically modified. All eyes were upon her.

She had them bewitched and ready to do her bidding.

"This firm are coming to my Mickey's funeral to kill a woman reporter. They don't know that we know they are coming. It's important to me that she be at the funeral as bait for those fuckers to turn up." She handed a post it note to one of the nearby thugs. "We had a tip off and this is where and when to pick her up. Take shooters in case it's a trap. At the funeral, when the shooting starts, she is to be protected, understood?" They all grunted their agreement.

"You all got your gloves, masks and umbrellas?" They all grunted in unison.

"Yes Mave."

She placed the black net veil over her face. Despite the distortion, they could all make out her blood red lips as she spoke.

"They all die... and anyone who tries to stop you."

Chapter 110

Jim briefly popped home to his flat to pack a small toiletry bag, for tonight he would sleep at the bunker. This would be his last chance to contact the reporter and her scary tramp friend. At first her line was engaged when he had rung her at the arranged time of 4pm. His heart pounded in his chest as so much was riding on her involvement. If she didn't play ball or just failed to answer the call, Jim would have to go through with Congressman O'Brien's assassination at the Dali exhibition and then the chances of him escaping this nightmare were nil. He would be a political assassin, not some conscripted innocent, fearful of his own life. If this nightmare did end and he did have to answer to the police, his freedom would be akin to swapping seats on the Titanic.

Once the call finally connected he spat out, at break neck speed, the number of armed personnel that would be in place at the bunker and how to locate certain targets requested by her soldier friend and how to locate the bunker's makeup technician Julian, and also the location and time to be picked up by Mave's bodyguards to be taken to the funeral. But most importantly, his flat address to escape to as a safe house once the shooting started.

Oh, and there would be shooting, his second phone call to Mave made very certain of that. How did he feel setting up 39 of his own "colleagues" to walk into a certain armed ambush? What was he supposed to feel at causing the deaths of 39 men who were going to murder one innocent woman? That's if they die at all. He didn't know what sort of arsenal Mickey Mullet's firm had, but for the reporter's sake, he hoped it was more than catapults.

During desperate moments of madness, Jim had thought, wouldn't it be easier just turning himself into the police? The Reapers would be stopped and he would be free. Free... after explaining he had been murdering people for money... because let's face facts a trained barrister would spot the fact that at no point did Jim give his wages of death over to Live Aid, Holidays for Heroes or surgical trusses for prolapsed ex-Sumo-wrestlers. Then there was the matter of the ex-CID-officers working for them at the bunker, ex-SAS-captain, hackers who could access any data base they want and ex-Police-pathologists. Any of them could still have buddies working for the authorities. There was also the issue of Jim and his late friend Simon Wilson's recruitment into the Reaper project. For years he had wracked his brain as to the common denominator that lead to them both being recruited. Why and how they were picked. Then he remembered their first words as the bunkers two thugs first came for him:

"We're from MI5"

Both he and Simon had applied to join MI5 during a government recruitment drive. Add onto this the current Head of section is reputed to be ex-MI5. So, there it was, these bastards must have someone in that security service who is screening applicants and passing suitable "candidates" on to the Reapers. Sir Hugo is a major arms dealer and his resources and contacts must be as vast as his humongous arse. So, to call the cops would result in certain incarceration or possible betrayal by the friends of the police and death. Jim fancied neither and planned his own version of escape.

He had done as much as he could; everything was in place for his escape. At the flat he checked the gnome in the garden was still in place. The little ceramic sentinel that marked the spot where only a foot below was buried an empty coffee jar containing the railway station locker key, that held the bag of money that Mavis Davis gave him. Add on to that all his "wages of sin" from his Reaper contracts he had been squirreling away and the business card from Joshua Goodchild he had hidden in his sock, he felt his freedom was beckoning.

The electronic door lock of the bunker's outer door clicked as Jim entered for possibly the last time. There was just one last person to speak to before he brought down this house of cards.

Chapter 111

Jim had only seen documentaries about behind the scenes big stage costumed performances. Italian operas, musical theatre and Shakespearean tragedies, and the one theme that always resonated with him about such productions that he had viewed, was organised chaos. You had armies of people shouting, rushing about like headless chickens all seemingly doing their own thing as they relentlessly bumped into each other. To the untrained eye it seemed like mass panic as someone pours a kettle of boiling water on a nest of ants, yet all the people in these costumed performances were all working in unison towards one singular goal:

The show.

As Jim looked around the killing floor he saw just such a dark opera production unfolding. Various Reapers half dressed as Rabbis with no trousers awaiting alterations on their costume fittings. Others eating sandwiches through huge false beards as they inspected and loaded Glocks with designer dum dum bullets. In the distance, down the ending bunkers corridors, the muffled but distinctive sounds of said Glock being fired for last minute target practice at the range.

The huge digital screen on the killing floor along with all the Reapers desk laptops were strangely blank. No constant intel filling them with upcoming or past kills.

No need today, as there was to be only one target.

In the bunker's history, this was unprecedented. The Reapers have only hunted solo, or if you were a novice, or quite shit at your job like Jim, in pairs.

Jim passed the tech boys who were busy hacking into all the CCTV cameras that lined the route of Mullet's funeral and any that may cover the Reaper's arrival or departure after the reporter was slain. For good measure, they hacked into the electronic control centre that regulated traffic signals at certain junctions within five miles of the graveyard. They planned mass gridlock so the gun battle would go off safe in the knowledge that the Calvary would be stuck firmly in traffic miles away as the only free road out, would be the one the transport carrying the Reapers would escape from. These tech boys remained at the bunker during the shooting, coordinating the safe return of all 39 without hindrance from the commuters and authorities alike. Jim smiled as he thought of these keyboard warriors facilitating real cold blooded murder, safe from all the carnage that their actions had enabled, not realising that tomorrow... a real life warrior and trained killer would be visiting the bunker and bringing the full horror of what they did right to them.

Sleeping bags, pillows and small rucksacks littered the floor everywhere, all along the corridors for the most ghoulish sleep over in history. Like Jim, all the Reapers would sleep here tonight, as nothing would be left to chance. Sir Hugo Montgomery's worldwide Reaper project would not be jeopardised because someone's alarm clock never went off.

The queue of Reapers dressed as rabbis grew, the nearer Jim got to Julian's makeup technician's office. Inside, a quite stressed Julian was adjusting the sleeves of a robe with coloured dressmaker's pins sticking out of his mouth.

The Reaper Julian was attending to was loving all the attention, behaving like a right Diva. In his eyes he wasn't a low-level underachiever being disguised to murder a woman; he was Beyonce Knowles on his fourth costume change before he went back on stage to shake his money maker at the Super bowl half time show.

"For god sake! You stabbed me with the pin then, you fucking idiot!"

Justin attempted to apologise yet again when Jim interrupted him.

"Julian, can I have a word outside please?"

The Reaper took great offence at this interruption of his pampering.

"No, he bloody can't! Wait your turn!"

Normally, Jim wouldn't engage with his colleagues on any level, let alone an adversarial one... however, today wasn't a normal day. And tomorrow was going to be an extra ordinary one indeed. Jabbing his finger at the Reaper, Jim snarled,

"Listen here you ugly, little prick! After tomorrow there are going to be some managerial changes around here. Yeah, you've heard the rumours... I'm going to be the new Head of Section here at the bunker."

Jim knew the other Reapers lined up for their fittings outside could hear him. He wanted them to, wanted the gossip to filter back... all the way back to the office. Wanted to cement in their mind their "boy" was going to kill O'Brien, because he wanted the top job as his reward. As long as they thought he was gladly here to stay, that would give him enough of a distraction when he ran.

The Reaper withered and apologised as Julian followed Jim out the room and down a quieter stretch of corridor to an old storeroom.

"Don't talk, just listen. We spoke recently about your desire to escape."

Julian tried to speak, but Jim cut him short by holding up a silencing hand.

"I told you last time this isn't a test or a trap. If it was, you'd be dead by now. Do you accept that?" Julian nervously nodded.

"Out of everyone in here, you are the only one who hasn't killed or been directly involved in helping or covering up killings. So, when the police do come... you are the only one walking out of here free. Do you accept that?"

Again, Julian nodded.

"Tomorrow, if you do exactly as I say... you will be free. Your old life not only back, but from TV, newspaper and most probably film deals... you are going to be a very rich free man." Julian's eyes started to moisten.

"Carry out all your duties exactly as they want you to, to the best of your ability, today and tomorrow. But at some point tomorrow... all hell will break loose. Lock yourself in your makeup cupboard in your room and stay there until someone comes for you. When he does, you'll be free. I know you won't betray me and run back to the office and repeat this conversation, because even if you think such loyalty born out of fear will get you rewarded, it won't.

They'll wrap you in plastic along with me... you know this. I'm offering you your only ever way out of this Julian." Jim handed Julian a tissue to dry his eyes.

"Now... at some point when the police do talk to you, here's what I want you to tell them."

Chapter 112

Mervyn Foster resisted the urge, yet again to calm his rattled nerves and sink another Scotch whiskey. Sat in his penthouse alone. The only source of distraction was the GPS tracking equipment, with detailed digital map of London on his laptop linked to his phone. The phone he stared at, wishing it would ring. But it wouldn't, not till at least 10pm, for that was the agreed time that his ace on the run reporter, Cassandra agreed to call him.

Many newspapers' editors' bullshit and lay claim to having second sight and predicting up and coming trends and world events. Yet all these right-wing purveyors of pornography or corporate propaganda are all just low level chancers. Mug punters guessing which horse will win. The only ones who can lay claim to being "ahead of the curve" are certain stockbrokers who nearly always come out on top. Alas, as recent high court trials have shown, far from being men of wisdom who have mastered the secrets of the mystics, these brokers have been indulging in "insider trading" which is basically low-level white-collar criminality at its best.

But Foster did have foresight. He did know what was going to happen tomorrow, before it happened. He knew, because his old buddy and now his nemesis, Sir Hugo had told him in this very office. Tomorrow, at Mickey Mullet's funeral, Hugo's men were going to kill Cassandra... and Mervyn was going to set her up. His eyes darted to his children's photo, the children Sir Hugo threatened to murder, then to the huge damp patches on his beige office carpet. Where Hugo's clean up squad had eradicated every last trace of his half-decapitated hacker's bleeding corpse.

They were very thorough. They went to the hackers flat and stripped every shred of Mervyn's involvement with him. They packed him a suitcase, emptied his bank account and bought a cross Channel ferry ticket and a six month Euro rail pass, locked up his flat and paid six months advanced rent by direct debit.

Hugo had taken the editor's laptop with the incriminating murder footage of Marty by Hugo's gunman... but Mervyn did not rise to the top of this nest of vipers in Fleet street by being a fool, naïve or giving his enemies a chance to strike him down. Mervyn made copies of the files that Hugo took. Sir Hugo may be one of the world's biggest arms dealers, but those files were the armour-piercing rounds that would cut that over-privileged, gut of his to ribbons.

But the bullet that would destroy the peer would be at Mullet's funeral... and Foster had no intention of letting her die before she could finish him.

Chapter 113

Whilst Cassandra was safely deposited in Bobby's shack under the motorway bridge, the ex-soldier did a spot of shopping in his canvas weathered Bergin army rucksack. Tinned food mainly, bottled water, various women's toiletries and sanitary products (these did raise a few eyebrows at the till) until he moved on to the more useful items he would need for tomorrow. The hardware store furnished him gladly, with the industrial dust mask, half face respirator and the white spirit (the shopkeeper even jested that Bobby mix it with lemonade to make a poor man's James Bond Martini... hands shaken, and vision blurred)

Yet the nearest the ex-soldier got to sarcasm was in the sports shop when he purchased the swimming goggles. Next to the serrated knife, the googles would tip the balance in favour of his success tomorrow.

As he strode purposely down the road he went over and over again in his mind his plan of attack. Starting at the observation post across from the bunker, then storming the bunker itself. He had planned and executed such raids endless times on different terrains, compounds and buildings... but always as a four-man team. Never solo. His opponents were mainly amateurs, a gang of nerdy hackers, a few mop-up squad dog's bodies, some ex police, the Head guy ex MI5 all possibly armed. Jim had informed him the bunker was well stocked for guns and ammunition and where it was all stored. His only real concern is the one ex SAS captain guarding the bunker's entrance. Whereas Bobby would have a fighting chance of minimising casualties with superficial wounding, depending upon how hard these fuckers fought back... the SAS captain would fight to the death.

He would have to be killed swiftly, no warning.

Chapter 114

Bobby had pulled out all the stops and cooked him and Cassandra a hearty supper of beans and sausages in a tin. The host even splashed out on a cheap bottle of Prosecco, which although in reality tasted like a sample from a clap clinic... in her alcohol starved state, tasted like fine French Champagne. She drank the wine very quickly and wanted more. The soldier noticed this and said nothing, just continued sharpening his serrated knife on the sharpening steel he had stolen.

"I know it looks bad, but it calms the nerves."

He handed her a bottle of water as they sat by the flickering light of the shack's mini stove.

"Drink this; you'll need your wits about you when you ring Foster later."

Staring at the blade she spoke tentatively, "Bobby, what are you gonna do tomorrow at the bunker?"

"I'm going to get to the head guy, capture him and make contact with our inside man. Then wait for the police to arrive, then it's over."

She took a long gulp of water. "What? Just like that? Jim said they are all armed"

"Not all, some are just support IT staff, some..."

"You know what I mean!" She interrupted. "You could die! That bread knife isn't going to help you when the shooting starts." She softened her tone, "Look... I'm not doubting your abilities, but you're outgunned and fighting an army."

He flashed a reassuring smile and handed Cassandra her coat.

"I've done this before, and I don't intend to stay unarmed for very long. Now, put this on we need to go find a call box and ring Foster."

Chapter 114

It was quiet now in the bunker, the main lights turned off, most of the Reapers had bedded down for the night in their sleeping bags. Some snoring like pigs, some farting like warthogs in a tar pit. A few chatted quietly amongst themselves, whilst others giggled like schoolgirls at private jokes passed amongst them. Apart from the dull glow of the emergency lighting, the only real bright light source came from the Head of Section's Porto cabin office, high on the gantry. Whilst the children down below were sleeping, the adults above were talking.

The three rats scurried around their small cage, as Singen fed them cheese and onion crisps. Jim politely sipped his whiskey as the Head of Section poured himself and Singen another. Singen took his whiskey then addressed them both.

"Two days ago, one of our Reapers went to the Dali exhibition and before he left, he informed the dim-witted girl on the till in the gift shop, that he had seen a rat next to one of the exhibits. Then yesterday before closing we had another of our guys do the same. They have been primed for tomorrow when we turn up with these beauties and we get access to the upper levels of the gallery."

The older man placed on his desk an old mobile phone with a lead plugged into it that ended in a blunt shiny jack plug. Next to this he placed what looked to be a small grey bar of hotel soap.

"Sir Hugo has kindly supplied us with a quantity of military grade C4 plastique explosive. Not enough to bring the roof down... but enough to sheer the restraining bolt that holds in place the five tonne bronze statue of The Abortion of Damocles... just as Congressman Daniel O'Brien stands directly underneath it."

Both he and Singen clinked glasses in agreement.

They both turned to Jim. Were they searching for doubt in his eyes? A sense of disgust at the impending assassination? They waited...

"I take it the lead from the phone is to a detonator that is placed into the C4 and then detonated remotely via a text or call... by me?"

They both smiled.

"Well done Jim" said Singen "And to think I doubted you had not only the grey matter but the balls to pull this off... then, a little bird told me today you nearly ripped him a new arsehole when he doubted your new position... as Head of Section."

He was playing games. Now wasn't the time to show weakness, only strength.

"Are you gentlemen trying to tell me you are going back on your word, that once I kill Daniel O'Brien... that I am not going to be made Head of Section here?"

Again, they both looked at each other, seemingly genuinely shocked at Jim's reply.

The Head of Section laid a reassuring hand on Jim's shoulder and smiled.

"Jim, I promise, once you've killed Congressman O'Brien, you'll get everything that's coming to you."

Chapter 115

It had been quite a restless night in Bobby's shack. The mini stove was still lit and the smell of wood and burning linoleum was now starting to grow on her. As toxic a combination as that was, it kept her warm and that is all she cared about. Their late-night jaunt round London trying to find a discreet phone box that wasn't vandalised or so full of piss that you would need water wings and a snorkel just to make a call was a task in itself... but in that bitter cold, it was leaving her legs shaking like Elvis with Parkinson's disease.

Foster had poured his heart out to her about his fear for his kids and his past dealings with Hugo. She constantly interrupted him and fired questions back, her old journalist instincts tearing through any guard or armour Foster had left. He couldn't lie to her, he had more to lose. He wasn't lying about his kids, she could hear it in his voice, and he was genuinely terrified. It was a gamble and she needed to make a choice; if he was lying and she turned up to an ambush she could die. Or, Mavis's gangster army would protect her and she, along with the army of reporters Mervyn promised he would send would capture the whole thing and publicly bring Hugo down. She would get her life back... her career back. The other alternative, don't go, run and hide... until they eventually did catch her and put her out of her misery.

Outside the wind howled and the chorus of night creatures filled the air with drunken menace. As frightening as these urine reeking demons sounded, they would not dare enter the abode in which she slept. For there was a terror far worse than soap waiting for this army of inebriated, inside the shack... Bobby Mcvie. If she ever doubted any of his claims about being ex Special Forces before, the pair of rat boys who he smashed to pieces on the bus soon put these doubts to rest. And tomorrow he planned to take on multiple armed killers... on his own. She had spent most of the night clutching the serrated knife for security from home.

Home.

It seemed like a distant memory now. Three days of sleeping rough. Well, Bobby had made his home comfortable and warm, but it was rough for her. The bundle of £5,000 bank notes wrapped in a jumper made a lumpy pillow. Cassandra managed a humourless smile, the contents of her pillow could secure her a suite at the Hilton, yet here she lay on pallet boards under a fucking motorway.

Yet Bobby did tell her that at least here, she was safe.

Was this to be her life now? Perpetually on the run? She gritted her teeth as she sat up and dragged a hairbrush through her bedraggled hair. God she'd kill for bath... and a bottle of Merlot. Make that three. Sighing desperately now, had the booze got such a hold on her? Here she was, hunted by armed assassins and instead of her heart pounding, her liver was screaming "feed me!"

She had no choice... she would go to the funeral. Death had to be better than this?

Jim's brief phone call on the bus told her where to be tomorrow to be picked up by Mullet's men to be escorted to the funeral. She lay down and tried to sleep. Something Bobby had been doing for hours.

Chapter 116

Bobby was awake early before her, cooking more beans. It was a good job neither of them smoked or the resulting methane eruption would look like a Cockney version of Hiroshima. Then in a bizarre twist of fate she watched this tramp transform into a stockbroker. Well, a stockbroker in another man's suit, a fat man... who liked pies... lots of pies. She on the other hand, despite going 16 rounds of pure MMA cage fighting grappling with her hairbrush, her hair resembled something children would adorn the top of their bonfires with, in November. After escorting Cassandra to her agreed rendezvous, Bobby stayed until Mullet's boys arrived in their gangster mobile, then he disappeared like smoke.

The door to the black Mercedes opened and a black suited thug pointing a gun at her snarled, "You Cassandra?" She duly nodded and took her seat beside him.

Fifteen minutes later she was at the mansion and stood before the demure widow. "What the fuck are you wearing? You look like a manky toilet! You ain't goin' to my Mickey's funeral with a head lookin' like a lesbian's armpit! Cassandra's eyes screwed up at the next roared octave.

"RICKY!"

The lumbering giant appeared. Mavis made her intentions clear.

"Oiy! Take this filthy cow upstairs! My sisters are up there, get 'em to boil this manky toilet and sort her barnet out! She can use some of my clobber."

Ricky gently led Cassandra upstairs for an Essex make over.

At last... a shower! She gratefully accepted her hostesses' gracious hospitality.

"And make sure she shaves her legs! Don't want the press to think we've got yetis in the family!"

Chapter 117

For the third and Bobby hoped the last time, he ambled down the deserted backstreet that led to the observation post opposite the bunker's entrance. Last time he used an incendiary device to slip past the observation post's gaze; to use the same ruse twice would seriously arouse suspicion. He was banking on the angle he would be at, directly under the three stories high window with its wooden sill, would be a natural blind spot. To see past this, they would need to open the window and look down. They daren't risk giving away their position for the sake of curiosity.

The gamble paid off. The stolen credit card again easily slipped the latch on the outer door... and he was in. Again, he stood perfectly still and waited for rushing footsteps as his eyes adjusted to the dimly lit staircase. To the left of the staircase, which although he noticed it last time, he paid no heed, because his focus was three floors up, was an ajar door to an abandoned office. Pulling the serrated blade from out the back of his trouser belt, he edged the door slowly open. Thankfully it didn't creak and made no sound. There was damp and mustiness of 75 years of decay and neglect in this empty room, whose only feature was an ornate art Deco fireplace that the Antique's road show would bite your arm off to restore.

It was the boarded-up window that he was more interested in. From the outside, the old boards had cracked and perished after 75 years of blistering cold and relentless rain soaked British weather. This had caused the boards to crack and splinter. Over time the damp swollen wood had expanded these cracks with some centimetres long and in places ten centimetres high. From the outside, these cracks were barely noticeable, but from the inside it provided Bobby with the vantage point of the street he needed. Using the sleeve of his stolen suit he wiped away decades of dust from the cracked window and squinted for a better view of the street outside.

He checked his watch, and just as Jim said, two white coaches with tinted windows drove up and parked opposite the entrance to the bunker.

Then the most surreal scene Bobby had ever witnessed unfolded as the Reapers filed out, regaled in long dark coats, Homburg hats, curly wigs with trailing ringlets and long wiry beards. He counted 39 costumed Reapers clambering onto the transport.

One was missing.

Nine boiler suited mop up squad lackeys loaded heavy kit bags into the back of the coaches, which Bobby surmised to be weapons, before they drove off.

The street was silent. No movement.

Bobby put on his respirator and swimming goggles and stealthily climbed the staircase, knife in hand.

Chapter 118

She looked like a painted whore. Sat in the back of the back of the immense funeral car, that was more Hollywood stretch limo than a widow's chariot. Cassandra was quite unrecognisable in the black silk Gucci jacket and knee length skirt, black tights and Italian hand stitched high heels. Her hair was pulled taut into a ponytail and her makeup resembled a high-class call girl. Mave's two sister's Tania and Chantelle sat either side of her like two immaculately glamorous perfumed rottweilers guarding her.

It was these two demure ladies with huge, augmented breasts who had transformed Cassandra in under an hour, from diligent investigative reporter/tramp, into something six sub-literate Premiership league footballers would pass round a hotel room like a woodbine. Although extremely grateful for the shower, the extreme make over was traumatising. At first Cassandra tried to reason with the ladies as they set about her with wax strips and lip gloss, then she soon learned that Tania was the more violent of the two.

She regaled the reporter of how she beat her ex-boyfriend to a bloodied pulp with a foot-long rubber dildo, for daring to criticise her new bloated collagen enhanced pout. Indeed, by all accounts when the five-foot-high Tania finally finished her frenzied phallic fencing, her ex had a pair of lips himself like Mick Jagger eating chilli. Cassandra didn't fancy sharing his fate by upsetting this petite psychopath. Then it hit her (not Tania, an epiphany) although the reporter may not approve of coming second in a Transvestite of the year pageant, she did have to blink twice when she looked in the mirror at the hussy facing her. It was perfect, she looked nothing like the newspaper photo her readers knew her by, or that the Reapers would no doubt have been given for identification of their target.

Camouflage.

Mave wore her widow's black silk mini dress and jacket like a film star attending the Oscars. The black fedora brim low over her face so only her blood red lips were visible through the veil. Ricky and another colossal black suited brute flanked her. Both were loading handguns.

On the floor of the car between them was a long open flower box containing a Mossberg shotgun. Next to that were six black golfing umbrellas.

Mave's hand was under her veil as she spoke on the phone.

"Wally's bringing fifty-three down from the Newcastle firm, Mad Tony has thirty boys from Glasgow, Dirty Dick's mob got in from Liverpool last night with machetes and hatchets. I know! I told them Billy, what good's a fucking bread knife in a gun fight? I'm surprised the knives haven't still got butter on them. Heh! It's like the fucking third world up there! Yeah, O'Riley has promised eighty-two lads are coming across from Belfast. But you are going to have a bleeding word with him, Billy. He wants to shoot all the coppers first. I told him, it's my Mickey's funeral and he can show a bit of bleeding respect. If he wants to kill the old Bill, he can bleeding do it on his own time! What the police dogs? Oh no, that's sorted. Matty and his brothers are bringing his 8 Doberman's down from the farm. Yeah, gonna be dog eat dog!"

Cassandra sat back in silence and was in awe of the transformation of the Mave she thought she knew from her dim-witted celebrity persona, to fully fledged gangster's moll. Not so much satisfied at being a dick ornament to a villain... but now being a villain in her own right. Only a week ago she was planning how many men she could take on in a record-breaking gang bang porno. Now here she was, cool as ice, planning an all-out war and gangland execution of 39 men in public at her husband's funeral.

Cassandra mused, if she lived through this day, this story would be her pension.

Their car travelled at a snail's pace behind the hearse. In front of which the head mourner, walking ahead of the hearse on foot, regaled in top hat through Mickey's old manor. And they all turned out in their thousands along the route. Some to pay their last respects at a local legend that had passed, others to secretly rejoice that the scourge of their community was now dead. The majority turned up to be seen to curry favour with the departed's criminal gang and his widow, who in all reality was now their new ruler.

Although the Metropolitan police pontificate in the media that they keep law and order on the streets, anyone who actually lives on those streets will inform you that this is as believable as that book with the talking snake. Those streets are not and never have been ruled by law... but they have always been ruled by fear.

No, not one of those dour faced flash mob of mourners who turned up to watch Mickey take his last car ride through his old manor did so out of "respect," but every last one of them turned up out of fear. Fear of reprisals. As one Newsagent, whose shop just happened to be on the funeral cortege route, found out when he refused to close his shop as a mark of respect to the late extortionist. The newsagent took great exception to closing his business for the man who would extort protection money from him every week for 10 years. The irony was lost on him now as the car passed the blackened remains of his freshly petrol bombed shop.

It wasn't only the police helicopters that buzzed the sky that morning. A two-seater plane that carries sky banners passed the 50 car procession several times. Usually these banners proclaim life and love: "Marry me Ethel!" or "It's a boy!"

Today this aerial billboard informed all the subjects of his Kingdom that:

"Mickey Mullet, Brown Bread ".

Cassandra wanted to smile at the sheer monstrosity of tackiness about the whole affair. But she feared to actually show any mirth on her lips may risk hers imitating The Rolling Stones' lead singer, if Tania pulled that rubber dildo out of her Gucci handbag again.

Mave ended her call and addressed Cassandra.

"Right you! We've been told the firm that killed my Mickey want you dead. They've got some fucking bottle turning up to his funeral just to kill you. Why are you so important?"

The reporter cleared her throat, acutely aware all eyes in the car were upon her.

"A friend of mine... had some evidence on them. That they were killing people. He spoke to me about it, they found out... and murdered him. Now, they want me dead too. My editor wanted me to cover the funeral because I've met you both. You briefly Mave, at our offices, but I did do a longer interview at your home with Mickey. I didn't want to do it as I've been hiding, but my boss said I'd be safe amongst you."

The best lies are always hidden amongst the truth. Although everything she told Mave was the truth, there was the lie of omission... her involvement with Jim. To say to this grieving woman that she was in cahoots with the man who murdered her husband would see Cassandra shot dead in a ditch. If Mave's boys found and killed Jim, the 39 Reapers would still be out there hunting her for the rest of her very short life. From what Jim had told her, the Reapers had people working for them from MI5, Special Branch, ex-Special Forces and hackers who could infiltrate any electrical device. Realistically, going to the cops, would also see her shot dead in a ditch.

"As I see it..." said Mave, "...no one's heard of this firm. Not even in Romford. They popped up from nowhere, kill my Mickey... in my own fucking house! Then swan out the door with a huge bag of my cash. They've mugged us off! No one knows how to get hold of 'em. Yet we get a tip off they are gonna be here at the funeral today, just to kill you."

She jabbed her finger at Cassandra.

"Oh, you are going to be there lady. You're our one chance of killing these fuckers!"

Chapter 119

Jim shivered in his big, dark winter coat as he walked along the banks of the Thames. It wasn't so much the cold wind that threw up fallen leaves that caused his involuntary shaking, but the stakes were so high now he was close to escape. He felt like a rabbit transfixed in the headlights of an oncoming car, almost paralysed with fear to move. In a moment of empathy, he almost understood now why all his fellow Reapers didn't try to escape.

It was just easier not to.

The huge seven-meter-high bronze elephant with long thin stilted legs glared down on him. Even though the London Eye towered above it, Jim's eyes were drawn to the malevolent colossal sentinel that guarded the entrance to The Dali Universe exhibition.

Singen walked briskly beside Jim like a man with not a care in the world. Within an hour, an innocent man would be murdered and Singen was positively drooling at the prospect.

They passed the bronze statue of a barren tree with a melting clock draped in its branches. The clocks numbers were running down the face of the dial.

Time was running out.

Jim shivered again.

Inside the exhibition they were greeted by the soothing sounds of soft, Spanish Flamenco guitar music, being piped out from hidden speakers throughout the gallery. The gallery itself spanned 3000 meters with over 500 artworks, sculptures, and surrealist furniture from the late artist. The collection, which was one of the largest in the world and took over forty years to compile, was split into three main sections:

Dreams and Fantasy

Sensuality and Femininity

Religion and Mythology

For the purposes of this execution, their prey would be found in Religion and Mythology.

Singen casually swung his black attaché case as he walked. The one that contained the silenced handgun in the secret compartment. That case also contained three live black rats. Jim imagined them being tossed around in the darkness of the case as Slimey strode past a sculpture of a melting clock. The vermin would be bashing into each other, biting out of fear and desperation. Tearing at each other in a frantic bid for survival. When they finally were released, they would go absolutely wild looking for a way out. Slimey was banking on that.

Like a little lap dog, he followed Slimey across the dark shiny gallery's parquet floor. He came to a stop in front of a golden statue of a woman with a skipping rope and roses where her face should be.

"So, what is your take on Dali's 'Alice in Wonderland' sculpture?"

410

Jim looked over his shoulder at the groups of tourists and art lovers milling about and replied, "It's well done, but it's not really my thing."

Singen still looking at the stature through tinted glasses that replaced his opaque sunglasses scoffed, "Oh Jim, you really are a little conformist, aren't you? You pretend to be a bit of a rebel, but take you out of your comfort zone..."

A cocktail of emotions bombarded Jim. This little shit was goading him. Normally Jim would retort and verbally wipe the floor with him, but today wasn't a normal day. If he lashed out, Slimey may deduce he hadn't changed and accepted his role as a Reaper. This would naturally cast doubt on his desire to carry out this execution that would spur his promotion. The promotion he had to convince Slimey he really wanted. He couldn't take the bait now; he was too close to freedom.

"It's true, comfort is desirable. But I'm tired of fighting, struggling. I want security, a future... and this promotion will offer me that." Slimey looked genuinely shocked as he turned to face Jim.

"Look Singen, I know we haven't got on. And I could've made more of an effort with you. I really could. After all, all you've ever done is tried to encourage me and mentor me. And, I've been a bit of a fucker, if I'm honest."

Jim sighed; he had to make this sound convincing. Even though he was far more intelligent than Singen, his nemesis had the cunning and savagery of the very rats he had trapped in his case. One hint that he didn't believe him, and it was all over for Jim.

"I mean, what am I gonna do, go back into teaching and train the Costa coffee wage slaves of the future? And...

when I'm Head of Section I won't have to personally kill anyone anymore. Others will do that for me."

Slimey raised his eyebrows.

"Well... you don't want blood on your hands, yet you'd gladly delegate wet work to others? So instead of being the conscientious objector you always have claimed to be... you're just fucking gutless?"

"Call it squeamish." replied Jim.

Slimey broke into a genuine wide smile and laughed.

"Ha! I'll accept that." He slapped Jim on the shoulder and gently nodded towards a door marked "Staff Only." He lowered his voice as more tourists passed behind them.

"Behind that door is a staircase to the storerooms above and the tungsten steel bracket in the floor that holds The Abortion of Damocles sculpture in place, above this gallery. The four security cameras around us have been hacked and will be remotely turned off for ten seconds, in five minutes time." He looked briefly at his watch and then vigorously shook his attaché case.

"Then it's time for our little friends here to make their grand entrance."

Chapter 120

Throughout her illustrious, former career as a serious investigative journalist, Cassandra had listened to the eulogies of many a great, departed individual. Some virtuous politicians, some inspirational and courageous civil rights activists and some beloved film stars and comedians. Throughout all of these heartfelt obituaries she always felt a lump brought to her throat. But as she listened to the eulogies at Mickey Mullet's funeral service, the only thing brought to her throat was vomit. It was almost like the world championships for the biggest lying bastard competition were being held in this very church.

Various shaven headed, flat nosed monstrosities, in black suits stood up and all sang the praises of Britain's most violent drug lord, as if they were talking about the death of Father Christmas. They all spoke with the sartorial eloquence of a rectal retch in an echo chamber. With the delivery that they all gave in a court room, "What, throw a grass off Beachy Head? Cor, not me Guvner, I was at a Mongolian nose flute recital at the time." "Nah, yer Honour, at the time you said I was strangling him with twenty two foot of his own duodenum, I was watching a documentary on Bolivian tree frogs with my old Nan."

Cassandra's eyes blinked several times as this tidal wave of sycophantic shite washed over her, until she felt like she would surely drown in Cockney rhyming bollocks. Also, the hymns were replaced by "Maybe it's because I'm a Londoner," "Knees up Mother Brown" and this pantomime had now turned into a musical.

The warmup acts had all lumbered back to their seats, or outside to inhale cocaine behind the gravestones, like an angry ant eater with flu. It was time now for the main speaker. Not Mave, for she sat tranquil and silent like an elegant statue, with circus tits. The widow, flanked by her massive thugs, delegated that particular honour to the aging, ex gangland boss of the East End, Billy Whelks.

Billy Whelks stood up as much as his five-foot-high frame would allow him. His head barely cleared the priest's podium, which gave him the eerie optical illusion of being a talking dismembered head, with half his ear bitten off. Then there was the question of his dyed unfeasibly black as coal swept back hair and the image of farce was complete. The subject of his coloured mane was a total taboo subject amongst the underworld. The fact an 80-year-old man had hair darker than a panda's arse, was a topic of conversation that no body dare raise. Just like salad on a fat woman's plate... it was left untouched.

"Mickey Mullet is bigger than Jesus."

Cassandra nearly choked trying to stifle a laugh.

"I mean, Jesus fed 5000 geezers with a kipper and a loaf of Hovis. Now Mickey, he's fed half of London in his time... and when it was called for, he fed a few wrong 'uns to the fishes."

414

This witty repartee drew a few throaty chuckles amongst a congregation who would seriously struggle remembering the lyrics to "Happy Birthday to you."

The tiny terror continued, "So I know when Mickey's up there in Heaven, there'll be a few changes round the gaff. For a kickoff, the letters MM will appear on the pearly gates to let the riff raff know whose Manor it is now."

At this revelation the listening priest looked quite disturbed. But not quite disturbed enough to rebuke the blasphemous Billy for disrespecting his employer. For these assembled vermin had paid for the very roof to be replaced in drug money, even though in reality some of them did steal the lead off the old one.

"And now Mickey's in charge of Heaven, there's gonna be a strict door policy... if yer name's not dahhrn, yer not coming in. And let me tell you sumfink, no farrrkin' old bill are getting into Heaven neither!"

This last pearl of wisdom brought about rapturous applause, whistles and stamping of size eleven feet. To illustrate his next point, he swished his open palm through the air.

"And if God doesn't like it or do as he's told... he's gonna get a dry slap!" As one, the whole congregation all swiped their palms through the air and parroted:

"Dry slap!"

Cassandra placed her hand over her mouth as she seriously couldn't trust her face not to betray her true feelings, with such provocation from Billy Whelks. The reporter sat again, sandwiched in the packed church, in between Mave's sisters Chantelle and Tania. The pew in front held Mave, flanked by eight huge bodyguards. Cassandra recognised one as Mickey's head bodyguard

Ricky, who had a small earpiece from a radio microphone trailing down into his collar. Suddenly, Ricky touched his earpiece and tilted his head slightly to one side like a cocker spaniel that's just heard the word "Walkies!" He nodded his head several times then leaned and whispered in Mave's ear.

Mave slowly turned around in the pew to face Cassandra.

"They're here for you... they're outside."

Chapter 121

"These are made by rolling between a virgin's soft nubile thighs." Said the older security officer Jenkins, in the observation point across the street from the bunker, as he exhaled a cloud of cigar smoke.

The younger officer, Darren, looked unconvinced as he studied the Cuban cigars with suspicion that they were both smoking.

"What, so as a recruitment policy, the state-owned tobacco company in Cuba will only employ "virgins" to individually roll their cigars between their legs?"

The older man enjoyed these rare moments of baiting his annoying junior and nodded sagely, as he inhaled another lungful of Cuba's finest export.

"My arse! How the hell would that interview even pan out? What if she was a manky slapper who had been with gangs of unwashed bin men and just lied on her C.V.?"

"You'd be able to taste the difference." was Jenkins sardonic reply as he blew more clouds of smoke into the air. He then pulled out his ace that he knew would push his junior's buttons.

"If you don't believe me… Google it."

He grinned as Darren puffed angrily on his own cigar and reached for his phone. Jenkins knew his pile of old cobblers he'd spun his colleague would not be verified by the search engine... but loved the fact that the youth of today would bounce signals off satellites to quantify the most outrageous shite fed to them, instead of trusting their own instinct. An old dog can teach a pup new tricks. These frivolous moments in the observation point were rare indeed.

Constantly on guard, forever vigilant. Watching the entrance to the bunker and overseeing the safe passage of the Reapers arrival and departure from the bunker. But today at least, they could take their foot off the gas. All 40 Reapers had left the bunker. 39 bussed out to Mickey Mullet's funeral and 1 sent to kill Congressman O'Brien at the Dali exhibition. There would be no drama here for at least 4 hours. He puffed again on the fine Cuban cigar that he had been saving for this occasion. After today, the Reaper project would expand into America and into Europe. And Jenkins planned to join the Head of section in the States training up the Yank Reapers. Then the Googling gobshite Darren on the phone before him would disappear like the cigar smoke that was slowly filling the room.

He blinked rapidly as the sweet cigar smoke was now starting to sting his eyes. Indeed, the room was filling with smoke, but far too much to be coming from two fat cigars. He stood up sharply and stared towards the locked front door... there was smoke pouring from under the door. Barging past the younger man he quickly unlocked the door and flung it open.

Only to be confronted by billowing black smoke... and a glass eyed demon.

Chapter 122

Bobby stared intently through the keyhole at the two-armed men smoking cigars. He packed the underneath of the door with paper and rags, doused it with lighter fluid and held the serrated knife tightly as he lit his diversion. The soldier wondered which one would reach the door first. The younger would be trigger happy and fitter; the senior would be more experienced but slower. It didn't matter; he only needed one of them to gain entry to the bunker.

The first one to open that door would die.

The builder's respirator and swimming goggles protected him from the worst of the smoke as the stairwell started to fill. His eyes adjusted to the darkness, theirs would not be. The smoke was not quite as effective as the flash bang stun grenades he had trained with in Hereford, but it would disorientate long enough to make the first kill. All senses were heightened as his training kicked in and he was suddenly switched on.

The panicked rattling of the key in the lock, the door flung wide open and the wide staring eyes of the older man as Bobby plunged the knife deep into his fat stomach, twisted it then grabbed the gun from his holster. Keeping the quivering man still on his blade and using him as a human shield, Bobby knew all the younger man would be able to see would be smoke billowing in from the stairwell and his boss' back.

He never gave the younger man time to react; Bobby drew a bead on him and shot him in his thigh.

Before he had hit the floor, the soldier had pushed the stabbed man to the ground and disarmed Darren. As both men writhed in agony, Bobby used the water from the kettle to douse the small fire and he relocked the door.

The shot officer was shaking as he tried to stem the flow of blood from his leg.

"First time being shot?" Smiled Bobby. "Not quite like in the movies, is it fella? All the fight has gone out of you now, hasn't it?" He removed his goggles and respirator.

"It's okay, seriously, you're not going to die... he is though." Pointing with his gun to the wheezing senior officer whose blood was pooling around him.

Bobby jabbed the cold hard muzzle of the Browning high power into Darren's bullet wound until he screamed.

Again, he smiled.

"Trust me, this is nothing to what I can do to you. I want entry into that bunker over the road. You are going to get me inside."

Chapter 123

Cassandra walked close to bodyguard Ricky, as instructed by Mave, because as she so succinctly put it, "When the shit hits the fan, Ricky's wearing body armour." The police, although crawling all over the area and hovering above in their helicopters, stayed completely out of the cemetery. Not out of some begrudging respect for a fallen adversary, but on orders from their commanding officer, who warned these highly volatile grieving villains could turn a funeral into a full-scale riot, if provoked. So apart from a reporter and a priest, the graveyard was full of assassins and gangsters.

The priest waffled on at the grave side about ashes to ashes as Cassandra saw the Reapers spread out in an arc about fifty yards away. Each stood beside or peered out from a gravestone or monument; all wore dark clothing and sported long beards. Like the creepiest ZZ Top convention ever created. Normally, this would bring a smile to her painted lips, yet all of them seemed to be staring straight at her. How the fuck could they possibly know it was her in this outfit and makeup? She shuddered and stood a bit closer to the man mountain Ricky, as she noticed every black suited villain in the graveyard was carrying a black umbrella. What, were these ultra-tough gangsters fucking soluble? Mused Cassandra. It wasn't even forecast rain. She looked up at the clouds and saw three helicopters, two police and one from Sky news.

Two large black transit vans were parked close to the graveside on the path, fifty yards apart, side on facing the Reapers. The reporter surmised these were part of Mave's firm. By a monument to fallen soldiers stood a group of troll-like men, doing their best to restrain eight snarling Dobermans, who seemed hell bent on tearing flesh.

Mave laid a wreath on Mickey's coffin, as countless flat nosed gangsters either talked into earpieces or mobile phones. Their free hands clutched their umbrellas. All of the gangsters stared incessantly at the Reapers.

The Reapers never took their eyes off Cassandra.

Ricky laid the long, white flower box down at Mave's feet respectfully and then stood back in front of the reporter.

The priest had finished his sermon and walked briskly back to the church. He wasn't stupid and had buried enough gangsters in his time to know when trouble was brewing. His normal flock were lambs... these were a pack of rabid wolves.

One by one, the Reapers were touching their ears, and then they delved into their long coats. Orders had been given. Mave gave hers first.

"Now Ricky."

All as one and on cue, the assembled cream of British underworld all put up their automatic, black golfing umbrellas covering a vast swath of the graveyard in a black nylon canopy. This basic anti-surveillance technique rendered them invisible to the helicopters hovering above. The gangsters wasted no time and all donned stocking masks and pulled out their various handguns and machine guns.

The Reapers had their own anti surveillance strategy, as the first of 39 smoke grenades was tossed into the air... and all hell broke loose.

Chapter 124

Slimey counted down the last few seconds until the hackers would turn the CCTV cameras off in his section of the Dali museum. He held the attaché case flat on his knees away from him, as he gripped the small spray bottle close to the opening. Jim watched, bemused, as soon as Slimey knew the cameras were off and he opened the case a fraction. Wild gnashing teeth and hairy snouts poked out of the tiny opening in the case. Slimey immediately used the spray on these snouts and after a few vigorous bursts he opened the case wide and the rats shot out and ran for their lives. As various tourists screamed and ran at the sight of the demented vermin, Slimey removed his surgical gloves and calmly walked towards reception.

"Aren't you afraid they'll close the exhibition until they catch them? We'll lose our chance at O'Brien then" Jim enquired.

Singen removed his overcoat to reveal workmen's overalls, Jim did likewise.

"Normally yes, dear Jim. But I've just sprayed those little blighters with cyanide before I released them… so they only have about a minute or so to create our window of opportunity before they die." By the time they both reached the reception with their fake I.D. word of the infestation had spread, and they were grateful of the cavalry's swift response.

"Ah hello Madam, Westminster pest control. We have had reports that several properties in this sector have experienced problems with vermin."

It took them five minutes to find and dispose of the dead rodents, but a further twenty minutes to check the upper levels to make sure there were no nests or further wee beasts lurking about.

The thankful exhibition's manager gave them all the security keys and let them go exploring the storerooms alone. After all, no fucking way was she going up there with them if there were more rats about.

On the first floor, in a dusty storeroom full of stored canvasses and upturned chairs they found what they were looking for in the middle of the floor; the tungsten restraining bolt that held the five-tonne bronze statue of The Abortion of Damocles suspended above the gallery floor below. Normally this bolt would be hidden under a floorboard but seeing as it was housed in a locked storeroom where the public would never see it; a decision was made to leave it uncovered for access, should the exhibit ever be taken down. The blueprints to this building, the architects and structural engineer's drawings and specifications in mounting this humungous sculpture were all attained by the bunker's hackers and were now on Singen's smart phone. But more importantly, the strength and dimensions of the restraining bolt and housing and how much C4 plastique explosive it would take to sheer it and drop the statue upon the head of Daniel O'Brien.

Singen took a lump of grey explosive from his case the size of a golf ball and moulded it around the base of the large nut and bolt in the floor. He then took out a mobile phone and connected one end of the jack plug to the phone and the larger detonator rod into the military grade soft explosive. He then gently placed the phone next to the bolt.

"Come on Jim, we want to get a good ringside seat for the show."

It was now or never. Jim looked suddenly alarmed and held his finger to his lips.

"SSSSHHH "Listen... I think there is someone outside the door."

Singen jumped up and listened at the door. Then yanked it open and looked outside. He scanned the empty corridor before peering back inside. Jim stood there nervous next to him holding his case.

"Sorry, nerves... I'm shitting myself we'll get caught... come on let's go."

Singen smiled at this spineless sign of weakness as he locked the storeroom door behind them and they both went downstairs.

Once at reception, Singen showed the disgusted manager the three dead rodents and reassured her building is now rat free before handing back her security keys. Five minutes later, Congressman Daniel O'Brien, Miles his secretary and Marine bodyguard Ronnie entered the building.

Chapter 125

Desi Shanks, the portly head of the Reaper's mop up squad was sat at the reception desk, just inside the bunker's main outer door. This was not his normal duty, but Captain Jeremy Naylor was having a meeting downstairs with the Head of section and Desi was asked to hold the fort. Desi envied Naylor, ex SAS captain in charge of bunker security. And what was Desi head of? Mopping up after incompetent fuck wits or carting off half dead tramps that the bunker's military attack dog, Wolfgang, had torn to bits. That reminded him, he must arrange to go out and have a pint with Chris, Wolfgang's owner soon. He was a good laugh, not like the fuckwits he worked with on a daily basis here.

His train of thought was broken by the phone ringing. It was the observation post.

"Hello... what?... not another tramp! Wh... why the fuck did you shoot him Darren yer mad prick! What the fuck do you think we've got Wolfgang for? You sure he's dead? Okay, as long as one of you is still in the observation post, bring him over."

Desi ended the call and considered calling Naylor... but what would Naylor do? Would he call for advice or assistance? No, he'd deal with it like the professional that he was. He replaced the phone and watched the monitors as the younger security officer who was limping, carried a man in a fireman's lift up to the outer door. Desi buzzed them in.

With head hung low as to not be detected by the bunker's alleyway CCTV cameras, Bobby draped himself over the bleeding Darren's shoulders whilst prodding the man's lower spine with the Browning high power to ensure his acquiescence.

Once inside he jumped off the man's shoulders, turned and with both hands fired two bullets into Captain Naylor's head. Except, it wasn't captain Naylor as Jim informed him it would be, but portly Desi Shanks who just happened to be in the wrong place at the wrong time. As far as Bobby was concerned, he couldn't fight or disarm an ex trooper, only kill him. Before his bleeding accomplice could inform him of his mistake Darren was knocked unconscious with the butt of the gun and cable tied. The two MP5 machine guns were under the desk as instructed. They were checked, one slung over his shoulder as he tentatively descended the stone stairwell to the bunker below.

Chapter 126

Cassandra couldn't believe the surreal scenario surrounding her. Here she stood at a gangster's funeral, under a pop-up shanty town of 700 plus black golfing umbrellas. As much of an aerial spectacle as this was to the police helicopters above... there was the matter of the 39 Reapers dressed as rabbis who had all thrown smoke grenades... and had now all drawn guns. The noise around her was deafening. Unlike the Reapers, Mave's firm did not possess silencers for their weapons. Cassandra ducked behind the colossal Ricky who fired an Uzi sub machine pistol at the Reapers. Empty cartridges hit the marbled head stones like a metallic tinkling piano.

Two Reapers spun in mid-air as high velocity rounds hit them. Another five seemed to spontaneously combust in a shower of crimson and bone. Brains splattered the gravestones and the wounded lay screaming. Stone crosses shattered after multiple rounds destroyed them. The villains weren't that good a shot, but they didn't need to be... for both doors of the black vans had opened and both M134 mini guns mounted on tripods were tearing up the graveyard, dispensing 6000 rounds of hot lead a minute through bone and sinew like two angry fire breathing dragons. Both vans rocked and shook at the velocity of these helicopter gun ship Gatling guns. Five more Reapers fell, and it would've been a complete massacre if it wasn't for the Reaper's smoke grenades. The air was thick with red smoke now and the helicopters above scattered for fear of crashing into each other. To her left she saw a gangster's chest explode in crimson as three bullets hit him. It was impossible to see now beyond ten feet; the Reapers were totally obscured. The graveyard was littered with blood, dropped umbrellas and slain masked villains. Some missing their faces. At the sound of gunfire, even the gangsters devil dogs had seriously shit themselves and ran for their lives. The ferocity of the shooting had slowed down now, as both sides conceded that to fire indiscriminately into a cloud of smoke was futile for fear of shooting their own. Even the M134 mini guns had stopped firing.

Mave had squatted with her back to a gravestone holding the large flower box and looked across at Cassandra who was crouched behind Ricky.

"You alright babe? Told yer you'd be safe behind Ricky, didn't I?"

Just then, two rounds hit Ricky square in the chest and sent him staggering backwards. Cassandra gasped, as the man mountain clutched his chest and then smiled. "Heh! It's ok girl, I'm wearing a bullet proof..."

The high velocity exploding round entered his left eye socket and erupted out the back, taking Ricky's liquidized brain and shattered skull with it. He stood there, like a huge confused Cyclops with half a head and looked directly at Cassandra... before his lifeless corpse slumped to the ground in front of her.

Lumps of stone exploded on a head stone next to her only she heard no gun fire. The Reapers must have silencers for their weapons. She ducked down behind the now lifeless Ricky as she felt his body judder as more bullets hit him. The red smoke was quite dense now, yet the bullets kept grouping around her. She heard the odd scream, as more of Mave's boys were being cut down silently in the crimson mist. The gangsters were stumbling about, shooting indiscriminately, whilst the Reapers picked them off with surgical precision one by one.

Then, the unmistakeable sound of the M134 mini gun starting up once again. Only this time, more of Mave's boys were screaming as the military cannon blew them to pieces. It was obvious that the Reapers had in the mist, killed the M134 mini gun's operator and were turning this fearsome tripod mounted weapon upon London's underworld. The gangster's ear-piercing screams were now drowned out under the deafening roar of its rotating barrel, until a huge explosion off to Cassandra's right shook the very earth she lay cowering on, behind the bleeding corpse of Ricky. The bumper and number plate from the second black van containing the other M134 mini gun landed a foot from Mave.

More bullets silently thudded into the dead bodyguard as Cassandra wondered how much longer her human shield would protect her.

Apart from the odd scream, and several panicked random shots, the graveyard fell eerily quiet. It was Cassandra who broke the silence. She whispered to Mave who still sat huddled behind a gravestone clutching the long white flower box.

"Mave! I... I think they can see us. Somehow they can see us in this smoke."

"How? I can't see a bleeding thing!" Replied Mave.

As Cassandra slowly peered up over the corpse of Ricky, she had her answer.

In the midst of the billowing red smoke she saw them; faint at first then clearer the nearer they approached. Two phosphorescent green eyes peered at her out of the impenetrable cloud. Another set of ghostly eyes appeared off to her left and another four pairs loomed in from the right. Soon the eyes merged into dark silhouettes, silhouettes of men who were clearly carrying silenced handguns. She turned her head behind to look for a way out. In the thick fog she could make out the yellow glow of the exploded black van and decided this was clearly a light source and a point to aim for if she ran.

She had to warn Mave before it was too late. As she raised her head above the slaughtered bodyguard, she saw six Reapers stood silently in a semicircle all dressed as rabbis, all wearing military issue night vision goggles... and all pointing silenced Glocks right at her head.

Slowly she stood up and instinctively held her hands up in surrender. The green luminous lenses of the covert goggles gave the Reapers an added sinister air of menace that they clearly didn't need. There seemed to be no leader, no one spoke, no one moved. They focused all their attention on her and appeared not to have spotted the buxom widow still crouched behind a gravestone.

"W... wait, you don't have to do th..."

She was cut short by the loud bang of a Mossberg 500 tactical pump action 12 gauge shotgun blowing one of the Reaper's skulls to pieces. Shocked, they all turned to the source of the noise, as another Reaper was sent flying backwards as the shot gun's cartridge punched a hole in him the size of a dinner plate. Each held their hand up to their eyes and stumbled about confused, firing their own silenced weapons and wildly missing their target, as another three had their spines erupt from the back of their coats. The last Reaper had his gun arm blown clean off at the elbow and he now lay screaming by Mickey Mullet's open grave.

Cassandra cowered behind Ricky's corpse as it dawned on her why Mave was able to kill five armed men so easily whilst they struggled to see her. The infra-red googles they wore, the very objects that enabled them to see and kill Mave's boys in the dense red smoke, were all rendered useless in the bright muzzle flash of the Mossberg shot gun. Mave reloaded the smoking shot gun and pointed the barrel directly at the one-armed Reaper by her late husband's grave as he rose to his knees.

"You killed my Mickey..."

He held up his remaining hand, but this disintegrated, as did his face when the widow fired twice, and his mangled body was catapulted backwards where it landed on the Oak coffin six foot below.

Mave took a pair of night vision goggles from one of the dead men and put them on. She then adjusted her black veil over her face so that all that could be seen were her trademark blood red lips and two demonic luminous green eyes. She chambered a cartridge into the shot gun and turned to Cassandra.

"Right, you've got yer story... fucking make sure this bit doesn't appear in it... no one likes a grass!"

Cassandra nervously nodded as Mave disappeared into the fog to complete her revenge. Cassandra stood and ran towards the glowing yellow of the exploded van determined to find a way out of this nightmare, as in the distance men screamed and a shot gun repeatedly fired.

Chapter 127

Bobby peered out from the bunker's main concrete staircase and surveyed the killing floor. Four rows of empty desks in a semicircle, huge digital monitor covering the whole back wall and a metal staircase leading up to a Porto cabin office. Outside this office stood two huge black suited guards. His target would be inside. He would need him alive. Anyone who hindered him would be regarded as collateral damage. If the Intel from Jim was accurate, the two guards and head of section would be armed. Possibly a couple of the mop up crew that may still be here. The hackers would give him no problems, nor would the two forensic pathologists they employed here. But the two ex CID advisors, would they be armed? He would try to keep alive as many as he could, after all, when they do arrive, the police would need witnesses, not a massacre and one gun-toting tramp.

The armoury lay off to the tunnel to his left, as did the hackers and his second target, Julian the makeup artist.

The hacker guzzled on his energy drink that contained about 72 ladles full of caffeine. His greasy hair hung over his face and his wacky T shirt had the anarchy logo emblazoned on it, to proclaim to the world that he was a unique non-conformist who wasn't like anyone else, a total individual who didn't follow the herd. The T shirt company has sold 17 million of these shirts... to individuals just like him. His fingers were like lightening on the keyboard as he remotely hacked the security cameras at the Dali Universe exhibition, to aid in Congressman O'Brien's execution. His five colleagues were all too busy to notice on the Play station in the corner murdering space midgets with chainsaws.

"Ladies... don't move."

They all turned in their seats to see a man in a baggy suit pointing a machine gun at them.

High on the metal gantry, outside the Porto cabin office the two suited guards looked bored.

"I'm gasping for a smoke." Said Tony.

"Heh! Yeah, well you'll have to gasp sunshine, if his nibs catches you, he'll tear you a new arsehole. You know it's no smoking down here." Replied Gary.

Just then, something caught his eye and he furrowed his brow.

"Eh? What's he playing at?"

The second guard looked in the direction of his interest. There across the killing floor, peeking out from the entrance to one of the tunnels that led to the tech room was one of the hackers waving at him.

"What's that long streak of piss want? Besides a fucking good wash."

Tony silently mouthed the word "what?" at the hacker as he did not want to shout and disturb the meeting inside the office and incur his boss's wrath. Yet the hacker just franticly waved and silently beckoned him to come down.

"Do you think his fucking PlayStation has broken?" said Gary.

"I'll be back in a minute Gary, do you want a coffee while I help the virgin look for his joy stick?" He angrily stomped down the metallic stairs and disappeared down the tunnel towards the hacker.

For the second time now, the hacker beckoned the remaining guard up on the gantry. He too looked pissed off and glared at the IT guy below.

"H… he's not going for it. I think he's suspicious."

Bobby who hid behind the hacker whispered,

"If he doesn't, I'll blow your fucking head off." He pressed the barrel of the MP5machine pistol into the base of his cranium.

"Try again."

The hacker waved again at the guard who now stormed down the steps towards him. Gary was angry now at this greasy little Herbert who was pissing him off and wasting his time. And where was Tony with his coffee? Can't take two of them to boil a kettle surely? He lumbered down the corridor and barged into the IT room.

"Right, you time wasting prick..."

On the floor were 5 hackers cable tied face down with gaffer tape on their mouths, Tony was trussed up the same the same only he was bleeding from his left eyebrow. The hacker who summoned him was on his knees with his arms behind his head. A low menacing voice from behind the door stopped him in his tracks.

"If you make me, I'll shoot you in the face just to teach these fuckers a lesson. Kneel down slowly and you won't have to die." Gary turned his head to see the weapon pointed at him by a man in a baggy suit.

Naylor reluctantly accepted the Malt whiskey from his boss. He was on duty as head of security at the bunker and as such, this was unprofessional. He left the SAS over a decade ago before Sir Hugo recruited him, yet his military discipline had never left him. He should be back at his post instead of letting that fat buffoon Desi Shanks guard the fort. But that was not his decision; it was his Masters who now summoned him to this meeting.

"Jeremy, I can't thank you enough for your diligence and sacrifice in working on the Reaper Project. Sir Hugo has shown great foresight in your recruitment. The secrecy and security of this facility that has allowed our Reapers to carry out their vital work is only possible, because of you."

As nice as these platitudes were, Naylor was a military man. And as such, his training had taught him that all praise from a senior officer always came with a catch; foreplay inevitably came before someone got fucked.

His training had also taught him that the dark looming shadows against the closed office Venetian blinds of Tony and Gary had been missing now for ten minutes. His own Glock lay upstairs at the reception desk with that fat fuck Desi Shanks.

"Gun?" Naylor gestured wildly at his boss.

"Pardon? Jeremy, what are..."

Naylor hissed, "Your guards are missing, where is your gun?! Is it in here?"

The Head of section clicked open his black attaché case on his desk and opened it up. Naylor got his hand to the silenced pistol just and the office door was booted in. He turned and got off two shots as both men fired at the same time.

With all stragglers cable tied and gaffer taped, Bobby ran up the metal gantry steps two at a time and burst open the office door with one almighty kick. Pieces of door frame flew as Bobby saw two men, one older behind the desk in a suit, and a younger man in dark boiler suit who turned to face him with a gun.

Bobby fired first and the machine gun shook in his hand until the pain went through him like lightening. Nine bullets tore through Naylor's rib cage puncturing his lung and shattering part of his spinal column; his body lurched backwards over the desk and crashed into the older man behind it. The one bullet that did strike Bobby hit his collar bone sending him sprawling out of the office where he lay stunned on the gantry floor, both his machine guns fell from his grip and clattered down the metal staircase. Stemming the flow of blood from his shoulder with one hand, he tried to get to his feet. He stumbled and managed to get to his knees. He bowed his head and gritted his teeth as another wave of pain came from his shoulder.

The unmistakeable sound of the hammer being cocked on the silenced Mauser pistol made him slowly look up.

"Who the fuck are you?" snarled the Head of Section, whose crisp grey suit was now smeared in Captain Naylor's blood and vertebra.

"I'm a friend... of Declan Hannah."

The older assassin looked confused and irritated at the same time. Bobby needed time, just enough time to slowly get his hand on the rigid object tucked into the back of his trouser belt. "Who the fuck is Declan Hannah?" The older man reinforced his threat by pointing the gun even closer to the soldier's head.

Good, that is exactly what Bobby wanted him to do. He was taught that, whenever faced with an armed opponent and you were unarmed... you had to close the gap. Ten foot or more and you would be dead before you could move. But when a gun is pointed right at your head, you only have to slap it to one side a couple of inches for it to miss. It is always worth the risk.

"Declan... Hannah..." said Bobby, deliberately dragging it out, making the Head Reaper assume he was dying, so as to not suspect an attack. "...was the old tramp you had torn to pieces... by an attack dog."

There was a look of bewilderment in the older man's eyes as Bobby tightened his grip on the serrated knife's handle behind his back.

"The tramp?! The tramp outside?!"

In his rage he never saw it coming. With his blood-soaked hand, Bobby slapped the pistol outwards and it instantly fired a bullet inches past his head. With his other hand he stabbed upwards into the outstretched triceps loosening the Reaper's grip on the gun. Bobby viciously twisted the serrated knife deep into the arm twice to make sure the gun was dropped into his waiting palm. Still holding the man skewered on his knife as he jabbed the gun hard into the Reaper's neck he hissed

"His name... was Declan!"

Chapter 128

All day, Julian the bunker's makeup and latex technician had been close to a nervous breakdown. So sure his conversation with Jim about escaping would find its way back to the office, and Julian would find himself full of bullets. Even when the last of the Reapers had left for Mullet's funeral and the bunker became eerily quiet with only support staff left, he still felt they would come for him. He had vomited quietly in the toilets three times in the last hour as his anxiety verged on hysteria. Then, he heard it. The gunfire.

All Hell had broken loose.

As instructed by Jim he hid in his makeup cupboard and crouched down low in the darkness. Tears welled up and he started to shake uncontrollably. The gun fire stopped. But he dared not move, he was instructed otherwise. It seemed like an eternity waiting there in the very depths of despair for salvation... or execution.

He was suddenly bathed in light as the cupboard door was yanked open.

The man in the baggy suit was bleeding from his shoulder and carrying a silenced pistol. Julian held up his hands to shield himself from the light... or bullets, or both.

"Are you Julian?"

"Y... yes." He stammered.

"Jim said you'd be here. You're safe, it's over... but we need to get our stories straight before the police get here."

Chapter 129

Miles gave a wry smile as he watched his boss, Daniel O'Brien glide around the Dali exhibition like a giggly schoolgirl. The Congressman was an uncompromising politician, who championed the poor and took on the right-wing lobbyists like a bare-knuckle street brawler. Some had foreseen greatness in him, and he was even likened to a latter-day JFK. Whether he shared his destiny for high office or his enemies on the right would cut him down... time would tell. Miles had seen them come and go. Some were vanquished; some were totally corrupted and owned by the lobbyists. But with O'Brien it felt different. Myles for the first time in his political career felt he was on the winning team. It would seriously need a man of Daniel's calibre to take on Senator Joshua Goodchild once they got back to Washington.

Miles never understood his boss's obsession with the late surrealist painter. It was all a bit too trippy, like a guided tour through a mad man's mind. Indeed, to reinforce Miles's opinion, he saw a quote by the artist emblazoned above a golden statue of a melted clock.

"The only difference between me and a Madman, is that I am not MAD!"

Ronnie, the ever-alert Marine looked for danger and assassins everywhere as they entered the Religion and Mythology section of the exhibition.

Congressman O'Brien stopped dead in his tracks when he saw it... The Abortion of Damocles. The grotesque bronze sculpture of Dali's infamous lost sketch. Three French tourists all stood under the suspended bronze which was tethered to the ceiling via a tempered steel chain.

Like a nervous schoolboy this seasoned politician waited his turn to stand in the white painted circle on the floor and look up at the razor-sharp, coiled umbilical cord that emanated from the huge cherub's bloated bronze belly.

Ronnie scanned the crowds in "the kill zone," an area twenty foot surrounding his boss. Any gun man or crazed maniac with a knife would be in this area. As long as Ronnie patrolled and dominated this area, the Congressman would be safe. If Ronnie had only cast his gaze a further thirty feet back, he would've spotted two pairs of furtive eyes watching them with a remote-controlled explosive, which planned to drop that five-tonne bronze monstrosity right on top of his employer.

Singen's nostrils flared as his excitement increased. His prey had now just stepped into the trap. Slowly, he took out the mobile phone and brought up the desired number. The number of the phone attached to the detonator that was imbedded in the C4 military explosive, which would destroy the housing bracket and restraining bolt and drop five tonnes of bronze onto Daniel O'Brien below. As much as an orgasmic kill as this would be, that honour would not be his... he handed the phone to Jim.

"When I say..."

Jim gulped hard as the next ten seconds would change his life forever.

"Now!" Singen hissed.

Jim pressed the call button. O'Brien looked up beneath the huge statue and stood there for what seemed an eternity.

Singen wildly looked at Jim. "Fucking press it!"

Jim pointed feebly at the phone and showed Slimey the screen. The number was ringing. Slimey turned to face O'Brien, who still stood beneath the statue without a care in the world. In desperation and anger, Singen snatched the phone from Jim, quickly cancelled the call and dialled the number again. This time he would take no chances and pressed send himself as his eyes bore into his target. He looked at the screen, it said "calling..." He cancelled it and redialled in wild panic as he saw O'Brien start to walk from beneath the statue. He looked down at the phones screen and then around at Jim.

But Jim was gone.

He looked around in fury for the Reaper, but he was nowhere to be seen amongst the crowds. Congressman O'Brien walked out from beneath the statue as in the background soft flamenco guitar music was soon replaced by the loud electronic sound of a fire alarm. Curators and security staff quickly ushered visitors out of the building. In the hustling crowds, Singen could only passively watch as his target's bodyguard removed him at speed from the building, before he himself was herded outside. Above the sea of heads, he briefly saw O'Brien entering a black car only to swiftly disappear.

Nearly as quickly as Jim disappeared.

Singen gripping his attaché case tightly, heard the fire engines approaching as he melted into the crowds boiling with rage.

Chapter 130

Cassandra removed the ridiculously high heels she had borrowed from Mullet's widow and gently massaged her aching feet. She had been waiting inside the stairwell to Jim's flat for forty minutes now. She hoped the address he had given her during their brief phone conversation on the bus was correct, because she had seriously run out of options. Her protector Bobby was off on some suicide vendetta at the bunker and she seriously didn't think without her homeless guide she would ever really find his shack, that had been her bolt hole for the last week. If the Reapers had survived Mave's vengeance, they would go to her flat or round to Mervyn Foster's newspaper looking for her. Until she knew who to trust, the police could never be an option. Realistically, there was only two people in this whole nightmare she could trust; one was possibly dead taking on an army single handed... and the other owned the flat she now loitered outside.

Just as she felt her situation was hopeless, the communal door burst open and Jim ran through it. He was out of breath and sweating. Scrabbling for his keys he gasped, "Come on, we haven't much time!" Slamming the flat door behind them they entered the flat and then stopped in their tracks.

"Oh my god..." Said Cassandra.

On the walls of Jim's living room were newspaper cuttings and photos of Congressman O'Brien. Dozens of them all stuck to the walls. One of them relating to his intentions on visiting the controversial Dali sculpture in London. But dominating the whole wall were four huge dates written crudely in red paint, which dripped down the walls in long streaks. Cassandra was puzzled as she scanned these dates trying to make sense of it

14th APRIL 1865

28th JUNE 1914

22nd November 1963

"I don't understand... what this is?"

"Assassination dates." replied Jim. I briefly taught history, before all this...

14th April 1864 John Wilkes Booth shoots Abraham Lincoln. 28th June 1914 Gavrilo Princip shoots Franz Ferdinand and 22nd November 1963, Lee Harvey Oswald... well, you know where this is going."

Cassandra pointed at the last date "Th... that's today!"

"Yeah, obviously I'm being set up, as all this was meant for someone to find. Lone crazed killer." He wrinkled his nose at the foul smell in his flat that he couldn't quite decipher. It seemed to be coming from the walls or more to the point, the red paint on the walls. Jim followed the red streaks down to the skirting boards where they both saw the source of the foul-smelling paint.

It was a cat... or to be precise, a headless cat.

Cassandra held her hand to her mouth "Jesus, I feel sick!"

Jim went instinctively to the fridge to get her a cold drink... and inside he found the cat's head staring back at him.

Great lengths had been taken to create this scenario as it dawned on Jim... he was never meant to escape after O'Brian's assassination. These walls were his statement to the police... a dead man's confession.

Panic gripped him and he grabbed her wrist.

"We've got to leave! They were never going to let me go!"

He yanked open the front door... and Singen's silenced Glock was pointed right at his head.

"Oh, you treacherous little bastard!"

Chapter 131

For the second time that day Cassandra had a gun pointed at her head. Singen slowly closed the front door and led her and Jim back into the flat.

"You pulled the detonator out of the C4 explosive, didn't you?" The words were icy cold and dripped with menace from Singen's lips. Jim nervously nodded; it was futile to lie.

"And the fire alarm?"

Jim nodded again.

Singen pulled the hammer back on the gun. Cassandra gasped.

"It's ok... he won't shoot." said Jim trying to reassure her.

Singen raised his eyebrows quizzically and smiled.

"When the Reapers kill, it is always meant to look like an accident. 'Death by misadventure'. That way no serious murder squad detective would give the death a second look. This... is an execution. Questions would be asked. And that's why he won't shoo..."

The silenced gun jerked once in Singen's hand as the bullet tore into Cassandra's thigh and exited into the wooden floor below. She cried out and instantly dropped to the floor clutching her leg.

"Not very good at gambling, are we Jim?" The gun was now levelled at his chest.

Jim's heart was pounding now as he stood there and waited to die. Then, a phone rang. Not for a second did Slimey take his eyes off Jim or the shot reporter as he answered the call.

"What?... no, he got away... thanks to your boy who let him escape... well I fucking warned you that you couldn't trust him! It's ok, I've got him... and the reporter at his flat right now. Yes, I'll deal with it!"

He abruptly ended the call and readdressed Jim.

"That just now on the phone was a dead man. You see, thanks to your fucking stupidity, Congressman O'Brien will go back to Washington and chair a Senate committee hearing into our American benefactor Joshua Goodchild's private mercenary army. We were given the job... or YOU more importantly, were given the job of killing O'Brien whilst here in London. Goodchild will no doubt have Sir Hugo killed for his failure to uphold this contract. And now... I'm talking to a second dead man."

Jim held up his arms.

"Wait! What's the point of killing us? It's over, if Hugo and Goodchild are finished, what is the point of carrying on? You don't have to do this." Singen smiled a cruel smile and replied,

"Finished? Oh no, dear poor deluded Jim, we are far from finished. This is damage limitation. Yes, the American side has gone, but we will find another benefactor in Europe, one who shares our vision of sustainable covert population control. All you have done is delay our global expansion. You were only ever a pawn in that game, never a player." He glanced down at Cassandra who was moaning on the floor as she tried her best to stem the flow of blood from her wound.

"Have you ever wondered how, or why you were recruited Jim? For our Reaper project we needed loners who fitted a specific psychological profile. You applied to join MI5 with your late friend Simon Wilson, didn't you?" He smiled again.

"MI5 never got your application; it was intercepted by a friend of ours who works there in recruitment, who is very loyal to our cause. He passed your details on to us and we came for you." Singen frowned now.

"But you caused us certain problems Jim. You see, after your friend Simon Wilson refused to work for us and we wrapped him in plastic, a vacancy needed to be filled... and you went straight to the top of the pile. Alas, for security purposes, all our Reapers had to be loners... no family to come looking for them, asking awkward questions once we snatched you off the streets." Jim needed a way out, a weapon, anything. Then he spotted it on the table next to him amongst house keys and various clutter. Not ideal, but a drowning man will clutch at anything to survive... and Jim was close to death. He slowly lowered his hands and brought them down to his sides.

"But you weren't a loner, were you Jim? You still had a father. Yes, he was ill in hospital, but for the purposes of your recruitment... he was the missing piece in your psychological profile."

Jim went suddenly cold.

Singen continued,

"You see we needed you to start immediately, yet your dad being alive did sort of bar you from entrance into our little club."

Jim shook his head and rested his hand on the table next to the shiny pointed object. Singen took this as a posture of shock and didn't seem to notice.

"Yes, that's right Jim... I suffocated your father in his hospital bed with a pillow so we could recruit you... I actually volunteered for it."

Jim's breaths were coming out in gasps now as his eyes moistened. The man who raised him and guided him through life, his rock... was murdered by this evil little bastard. The tears welled in his eyes now, burning as the rage welled up in his chest. His breaths were coming out in short gasps. He gritted his teeth as a tear ran down his cheek. His hand edged nearer to the silver pen.

"So, when the police find you dead here in your lair along with the valiant reporter who tried to stop you, it will tick every criminal psychologist's box."

He now flippantly addressed the prone Cassandra. "And you my dear, shall be hailed as a heroine... a martyr to all the things you couldn't be in life. And while you get your feeble ten seconds of fame... we will silently start up again on the continent."

His mocking eyes were on her, Singen removed his tinted sunglasses to reveal those bloodshot pupils basked in crimson.

The object was now firmly in Jim's palm, only the point stuck out from his now clenched fist. Singen brought the gun up and aimed at her head. In that split-second Jim lunged at him and Slimey turned the gun away from Cassandra at his new target. He grabbed Slimey's wrist and shoulder charged him into the wall. The gun went off and plaster erupted from the wall opposite. Both men wrestled as Jim held the gun arm away from his face as it fired again. Singen was strong and curled his wrist inwards to aim at Jim's head. He smiled again, his evil red eyes inches from Jim's. The gun was now in range...

With all his strength, Jim jabbed the silver fountain pen he had secreted in his other hand deep into the side of Singen's neck. Blood instantly spurted out in a hot jet. Singen, let go of the gun and it skidded along the wooden floor and he instinctively grabbed his neck as he fell forward onto Jim, pinning him to the floor.

Singen, injured and mad with rage, resembled a dying bull in a Spanish stadium with a sharp implement hanging out of his gushing neck, grabbed Jim's throat with both hands and squeezed as he straddled him. Jim grabbed Singen's wrists, but he was getting weaker the more he squeezed.

"You stupid little prick! All your clothes we supply have tracking sensors in them... its GPS linked to my phone. That's how I found you so quickly!"

He could feel Jim's grip loosen, as his tightened.

"I put your Daddy down like an old sick dog... and now I'm going to put down the fucking RUNT of the litter!"

Singen's head jerked back violently as one of Sir Hugo's designer dum dum bullets entered his big angular nose, before erupting in a kaleidoscope of nasal cavity, brain and skull fragments as its shock wave churned everything up in its path in a maelstrom of blood and splattered the wall behind him.

His grip loosened on Jim's throat as he just sat there wide eyed as blood poured from his open mouth, the wall

454

behind was clearly visible as the back of his head was now gone.

Then, he slid slowly sideways with a wet squelch as his head hit the floor.

Jim coughed and choked as he gasped for air as he pushed the corpse from off him, then turned to face Cassandra.

She was pointing the silenced Glock right at him.

He climbed to his knees and held up his bloodied hand to her.

"I… I'm not like him. I… I saved you. He wanted you dead, you threatened everything. I gave you money to escape. I couldn't kill you."

Cassandra held her bleeding thigh, but still held the gun on Jim.

"You've killed before… I have you on tape."

Jim let out an exasperated sigh as he rubbed his bruised throat.

"Y… yes, but as I've told you… I was forced to, or they would've killed me. But I could never kill a woman… that's why you're still alive."

Cassandra furrowed her brow at this latest statement from the man she had been hunting for so long. Her prey… now in her sights.

"Lorraine Fuller… ring any bells? Laundrette, late at night… suffocated in an industrial tumble dryer… by you. I have you on street CCTV footage entering the laundrette, then leaving after she was dead."

Of all the deaths committed by the Reapers, Lorraine Fuller's still resonated with her. Maybe she somehow felt a kindred spirit with the dead single woman who lived alone.

An unspoken debt to find her killer... and now she pointed a gun right at him.

Jim coughed as his throat was still aching.

"That wasn't me... it was him!"

Cassandra shook her head in disbelief.

"L... look if you have footage... go look at it again. There were three people in that laundrette, me, Miss Fuller... and him. He was dressed as an old woman. He got there before her. Yes, I was sent to kill her, but with my track record, they knew I'd lose my nerve. That's why they sent him along. When the time came, I... I just couldn't. But HE did. I couldn't watch, so I left as he grabbed her. If you are going to shoot me... do it because I was too much of a coward to stop him. Because I didn't want to die."

Maybe it was a mixture of the loss of blood, the shock of being shot... or just the pain and misery she saw in his haunted eyes... she slowly lowered the gun to the floor. Jim instantly jumped up and dashed into the bedroom, grabbed a bag, some towels and a first aid kit out of the bathroom cabinet. Without asking, he tied a silk tie high around her thigh above the bullet wound and then with a wet squelch, pulled the silver pen out of Singen's neck and twisted it around under the tie to form a tourniquet. He then applied gauze pads to the entry and exit wounds and bound this tight with Elastoplast tape off a roll. He used the towels to mop up her blood, so she wasn't sat in it and then handed her Singen's mobile phone.

"I can't turn myself in to the police. As you said... I have killed. Exactly like you've just done. You'll get away with it... I won't. The mitigating circumstances don't concern the authorities. I would just be swapping one prison for another. I had one choice: kill or be killed. As for you... you

456

have three. You have a gun and a phone. You can shoot me dead, phone the police and I'll die in prison... or, you can let me go." Jim picked up his bag and then slipped a small white piece of card into Singen's pocket.

"All I ask is that you wait fifteen minutes before you ring the police... the tourniquet on your leg should hold the blood loss, you'll be fine." He opened the door and turned.

"If you do decide to let me go, your source who broke the story and your inside man at the bunker is a makeup artist called Julian. As far as the police need to know, I never existed... I'm a ghost."

And with that, he was gone.

Chapter 132

It had been over two months now since she had been shot. The stitches had been removed and the scaring was less noticeable at the front as opposed to the mess it was round the back. Still, that's what a dum dum bullet will do for you or so the overly chirpy surgeon, who used to work in Belfast told her. Apparently, she was lucky it went straight through and not shattered inside the wound. She had lost a section of her quadricep in her left leg that had left her with a permanent limp. Again, the Belfast surgeon informed Cassandra, that without that makeshift tourniquet, she could've lost her leg. The Merlot helped with the pain, but she knew secretly that the stick she now used was needed much more than her old preferred alcoholic crutch. She was slipping back into her old ways.

The tourniquet had saved her leg... and Jim had saved her life. In every aspect.

She no longer worked for Mervyn Foster at his porn rag. She had so many offers for work and her story that realistically; in three months... she would never have to work ever again. The plush two bedroom flat in Kensington, bought outright by the serialisation and rights to her story, on how she took down an evil peer of the Realm and his secret army of assassins. The royalties off this alone, ran into millions of pounds. And that was just off Foster for the newspaper rights. The lecture tours and chat-shows both here and America had left her a very rich lady indeed. For the United States' very own Baptist butcher Senator's, involvement meant there was not a TV network over there that did not know her name.

She rubbed the wound as it gave her a twinge of pain as she limped to her desk where her laptop sat. She logged on again, for the fiftieth time she rechecked the black and white CCTV footage that her dead friend Marty had supplied of the Loraine Fuller killing. Jim was right. Before Loraine and Jim went into the laundrette and again after Jim left, there was an old woman. Cassandra zoomed in on the digitally enhanced still and it was unmistakeable, the angular nose, those evil eyes... it was the Reaper who she shot in Jim's flat. And to think... she nearly killed Jim over this. As it was, she had inadvertently given Lorraine Fuller and her friend Marty some belated justice.

She closed the file and checked the daily news feed online. Apart from the odd hurricane turning Florida into porridge or a Maori warrior shaking his cock at a red-faced visiting Royal, 90% of the mainstream news was about the Reapers. Each day more and more revelations and links to this story since the police got involved. Wall to wall coverage both here and in Washington, turned the whole nightmare into a tidal wave that nobody who owned a TV or smart phone could avoid.

The BBC reported that 23 arrests were made at two locations, one, Brookwood cemetery in London and the other at a secret location that for matters of national security, they could not disclose. Mainly, because Her Majesties government had unwittingly sold an ex Ministry of defence bunker, to a gang of assassins led by an MP who was given a seat in the Lords by the Head of state herself. Despite trying, the government's press gagging orders failed, as the world was informed quite vigorously, with the help of Foster's paper that a Peer of the Realm was secretly executing the Queen's subjects and with the aid of Joshua Goodchild, he planned to cull the Americans as well. The high-resolution photos taken from Fosters photographers hiding in the graveyard at the massacre were used in court as exhibit A.

Goodchild tried to deny with his viper's tongue, but when it was revealed that half of one of his business cards with a handwritten message to Sir Hugo was found at the scene of a remote-controlled bomb in a London exhibition, it sealed his fate. The fact the man that bomb was meant to kill was chairing a Senate Committee hearing right in front of him, when the Feds and swat teams burst into the chamber, showed the Commander in Chief that his favourite attack dog just too unpredictable and dangerous to be outside of a cage.

DNA testing on the torn business card and the handwriting and ink forensically matched the ink in Goodchild's monogrammed pen. Encrypted phone records showed a direct line was opened to Sir Hugo. The dead Reaper in the flat had the second half of the business card in his pocket and Joshua and Hugo were linked in a Faustian pact, conspiring to commit political assassination. If it wasn't for Jim leaving the card at the scene, pulling out the detonator and hitting the fire alarm for the fire brigade to find the bomb, it wouldn't just be O'Brien that would be dead that day. The Reapers would've gone on to kill millions in America and Europe.

As the armed response unit smashed the door of Sir Hugo's private study in at his stately home, he was well aware that the media onslaught from the story, fuelled by his old buddy Mervyn Foster would be the end for him. Politically, and literally when Goodchild's men got hold of him. So, for the first time in his rabid life he decided to do the honourable thing and fall on his sword. Or blow his upper set of dentures through the top of his skull with one of his designer dum dum bullets he was so proud of.

Only two of the Reapers survived the wrath of Mave, who slaughtered her way through the smoke engulfed graveyard. By the time the dense crimson mist had cleared for the police to move in and arrest anyone, there were a lot of dead and no witnesses. All the living had stashed their guns and walked out with the crowds. The police could only mop up the mess as anybody who could testify, were either dead or a hardened criminal. The police had nothing as any evidence of murder disappeared with the red smoke.

Mavis the mammary monster did exceptionally well out of the funeral massacre. She has achieved her life's goal and is now an A list celebrity hosting her own chat show in America and Hollywood want to make two movies about her; one you can take your granny to and one you can show at a stag do.

Meanwhile her antics at her late husband's graveside, with a Mossberg shot gun have cemented her place in the gangland narcotics trade as the undisputed drug lord of all London. Whereas nobody ever fucks with her... unless it's in one of her movies.

The bunkers zealots, support staff, guards and Head of section as he was euphemistically, called were all put on trial. Along with the two surviving Reapers from the funeral and various mop up squad lackeys. Most tried to cut a deal and squealed like a stuck pig to save their own hides by sacrificing others. Unfortunately, they all did this to each other so their deals with the judge were null and void. They each received twenty years imprisonment. The Head of section acting like the captain of the Titanic went down with his ship. It transpired he was ex MI5, it surprised nobody that since the time of his arrest, right the whole way through his trial, he never uttered a single word. He got thirty years and would in all likelihood die inside.

The only one from the bunker to walk away free was the prosecution's star witness, and "inside man," Julian the makeup technician. He was able to fill in all the gaps where electronic data couldn't corroborate complicities in murder or aiding and abetting genocide. By the end of the month long trial enough evidence was gathered to incarcerate, not only all who were involved with murder, but warrants were issued for more arrests. The officer in recruitment at MI5 who helped the Reapers conscript new assassins went on the run and the whereabouts of Chris the attack dog handler were, as of yet, still unknown.

Cassandra gave a troubled smile at this last report as there was a story a month ago about a man fitting Chris's description found dead in the basement of his flat. His huge Alsatian dog had eaten both his legs and fingers before tearing out his throat. The man was bound and gagged. After the dog was destroyed, the autopsy revealed that apart from his owner's limbs, there were traces of steak infused with a powerful sedative. The police report stated that the dog had been fed drugged meat through the letter box. The owner was overpowered and carried down to the basement along with his dog. Now, Cassandra couldn't prove that this was the soldier Bobby Mcvie who deliberately left that man to be eaten by his own dog over 5 days, to avenge his old tramp friend who the Reapers had the Alsatian tear him to bits. Yet the canine did have a dog tag on it that read WOLFGANG, and the owner was cable tied and gagged with gaffer tape exactly how the police found the staff at the bunker.

She thought of asking Bobby about this when they briefly met in the green room of a news TV studio two weeks ago, but then thought... let sleeping dogs lie.

He too has totally turned his life around with the army removing his court martial and inviting him back to be a trainer at Hereford. With the media painting him as a national hero, even billionaire Cates has had to reluctantly drop his vendetta against him. That and the fact the billionaire's business dealings with Joshua Goodchild could be construed as linking him with the Reaper project. Bobby declined the Regiment's kind offer and instead went to work on the Circuit. An organisation that employs ex Special Forces to guard industrialists, oligarchs and Saudi royal princes. He sent her a post card from Dubai on Tuesday as they agreed to keep in touch.

Cassandra poured another glass of Merlot and clicked on another article relating to the story, regarding a police inspector talking about anomalies in the case. All the Reapers were only ever known by their first names and they all disappeared from any data base well over a decade ago, so little if anything is known of their true identities. Notably one name that kept cropping up that the police could not account for... a man called Jim. The prosecution's star witness Julian informed them that this was a cover name given to a Reaper that they had specifically chosen for a political assassination, called Simon Wilson. Cassandra smiled as this was the name Jim had supplied to Julian for when the police arrived. In gratitude for Jim saving him, he stuck to this story right throughout the investigation and subsequent trial. He and Cassandra both agreed for him to be named as the inside man that broke the story to Cassandra, thus letting Jim disappear into the shadows and catapulting Julian into stardom and lucrative media deals for his story.

Even though conflicting reports from the convicted bunker's technical staff all say that Simon Wilson was shot dead five years ago for not joining them, the police chose to believe Julian. Afterall, he was the only one not implicated in actively aiding and abetting murder. Just a terrified makeup artist frightened for his life. Whilst the bunker's staff were all trying to save their own skin, Julian had no reason to lie. Cassandra told the police she didn't know the identity of the Reaper who put the tourniquet on her leg and gave a useless vague description; they put this down to the shock of being shot. The cops however took the inscribed pen from the tourniquet and when the name matched the one Julian had given them... they had their missing Reaper. So immediately the police launched a worldwide man hunt for Simon Wilson.

Chapter 133

Jim felt the cool breeze ruffle his hair as the open top sports car sped along a Spanish mountain road. He could see the yachts moored in the harbour in the hot Mediterranean sunshine that felt glorious on his suntanned skin. He opened the glove box and next to the 38 Smith & Wesson revolver lay a small bottle of water. He flipped up the bottle's lid and drank deeply. He felt good. Full of a sense of peace and security he had not experienced in a long time. The huge bag of money in the boot gave him the peace... the 38 Smith and Wesson in the glove box gave him the security. For the first time in his life he felt positive about the future. It had been over two months now since he escaped the Reapers and lived as a free man. Jim's mind drifted back to the day he ran.

The small dirty fishing boat lay in a quiet jetty at the end of Tilbury docks, Essex. Jim had chartered the boat to take a solitary foot passenger on a one-way trip across the Channel, no questions asked. Jim paid the captain handsomely up front three days before the O'Brien assassination attempt. Win, lose or draw... Jim was getting on that boat. All he took was a full change of clothing... that had no tracking sensors in, and a bag... a fucking big bag. Once on French soil he hitchhiked across France, sleeping in fields and staying away from people as he constantly scanned his portable radio for news on the erupting story he had escaped from. Day after day the story spread like wildfire, from London to Washington. The media went wild with a gangland funeral massacre, porn stars, Peers of the Realm, genocidal assassins, mercenaries and even an American Senator involved. There were arrests in London and in Washington. People were named, convicted and with warrants issued.

He listened intently for his own name.

Instead, a manhunt was launched for the last on the run Reaper... Simon Wilson.

When Jim heard this, he jumped for joy. Both Cassandra and Julian had kept their word and not named him. Even in death, his late friend was still helping him. With the whole of Interpol now chasing a man who died five years ago, Jim felt safe using his passport to board a train for Spain. He had been here ever since.

Nearing the harbour now, Jim approached a roadside bar overlooking the sea. Outside there were several very rowdy ex pat Brits being very loud and obviously drunk. One of them a huge brute with beige cargo pants and a Union Jack vest on suddenly lurched into the road and caused Jim to screech on the breaks, stopping inches from him. The shaven headed troglodyte waved his tattooed arms at Jim and then threw his pint glass at his car where it shattered on the bonnet.

"What are you fuckin' lookin' at you prick? Do yer want some? Do yer, eh?"

Jim said nothing; he just calmly put the car in reverse and backed it up fifty feet.

The brute stood defiantly in the road, putting two fingers up to Jim.

Jim opened the glove box and looked at the gun. He then slammed it shut and gunned the engine. Going through the gears at a rate of knots, the high-performance sports car accelerated straight towards the thug. Instead of moving, the skin head stood transfixed... unable to move as the car drove straight at him. It was too late now, even if he chose to run, the car was too close and travelling too fast. His beige cargo pants turned darker as the urine just gushed from him and he waited to die. He could see Jim's eyes and they were full of death as they bore into his.

Then, at the last second... the car swerved right round him spraying him with gravel as it roared off into the distance.

In his rear-view mirror, he could see the dark stain on the crotch of the thug who roared after the speeding car,

" Y... you fuckin' idiot! You could've killed me!"

Jim smiled to himself and said out loud,

"Yeah, I could've... couldn't I?"

The End

Acknowledgements

I'd like to thank all my friends and family for their love and support over the years.

I'd also like to thank Taryn Johnston and all the hard working people at Chronos Publishing for all their help and guidance and to their designer for the excellent front cover illustration replicated from my sketch.

A special thank you goes out to fellow author Graham Hey, a good friend of over 30 years who has always nurtured my creative endeavours and encouraged me to write.

My idol is the late surrealist painter Salvador Dali whose work appears within the pages of this novel. His work broke all boundaries and inspired me to draw differently... and think differently.

About the Author

Paul Kelly is a freelance cartoonist, illustrator and comedy writer who has worked on comedy publications for over 20 years. During that time he has produced comedy scripts and artwork for adult publications: *Zit, Scurvy Dog* and *Spit!* comic. The latter, he went on to become editor.

He also wrote for a successful comic strip in the *Daily Star* newspaper called the *Star Birds* and was a comedy script writer for a weekend football fanzine also at the *Daily Star*. He has had a solo artwork exhibition at the Royal Jersey Opera House and is kept busy on the corporate caricature circuit and private commissions. In his spare time he likes to indulge in his two main passions by going to comedy clubs and travelling the world to view renaissance art in all its glory.